James Cotter Morison

The Life and Times of Saint Bernard of Abbot of Clairvaux

James Cotter Morison

The Life and Times of Saint Bernard of Abbot of Clairvaux

ISBN/EAN: 9783337337520

Printed in Europe, USA, Canada, Australia, Japan

Cover: Foto ©Raphael Reischuk / pixelio.de

More available books at **www.hansebooks.com**

THE LIFE AND TIMES

OF

ST. BERNARD.

THE

LIFE AND TIMES

OF

SAINT BERNARD,

ABBOT OF CLAIRVAUX.

A.D. 1091—1153.

BY

JAMES COTTER MORISON, M.A.,

LINCOLN COLLEGE, OXFORD.

London:

MACMILLAN AND CO.

1884.

LONDON :

R. CLAY, SONS, AND TAYLOR,

BREAD STREET HILL.

TO

THOMAS CARLYLE

THIS

𝕭olume is dedicated

(BY PERMISSION)

WITH DEEP REVERENCE AND GRATITUDE.

CONTENTS.

BOOK I.

CHAPTER VI.

CHAPTER VII.

CHAPTER VIII.

CHAPTER IX.

BOOK II.

CHAPTER I.

CHAPTER II.

CHAPTER III.

CHAPTER IV.

CHAPTER V.

BOOK III.

CHAPTER I.

CHAPTER II.

CHAPTER III.

CHAPTER IV

CHAPTER V.

CHAPTER VI.

BOOK IV.

CHAPTER I.

BOOK I.

THE LIFE AND TIMES

OF

ST. BERNARD.

BOOK I.

CHAPTER I.

SAINT BERNARD'S BIRTH—PARENTS—THE FIRST CRUSADE—DEATH OF
ALITH, HIS MOTHER.

SAINT BERNARD was born A.D. 1091, and died A.D. 1153.
His life thus almost coincides with the central portion of the
Middle Ages. He witnessed also what may be regarded as
especially mediæval events. He saw the First and the Second
Crusades; he saw the rising liberties of the communes; the
beginnings of scholasticism under Abelard were contemporary
with him. A large Church reformation, and the noblest period
of growth and influence that monasticism was destined to
know, were social facts with which he was not only coeval,
but on which he has left the deepest marks of his action
and genius.

Saint Bernard was a Burgundian. Not far from Dijon, in
full view of the range of the Côte d'Or hills, was a feudal
castle, situate on a small eminence which went by the name
of Fontaines.[1] This castle belonged to Saint Bernard's father,

---

[1] An old round archway is still
shown at Fontaines as a relic of
Tesselin's castle. Louis XIII. built
(on the same site, and using portions
of the old walls) a church for the
Reformed congregation of Feuillants

B

Tesselin, a knight, vassal and friend of the Duke of Burgundy. Tesselin had the surname of *Sorus*, which meant, in the vulgar dialect, reddish, almost yellow-haired. He was rich. He followed his suzerain in his wars, and it is said that when he did so, victory always attended the arms of the duke.

But Tesselin was not simply a fighting baron ; he belonged to a class of men who were not so rare in the Middle Ages as we are apt to suppose—men who united the piety of monks to the valour of crusaders. Of Tesselin we read that his manners were gentle, that he was a great lover of the poor, of ardent piety, and that he had an incredible zeal for justice. He used to wonder that men found it difficult to be just ; or that fear or covetousness should make them forsake the justice of God.[1] He was a most brave knight ; but he never took up arms except for the defence of his own land, or in company with his lord of Burgundy. On one occasion he was drawn into a quarrel, and a single combat was arranged between him and his adversary.[2] The day and place of meeting were fixed—

in 1619. It was desecrated at the Revolution, and used as a smithy. The chapel was restored by Louis Philippe.

[1] " Inter quos [proceres] excellebat Tesselinus quidam, cognomento Sorus ; quo nomine, vulgari lingua subrufos et pene flavos appellare solemus. Erat autem vir iste genere nobilis, possessionibus dives, suavis moribus, amator pauperum maximus, summus pietatis cultor, et incredibilem habens justitiae zelum. Denique, et mirari solebat, quod multis onerosum esse videret servare justitiam ; et maxime, adversus quos amplius movebatur, quod aut timore aut cupiditate desererent justitiam Dei. . . . Nunquam armis usus est, nisi aut pro defensione terrae propriae, aut cum domino suo duce, scilicet, Burgundiae, cui plurimum

familiaris et intimus erat ; nec aliquando fuit cum eo in bello quin victoria ei proveniret."—St Bern. *Op.* vol. ii. col. 1275.

[2] See Ducange, *voc.* ' Duellum,' for a long and interesting article. The combatants were obliged to swear that they would use no magic arts against each other. *Consuet. Norman.* part ii. cap. 2 : " Primo jurabit defensor quod nec per se, nec per alium, in campo sorcerias fecit aportare, quae ei possint et debeant juvare, et partae adversae nocere." *Lex Rothar.* cap. 371 : " Nullus campio praesumat quando ad pugnam contra alium vadit, herbas quae ad maleficia pertinent super se habere, nec alias similes res, nisi tantum arma sua quae conveniunt." They fought with uncovered heads and feet : " Quantum voluerint de

the enemies appeared. Tesselin was by far the stronger man, and his victory would have brought him no little advantage. His courage was undoubted. But the feeling that all this was radically wrong overpowered every other. Divine exhortations to charity and peace, divine condemnations of violence and strife, crowded on his mind. He determined to be "reconciled to his adversary." He offered terms which he knew would be accepted. He relinquished the point in dispute. In that stern time, when force was generally law, a man must have been very sure both of his courage and piety to act thus. Gentle yet brave, modest yet strong and rich, such a man was Saint Bernard's father.[1]

Tesselin's wife was a fitting partner for such a man—earnest, loving, and devout. Her name was Alith. She was a great favourite with the monkish historians of her illustrious son, and they have left a portraiture of her, pale and shadowy indeed, yet presenting a conceivable image. She bore Tesselin seven children, six sons and a daughter. Her boys she offered to

corio et lineo induant, dummodo capita atque pedes permaneant enudati." Plebeians were obliged to have their hair cropped above the ears before they were allowed to fight : " Et chascun doit estre roingnez par dessus les oreilles." A champion in his own cause, if conquered, suffered only a fine or imprisonment ; in the cause of another, he suffered mutilation : " Pugil conductitius, si victus fuerit, pugno vel pede privabitur."

[1] " Cum, quodam tempore, vir memoratus, diversis emergentibus causis (sicut inter saeculares frequenter contingere solet), cum quodam sibi adversante, multo inferiori genere, et substantiae minoris, monomachia firmaverat decertare ; adest statuta dies et praefixa certamini. Convenitur utrimque. Recordatus autem vir venerabilis Tesselinus timoris Dei, et judiciorum divinorum," &c.—St. BERN. Op. vol. ii. col. 1282.

I use Mabillon's 2d edition of Saint Bernard's Works, 1690, in two vols. fol. The Abbé Migne's reprint is also extremely convenient, and has the numbers of the columns as they stand in Mabillon's edition inserted in the text ; so that the reference is good for either Migne or Mabillon. As regards Tesselin's character for gentleness, it would seem to have been a recognised trait of the ideal knight. Thus Chaucer,—

" And though that he was worthy he was wys,
And of his port as meke as is a mayde.
He never yit no vilonye ne sayde
In al his lyf unto no maner wight.
He was a verray perfight gentil knight."
              Canterbury Tales, Prologue.

B 2

the Lord as soon as they were born. Piety and humbleness of mind distinguished her even more than her husband. Charity, too, of the most practical kind she exercised in her neighbourhood. She sought out the poor in their squalor and misery, attended to and relieved their sick, cleansed their cups and vessels with her own hands. The latter years of her life were passed in devotions and austerities, which were monastic in all but the name. By scantiness of food, by simplicity of dress, by the avoidance of worldly pleasures, by fasting, prayer, and vigils, she strove after that ideal of self-sacrifice and holiness, which was alone attractive and beautiful in that age.

Such were the parents of Saint Bernard—of his mind and character no less than his bodily frame.

One of the earliest remembrances in Bernard's life must have been the First Crusade. In the year 1095 Peter the Hermit was going about Europe on his mule. In November of that year Pope Urban II. made his speech at Clermont, and all Christendom was in a ferment of preparation for the Holy War. Every class and station shared in the general enthusiasm. That year had been one of scarcity, so that even the rich endured privations.[1] Suddenly so great was the emigration, that the sellers of provisions became more numerous than the buyers, and unusual cheapness ensued. Men passed rapidly from apathy or hostility towards the movement, to vehement and practical advocacy of it; and accompanied those whom just before they had laughed at or opposed. The "way of God," as it was called, seemed the only thing or enterprise which could rouse sympathy and interest. A strange scene

---

[1] " Erat ea tempestate, pro generali defectione frugum, etiam apud ditiores magna penuria, . . . diversae plurimorum copiae deferuntur in medium, et quae chara videbantur dum nullus movetur hominum, commotis ad hoc iter omnibus vili pretio traduntur venum, . . . dat quidquid habere videtur, non pro sua sed pro taxatione ementis, ne Dei posterior aggrediatur viam." — GUIBERTUS NOVIGENSIS, *Gesta Dei per Francos,* lib. ii. cap. 3.

must have been this pilgrimage of nations.   From all parts of Christian Europe they came in troops : the Scotch made their appearance in rough cloaks ; others arrived, no one knew whence, who spoke an unintelligible dialect, but conveyed their meaning and purpose by placing their fingers in the form of a cross.   Men, says a contemporary, sold their lands for a less sum than at other times they could have been induced to take even to ransom themselves from a most horrible captivity. Any means were adopted to get away.   From the powerful baron with his retainers down to the subdued and humble serf, all had a common tendency and hope.   "Christ had thundered through the ears of all minds,"[1] and the only fear was that of being the last on the road.   An odd and yet touching sight was afforded by the conduct of many of the ignorant poor. Harnessing their oxen to their farm carts, they placed therein their goods and little ones, and started in all simplicity for the Holy City.   Bad were the roads then, and long the journey, even from province to province.   Slowly moving and creaking over marsh and moor, as town or castle rose in sight, the children would ask, "Is that the Jerusalem we are going to ?"[2]

This grand procession of the Crusade went thus gradually by, to disappear at last beyond the seas.   For four years came back tidings of disasters, of successes, of the terrible siege of Antioch, of the perished thousands on the plains of Asia Minor, till at last it was told how, after toils and dangers beyond belief, Godfrey, on Friday, 15th July, 1099, at three in the afternoon, had stepped from his wooden tower on to the walls of Jerusalem ; and how the steel host of Crusaders, reduced from a mob of half a million to a few thousand seasoned soldiers, had gratified their piety and revenge by a week's massacre of the infidels, till "our people had the vile blood of the Saracens up to the knees of their horses."[1]   But Europe was again ready to send forth another wave of armed men to overwhelm the East, and in the first year of the twelfth century a multitude of five hundred thousand departed for the Holy Land.   The Duke of Burgundy was one of the chief leaders.   He never returned alive.   One of his last wishes was that his bones might rest in the cemetery of some poor monks recently settled at Citeaux, a few miles distant from Dijon.   He had befriended these monks, and often prayed in their humble oratory, and even built himself a residence in their neighbourhood.   His body was brought home and placed where he had desired it to be.   The great feudal lord had chosen the poor, well-nigh wretched Citeaux, before the sumptuous and wealthy abbeys of his dominions.   A vassal so near the duke as Tesselin was could hardly have escaped some connexion with the rites and offices of his suzerain's burial ; and, if so, it is probable that the topic would not be unnoticed or untalked of around the hearth at Fontaines. The good Alith, who offered her sons to the Lord, would easily draw a moral from these facts—the great Crusader going forth with his armies in full panoply, returning coffined and still to the cemetery at Citeaux.   In any case, Bernard's earliest years were passed in scenes and emotions among the most vivid the human race has known.

When he was old enough, the little Bernard went to school at Chatillon, a place with which his father had family rela- tions.   He soon fulfilled his mother's hopes by his proficiency. Studious and retiring, he loved to be alone, and was "mar- vellously cogitative,"[2] we are told.   Another account, perhaps not less authentic, describes him as zealous and ambitious of

---

[1] These words are in a letter written to the pope and bishops by Godfrey and other Crusaders. (See Michaud's Hist. of the Crusades, book iv.)

[2] "Mire cogitativus." (St. Bern. Op. vol. ii. col. 1063.) It will be seen further on how Bernard's lite- rary tastes were made a matter of reproach to him by his adversaries.

literary fame, and as carrying on a vigorous rivalry with his
fellows in verses and repartees.

Saint Bernard was passing from boyhood to youth when his
mother died.   It was her custom on the festival of Saint
Ambrose (the patron saint of the church at Fontaines), to
assemble a number of clergy in her house, and "to the glory
of God, the Blessed Virgin, and the above-mentioned saint,
solemnly to refresh them with food and wine on that day."   A
few days before the anniversary, which was the last she was
destined to see, it was revealed to her that she would die on
the festival.   On the vigil of the feast she was taken ill with
fever.   The next day, after the celebration of mass, she asked
most humbly that the Body of the Lord might be brought to
her, and received the sacrament of Extreme Unction.   She
then bade her friends proceed to their entertainment as usual.
But while they were at meat she sent for her eldest son Guido,
and requested him, as soon as the feast was over, to bring the
guests to her bedside.   They assembled around her, and she
told them that her death was near.   They immediately began
to chant a litany, supplicating God for her soul.   She joined
in with them, and sang devoutly till her very last breath.
When the chorus of voices toned forth the words, " Deliver
her, O Lord, by thy Cross and Passion," in the act of making
the sign of the cross, her life and psalm of praise ceased
together, and, after her breath had fled, her hand remained
erect and fixed as she had elevated it to perform her last act
of faith.[1]

When the report of her death was noised abroad, Gerannus,
Abbot of Saint Benignus of Dijon, came to Fontaines and
begged the body of Alith, "regarding her remains as a most

---

[1] "Cum vero chorus psallentium
jam pervenisset ad illam litaniae sup-
plicationem,—Per Passionem et Crucem tuam libera eam Domine, . . .
elevata manu, signans se signaculo
sanctae crucis, in pace reddidit spiritum.   Manus sicut erat erecta ad
indicandum signum crucis sic re-
mansit."—St. Bern. *Op.* vol. ii.
col. 1283.

precious treasure." His request was granted out of deference to
his worth, and forthwith he himself, and several with him, carried
back to Dijon on their own shoulders the " holy body." On
their way they were met by a large concourse of people bearing
crosses and tapers, who, with great joy and veneration, accompanied them to the church of the blessed martyr, Benignus,
where the pious mother of Bernard was buried. " The said
abbot also caused six images to be made and placed upon her
tomb, in memory of her six sons, where they may be seen to
this day." [1]

We are told how she was wont to appear to her sons after
her death, how she exhorted Bernard to persevere in the good
work he had begun when he became a monk. These fond
credulities of an unscientific age are little tolerated in our time.
Yet we may accept the legend as conveying or veiling a known
fact of human nature, and acknowledge that the tomb gives a
robe of beauty unseen in the sunlight, and that the words of
the departed acquire a strange reverberating echo from the
vaults wherein they sleep.

[1] St. Bern. Op. vol. ii. col. 1284.

CHAPTER II.

CHOICE OF A CAREER.—TEMPTATIONS FROM LOVE OF LITERATURE.—
TRIUMPH OF FAITH.—CONVERSIONS.—CITEAUX: ITS ORIGIN.—SAINT
BERNARD'S AUSTERITIES.

AFTER his mother's death, Bernard was left free to choose his
own occupation in life.[1] There is no reason to disbelieve the
testimony borne to his great beauty of person, while his charm
of manner, and the power of his facile eloquence, rest upon the
concurrent testimony of contemporary history. But what shall
his calling be? After all, there is no great choice. A gentleman and a knight has a well-defined career before him, and all
know what it is. Father Tesselin is a knight, and even he
cannot keep clear of single combats, and following my lord of
Burgundy to his wars. Brothers Guido and Gerard are knights,
and what are they even now doing? besieging the castle of
Grancy with the new lord of Burgundy, Hugh II, surnamed the
Pacific, son of him who lies buried at Citeaux. So is everybody slaying or being slain, blockading or being blockaded,
attacking or being attacked. It is a fierce world. The
thoughtful and refined natures have little hesitation in quitting

---

[1] " Ex hoc, suo jam more, suo
jure victitare incipiens, eleganti corpore, grata facie praeminens, sua-
vissimis ornatus moribus, acceptabili
pollens eloquio, magnae spei adoles-
cens praedicabatur.   Obsidebant
autem benignum juvenis animum so-
dalium mores dissimiles et amicitiae
procellosae, similem sibi facere ges-
tieutes."—ST. BERN. Op. vol. ii.
col. 1065.

it.   Dukes and princes, peasants and paupers, are ready to leave their luxury or their misery, and to seek a haven of shelter where, during this short life, they may say their prayers, and lie down for the long sleep in peace.

And such a haven was then open, and inviting to all.   Between the clash of arms and the din of wars, comes a silvery peal of convent bells.[1]   In the deep, hushed winter's night, the chorus-song of matins is heard in measured cadence, and the last chant of compline goes forth as the summer sun approaches the horizon.   There, in the thick woods, sleeps the monastery, from whence these voices and bell-tones are heard.

Calm and holy it looks, casting long rays of light into the dark air, as the "'lated traveller" hastens to its welcome shelter. For a young, ardent spirit, entering the world, the choice practically was between a life of strife, violence, wickedness, of ignoble or ferocious joys and sorrows; or of sober, self-denying labour and solitude, with a solemn strain in the heart, lightening and prospering the work of the hands.

Bernard had now made trial of a secular life for some years, when, as his friend and biographer says, "he began to meditate flight."[2]   But whither?   There were abbeys and priories all round him at Fontaines, at the doors of any of which he would have been welcome.   But this new establishment at Citeaux must surely be the very one of all others where what he seeks for is to be found.   The monks are austere, devout, and can hardly keep alive for poverty.   These men must be in real

---

[1] "Ce n'est guère qu'à dater du XIII⁰ siècle," says M. Viollet le Duc, "que l'on donna aux cloches des dimensions considerables.   Les cloches donnees par Rodolphe abbé de St. Trond, au commencement du XII⁰ siècle pour l'église de son monastère pesaient depuis 200 jusqu'à 3,000 livres."—*Dict. de l'Architecture,* vol. iii. 'Cloche.'

[2] The following, in reference to a certain class of temptations, and the way he subdued them, is characteristic :—"Stagno quippe gelidarum aquarum collo tenus insiliens, tamdiu inibi permansit, donec, pene exsanguis factus, a carnalis concupiscentiae calore totus refriguit."—ST. BERN. *Op.* vol. ii. col. 1065.

earnest, and have gone there for what he so longs.   To Citeaux
it shall be.

But here a great and unexpected obstacle arose.   When his
friends and brothers knew of his intention they strongly
opposed it, and with such well-chosen reasons that Bernard
himself acknowledged they almost succeeded.   They, doubtless, had no hopes of making a knight of him—he was too
delicate and fragile for that—so they strove to rouse an
ambition of another kind, more engrossing, more lasting, and
more insidious than any military glory could gratify in that
age.   If he would not be a fighter let him be a disputer,[1] let
him study this new and surprising philosophy which is bringing
such renown to its votaries.   At this time, William of Champeaux, the great Paris doctor, is celebrated throughout France
for his admirable Dialectics ; and now, behold ! a young rival,
once his disciple, has challenged him, and these two are having
as eager and ferocious a tournament as any mailed knights
could exhibit.   The new and audacious champion, who has
entered the lists with the old veteran, is a young logician-errant
from near Nantes in Brittany, named Master Peter Abelard,
who has fought his way up to Paris in many an encounter,
and is now going to carry off his crowning victory amidst the
plaudits of assembled Europe.[2]   There was much in such a
prospect to tempt an ardent, intellectual youth, whose mind,

[1] " Omnimodis agere coeperunt,
ut animum ejus ad studium possent
divertere literarum ; et amore scien-
tiae saecularis, saeculo arctius impli-
care.   Qua nimirum suggestione,
sicut fateri solet, propemodum re-
tardati fuerant gressus ejus.   Sed
matris sanctae memoria importune
animo ejus instabat, ita ut saepius
sibi occurrentem sibi videre videretur,
conquerentem quia non ad ejusmodi
nugacitatem tam tenere educaverat,
non in hac spe erudierat eum."—ST.
BERN. *Op.* vol. ii. col. 1066.

[2] When this great battle came
off, I have not seen mentioned, but
it must have been somewhere near
the year 1108. "Guillelmus melioris
vitae cupidus, ad cellam veterem in
suburbium Parisiorum, ubi erat aedi-
cula quaedam Sancti Victoris, cum
discipulis aliquot migravit, anno
1108."—*Gallia Christiana*, tom. ix.
He became Bishop of Châlons in
1113 ; so that his defeat and Abelard's victory would come very
near St. Bernard's seventeenth or
eighteenth year.

however religious, had not yet received from habit and reflection a decided bias. Bernard acknowledges that his spiritual progress was almost stayed by this snare. To what extent he yielded we do not know. Such an impetuous character would not be likely to bring lukewarmness to studies so popular and so exciting. At such a time, too, of intellectual activity following a long apathy, the novelty of study and the attraction of knowledge are intense, even violent. Crowds, amounting to thousands, crossed high mountains and broad seas, and endured every inconvenience of life, to enjoy the privilege of hearing Abelard lecture. Men long debarred from the tree of knowledge, hardly knowing that there is such a tree, when first they see its golden fruit, " pleasant to the eyes and to be desired to make one wise," are inflamed with a passion for mental food, which more instructed generations can hardly appreciate. Now, that is exactly what would have sufficed to alarm so sensitive a conscience as Bernard's. When he felt the impulse himself, or saw it in others, the third chapter of Genesis would be at once present to his mind. While still undecided as to his ultimate course, he was proceeding to join his brothers, who with the Duke of Burgundy were at their usual occupation of besieging a castle. He, doubtless, felt he had fallen from the high resolves and aspirations of his early youth. The life of holiness and prayer, which had seemed to open before him under his mother's example and conversation, had faded away now, and although he was not a knight, killing and plundering, he was still in the world and of the world, loving knowledge and its human rewards. Self-reproach and shame at this spiritual retrogression filled his mind with heaviness and grief. In this mood he rode along over the bare moor or through the tangled forest, thoughtful and sad. Presently he came to a church. But by this time the dark cloud of doubt and wavering had broken and vanished before the rising sun of Faith. On his knees in that wayside church.

and in a torrent of tears, "he lifted his hands to Heaven, and poured forth his heart like water, in the presence of his Lord."[1] From that hour his purpose of entering the monastic life never faltered.

The instinct which leads us to eagerly impart to others a spiritual truth which has taken strong hold of ourselves; the impulse to preach, to exhort, to labour, to convert, subject though it be to fearful perversions, is yet one of the most beautiful in our nature. A sympathetic, vigorous character, like Bernard's, was sure to feel it strongly; and when, at this time, he determined to induce his brothers and friends to follow him into the cloister, he completely succeeded. He at once displayed that commanding personal ascendancy, that overpowering influence of spirit, which hardly met with a defeat during his whole life. His uncle, "a worthy man and powerful in the world," lord of the castle of Touillon, yielded at once. Bartholomew and Andrew, both his juniors, made but small resistance to their brother's earnest appeal. But the eldest, Guido, who was married and had children, and who, through his position and his age, was firmly settled in the world, presented a conquest of far greater difficulty. At first —and it cannot surprise one—we are told, Guido hesitated at the proposition to leave his wife and daughters and enter a monastery. Then he agreed to do so if his wife would give her consent.[2] Bernard, "conceiving a livelier hope of the

[1] "Cum aliquando ad fratres pergeret, in obsidione castri quod Granceium dicitur, cum duce Burgundiae constitutos, coepit in hujusmodi cogitatione vehementius anxiari. Inventaque in itinere medio ecclesia quadam, divertit, et ingressus oravit cum multo imbre lacrymarum, expandens manus in coelum, et effundens sicut aquam cor suum ante conspectum Domini Dei sui · ea igitur die firma-
tum est propositum cordis ejus."— ST. BERN. Op. vol. ii. col. 1066.
[2] "Primo fratres aggreditur . . . deinde cognatos, et socios, et amicos, de quibuscunque poterat esse spes conversionis. . . . Guido primogenitus fratrum, conjugio jam alligatus erat, vir magnus, et prae aliis jam in saeculo radicatus. Hic primo paululum haesitans, sed continuo rem perpendens et recogitans, conversioni

mercy of God, announced to him "—as a fact likely to dispel
his hesitation—" that his wife would either die or consent to
the separation." Even this did not persuade the young wife
to regard the matter in a proper light, and she still refused.
Guido, between the brother he feared and the wife he loved,
was in sad perplexity. Might he not try a middle course—
give up the wickedness of the world, its soldiering and jousting,
take to a peasant's life, and support himself and wife by his
own labour? No small concession for a gentleman and a
knight to make. But it would not do. Bernard had left the
disobedient to the fate he had foretold to them, and was active
in all directions collecting his spiritual recruits. And now
came the woe he had announced. "Guido's wife was chastened
by a heavy infirmity," but her eyes were opened at the same
time, and "she saw how hard it was to kick against the
pricks." She sent for Bernard, implored his forgiveness, and
was the first to ask for a religious separation. She went
into a convent near Dijon, and Guido was free to follow his
brother.

The second in age after Guido was Gerard. He, too, was
a bold knight, and inclined to take a worldly, compassionate
view of Bernard's enthusiasm.[1] "Ah!" said the young preacher,
"I know that tribulation alone will give thee understanding,"
and, placing his finger on his brother's side, "the day will
come, ay, and quickly come, when a lance shall pierce thee
here, and make a way to thy heart for that counsel of salvation
which thou now despisest. And thou shalt fear greatly, but

---

consensit, si tamen conjux annueret :
. . . Demum cum omnimodis illa re-
nueret, vir ejus magnanimus, . . .
virile concilium, Domino inspirante,
concepit ; ut abjiciens quidquid habere videbatur in saeculo, vitam
institueret agere rusticanam."—St.
Bern. *Op.* vol. ii. col. 1066.
   [1] "Secundus natus post Guido-

nem Gerardus erat, miles strenuus
. . . ut mos est saecularis sapientiae,
levitatem reputans, obstinato animo
salubre concilium et fratris monita
repellebat. Tum Bernardus fide jam
igneus, 'Scio, inquit, sola vexatio
intellectum dabit auditui.'"—Ibid.
vol. ii. col. 1067.

shalt in no wise perish." A few days after, Gerard was surrounded and overthrown by enemies, and carried off captive, with a spear in his side. "I turn monk," he exclaimed, "monk of Citeaux!" a vow which, on recovering his liberty, he hastened to fulfil.

Soon after, Bernard and his converts were assembled together in a common spirit of devotion, and presently they entered into a church, and, as they entered, this verse was being read, "God is faithful, and He that hath begun a good work in you the same will perform it unto the day of Jesus Christ." From this time he gave himself up more unreservedly to preaching ; he began to put on "the new man ;" and to those whom either literature or worldly concerns brought into relation with him, to speak of serious matters and conversion of heart ; showing that the world's joys were fleeting, and life full of misery ; that death was imminent, and after death, in weal or woe, would be life eternal.[1] The effect of his preaching was, that "mothers hid their sons, wives their husbands, companions their friends," lest they should be led away captive by that persuasive eloquence. At last, having assembled a company of about thirty chosen spirits, he retired with them into seclusion at Chatillon, where for a space of about six months they devoted themselves to self-preparation for the great change that was at hand. Their remaining worldly business was soberly and definitely disposed of, leave was now taken of friends, and a semi-monastic life begun during this retreat.[2]

At last, when all arrangements were completed, in the year

[1] "Coepit novum induere hominem, et cum quibus de litteris saeculi, seu de saeculo ipso agere solebat, de seriis et conversione tractare ; ostendens gaudia mundi fugitiva, vitae miserias, celerem mortem, vitam post mortem, seu in bonis, seu in malis, perpetuam fore."—ST. BERN. *Op.* vol. ii. col. 1068.

[2] "Erat enim eis Castellioni domus una propria et communis omnium. . . . Ipsi vero quasi mensibus sex post primum propositum in saeculari habitu stabant, . . . dum quorundam negotia per id temporis expediebantur."—Ibid. vol. ii. col. 1069.

A.D. 1113, Bernard being then twenty-two years old, he and
his companions knocked at the gate, and disappeared within
the walls, of Citeaux.

Citeaux had been founded fifteen years before, and had had
a chequered existence of good and evil fortune, the adverse, on
the whole, preponderating.[1] In the first curiosity and interest
excited by Robert of Molême and his few monks, the patronage of the great Duke of Burgundy had been extended to
them, and, as has been seen, he had desired that his remains
should repose in the humble cemetery of these austere monks.
His son Hugh, also, was well disposed to Citeaux, and
frequently attended the abbey-church on great festivals. But
the Abbot of Citeaux at this time was a very remarkable man,
and did not regard the condescending patronage of the great
as the object of a religious house ; he thought it might even
defeat the object of a religious house. He made it understood,
then, that neither duke nor any other grandee should ever hold
his court at Citeaux for the future. Stephen Harding—for
that was our abbot's name, an Englishman, originally from
Sherborne, in Dorsetshire—and his monks were quite free now
from noisy interruptions from knights and courtiers, or troublesome visitors of any kind ; but the danger was that they would
be left alone altogether ; that their small community, gradually
thinned by death, would at last pass out of the world quite
unnoticed, and never cause to spread that grand scheme of
monastic reform which Abbot Stephen has got matured, if he
had but the monks to do it. For these monks at Citeaux,
though very wonderful, do not tempt one to join. They
actually keep the whole of St. Benedict's rule literally, not
conventionally and with large allowances, as is usual in the

---

[1] In reference to the early history of Citeaux, nothing can surpass
the account given in the "Life of
Stephen," in the series published
under the superintendence of Rev.
J. H. Newman. I make a general
reference to that beautiful little
volume with regard to the small
amount I have to say about Citeaux.

strictest houses.   They eat but one meal a day, and have risen
twelve hours from their hard couches, and sung psalms, and
worked in the fields before they get even that.   They never
taste meat, fish, grease, or eggs, and even milk only rarely.
Their dress consists of three garments, and those of the
coarsest wool.   Their church shows no attempt towards
picturesque beauty, but, on the contrary, in all things aims at
the austerest simplicity.   It is not wonderful if, even in that
age of monkish enthusiasm, St. Stephen, and St. Alberic before
him, had had to wait doubtfully anxious as to whether what
they were attempting would prove a noble reform or a pitiable
failure.[1]   And, now, to their voluntary privations was added a
scarcity bordering upon famine.   This left them only a too
easy prey to an epidemic, and all hope of Citeaux seemed at
an end.   It was just at this juncture that Bernard and his
friends presented themselves, and begged to be admitted as
novices.

It was usual when any one wished to become a monk at
Citeaux to make him wait for four days before he was taken
to the Chapter in presence of the assembled convent.[2]   After
this, on entering, he prostrated himself before the lectern, and
was asked by the abbot what he wanted.   He replied, "God's
mercy and yours."   The abbot bade him rise, and expounded
to him the severity of the rule, and inquired of his intention

---

[1] " Vides   in quanto taedio
et defectione mentis versamur qui
arctam et angustam viam, quam in
regula nobis beatissimus pater noster
Benedictus proposuit, utcunque in-
gressi sumus.   Sed utrum haec nostra conversatio Deo placeat necne
non satis nobis constat."— *Exor-
aium Magnum Dist.* 1, cap. 16.
This is part of an address by St.
Stephen to a dying monk, who
was requested to come and tell
him after death what the fate of the
order would be, which he did very
accurately.

[2] " Monachus quis fieri volens,
facta petitione, non nisi post quatuor
dies ducatur in capitulum ; qui dum
adductus fuerit prosternat se ante
analogium.   Interrogatus ab abbate,
quid quaerat, respondeat, 'Misericor-
diam Dei et vestram.' . . . Tertio vere
die ducatur in cellam novitiorum ;
et abhinc annus incipiatur proba-
tionis."—*Usus Ord. Cist.* pars iv
cap. 103.

again, and if he answered he wished to keep it all, the abbot said, " May God who hath begun a good work in thee Himself accomplish it." This ceremony was repeated three days, and after the third he passed from the guest-house to the cells of the novices, and then at once began his year of probation.

The following was the ordinary routine in the Cistercian monasteries in Bernard's time : At two in the morning the great bell was rung, and the monks immediately arose and hastened from their dormitory, along the dark cloisters, in solemn silence to the church. A single small lamp, suspended from the roof, gave a glimmering light, just sufficient to show them their way through the plain, unornamented building. After short private prayer they began matins, which took them about two hours. The next service—lauds—did not commence till the first glimmer of dawn was in the sky, and thus, in winter at least, a considerable interval occurred, during which the monk's time was his own. He went to the cloister and employed it in reading, writing, or meditation, according to his inclination. He then devoted himself to various religious exercises till nine, when he went forth to work in the fields. At two he dined, at nightfall assembled to vespers, and at six, or eight, according to the season, finished the day with compline, and passed at once to the dormitory.[1]

Bernard found these practices and austerities inadequate to satisfy his zeal and spirit of self-mortification. He determined to subdue not only the desires of the flesh, which arise through the senses, but even those senses themselves. His days were passed in ecstatic contemplation, so that seeing he saw not, and hearing he heard not ; he scarcely retained any taste, and hardly perceived " anything by any sense of his body." [2]   Time

---

[1] Usus Ordinis Cisterciensis, pars iii.

[2] " Totus absorptus in spiritum, . . . videns non videbat, audiens non audiebat ; nihil sapiebat gustanti, vix aliquid sensu aliquo corporis sentiebat."—St. Bern. *Op.* vol. ii. col. 1242. . . . " Nullum enim tempus magis se perdere conqueri solet, quam quo dormit, idoneam satis

given to sleep he regarded as lost, and was wont to compare
sleep and death, holding that sleepers may be regarded as
dead among men, even as the dead are asleep before God.
The visits of those of his friends who were still in the world
were a great source of disquiet to him. Their conversation
brought back thoughts and feelings connected with that evil
world which he had determined to leave for ever. After their
departure, on one occasion, he went to attend the office of
nones, and as usual lifted his mind to prayer, but immediately
found that God's grace and favour were not vouchsafed as
before. That idle talk was evidently the cause. But the next
time his importunate friends came he was prepared; by carefully stopping his ears with little wads of flax, and burying his
head deep in his cowl, though exposed for an hour to their
conversation, he heard nothing, and even spoke nothing except
a few words to edification; and by this ingenious device
escaped the evil he had before experienced.[1] The same
austerity marked all his actions. As regards vigils, his rule
was not to pass the whole night sleepless.[2] For food he had
lost all desire, the thought of it seemed to give him pain, and
nothing but the fear of fainting ever induced him to take any.
A weakness of stomach, caused or increased by these severities,
now attacked him to such a degree that he could scarcely
retain any aliment, and what he did digest seemed rather to
defer death than sustain life.[3] Still his dauntless spirit never

---

reputans comparationem mortis et
somni; ut sic dormientes videantur
mortui apud homines, quomodo apud
Deum mortui dormientes."—GUIL-
LELMUS, *St. Bern. Op.* vol. ii. col.
1071.
[1] "Sed et alii venerunt visitare
eum. . . Et cum ad eos duceretur
accepit stupas, et misit sub capucio
in aures suas, ita ut hoc artificio
. . . fuit cum eis per totam horam

et nihil audivit."—J. EREMITA, *St.
Bern. Op.* vol. ii. col. 1285.
[2] "Quantum enim ad vigilias,
vigiliarum ei modus est non totam
noctem ducere insomnem."—GUIL-
LELMUS, *St. Bern. Op.* vol. ii. col.
1071.
[3] "Sic accedit ad sumendum
cibum quasi ad tormentum, . . . cor-
rupto stomacho crudum continuo per
os solet rejicere quod ingeritur.

yielded.   When from bodily weakness he could not join in the
hard manual labour of the monks, he betook himself to "other
and more menial offices, that he might supply by humility his
deficiency in labour."   But if only his inexperience stood in
the way of his imitating his brethren, he at once sought some
employment equally arduous, and devoted himself "to digging,
or hewing wood, and carrying it on his shoulders."   And thus
did Bernard apply himself to the observance of the very letter
of his rule of life.[1]

But, even according to his own showing in after life, there
was another influence to which he owed more than to all his
austerities, and that was his love of, and communion with,
Nature.   His ardent imagination, which gave a mystic and
manifold meaning to outward facts, his love for peace and
meditation, his truly Christian and jubilant heart, which ever
gave thanks for all things, all contributed to give him this
fond delight in Nature, and made him say to a friend and
pupil, "Trust to one who has had experience.   You will find
something far greater in the woods than you will in books.
Stones and trees will teach you that which you will never learn
from masters.   Think you not you can suck honey from the
rock, and oil from the flinty rock?   Do not the mountains
drop sweetness, the hills run with milk and honey, and the
valleys stand thick with corn?"[2]   In fact, Theology and
external Nature were Bernard's only subjects of intellectual
meditation.   In the world of thought, Theology reigned with-

---

Si quid autem residuum est, ipsum
est alimentum corporis ejus quale-
cunque non tam ad vitam sustentan-
dam quam ad differendam mortem."
—St. Bern. *Op.* vol. ii. col. 1071.

[1] " Fodiendo seu ligna caedendo
propriis humeris deportando. . . .
Ubi vero vires deficiebant, . . .
laborem humilitate compensabat."
—Ibid. col. 1072.

[2] "Experto crede : aliquid amplius invenies in silvis quam in libris.
Ligna et lapides docebunt te quod a
magistris audire non possis.   An non
putas posse te sugere mel de petrà,
oleumque de saxo durissimo?   An
non montes stillant dulcedinem, et
colles fluunt lac et mel, et valles
abundant frumento?"—St. Bern.
Epist. 106.

out a rival. Religion filled every mind which thought at all.
It had no competitor for men's attention. Those vast fields
of knowledge, rich with golden harvests through the labour of
generations of thinkers, which are now seen from every day
and action of modern life, were far removed from the man of
the twelfth century. The great past civilization of Greece and
Rome was to him little more than a blank, across which moved
the shadows of great names. A dim religious light prevailed
in the world of thought, as well as in the solemn cathedral
aisles.[1] But of all the states of mind suited to enjoy and
delight in external nature, the religious and emotional, un-
chilled by systematic, scientific thought, is perhaps the most
calculated. One can conjecture the procession of burning
thoughts, the rapture of ecstatic, admiring love, which would
command Bernard's mind when he entered the gloomy forest,
or watched the sailing clouds, or gazed at the setting sun
filling the west with liquid fire. No cold abstractions came
between him and those marvels. He thought of no " theories,"
" causes," or " effects ; " and " laws " and " phenomena," in

---

[1] The study of any writings not
of Christian authorship had up to
this period been neither practised
nor recommended. The following
anecdote of St. Odo of Cluny well
illustrates the prevalent feeling :—
" Cum Virgilii voluisset legere car-
mina, ostensum fuit ei per visum vas
quoddam, deforis quidem pulcherri-
mum, intus vero plenum serpentibus,
a quibus se subito circumvallari con-
spicit ; et evigilans, serpentes doctrinam poetarum, vas Virgilium intel-
lexit."—*Vita St. Odonis*, 'Annales
Ordinis St. Benedicti,' Saec. V.
John Foster, the essayist, would
doubtless not have felt himself
flattered at any resemblance he
might bear to a Middle Age Saint.
Yet his essay on the " Aversion of
Men of Taste to Evangelical Re-

ligion " contains passages which St.
Odo might have cordially praised.
Homer he thinks a most injurious
author. " Who can tell how much
that passion for war may have been
reinforced by the enthusiastic admiration with which young men read
Homer? As to the far greater
number of readers, it were vain to
wish that pure Christian sentiment
might be sufficiently recollected and
loved, to accompany the study, and
constantly prevent the injurious impression, of the works of pagan
genius. A few maxims of Christianity
will but feebly oppose the influence.
The spirit of Homer will vanquish as
irresistibly as Achilles vanquished."
(Let. 5.) St. Odo was even more
moderate than this in his disapproval
of the " doctrina poetarum."

their modern sense, never crossed his mind. This glorious
phantasmagoria of creation, what was it? The result of a
word from God. This overwhelming and inconceivable
beauty of river, and tree, and mountain ; it was all to vanish
one day ; but they had been pronounced "very good," and
prophet, psalmist, and patriarch had rejoiced in their loveli-
ness. It is true that these gorgeous heavens are to pass away
like a "scroll when it is rolled together," and a fervent heat
shall dissolve this green earth and its products ; but Nature
is not less lovely for being fellow-mortal with man—is rather
endowed with the grace of a friend with whom we know our
sojourn is brief, and that we shall see his face no more. And
thus Bernard glanced from Nature to his Bible, and from his
Bible to Nature, the one helping him to understand the other.
He was accustomed to say that whatever knowledge he had of
the Scriptures, he had acquired chiefly in the woods and fields;
and that beeches and oaks had ever been his best teachers in
the Word of God.[1]

---

[1] "Quidquid in Scripturis valet, quidquid in eis spiritualiter sentit, maxime in silvis et in agris meditando et orando se confitetur accepisse, et in hoc nullos aliquando se magistros habuisse nisi quercos et fagos joco illo suo gratioso inter amicos dicere solet."
—ST. BERN. *Op*. vol. ii. col. 1072.

CHAPTER III.

(A.D. 1114.   AETAT. 23.)

GROWTH OF CITEAUX—FOUNDATION OF CLAIRVAUX—ILLNESS OF BER-
NARD—WILLIAM OF CHAMPEAUX—WILLIAM OF ST. THIERRY—PETER
DE ROYA.

A YEAR after he had entered Citeaux, Bernard's noviciate was
over, and he solemnly made his profession.   This ceremony
was a very important business, and was surrounded with all
that could impart to it awe and majesty.   The novice was
called into the chapter, and, before the assembly, made disposal
of any worldly goods he might possess.   His head was shorn,
and the hair burnt by the sacristan in a piscina used for this
purpose.   Going to the steps of the presbytery, he then read
the form of profession, made over it the sign of the cross,
and, inclining his body, approached the altar.   He placed the
profession on the right-hand side of it, which he kissed, again
bent his body, and retired to the steps.   The abbot, standing
on the same side of the altar, removed from it the parchment,
while the novice on his hands and knees implored pardon,
repeating three times the words, " Receive me, O Lord."   The
whole convent answered with " Gloria Patri," and the cantor
began the psalm, " Have mercy on me, O God," which was
sung through by the two choirs alternately.   The novice then
" humbled himself at the abbot's feet," and afterwards did the
same before the prior, and successively before all the religious
present, even going into the retro-chorus and prostrating him-

self before the sick, if there were any.   Towards the end of
the psalm, the abbot, bearing his crosier, approached the
novice and made him rise.   A cowl was blessed and sprinkled
with holy water, and the abbot, removing from the novice his
secular garments, replaced them with the monastic dress.   The
Credo was said, and the novice had become a monk, and took
his place in the choir.[1]

The arrival of Saint Bernard and his thirty companions
proved a turning-point in the history of Citeaux.   The monastery
grew in fame, both through the praise of its friends and the
detraction of its enemies.   Out of the numbers which curiosity
attracted to view, perhaps to criticise, the new order, many
remained as monks who had come as scoffers.   The small
monastery had soon more inmates than it could conveniently
hold.   A colony of monks was dispatched, under the guidance
of an aged brother named Bertrand, to found the Abbey of
La Ferté.   Stephen selected the name "Firmitas"—"endurance"
or "strength"—as symbolical of the career he and his monks
had had, and of the fair fruit which in due time was sure to
come of perseverance.   Hugh of Macon in a short time was
the leader of another band, who established a house at Pontigny.   And already, in the year A.D. 1115, that is, two years
after the arrival of the thirty novices, it was necessary to look
out for the means of founding another offshoot of the now
prolific Citeaux.

Stephen, notwithstanding his religious enthusiasm, always
displayed a most practical and penetrating mind, quite worthy
of his English origin.   Of all qualities requisite in a ruler, a
ready and deep perception of character is one of the most
important: of this power the Abbot of Citeaux often gave
proof; but he never exercised it with more effect than when
he selected out of all before him the young Bernard, just
turned four and twenty, to be the head of the new community

---

[1] Usus Ord. Cist. cap. 103.

The choice gave surprise in the abbey, and to ordinary observers there was little to recommend it. An abbot, like a bishop, needed to be something else besides being a merely good man. He was required to be a man of energy, experience, and personal influence. On him depended much of the welfare, and even safety, of those under him. He was often brought into rude, even hostile, collision with the secular power around him. In every case, years and a matured character would appear all but indispensable for the arduous task of founding a monastery. The accumulated experience of Alberic and Stephen together had only been sufficient to accomplish it in the case of Citeaux. Such reflections naturally arose on the occasion of Bernard's selection.[1]

Twelve monks and their young abbot—representing our Lord and His apostles—were assembled in the church. Stephen placed a cross in Bernard's hands, who solemnly, at the head of his small band, walked forth from Citeaux. The monks who were to remain accompanied them to the abbey gates, for Bernard's powerful and assimilating nature had won all hearts, and the day of his departure was a sad one in Citeaux. Till they reached the limit of their own land they walked so closely together that it was not easy to say which were going and which were to remain ; but the gateway revealed the emigrants. A Cistercian monk might not leave his own grounds on any pretext without permission. Bernard, cross in hand, passed over the prescribed boundary, and his allotted troop were severed from their late companions.[2]

---

[1] " Misit Deus in cor abbatis Stephani ad aedificandam domum Clarae-Vallis mittere fratres ejus. Quibus abeuntibus ipsum etiam domnum Bernardum praefecit abbatem, mirantibus sane illis, tanquam maturis et strenuis tam in religione quam in saeculo viris, et timentibus ei tum pro tenerioris aetate juventutis, tum pro corporis infirmitate, et minori usu exterioris occupationis."—ST. BERN. *Op.* vol. ii. col. 1073.

[2] " Duodecim monachi loco xii. Apostolorum cum tertiodecimo abbate qui loco Christi eis praeponitur, ad novam abbatiam fundandam emittuntur. Crux enim dominicam ha-

Bernard struck away to the northward. For a distance of nearly ninety miles he kept this course, passing up by the source of the Seine, by Chatillon, of school-day memories, till he arrived at La Ferté, about equally distant between Troyes and Chaumont, in the diocese of Langres, and situated on the river Aube. About four miles beyond La Ferté was a deep valley opening to the east: thick umbrageous forests gave it a character of gloom and wildness; but a gushing stream of limpid water, which ran through it, was sufficient to redeem every disadvantage. In June, A.D. 1115, Bernard took up his abode in the valley of Wormwood, as it was called, and began to look for means of shelter and sustenance against the approaching winter. The rude fabric which he and his monks raised with their own hands, was long preserved by the pious veneration of the Cistercians. It consisted of a building covered by a single roof, under which, chapel, dormitory, and refectory, were all included. Neither stone nor wood hid the bare earth, which served for floor. Windows, scarcely wider than a man's hand, admitted a feeble light. In this room the monks took their frugal meals of herbs and water. Immediately above the refectory was the sleeping apartment. It was reached by a ladder, and was, in truth, a sort of loft. Here were the monks' beds, which were peculiar. They were made in the form of boxes, or bins of wooden planks, long and wide enough for a man to lie down in. A small space, hewn out with an axe, allowed room for the sleeper to get in or out. The inside was strewn with chaff, or dried leaves, which,

bens imaginem, a patre abbate datur ei in manus, quem de oratorio cum eadem cruce exeuntem duodecim ad hoc ordinati sequuntur, quasi Christum Apostoli. . . . Videres cum jam essent recessuri, in profundo silentio cadentes lacrymas omnium monachorum, et solas voces cantantium resonantes inter singultus . . . nec decerneres remansuros a discedentibus, quoadusque ad portam domus illos stantes a progredientibus cunctatio ipsa divisit. Haec Bernardo atque sociis abeuntibus, devota quidem sed tristis facies Cistercii fuit." —*Acta Sanct.* tom. iv. August. die 20, § 5.

with the wood-work, seem to have been the only covering permitted.[1]

At the summit of the stair or ladder, was the abbot's cell. It was of most scanty dimensions, and these were further reduced by the loss of one corner, through which access was gained to the apartment from below. A framework of boards was placed over the flight of steps, in such a manner that they were made to answer the purpose of a bed. Two rough-hewn logs of wood were his pillows. The roof was low and slanting, to such a degree that it was impossible to sit upright near the wall. It was also the sole means of obtaining both light and air; sometimes too easily, as, through its imperfect joining, wind, rain, heat, and cold, found a ready entrance. Such was the commencement of Clairvaux.[1]

The monks had thus got a house over their heads; but they had very little else. They had left Citeaux in June. Their journey had probably occupied them a fortnight; their clearing, preparations, and building, perhaps two months; and thus they would be near September, when this portion of their labour was accomplished. Autumn and winter were approaching, and they

---

[1] Joseph Meglinger, a German religious, of the monastery St. Maria de Maris Stella (Wettingen), in May, 1667, paid a visit to Citeaux (to attend the general Chapter), and has left a very curious account of what he saw there. He also proceeded on to Clairvaux, and, in a pleasant familiar way, tells us of the state in which he found the venerable relic of the great abbot,—viz. the first monastery at Clairvaux, which Bernard had himself helped to build.

"Ad antiquum monasterium pervenimus. Id Bernardus ac socii cum eo ex Cistercio missi propriis manibus fabricarunt. Uno tecto templum et habitatio monachorum operitur; una etiam contignatio comedendi et dormiendi loca separat. Infra refectorium nullo lapide stratum, nudam terram sanctissimis illis pedibus calcandam praebebat, . . . paucis et palmo non majoribus fenestris illud illuminantibus."— MEGLINGERI, *Iter.* cap. 66.

"Hinc per scalam ascenditur ad dormitorium, idem in longum latumque occupans spatium cum refectorio; in quo adhuc aliquot lectisternia supersunt, ex quatuor asseribus compacta; longa ad hominis proceritatem et dimidia parte minus lata; humili cistae ferme similia. . . stramini . . . aut aridis arborum foliis . . . loco plumarum utebantur."—Ibid.

[2] Ibid. cap. 67.

had no store laid by. Their food during the summer had been a compound of leaves, intermixed with coarse grain. Beech-nuts and roots were to be their main support during the winter And now to the privations of insufficient food was added the wearing out of their shoes and clothes. Their necessities grew with the severity of the season, till at last even salt failed them ; and presently Bernard heard murmurs. He argued and exhorted ; he spoke to them of the fear and love of God, and strove to rouse their drooping spirits by dwelling on the hopes of eternal life and Divine recompense. Their sufferings made them deaf and indifferent to their abbot's words. They would not remain in this valley of bitterness, they would return to Citeaux. Bernard, seeing they had lost their trust in God, reproved them no more, but himself sought in earnest prayer for release from their difficulties. Presently a voice from Heaven said, "Arise, Bernard, thy prayer is granted thee." Upon which the monks said, "What didst thou ask of the Lord ?" "Wait, and ye shall see, ye of little faith," was the reply ; and presently came a stranger, who gave the abbot ten livres.[1]

On another occasion he said to Brother Guibert, "Guibert, saddle the ass, go to the fair, and buy us salt." Guibert answered, "Where is the money ?" "Believe me," said Bernard, "I know not the time when I had gold or silver. He is above who holds my wallet and my treasures in His hands." "If I go forth empty, so shall I return." "Fear not, my son, go in peace. He who holds our treasures will be with thee in the way, and will grant thee all those things for which I send thee." Guibert received his abbot's benediction

---

[1] "Coacti vero fame, frigore, et aliis indigentiis, abbati suo conquesti sunt, quod pro nimia paupertate discedere cogerentur. . . . Abbas blande et leniter consolans eos, Dei timorem et amorem, spem quoque vitae eternae et remunerationis di-vinae, quantum potuit, insinuavit ; . . . demum convertit se ad oratio-nem, quo facto, audivit vocem de coelo dicentem sibi coram omnibus 'Surge, Bernarde, exaudita est oratio tua.'"—J. Eremita, *St. Bern. Op.* vol. ii. col. 1286.

and obeyed, though still more than doubtful of the use of his
errand. He proceeded on the ass—the solitary animal in the
possession of the community—to the castle of Risnellum,
where the fair was. As he approached his destination, he met
a priest. "Whence comest thou, brother, and whither art
thou bound?" He told his questioner the object of his
expedition, and drew a sad picture of the misery and suffering
to which he and all the monks under Bernard were reduced.
The tale so wrought upon the priest that he took him to his
own house, gave him half a bushel of salt, and fifty *solidi* or
more. Guibert soon hastened back to Clairvaux, and told
Bernard all that had occurred to him. "I tell thee, my son,"
said Bernard, "that no one thing is so necessary to a Christian
as faith. Have faith, therefore, and it will be well with thee
all the days of thy life." [1]

From that day forth, we are told, Guibert and the other
monks held the words of Bernard in greater reverence than
they had done before : a result which might well arise—not,
indeed, from apocryphal miraculous power attributed to him,
but from the native vigour and grandeur of his character,
which the trials they had just passed through had distinctly
brought out. Though the weakest in body, he had shown he
possessed the stoutest heart ; and men found it more profitable and more agreeable to obey than to oppose him.

After this crisis was over, a bright prospect opened on
Clairvaux. Indeed, it would seem that a new monastery was
in a measure bound o win its way to public fame, by first of
all nearly getting extinguished by cold and hunger. Molême
had done so ; Citeaux had done so ; and now Clairvaux had
followed these examples. The curiosity, first, then the
sympathy of the neighbourhood were attracted, and Clairvaux
was soon placed beyond the reach of those trials by which it
won its first renown.

[1] St. Bern. Op. vol. ii. col. 1285.

In the mean time Bernard had been solemnly consecrated Abbot of Clairvaux. His diocesan, the Bishop of Langres, being absent from his see, a substitute had to be found to perform the ceremony. "The good fame of the venerable Bishop of Chalons, that most renowned Master William of Champeaux, was soon heard of, and it was determined to go to him." Bernard therefore went to Chalons, taking with him a monk named Elboldo, a man of large and powerful frame. They entered the bishop's palace, and presented a striking, almost grotesque, contrast ; Bernard's attenuated body and emaciated countenance, his homeliness, not to say raggedness of dress, excited the mirth of the loungers and idlers about the bishop's house. There was no small question as to which of the two was abbot ; but the bishop, " a servant of God, was the first to recognise the servant of God," and received him accordingly. In their first conference, " Bernard's modesty of speech showed William of Champeaux, better than any eloquence could, the wisdom that was in him ; and the bishop appreciated the worth of his guest." The experienced master of the Paris schools, doubtless, soon perceived that in the threadbare, care-worn youth before him, a rare and ardent spirit was concealed. He prevailed on Bernard to pay him a short visit. Then, in the freedom of social conversation, the monk's demureness was cast aside, and the old dialectician could feel more distinctly the warmth of an enthusiasm which Bernard veiled from ordinary eyes. The foundation of a deep and lasting friendship was laid at this interview, and they afterwards visited each other so frequently, that Clairvaux became a sort of bishop's palace, and Chalons became in a measure another Clairvaux. William's friendship also made many others enter upon friendly relations with Bernard.[1]

---

[1] " Abiit autem Catalaunum, assumpto secum Elboldone monacho quodam Cisterciensi. Intravit, ergo, praedicti episcopi domum, juvenis exesi corporis et moribundi, habitu quoque despicabilis, subsequente

But these labours, anxieties, and powerful emotions, which his new duties had imposed upon him, in addition to his own excessive austerities, had well-nigh brought Bernard to the grave. The responsibility which rested on him, the love and devotion he bore to his flock, the difficulties and dangers he had passed through, all contributed to excite a restless, almost feverish, energy of soul. After matins, in the deep dark night he would wander forth alone, and pray to God with all his strength that what he did, and what his brethren did, might be pleasing in His sight. Then, while shutting his eyes, still in prayer, his over-wrought mind saw in vision the surrounding country, even to the slopes of the neighbouring hills, filled with an innumerable multitude of every rank and diversity of condition, so that the valley could not contain them.[1] A robust constitution must have succumbed to such incessant demands on the powers of life. Bernard's enfeebled frame was failing fast, when his friend, the bishop, came to pay him a visit. He found Clairvaux confused with grief at the condition of its abbot. He was told there was no hope, that either death, or a life that was worse than death, must be expected for Bernard. William did not take quite so desponding a view of the case. He said he had hopes not only of Bernard's life, but even of his health, if he could be induced to spare himself a little, and take rest. Yet he fully appreciated the danger of his condition, more especially as he found Bernard quite inflexible with regard to the required change. William resorted to a stratagem which was as credit-

monacho seniore, et magnitudine et robore corporis eleganti, aliis ridentibus, aliis irridentibus, aliis rem sicut erat interpretando venerantibus. . . . Ut propria esset domus episcopi Clara-Vallis; Claraevallensium vero efficeretur non sola domus episcopi, sed et per ipsum tota civitas Cata-

launensis."—St. BERN. *Op.* vol. ii. col. 1076.

[1] "Contigit autem . ut aliquando temperius solito surgeret ad vigilias . . . egressus foras, et loca vicina circumiens, orabat Deum, ut acceptum haberet obsequium suum et fratrum suorum."—Ibid. col. 1073.

able to his subtlety, as its motive was to his heart. He started off at once for Citeaux. He found the Chapter assembled, and entering, prostrated himsel.—bishop as he was —before Stephen and the abbots around him. William begged, and obtained leave, to direct and manage Bernard for one year only. So provided, he hastened back to Clairvaux, and now found its abbot as obedient as he had before been unyielding. He caused a small cottage to be built outside the monastery walls ; in this he ordered Bernard to dwell, at the same time commanding that neither his food nor drink should be regulated by the monastic rule, while all care and responsibility as regarded the abbey were removed from his mind. The good bishop probably hoped that he had taken measures prompt and vigorous enough to ensure his object, and returned to Chalons, from which he had been so long absent for his friend's sake.[1]

In the mean time Bernard continued to do as he was told. The result of this passive obedience is related by an eyewitness, his friend and biographer, William of St. Thierry. William, in company with another abbot, had paid him a visit, and gives this account of it :—" I found him," says the affectionate chronicler, " in his hut, . . . freed by the order of the bishop and abbots from all care of the monastery, whether external or internal, at leisure for himself and God, and exulting, as it were, in the delights of Paradise. When I entered that chamber, and beheld the place and its inhabitant, I call God to witness, a feeling of veneration came over me as

[1] " Modico vero post tempore transacto, cum eousque infirmitas abbatis ingravesceret, ut jam nonnisi mors ejus, aut omni morte gravior vita speraretur, ab episcopo visitatus est. Cumque viso eo episcopus se non solum vitae ejus, sed et sanitatis spem habere diceret, si consilio ejus acquiescens, secundum infirmitatis suae modum aliquam corpori suo curam pateretur impendi . . . profectus episcopus ad Capitulum Cisterciense ibi coram pauculis abbatibus qui convenerant . . . toto corpore in terram prostratus, petiit et obtinuit ut tantum anno uno in obedientiam sibi traderetur."— St. Bern. *Op.* vol. ii. col. 1076.

if I had been approaching the altar of God. He, on his part, received us with joy, and we then inquired how he did, and how he liked his new mode of life. 'Excellent well,' he replied, in his own noble manner; 'I who have hitherto ruled over rational beings, by a great judgment of God am given over to obey an irrational beast.' This he spoke concerning an ignorant rustic, to whose care he had been entrusted, and who boasted he would cure him of the infirmity he was suffering from. As we sat at meat with him, I thought how carefully so precious an invalid should be tended. Yet presently we saw food placed before him by the agency of this doctor, which a healthy man, driven on by the extremity of hunger, would not have eaten. We could hardly restrain ourselves from breaking the rule of silence, and assailing that sacrilegious homicide with angry reproaches. But he to whom this was done took it all with indifference, and approved of everything. His sense of taste seemed altered or even dead, so that he could scarcely discern anything. For he is known to have eaten raw blood for many days, which, by mistake, had been given him for butter, and to have drunk oil, thinking it to be water, and many similar mishaps occurred to him. Water alone, he said, was pleasant to him, which, as he swallowed it, cooled the fever of his throat and mouth.

"I tarried with him a few days, unworthy though I was, and whichever way I turned my eyes I marvelled, and thought I saw a new heaven and a new earth, and the old pathways of the Egyptian monks our fathers, with recent footsteps of the men of our time left in them. The golden age seemed to have revisited the world then at Clairvaux. There you could see men, who had been rich and honoured in the world, glorying in the poverty of Christ." William continues, in a strain of enthusiastic admiration, to give a description of Clairvaux as it was at this time.—

" At the first glance, as you entered Clairvaux by descending the hill, you could see it was a temple of God ; and the still, silent valley bespoke, in the modest simplicity of its buildings, the unfeigned humility of Christ's poor. Moreover, in this valley full of men, where no one was permitted to be idle, where one and all were occupied with their allotted tasks, a silence, deep as that of night, prevailed. The sounds of labour, or the chants of the brethren in the choral service, were the only exceptions. The order of this silence, and the fame that went forth of it, struck such a reverence even into secular persons that they dreaded breaking it—I will not say by idle or wicked conversation, but even by pertinent remarks. The solitude, also, of the place—between dense forests in a narrow gorge of neighbouring hills—in a certain sense recalled the cave of our father Saint Benedict, so that while they strove to imitate his life, they also had some similarity to him in their habitation and loneliness."[1]

Another description of Clairvaux, but referring to its effects on the mind rather than its appearance to the eye, has come down to us. It is in a letter to the Provost of Noyon, by a young novice named Peter de Roya. A great deal of it is occupied with the conventional phrases usually produced after religious conversion. But presently come passages of real human feeling and perception.

" Often whilst I was at Noyon, dear friend, in the bishop's palace, and sat in the window, either alone or with you or with others, I contemplated the order and beauty of that house—a beauty which was fresh yesterday, to grow old and withered to-day—and, while doing so, I secretly turned the glance of my

---

[1] The reader will often meet with William of St. Thierry again. He was one of Bernard's most devoted friends. The biography we have by him of Bernard was never finished ; as he died before the Abbot of Clairvaux. The passage translated in the text is from the 7th chapter of his little book entitled Vita Prima, cap. 7.—St. Bern. *Op.* vol. ii. col. 1076, 1077.

mind's eye to that most orderly house which is in the heavens, whose glorious, indestructible, and ever new beauty passes man's faculty to imagine. . . . For, as I sat at the table of the bishop, our fellow-citizen and my host, I fed daintily off silver plate, and not unwholesomely as far as the fare was concerned. But, while I gathered with my bodily hand those sweet delicacies, with the hand of the heart, from the same silver platters, I was collecting a very different food. And you, my friend, although we sat near enough to each other, you did not know that I was so employed. Do I, therefore, blame those daily festive banquets or innocent plates and salvers? do I accuse the good wine, whose colour softly charmed the eye, and whose flavour gave a sweet response in the palate? do I accuse the silver goblets? God forbid. Neither the food, nor the wine, nor the cups were to blame. But in me, a potter's vessel, lurked seeds from which within I felt the sharp sting of a rising crop of thorns." This all ends in his going to Clairvaux.

"Although the monastery is situated in a valley, it has its foundation on the holy hills, whose gates the Lord loveth more than all the dwellings of Jacob. Glorious things are spoken of it, because the glorious and wonderful God therein worketh great marvels. There the insane recover their reason; and, although their outward man is worn away, inwardly they are born again. There the proud are humbled, the rich are made poor, and the poor have the Gospel preached to them, and the darkness of sinners is changed into light. A large multitude of blessed poor from the ends of the earth have there assembled, yet have they one heart and one mind; justly, therefore, do all who dwell there rejoice with no empty joy. They have the certain hope of perennial joy—of their ascension heavenward already commenced. In Clairvaux they have found Jacob's ladder, with angels upon it; some descending, who so provide for their bodies that they faint not on the way; others ascending, who so rule their souls that their bodies hereafter may be glorified with them.

"For my part, the more attentively I watch them day by day, the more do I believe that they are perfect followers of Christ in all things. When they pray and speak to God in spirit and in truth, by their friendly and quiet speech to Him as well as by their humbleness of demeanour, they are plainly seen to be God's companions and friends. When, on the other hand, they openly praise God with psalmody, how pure and fervent are their minds, is shown by the posture of body in holy fear and reverence; while, by their careful pronunciation and modulation of the psalms, is shown how sweet to their lips are the words of God—sweeter than honey to their mouths. As I watch them, therefore, singing without fatigue, from before midnight to the dawn of day, with only a brief interval, they appear a little less than the angels, but much more than men. . . . As regards their manual labour, so patiently and placidly, with such quiet countenances, in such sweet and holy order do they perform all things, that, although they exercise themselves at many works, they never seem moved or burdened in anything, whatever the labour may be. Whence it is manifest that that Holy Spirit worketh in them who disposeth of all things with sweetness, in whom they are refreshed, so that they rest even in their toil. Many of them, I hear, are bishops and earls, and many illustrious through their birth or knowledge; but now, by God's grace, all acceptation of persons being dead among them, the greater any one thought himself in the world, the more in this flock does he regard himself as less than the least. I see them in the garden with hoes, in the meadows with forks or rakes, in the fields with scythes, in the forest with axes. To judge from their outward appearance, their tools, their bad and disordered clothes, they appear a race of fools, without speech or sense. But a true thought in my mind tells me that their life in Christ is hidden in the heavens. Among

them I see Godfrey of Peronne, Raynald of Picardy, William
of St. Omer, Walter of Lisle, all of whom I knew formerly in
the old man, whereof I now see no trace, by God's favour.
I knew them proud and puffed up. I see them walking
humbly under the merciful hand of God.

"Such, my friend, is a brief account of Clairvaux. Greater
and better things remain untold; but this must suffice for the
present. My desire is that I may deserve to be joined with
these poor in Christ. In the meantime I undergo my probation,
and, by the grace of God, I am being established in their rule
and life so that, until I be joined to them, I may learn to watch
with them, and dream only in the Spirit. For the kingdom is
promised to him who watches; and he who sows in the Spirit
shall of the Spirit reap everlasting life. May I, a partaker of it,
behold you and the whole Church of Noyon, my mistress and
mother, by the mercy of God, reigning and living with Christ
for ever. On the Sunday after Ascension Day, I shall, God
willing, assume the armour of our monastic profession. Farewell! and think on your last days."[1]

[1] Epist. Bern. 492; Op. vol. i. col. 393.

CHAPTER IV.

(A.D. 1118. ÆTAT. 27.)

FOUNDATION OF THE ORDER OF CITEAUX—THE CHARTER OF CHARITY
—THE COMMENCEMENT OF ST. BERNARD'S CORRESPONDENCE— LETTERS
TO ROBERT—TO FULK—SERMONS ON THE ANNUNCIATION.

IT was said in the last chapter that William of Champeaux had
petitioned " Stephen Harding and the abbots around him at
Citeaux " to be entrusted with the care of Bernard for a twelve-
month.   The expression refers to one of the most important
facts in the history of monasticism—to one of the greatest and
wisest additions to the scheme of Saint Benedict ever made,
and such as almost entitles the English abbot of Citeaux to be
considered the second founder of cœnobitic life.

Saint Benedict's celebrated rule had reference solely to a
single religious house—it might almost be said to a single
monk.   It is a mixture of exhortation and command to lead
a life of self-mortification and prayer :—" Hear, O son, the
Master's words, and incline the ear of thine heart.   Accept
the counsel of a loving Father, and accomplish it thoroughly,
in order that thou mayest return to Him, through the labour
of obedience, whom thou forsookest in the wantonness of
disobedience.   To thee are my words directed, whosoever
thou mayest be, who, renouncing thine own self-will, and
assuming the strong and splendid arms of submission, art
ready to fight for the Lord Christ, the true King."   And this
immediate, personal tone of direction is rarely departed from.

Saint Benedict's ideal monastery is severed from the outer world completely, and has no necessary relations even with other monasteries.[1]

The result was that the position of monasteries in the Church was, for a considerable time, ill-defined and uncertain. Under whose jurisdiction did their supervision in the last resort reside? During the seventh, eighth, and ninth centuries, when the episcopate was ascendant in the Church, the bishops assumed the right of controlling monasteries, and even of deposing abbots. When the papacy rose into its vast authority, the convents made strenuous efforts to get relieved from a subjection which they found always irksome and sometimes tyrannical, and sought and obtained of the head of the Church immunities from episcopal dominion. Still the corruption and disorders, which were far from unknown in monasteries, rendered this one of the weakest sides of the institute. A few years sometimes, through the succession of a weak or wicked abbot to a wise and good one, were enough to witness the fall of an old illustrious abbey from an elevated piety to a degrading worldliness. The famous house of Cluny, as will be presently seen, was a conspicuous example of such a fall.[2]

Stephen Harding's experiences at Molême or elsewhere had shown to him the danger and malignity of this evil, and with the genius of a statesman he had devised a remedy for it. He conceived a plan of uniting in one compact whole all monasteries which sprang from the parent stock of Citeaux. A

---

[1] "Ausculta, O fili, praecepta magistri, et inclina aurem cordis tui : et admonitionem pii patris libenter excipe, et efficaciter comple ; ut ad eum per obedientiae laborem redeas, a quo per inobedientiae desidiam recesseras."—*Regula St. Benedicti,* Prolog.

[2] In two admirable lectures of his "Histoire de la Civilisation en France," vol. ii. lecs. xiv.-xv. M.

Guizot has developed the rise and progress of monasticism. He has adduced redundant proof of—1. The lay character and independence of the primitive monks. 2. Their gradual entrance into the clerical body. 3. Their humiliating subjection to the bishops. 4. Their slow emancipation, partly through help from the royal power, but principally from the papacy.

system of **mutual** supervision and control was the result.   As early as Bernard's illness, during his first year at Clairvaux, in A.D. 1116, a few abbots were assembled around Stephen, when William of Champeaux unexpectedly entered.   Three **years** afterwards a more encouraging **prospect** was before him.[1]   His Cistercians had so thriven that he was able to collect **twelve** abbots under his presidency at Citeaux.   These, as representatives of their abbeys, were to be **united** to one another, and to their **chief**, by common **hopes** and common **fears**, by a system in which **mutual** love, ambition, and envy should combine to further **one** and the same end—namely, the spiritual **welfare** and **independence** of the order.   The abbots of the order of Citeaux were assumed to be—and at this period doubtless were—animated by a pure zeal for religion and the **Church**.   But "if any—which God forbid—should attempt to forsake the sacred observance of the **holy rule**," hope is expressed that, "by care and solicitude, they **may be able to** return to rectitude of life."[2]

The general **Chapter** met **every year** in September, and lasted five days.   Every abbot of the order, whose monastery was in France, **Italy**, or **Germany**, was **bound** to attend annually.   Illness alone was a valid excuse, and then even a fit "**messenger**" must be sent to account for the absence of his chief.[3]   Abbots residing at a greater distance **from Citeaux** than those above mentioned were held to a **less frequent** attendance.   Those from **Spain every two years**; those from

---

[1] "Le chapitre général fut fondé en 1119.   Les Abbayes Cisterciennes étaient alors au nombre de treize.   D'abord les cinq abbayes-mères, Citeaux et Laferté, Pontigny, Clairvaux, Morimond ; ensuite Prully, Trois Fontaines, la Cour-Dieu, Bonnevaux, Bouras, Cadouin, Fontenoy, Mazan."—*Études sur les Abbayes Cisterciennes au* XIIᵉ *et au* XIIIᵉ *Siècle*, par M. D'Arbois de Jubainville, p. 148.

[2] *Charta Charitatis,* cap. i.

[3] "Omnes abbates de nostro ordine singulis annis ad generale Capitulum Cisterciense, omni postposita occasione, conveniant, illis exceptis quos corporis infirmitas retinuerit."—*Ibid.* cap. iii.

Ireland, Scotland, Sicily, Portugal, every four years; those from Norway, every five years; and those from Syria and Palestine, every seven years.[1]

The Charter of Charity, which this Chapter definitely promulgated for the guidance of the Cistercian order, is a brief but pregnant document. In five short chapters it provides for a system of government and mutual supervision of rulers and ruled which quite justifies and explains the discipline, organization, and success which attended it while it was carried out. The Abbot of Citeaux, lord and master as he is of all—so that to whatever monastery he comes, the abbot of that monastery, for the time being, abdicates his functions in his favour—even he is under the strict supervision of the four Abbots of La Ferté, Pontigny, Clairvaux, and Morimond. If he is remiss or vicious, they are to admonish him four times of his errors, and implore him to amend himself, or to see to the amendment of others. If all this avails not, they are to call a Chapter of the order and solemnly depose him.[2] On the other hand, the Abbot of Citeaux, at least once a year, shall visit all the abbeys which are of his filiation; and each of them, again, shall overlook the houses which have sprung from them. The great object is to keep the rule in its entire purity, and carefully to report and to suppress any the least deviation from it, either in the letter or the spirit. "If any abbot shall be found too lukewarm for the rule or too intent on worldly matters, or in

[1] Études, par M. D'Arbois de Jubainville, p. 150.

[2] "Domum autem Cisterciensem simul per seipsos visitent quatuor primi abbates, de Firmitate, de Pontigniaco, de Claravalle, de Morimundo, die quam inter se constituerint."—*Charta Charitatis*, cap. ii. § 9.

"Si forte, quod absit, abbates nostri ordinis matrem nostram Cisterciensem ecclesiam in sancto proposito languescere, et ab observatione regulae vel ordinis nostri exorbitare cognoverint, abbatem ejusdem loci per quatuor primos abbates, scilicet de Firmitate, de Pontiniaco, de Claravalle, de Morimundo, sub caeterorum abbatum nomine, usque quater ut corrigatur ipse, et alios corrigere curet, admoneant . . . virum inutilem ab officio suo deponant."—Ibid. cap. v. § 27.

any way reprehensible," he shall be "accused publicly in the Chapter—shall ask for pardon, and undergo penance commensurate with his fault." Thus the piety of good men, and the interest of worldly men, were alike enlisted on the side of regularity and rigour. A powerful corporate spirit was generated; width of view and largeness of sympathy were encouraged by the frequent and well-attended debates at Citeaux, which certainly, at this period, was an example of a self-governing community, or school for political experience, nearly, if not quite, unique in the world.

In the meantime, Bernard, at Clairvaux, had recovered his health, and resumed his duties of abbot. He did more. About the year 1119 he commenced that career of literary and ecclesiastical activity—that wide and impassioned correspondence—that series of marvellous sermons, which have won for him the title of the Last of the Fathers. His first essays— the first strong but untutored efforts of his powerful intellect— are curious, as being *his*, rather than for merits of their own. The vigour is abundant; but it is not directed by judgment and skill. The extracts which follow from his two first Epistles, and his Homilies on the Annunciation, are given, not for their own excellence, but as standards to show how much they were afterwards surpassed.

Among the thirty converts who entered Citeaux, under the leadership of Bernard, was a young kinsman named Robert. From Citeaux, Robert followed his cousin to Clairvaux, and, it is supposed, made his profession in the year 1116. The youth had been touched with the enthusiasm around him, and bound himself hastily to a mode of life, which before long he was glad to abandon. The severe, unrelenting discipline was more than he could bear. He was not without hopes of deliverance. His parents, in his childhood, had promised him to the monastery of Cluny; and Robert well knew the difference between the opulent and magnificent Cluny and the

LETTER TO HIS KINSMAN ROBERT.

poor austere Clairvaux. While he was in this state of mind an emissary from Cluny arrived at Clairvaux. Robert fled. This was a most painful incident to Bernard. It was a sort of defeat in the midst of his success. For a monk to leave Clairvaux—above all, for that monk to be a relation of the abbot—was necessarily a most untoward occurrence. Bernard wrote to the young deserter a long and curious epistle, in which genuine feeling and rhetorical bombast alternately contend for, and obtain the mastery. His wrath against Cluny, and his tenderness for Robert, struggle for utterance, in succeeding sentences, through four folio pages.

After taking full blame to himself for inadvertence in not tempering with more care the severity of the rule to the tenderness of Robert's age, he alludes to the artful temptations which were held out to him from Cluny.

" A certain great prior was sent, outwardly having sheep's clothing, but inwardly a ravening wolf. He attracted, he enticed, he flattered, and this noble preacher of the Gospel eulogised debauchery, condemned thrift, and voluntary poverty he termed misery. Fastings, vigils, silence, and manual labour he regarded as insanity, whereas idleness was with him contemplation, gluttony, loquacity, and every sort of indulgence was *discretion.* 'When,' he would say, 'is God pleased with our sufferings? where does the Scripture command any one to kill himself? and what sort of religion is that which consists in digging the ground, cutting timber, and carting manure? Wherefore did God create food, if we may not eat of it? why did he give us bodies, if we may not support them? In fine, to whom will he be good who is evil to himself? and what man in his right mind ever hated his own flesh?' "

This passage shows Bernard well knew what could be, and doubtless often was, said against his severe discipline. Indeed he appears to take a pleasure in a sort of rhetorical exaggeration of what might be urged against him, as if too sure of his ground to be doubtful of the issue. He proceeds to say how this "wolf of a prior" had succeeded, and carried off his victim to Cluny; how Robert was clipped, shaven, and washed; and his old rustic clothes were exchanged for new handsome ones.

"What then, will you find salvation in splendour and abundance of clothes and food, or in sobriety and frugality? If soft warm furs, fine and costly garments, long sleeves and an ample hood, downy couch and dainty coverlet, make a saint, why do I delay a moment? why do I not follow you to Cluny? But these are comforts for the sick, not arms for the men of war. Wine and the like, soup and fat things—these are for the body, not for the mind; not the soul, but the flesh is nourished by ragouts. Many brethren in Egypt served God a long time without eating fish. Pepper, ginger, sage, and cummin, and a thousand other spices, may indeed delight the palate, but they also light up the flames of lust; and think you youth can be passed in safety, surrounded by them? . . . . You fear our fasts, and vigils, and manual labour, but if you dwell on eternal flames, these will seem matters of small moment. The remembrance of outer darkness will banish all fear of solitude. If you reflect that account is to be kept of every idle word, silence will strike you as less appalling. That eternal weeping and gnashing of teeth, if brought before the mind's eye, will make a mattress or feather bed equally indifferent. If you watch by night, and attend to the Psalms as the rule directs you, that bed must be hard indeed in which you will not placidly rest. If you work as much as you ought, according to your vows, plain indeed must be the fare which you do not readily relish.

"Arise, then, soldier of Christ, shake off the dust, and return to battle whence you have fled; show more courage after this flight, in hopes of a more glorious triumph. Are you fearful? But why fearful when there is no cause for fear, and yet bold where all is terrible? Because you have deserted your ranks do you suppose you have escaped the enemy? Alas! the enemy will pursue you more readily in flight than he would resist you if you attacked him. Now you have laid aside your arms, and, at the very hour in which Christ rose from the dead, you are deep in morning slumber. An armed multitude surrounds your house, and yet you sleep. They are scaling the walls; they demolish the palisade; they will soon burst through the postern. Do you wish to be found by them alone, or with others?—naked in bed, or armed in the field? Up, seize your arms; hasten to your comrades whom you forsook. At what do you tremble when the united band of armed brethren will protect you, when angels will fight by you, when the commander, Christ, will go before you, animating His own to victory, and saying, ‘Be of good cheer, I have overcome the world?’ If Christ is for us, who can be against us? You may well fight without fear when you are certain to be conqueror. Safe indeed is warfare with, and for, Christ, for though wounded, prostrate, trampled on, killed, if possible, a thousand times, yet, if you fly not, you shall in nowise lose your victory. By flight alone you can lose it. Death will give it you. Death will crown you. But woe be to you if you lose, through flight, both crown and victory!"[1]

Bernard's passionate appeals were in vain, at least for the time. The "morning slumbers," the "ginger," and the

[1] Sanct. Bern. Op. vol. i. col. 1, epist. i. This letter was placed first, we are told by William of St. Thierry and the monk Geoffrey, on account of the miracle which attended the writing of it. Geoffrey intimates that Bernard not only accepted the authorship of the miracle when performed, but knew that it was coming beforehand: " Exiit autem " (says Geoffrey) " extra monasterii septa, ut dictaret secretius; et Guillelmus, qui postea in Angliis Rievallensem aedificavit abbatiam, quae dictabantur excipiens scribebat in charta. Subito autem, inundante pluvia, timuit qui scribebat; erant enim sub dio." William adds further detail: " Chartam reponere voluit. Cui venerabilis abbas,—Opus

"pepper" had charms for young Robert, which he found not in spiritual things when they were dwelt on in so severe a manner as at Clairvaux. He remained at Cluny for several years, in fact, till the death of the abbot, Pontius. The latter's successor, Peter the Venerable, restored the truant to Bernard.

Soon after this grief, Bernard had another of a similar kind. It had not, indeed, the additional sting of arising from a relation of his own ; but it was sufficiently mortifying to him as a Cistercian monk. The facts, as far as we know them, were these. A young man, of the name of Fulk, had made vows as a regular canon. He had an uncle a dean. The uncle was rich and old. He had long enjoyed Fulk's company ; but now, just when he wanted it most, he was deprived of it by the young man's taking vows as a regular canon. To whom he was to leave his garnered treasures was now a doubt and trouble to him. He had land, and horses, and vessels of gold and silver, and whose were they to be? So Fulk was induced to forsake his canons, and come back and live with his uncle. But what a horrid apostasy was this ! Fulk, who had renounced the world and all that belonged to it—who had made vows of obedience, poverty, silence, and mortification, to abandon all this, and merely at the temptations of an old uncle and worldly riches. Bernard's whole nature was shocked. He poured forth his sorrow, indignation, and reproof in a long letter, from which follow a few extracts :—

"I would say nothing of your uncle's crime if I could, in order to avoid, if possible, all useless offence. But I cannot pass one by whom I have ever found, as far as in him lay, an adversary of the Holy Spirit. He certainly strove to extin-

---

inquit Dei est ; fac quod facis. Res mira ! *Madebant vestes eorum*, et scribebatur grandis epistola, et chartam omnino non tetigit imber. Extat adhuc epistola ; et ego ipse primam eam constitui in corpore epistolarum, cum audissem tam grande miraculum ab ipsius ore, qui scripsit eam in pluvia sine pluvia."—St. BERN. *Op.* vol. ii. col. 1277.

guish all fervour in me when a novice. But thanks be to God, he prevailed not.

"But what shall I say of your **uncle's** malice, who withdrew **his** nephews from Christ's warfare **to take** them with himself to him? Is it thus he is **used to serve his** friends? Those whom **Christ calls to** abide for ever with **Him your** uncle recalls, that they may burn for ever **with him.** I marvel that Christ's wrath is not already kindled against him, and **ready to** say, '**How often have I** wished to gather your nephews even **as a** hen gathereth her chickens under her wings, **and you** would not.' . . . Christ says, 'Suffer little children **to come** unto Me, for of such is the kingdom of heaven.' Your uncle says, '**Suffer my nephews that they** may burn with me.' Christ says, '**They are mine, and Me they ought to serve.**' '**Nay,**' says **your uncle,** 'but they perish with me.'"

After **a good deal more of similar** declamatory exhortation, he thus describes the uncle's feelings and reflections, **on hearing** of Fulk having become a canon :—

"Woe is me! what do I hear? how blighted are my hopes. Is it right, lawful, just, or reasonable, that one whom I have brought up from a child should now, when a man, be the profit **of others?** My hair is white ; **alas!** I shall pass the remainder of life **in sorrow, now that the staff of my old age has for**saken **me. If my soul were** demanded of me to-night, whose would **my** hoarded treasures be? My garners are **full and** plenteous, with all manner of store. My sheep bring **forth** abundantly ; my **oxen are** strong ; but to whom will they remain? My farms, meadows, houses, vessels of gold and silver, for whom **were** they collected? I have obtained for myself some of the richest and most lucrative preferments in my diocese, and hoped to obtain more for Fulk. What shall **I do?** I will recall him if I can. But how? The deed is **done ;** the fact is known. Fulk is a regular canon. If he **return to** the world he will be branded with infamy. But this

is more tolerable than to be without him. Honour must give
way to convenience : modesty to necessity. Even the lad's
sense of shame had better suffer than my loneliness be
continued."

Bernard then gives the reasons why Fulk cannot be saved
if he remains in his uncle's house :—

"But how can any one hunger or thirst for Christ who is
daily filled with the husks of swine? You cannot drink from
the cup of Christ and also from the cup of demons. The cup
of demons is pride ; the cup of demons is slander and envy ;
the cup of demons is rioting and drunkenness—which things,
when they shall have filled your mind and belly, will leave no
place in you for Christ. Wonder not at what I say. In your
uncle's house you cannot be drunk with the fulness of the
house of God. Christ deigns not to offer to the mind His
wine—sweeter than honey—when He sees debauchery hic-
cuping in its cups. When there is a curious diversity of food,
when the colour and variety of rich furniture feed both the eyes
and the stomach, then the heavenly bread leaves the mind to
fast. . . . . These are they with whom you associate, and
whose evil communications corrupt a youth's good manners.

"But how long will you hesitate to come forth from among
them ? What do you do in a town, who had chosen a cloister ?
That you rise to vigils ; that you attend mass ; that day and
night you are in the choir at the appointed hour—is likely, is
commendable. By this means you do not get your prebend
for nothing. It is right that he who serves the altar should
live by the altar. It is permitted to you, if you serve the altar
well, that you should live by it. But not permitted that you
should luxuriate by it, nor, waxing proud through it, get golden
bridles for yourself, or embroidered saddles, or silver spurs,
or grey furs, trimmed with purple round the wrists and collar.
Whatever beyond necessary food and clothing you take and
retain from the altar is not yours—it is robbery, it is sacrilege.

" What do you in the town, a delicate soldier, while your
fellows, whom you have deserted, are fighting and conquering?
They knock and are entering.   They seize heaven and reign.
Whereas you, seated on your palfrey, clothed in purple and
fine linen, move about the streets and villages.   These are
the baubles of peace, not the defences of war.   Purple will
not repel lust, nor pride, nor avarice ; and, what is more,
and what you fear more, it prevents not fever, it saves not
from death.   Where are the arms of battles ? where the shield
of faith ? the helmet of salvation ? the breastplate of patience?
Why do you fear ?   More are with us than against us.   Seize
your weapons while the battle still lasts.   Angels are present
and protecting.   The Lord himself is there, the helper and
deliverer.   Let us hasten to the help of our brethren, lest, if
they fight without us, they also conquer without us, and enter
without us ; and at last, from the closed door within, it be
replied to our knocking, 'Verily, I say unto you, I know
you not.' " [1]

Allowing all due margin for exaggeration, this letter shows
that a reformer like Bernard thought himself justified in
speaking of the secular clergy as contented with a low standard of morals and religion.   Hildebrand's reformation had
done much.   But in an age when communication was difficult,
and public opinion non-existent, it is probable that much of
the old apathy and worldliness which the great Pope had so
energetically combated, still remained in many an unobserved
corner.   It was the vigilant and active supervision, and even
asceticism of the Cistercians, which made them such valuable
monitors and reformers throughout the by-ways of Europe.

It is probable, though not certain, that at or about this time
Bernard composed four homilies on the words of Saint Luke :
" The angel Gabriel was sent from God."   They are supposed
to be among the first efforts of Bernard in this direction.

[1] Sanct. Bern. Op. vol. i. col. 8.

E.

They are essays or pious discourses to be read rather than sermons to be preached. They are curious in many ways. The crudity, not to say horribleness, of some of the ideas; the ambitious and gaudy rhetoric; the conspicuous absence of high spiritual thought, make them interesting as evidence of what Bernard was, as contrasted with what he became. It is strange, and almost wonderful, that the same man who wrote these stiff, essentially *hard* homilies, afterwards poured forth the soft poetry of the Sermons on the Canticles.

In a short preface,[1] Bernard himself tells us their origin, which was in one of those numerous illnesses which at this period so afflicted him, and for the time prevented him from discharging his usual duties among the monks. Still he had much to do, most likely in the way of correspondence; and these homilies were written during the short intervals which the indefatigable abbot was able to steal from sleep. He thinks that if he does not neglect any duty which the brethren have a right to expect of him, they have no cause of complaint if he think proper to gratify his devotion by such a work; which was assuredly a humble way of putting it.

He chose for his subject the Annunciation. He treats it with a minute *external* exactness, which is very curious to a modern man. Every fact, and every possibility for supposing

---

[1] This little preface is the pleasantest thing about these homilies. "Scribere me aliquid et devotio jubet, et prohibet occupatio. Verumtamen quia praepediente corporali molestia, fratrum ad praesens non valeo sectari conventum; id tantillum otii quod vel mihi de somno fraudans in noctibus intercipere sinor, non sinam otiosum."—SANCT. BERN. *Op.* vol. i. col. 732. It is probable that this "corporalis molestia" is the same as that referred to in such graphic, but well-nigh horrible, terms, by William of St. Thierry. "Nam cum crebra illa ex corruptione stomachi per os ejus indigestae cruditatis *eructio aliis inciperet esse molestior*, maxime autem in choro psallentium, non tamen illico collectas fratrum deseruit; sed juxta locum stationis suae procurato et effosso in terra receptaculo doloris illius, sic aliquandiu, prout potuit, necessitatem illam transegit. *At ubi ne hoc quidem permisit intolerantia rei*, tunc demum collectas deserere, et seorsum habitare compulsus est." — Ibid. vol. ii. col. 1079.

a fact, is dwelt upon, and amplified, and turned, and drawn out, till it is difficult to recognise where one is. "Why," he begins by asking, "Why did the Evangelist mention so many proper names in this place? Do you suppose that any one of them was put in superfluously? By no means. If a leaf falls not from a tree, nor a sparrow to the ground, without the Heavenly Father, can I think a superfluous word fell from the lips of the holy Evangelist, especially in the sacred history of the Word? I will not think so. They are full, indeed, of supernal mysteries, and each runs over with heavenly sweetness, if only they have a diligent observer, who knows how to suck honey from the rock, and oil from the flinty rock."

This is his warrant for every imaginable microscopic examination of detail. As, for instance—

"He (the Evangelist) says then, 'The angel Gabriel was sent from God.' I do not think that this was one of the inferior angels, who, for any cause, are used to carry frequent messages to earth. And this is manifest from his name, which, being interpreted, means the 'strength of God.' And also, because it is not related that he was sent by any spirit better than himself (as was customary), but by God himself. For this reason, then, it is written 'from God.' Or this, perhaps, was the reason—lest God should be thought to have revealed His counsel to any of His blessed spirits before He did so to the Virgin, excepting the archangel Gabriel, who was found among his class to be of such excellence as to be worthy of this name and this message. Nor does the name disagree with the message. For who was more fit to announce Christ—that is, God's power—than he who was honoured by a similar name? For what is strength but power? Neither is it unfitting or incongruous for the Lord and the messenger to be called by the same name; as, although the appellation in both is the same, this similarity has not the same cause. In one sense is Christ the strength or power of God; in a different sense is

the angel called by the same name. The angel only nomi-
nally ; Christ substantively."

A series of remarks about Nazareth comes next. The more
direct object of the discourse, viz. the praise of the Virgin
Mary, is thus treated :—

" To that city, therefore, was the angel Gabriel sent by God.
To whom ? To a virgin espoused to a man whose name was
Joseph. Who was this virgin so venerable that she deserved to
be saluted by an angel—so humble that she was espoused to a
carpenter ? Beautiful is the union of virginity and humility ;
and very acceptable is that soul to God in which humility
commends virginity, and virginity adorns humility. But what
veneration is due to her whose fecundity exalts her humility,
and whose maternity consecrates her virginity ? You hear
she was a virgin ; you hear she was humble. If you cannot
imitate the virginity of the humble, strive after the humility of
the Virgin. Virginity is a laudable virtue, but more necessary
is humility. One is of admonition, the other is of command.
To one you are invited ; to the other you are compelled. Of
one it is said, ' He that is able to receive it, let him receive
it ;' of the other it is said, ' Unless ye become as little children, ye shall not enter into the kingdom of heaven.' One is
rewarded, the other is exacted. You may, in a word, be saved
without virginity. You cannot be saved without humility.
Humility may be pleasing even though it has lost its virginity ;
but without humility, I make bold to say, that even Mary's
virginity would not have been acceptable. ' *Upon whom shall
my spirit rest except upon the humble and meek ?*' Upon the
humble, He says, not upon a virgin. If, therefore, Mary had
not been humble, the Holy Spirit would not have rested on
her ; and if He had not rested on her, He would not have
impregnated her. For how could she have conceived of Him
without Him ? It is clear, then, that in order for her to conceive of the Holy Spirit, as she herself says, ' He regarded

the lowliness of His handmaiden' rather than her virginity; and if she pleased through virginity, she conceived through humility. Whence it is plain that her humility was the cause of her virginity being pleasing."[1] And so on to the end of the homily this one key is struck without intermission.

In the second homily the same subject is continued. "She, therefore, who was about to conceive and bring forth the Saint of Saints, that she might be holy in body, received the gift of virginity; that she might be holy in mind, the gift of humility. The royal Virgin, then, adorned with the jewels of these virtues, and radiant with the double glory of her body, and of her mind, known in heaven by her appearance and her beauty, attracted the gaze of the citizens of heaven upon her, so that she inclined the King's mind to desire her, and drew down from above a heavenly messenger to her. What a condescension in God; what excellence in the Virgin! Run ye mothers, run ye daughters, run all who since Eve and through Eve are born and bring forth in sorrow. Approach the Virgin's nuptial couch; enter if ye can the chaste bridal-chamber of your sister. For behold, God sends to the Virgin; the angel is speaking to Mary. Place your ears to the wall; listen to what he announces to her, if by any means ye may hear that whereby ye may be comforted."[2]

These are sufficient specimens of these homilies. Their intrinsic worth does not need discussion. But they are curious, and even valuable, as evidences of what effect a highly stimulating, objective theology will have on a passionate mind when unprotected by thought and knowledge of a non-religious character. In Bernard's time the mythology which had gathered round Christ's religion impelled and occupied, without rival or restraint, the warmest temperaments and most active intellects which rose at all above the level of feudal barbarism. The facts, and the supposed facts, of this mythology were regarded

---

[1] St. Bern. Op. vol. i. col. 736.   [2] Ibid. vol. i. col. 737.

as by far the most important in the history of the world. They
were dwelt upon as talismanic and miraculous, and symbolical
in themselves. Their moral meaning was forgotten in their
external character and influence. Although the age was so
credulous of spiritual, or rather supernatural, agencies, it was
essentially a most materialistic one in the groundwork of its
beliefs. Although the physical world was supposed to be incessantly invaded and subdued by the spiritual—insomuch, as we
shall see presently, that miracles were considered the natural
course of events—yet the spiritual was constantly apprehended
and interpreted in the most unspiritual manner. Moral goodness was thought to be imparted to physical objects. The
miraculous powers of a saint were transferred to his clothes,
or anything he had touched. Even sanctity itself was figured
as an odour. Hence the events of the Gospel history were
examined like the bones of a martyr—with awe-struck reverence, doubtless, but with a mystical belief in the magical
import and efficacy of the letter and external fact, to the
frequent neglect of the spirit and the life. Nothing was
without meaning, nothing but what enclosed a hidden virtue
if it could be got at ; hence tedious expositions such as the
above.

CHAPTER V.

(A.D. 1122. AETAT. 31.)

BERNARD'S FRIEND, WILLIAM OF ST. THIERRY—HIS ILLNESS—CURED MIRACULOUSLY BY BERNARD—MIRACLES IN THE MIDDLE AGES— SEVERAL EXAMPLES.

BERNARD had few more devoted friends than William, abbot of St. Thierry, who afterwards retired to become a monk of Signy. It was he who visited Bernard when William of Champeaux had placed the abbot of Clairvaux under the care of the rustic doctor. It is to him we owe an interesting account of Bernard's early life and education. He was a most humble, deeply pious, affectionate man, who looked up to his impetuous friend with feelings bordering on adoration. To be in Bernard's society was his great delight, and he often wished to be allowed to become a monk at Clairvaux ; but the austere abbot would never permit it. He was, for his time, an elegant writer, and composed several treatises, of which one, his Epistle to the Brethren of Montdieu, is remarkable for its thoughtful yet practical views on monastic life.[1] In time he grew weary of the cares of his abbey, and sought for solitude as a monk at Signy, and it was there that he composed during Bernard's life that valuable record which has furnished us with so many

---

[1] That the "Epistola ad Fratres de Monte Dei" ought to be ascribed to William, is Mabillon's opinion. At the same time it must be added that Dom Massuel has adduced facts and arguments which tend to prove that it belongs by right to Guigo, fifth prior of the Carthusians, to whom St. Bernard once paid a visit.

important facts. On one occasion he was very ill, and his friend Bernard sent his brother Gerard to him to ask him to come to Clairvaux ; at the same time promising, as an inducement, that he should either soon get well or else die. William was only too happy to go to Clairvaux ; it was an alternative of joys, as he says, either of dying with Bernard near him, or else of living some little time in his company ; and he declared he could not tell which he would have preferred[1]   However, it turned out that he got well. "Gracious God, what good did not that illness, those feast days, that holiday, do for me ! For it happened that during the whole time of my sickness *he* also was ill, and thus we two, laid up together, passed the whole day in sweet converse concerning the soul's spiritual physic, and the medicines which virtue affords against the weakness of vice.   He then discoursed to me upon the Canticles as much as that stage of my infirmity allowed, but only giving a moral exposition, and omitting the mysteries of that scripture, as it was thus I wished it, and had demanded of him.   And whatever I heard day by day I wrote down, lest it should escape me, as far as God permitted me and my memory helped.   I found that when he, with gentleness and love, expounded to me, and communicated his opinions and the results of his experience, and strove to teach my inexperience many things which can only be learnt from use and practice, although I could not understand what was presented to me, yet he made me better than usual comprehend what was wanting to me to make me understand it.

"It happened that as the Sunday which is called Septuagesima drew near, on the Saturday night previous I had improved in health so much that I could get out of bed alone, and even go in and out of doors without assistance.   I began

---

[1] "Ego vero quasi divinitus accepta vel oblata facultate seu apud eum moriendi, seu aliquandiu cum eo vivendi (quorum quid maluerim tunc, ignoro) profectus sum statim illuc, quamvis cum nimio labore ac dolore."—St. Bern. *Op.* vol. ii. col. 1085.

to make arrangements for returning home, which, when he
heard of, he at once forbade, and prohibited all hope or
attempt to return before Quinquagesima Sunday. I obeyed
readily, as both my inclination and debility led me to acquiesce.
Up to Septuagesima I had been eating meat; he had ordered
it, and it was necessary for me; now I wished to leave it off,
and this also he disallowed. But I would not yield to him in
this, and neither his advice, request, nor command influenced
me, and so we parted on that Saturday night—he in silence to
compline, I to my bed. When, behold, my malady revived in
all its fury and strength, and seized me with such violence, and
all through the night with such malignity did it torture me,
above all my strength, above all my endurance, that, despairing
of life, I thought only to live till the morning, and, if it were
but once, to speak with the man of God. After this night of
misery I sent for him, and he came not with his usual countenance of pity, but rather of reproof. At last, smiling, he
said, ' Well, will you eat to-day?' But I had already attributed
my affliction to my previous disobedience, and answered,
' Whatever you choose to order.' ' Rest still, then,' he replied,
' you will not die this time,' and went away; and at once all
pain went with him, except that, exhausted by the night's
sufferings, I could scarcely rise from my bed the whole day.
But what manner of pain was that? I never recollect anything
like it in my life. But the day after I was whole, and recovered
my strength, and a few days after, with the blessing and favour
of my good host, I returned to my own people."[1]

In this reverential and affectionate tone does the good
William always speak of his friend. Bernard, on the other
hand, with his strong nature, often treated his gentle admirer
with a roughness which vigorous characters not rarely manifest
towards weaker brethren. He who was so full of thought and
action, perhaps was not far from feeling the loving William as

[1] St. Bern. Op. vol. ii. col. 1085-86.

somewhat troublesome at times. William once wrote to tell Bernard that he was sure he did not fully return his affection for him, and he got this in reply,—it is hardly rash to suppose that he never made the same complaint again :—

" If no one knoweth the things which are in a man, except the spirit of man which is in him ; if man seeth the face only, but God searcheth the heart, I marvel—nor can I marvel enough—by what means you could weigh and measure our mutual love for each other, so as to express an opinion, not only of your own, but also of your neighbour's heart. It is an error of the human mind, not only to think good evil, and evil good, or true false, and false true, but also to take things certain for things doubtful, and things doubtful for things certain. It is, perhaps, true what you say, that I love you less than you do me ; but I am quite certain it cannot be certain to you. How, then, can you affirm that with certainty of which you are far from certain? Wonderful ! Paul does not trust himself to his own judgment ; but says, ' I judge not mine own self.' Peter bewails the presumption by which he deceived himself, when speaking from himself, he said, ' Although I should die with thee, yet will I not deny thee. . . .' David confesses his own self-ignorance ; and praying, exclaims, ' Remember not my offences.' But you, with I know not what boldness—not only concerning your own heart, but even concerning mine—openly declare, ' that loving more you are cared for less.'

" And these, forsooth, are your words—and I wish they were not yours, for I do not know whether they are true. . . . Whence, I ask—whence do you know that I am loved by you better than you are by me? Is it from what you add in your letter, that those who go from these parts in your direction do not bring you from me any proof of love or friendship? But what proof or token of love do you expect from me? Are you vexed that I have never answered even one of your numerous letters? But how could I think that the scribblings of my inexperience could ever delight the maturity of your wisdom? I remember who said, 'Little children, let us not love in word, neither in tongue, but in deed and in truth.' And when did you ever need my assistance and it was not given to you?"[1]

This letter was certainly not open to the charge of excessive tenderness, especially as it was an answer to several letters and kind messages on the part of William. However, the latter was quite content to bear with the occasional warmth of the impetuous abbot of Clairvaux. He never ceased to regard him with the fondest affection, and even to attribute to him super-human qualities.

In the above narrative of his own illness and recovery, it is evident that William ascribes much to Bernard's miraculous power, as exerted on himself; but he does so in a much greater degree, and with more outspoken emphasis, in other parts of his biography. In this he only resembled all the men of his own, and several ages, both before and after him. Miracles, ghostly apparitions, divine and demoniac interference with sublunary affairs, were matters which a man of the twelfth century would less readily doubt of than of his own existence. To disbelieve in such would have been considered good *prima facie* evidence of unsoundness of mind. The critical powers then were never for a moment exerted on an alleged case of miracle. If the matter could, by any interpretation, be brought into some kind of connexion with heaven or hell, with moral good or evil, it was assumed to be *natural*, not *unnatural*, that miracles should occur. The modern definition of a miracle, viz. a violation of the laws of nature, would have by no means commanded Bernard's assent. He would have said, " What are your laws of nature? I know them not. Miracle is the law of God." The men of that time believed that the air swarmed with angels; or, if not with angels, then with devils.

---

[1] St. Bern. Op. vol. i. col. 87-8.

They believed that fearful and perpetual strife was being waged between the adverse hosts—that armies of good and evil spirits were for ever on the wing—that they encamped in invisible companies to waylay and deceive, or to counsel and succour, the sons of men. They believed they heard the laughter of the fiends borne on the night gusts of the moaning wind, and gradually retiring before the chorus-song of rejoicing angels, swelling up on the morning air. They believed that all evil thoughts were whispered in the ear by the emissaries of the old enemy of man's soul, and that nothing but prayer, faith, and the help of the blessed saints would avail to avert or dispel them.

No expression of disgust or contempt is required now with reference to such a stage of human belief. The great majority of mankind have ever held opinions similar to or identical with the above. The exception is to hold the reverse, and to substitute for Miracle a reliance on Law. Intrinsically, then, these groundless beliefs are nothing but silly tales, with little merit of either variety or invention. But, regarded historically, as stages in man's mental development, they assume quite a philosophic importance. Even as fossil bones and shells to a geologist become hieroglyphics significant of far-off revolutions and convulsions of the planet, so to the historian the great but extinct modes of thought which have appeared in the intellectual world are really the most important of the facts and events he has to record. When Peter of Cluny tells us that " very often the devils disturb the monks during the hours allotted to sleep, in order that they may feel sleepy when they ought to be awake, and thus lose the advantage of holy vigils—that he had often heard such complaints from many, of whom some have had their bed-coverings pulled off them while they slept, and carried to a great distance ; some, after a struggle, had succeeded in wresting their coverings from the demons ; while others, when in the act of satisfying the wants of nature, had seen the devils stand before them in a mocking, ridiculing attitude;"[1]—we can regard the whole as an absurd fiction, if we choose, and in this light it is uninteresting enough. But, if we remember and reflect who the venerable Peter was—how wise he was, how good he was, and what a leader of thought he was in his day—then the fact that it was possible for such a man to hold such absurdities as literally true, assumes a different aspect. The minds of men of the twelfth century were in some sort the reverse of ours. What we think or well know to be possible and feasible, men of the Middle Ages would have regarded as the idlest dreaming. What we know to be simply nonsense, they looked on as a matter of indisputable truth. They were far removed from being "ministers and interpreters of nature." They did not worship the powers of nature as their pagan ancestors did, but they had fully the same belief in the capriciousness of their exercise; they had the same anchorless insecurity as to what the invisible world would next do to, and in, the visible world. The men they saw, the trees, the houses, the green earth, the forest, were alternately possessed and quarrelled over by the unseen powers of good and evil. And poor, feeble man had to pick his way in the midst of them; on either side of his

---

1 "Unde plerumque ita monachos in somnis inquietant, ut horis somno congruentibus amissis, cum vigilare debent dormiant, et sic sanctarum vigiliarum lucra amittant. Harum inquietudinum multorum multoties querelas accepi, quorum alii opertoria sua noctibus dum dormirent subrepta sibi atque longius projecta a daemonibus, dicebant; alii subripere volentibus violenter eadem tegmina se extorsisse, nonnulli dum in remotioribus naturae satisfacerent, eos sibi derisorie astitisse affirmabant. Praeterea quosdam nocturnis horis, aliis quiescentibus, sancta orationum iurta quaerentes, et eadam causa claustra et ecclesias peragrantes, multis aliquando terroribus appetebant, ita ut in eorum aliquos *visibiliter* irruerent, et ad terram verberando prosternerent."—*Petrus Venerabilis, De Miraculis,* lib. i. cap. 17.—The ludicrous is overcome by the pathetic in the sentence "aliis quiescentibus," &c. These sorrowful, sincere, anxious men, wandering about their cloisters and churches in the silent night, to make "holy thefts of prayer," getting troubled and "knocked down" by the fiend and his demons, form quite a melancholy picture.

path, at all hours of sleeping or waking, his mind and his heart were the desired prize of one or the other. The deliberately wicked man was given over for the time, in full property to the fiend. The good, the deeply holy man, was surrounded by choirs of angels ; and the devils were supposed almost to howl at his approach. He was changed, he was another creature to their believing eyes ; he was in direct correspondence with God ; the breath of the Divine love had robed him in beauty. Could there be any difficulty in thinking that to such a one—one on whom the smile of the Eternal was supposed to rest ; one whose thoughts moved, like the angels in Jacob's dream, to and fro between earth and heaven ; one whose future glory in the kingdom of the just was well assured —would it have been possible to doubt that to such a one the forms and things of this miserable, accursed earth would yield a swift obedience as of servants to their lord ? Could inert matter, which even the very devils were able to work upon, resist a holy man full of the Spirit of God ? Must not the earthly give way to the Heavenly ? Must not Christ be the conqueror of Satan ?

It was thus all but inevitable that a man in Bernard's position should have miraculous powers attributed to him. They had been attributed to hundreds before him, with far less warrant. It could not be a matter of doubt that he was a man spiritually endowed in a very extraordinary degree. By all the tests then in vogue, he was one of the most pious of men. Hence, as a necessary consequence, he must be supposed, sooner or later, to work miracles.

The only witnesses to his miracles whom it is now interesting to call, as evidence of the overpowering force of the popular belief, are his friends William of St. Thierry, Geoffrey his secretary, and himself. His own claim to miraculous power will be deferred to that portion of his life in which he made it, viz. just previous to the preaching of the Second Crusade.

But the narratives of the above-named biographers may as
well be dealt with now, as they refer, as far as can be judged,
to this part of his career.

And first, the reported conduct of his uncle Galderic, and
his brother Guido, is worthy of attention. We are told their
only fear was that his miraculous power would have an injurious
effect on his character, so much so that "he appeared to have
received these two relations as two thorns in the flesh, lest
by the abundance of his graces he should be exalted above
measure. Neither did they spare his tender modesty, exciting
him with harsh words, deprecating his good deeds, making
nothing of his signs, and afflicting the meek and unresisting
one even to tears by their harshness and insults. Godfrey, the
venerable Bishop of Langres, who was a near relative of the
holy man, a fellow-convert, and ever afterwards his inseparable
companion, used to say that on the occasion of the first miracle
which he ever saw him perform, the said Guido was present.
It happened as they were passing Château Landon, in the
territory of Sens, that a certain youth, having an ulcer in his
foot, begged, with many prayers, of Bernard to touch and bless
him. Bernard made the sign of the cross, and immediately
the lame was healed. A very few days after, as they returned
through the same place, they found him whole and well. Still
Guido could not be restrained, even by the miracle, from re-
buking him, and taxing him with presumption for having
consented to touch the lad, so anxious about him in the bond
of charity was his brother."[1]

[1] "Nec tamen in more carnalium,
in gloriam elevabantur humanam,
sed juvenili ejus aetati, et novae
adhuc conversationi, spirituali sollicitudine metuebant. . . . Neque
enim parcebant verbis durioribus
exagitantes teneram verecundiam
ejus, calumniantes etiam bene gesta,
signa omnia annihilantes, et hominem
mansuetissimum nihilque contradi-
centem, frequenter usque ad lacrymas
improperiis et opprobriis affligentes.
   Signatus autem, statim convaluit, et post paucissimos dies re-
gressi per idem oppidum, sanum et
incolumem invenerunt. Caeterum
saepe dictus beati viri frater ne ipso
quidem poterat compesci miraculo,

" All who knew Guido knew what gravity and truth were in him. Once upon a time, when we"—that is, William of St. Thierry and Guido—"happened to be together, conversing upon such subjects, I was asking him questions, when he, in his usual pleasant way with his friends, said, ' Of what I am ignorant I do not speak ; but one thing I know and have experienced, viz. that many things are revealed to him in prayer.' " And the unbelieving Guido then told William a story which he thought conclusive to his brother's gift of prophecy.[1]

Geoffrey, the secretary, relates how " he saw in the district of Meaux a knight offer the most heartfelt thanks to Bernard for having cured him instantly with a piece of consecrated bread. The knight had been suffering from a quartan fever for about eighteen months, and so violent were the attacks, that when they seized him he was like a madman, and did not recognise even his own mother. I have also heard Gerard, the venerable Bishop of Limoges, bear witness how a young man connected with himself was mortally wounded in the head : and, as he lay foaming and unconscious, a small mouthful of bread, blessed by the man of God, was placed between his lips ; and within that very hour he arose healed.[2] "

" Many people knew the illustrious young Walter of Mont- mirail, whose uncle became a monk at Clairvaux. When this Walter was very young indeed, not above three months old. his mother entertained Bernard as a guest. Full of thankful- ness and exultation that she was worthy to have such a holy man under her roof, she presented her infant to him to receive his blessing. Then, as was his wont, the man of God began to speak of the salvation of souls to those around him ; while

---

quominus increparet eum, et prae-   [1] St. Bernard, Opera, vol. ii. col.
sumptionis argueret, quod acquieverit   1087.
tangere hominem."—ST. BERN. *Op*   Ibid. vol. ii. col. 1138.
vol. ii. col. 1081.

the mother, holding her child in her lap, sat at his feet.   But, as he spoke, he now and then stretched forth his hand, and the infant strove to take hold of it.   When it had done this several times, it was at last observed ; and, as they all marvelled, the child was allowed to clutch the hand as it wished. Then, with the deepest reverence, holding it with both hands, it lifted it to its mouth and kissed it.   And this not once only, but as often as it was allowed to repeat the act."[1]

" I have known in even the smallest matters great things have occurred through him.   When he came to the dedication of the Church of Foigny, it happened that an incredible multitude of flies filled the place, and their noise and flying about became an intolerable nuisance to those who entered.   As no remedy seemed at hand, the Saint said, ' I excommunicate them ;' and in the morning they were all found dead.   They covered the whole pavement, and were shovelled out with spades, and so the church was rid of them.   This miracle was so known and celebrated, that among the neighbours—a large concourse of whom had been present at the dedication—the cursing of the Foigny flies passed into a proverb."[2]

" On another occasion, as Bernard was returning from Châlons, the wind and the rain were a great impediment to him and his company. Some of them, however, got in advance; and they, owing to the intense cold, not paying much attention to him, he followed almost alone. Now the horse of one of the two who alone remained with him, by some accident, got away, and ran about the open plain.   They tried to catch him, but in vain ; and the cold making any further delay for this purpose inexpedient, ' Let us pray,' said Bernard, and, kneeling with the brother who remained with him " (the other being after the horse, we suppose), " they were scarcely able to get through the Lord's Prayer, when behold ! the horse in all tame-

---

[1] St. Bern. Op. vol. ii. col. 1084.   [2] Ibid. vol. ii. col. 1083.

ness returned, stood before Bernard, and was restored to his rider."[1]

The above will be quite sufficient to give an idea of what Bernard's contemporaries thought of him. The constant recurrence of supposed miraculous events is so universal in the Middle Ages that it was necessary to state, with some explicitness, on what terms they would be treated here. It seems best to give them in their natural simplicity and crudity, not as true, but as significant. They are neither to be admired nor vituperated; neither to be accepted with credulity nor denied with fury. As belonging to the time, as much as feudal castles and mail armour do, they must form part of a picture of it. The intense convictions of men for several centuries are at least as much the property of history as their outward actions.

[1] St. Bern. Op. vol. ii. col. 1088.

CHAPTER VI.

(A.D. 1125. AETAT. 34.)

VISITS TO PARIS—TO LA GRANDE CHARTREUSE—INNER LIFE OF THE
MONASTERIES.

IT was Bernard's often expressed wish and resolution not to
leave his monastery except at the command of his superiors.[1]
The two journeys which about this time he made—one to
Paris, the other to La Grande Chartreuse—therefore, were in
all likelihood in some way connected with monastic or other
business, of which no record has been preserved. For although
to both of these journeys an interesting anecdote is attached,
in reference to him, yet their main purpose is not alluded to.

The Carthusian Order was founded by Saint Bruno, in 1084.
The prior thereof, whom Bernard visited, was named Guigo—
a man of most approved and conspicuous piety, and a friend
of the most devout persons of that age. He and Bernard had
been carrying on an epistolary interchange of pious sentiments
before this visit. Guigo and his monks were rejoiced to find
that the hopes raised in them by his letters were realized when
they met him in the flesh. But there was one drawback to
the general satisfaction, and it was this, that the saddle on
which Bernard had ridden to La Grande Chartreuse was, in

---

[1] It was a sentiment to which he
repeatedly gave utterance. "Cum
sciam mihi consilium esse et propositum, nunquam (si causa duntaxat
nostri ordinis non fuerit) exire de
monasterio, nisi aut apostolicae sedis
legato, aut certe proprio vocante
episcopo." — ST. BERNARD. *Epist.*
xlviii. See also *Epist.* xvii. vol. i.
col. 35.

the eyes of the Carthusians, far too magnificent and costly for a genuine disciple of Saint Benedict : and Guigo, the prior, was constrained to confess to one of the Cistercians, that he was astonished and even pained at such a spectacle. The criticism, in due time, reached Bernard's ears, who at once inquired, in equal surprise, what those trappings were which had given such offence ; that as regarded himself he had, it was true, sat upon them all the way from Clairvaux to La Grande Chartreuse, but had not, up to that very hour, noticed them in the least. The fact was, that the horse and saddle were not his own, but had been lent to him by his uncle, a Cluniac monk, and their nature had not been perceived by him during the whole journey. Guigo acknowledged his delight and pleasure at such an unexpected explanation ; and especially wondered at the depth of contemplation which had hidden from Bernard, for several days, what *he* saw at the first glance.[1]

Less pleasing than the above anecdote is the other regarding his absence of mind when travelling by the Lake of Geneva. After having passed a whole day in riding along its shore, in the evening when his companions were speaking about "the Lake," he inquired, "what lake?" to their no little surprise.[2] This is hardly consistent with what we have had, on William of St. Thierry's authority, respecting his love of nature.

His appearance at Paris about this time is just as sudden and unexpected as at La Grande Chartreuse, and survives only by a single anecdote, unconnected with any previous or subsequent event, still worth relating.

On his arrival in the little, thronged, dirty, ill-paved city,

---

[1] " Caeterum cum in reliquis omnibus aedificarentur, unum fuit quod praedictum Priorem Carthusiensem aliquatenus movit ; stratura videlicet animalis, cui idem vir venerabilis insidebat, minus neglecta, minus praeferens paupertatem. Nec silentio pressit aemulator virtutis quod mente conceperat : sed locutus uni e fratribus, aliquatenus super hoc moveri sese confessus est et mirari." —ST. BERN. *Op.* vol. ii. col. 1118.

[2] Ibid. vol. ii. col. 1118.

Bernard lodged with an archdeacon during his stay there, and, it is presumable, was principally in the society of ecclesiastical persons. They requested him to go into their schools, and lecture to them. He at once dilated on the "true philosophy," on a contempt for the world, and a voluntary poverty assumed for Christ's sake. This preaching did not have the effect which usually attended his exhortations. Not one of the clerks was converted. And it cannot be very surprising when we consider the different order of discourse which they were in the habit of hearing with extreme delight. The curious and irritating scholastic puzzles which were then attracting natives of every country in Europe to Paris, must have made a bad preparation for Bernard, with his austere doctrine of worldly renunciation. But Bernard was very sad about it. He returned to the house of his friend, the archdeacon, and immediately fell to praying. And as he prayed with great vehemence, he was overcome by such a torrent of tears, accompanied by sobs and groans, that he was heard outside. The archdeacon asked one of his friends what could be the cause of such grief to their guest. A monk named Rainald, who knew Bernard well, replied, "That wonderful man, heated by the fire of charity, and entirely absorbed in God, cares for nothing in this world save only to recall the wandering to the ways of truth, and to gain their souls to Christ; and because he has just sown the word of life in the schools, and has gathered no fruit in the conversion of the clerks, he thinks God is angry with him. Hence this storm of groans, and outpouring of tears; wherefore I firmly anticipate that a full harvest to-morrow will compensate for to-day's sterility."

The next morning he preached again, and with a very different result; for as soon as his sermon was over, several of his hearers expressed their desire to become monks. He at once determined to bring the results of his spiritual fishing to Clairvaux. He accordingly set out from Paris and reached

St. Denis, where he passed the night. The next day, however, when his friends expected he would continue his journey homewards, he said, "We must return to Paris, as there are still some there who belong to us, whom it behoves us to add to this, the Lord's fold, that there may be one fold and one Shepherd." As they were re-entering Paris, they saw three clerks at a distance, coming towards them; and he said to his friends, "God has helped us. Behold there are the clerks for whom we returned." When these approached and recognised Bernard, they rejoiced with a great joy, saying, "O most blessed father, you have come to us who desired you much. For it had been our intention to follow you, and we hardly hoped to overtake you." "I knew it, beloved," he replied; "we will now go together, and by God's grace I will lead you on your journey." They then proceeded onwards; and persevered under the discipline of his rule all the remainder of their lives.[1]

But these wide excursions were quite the exception with Bernard at this period. He over and over reiterates his determination not to leave the monastery except at the command of superiors, or else for some inevitable cause; and the two excursions just mentioned seem to have been the only infringements he made to this rule. At a later epoch of his life, when he shared in or guided every important event that occurred in the Church, he overran the greater part of Europe more than once. But at this time, and for a few years after this, he was still a secluded monk, of a new and humble order. His influence was, however, slowly spreading, and the commencement was being laid of that authority and estimation which enabled him to take the chief part in quelling a wide-spread schism, in opposing a renowned and formidable heretic, and in giving the strongest impulse to the Second Crusade.

[1] "Exordium Magnum Cisterciense."—*Dist.* ii. cap. xiii. ST. BERN. *Op.* vol. ii. col. 1202.

The principal means by which, at this time, Bernard's power and importance were felt, was his vigorous and persevering correspondence. He was the most indefatigable of letter-writers. He writes to persons of all classes, on all subjects—from kings and princesses down to poor virgins—on subjects ranging from the most elevated and spiritual raptures on the welfare of the soul, down to the stealing of pigs. Some letters, especially the earlier ones, are sermons directed to individuals, and by no means free from rhetorical exaggeration, as two specimens quoted above sufficiently prove. Others are the most terse and business-like conceivable, going direct to the point, with no verbiage ; and it is noticeable how, as years and occupations increased on Bernard, the exuberance of mediæval grandiloquence was sensibly curtailed. And this latter class of epistles is the most valuable portion of his writings. They are a wide repertory of indubitable facts. They are generally, almost invariably, written with a distinct practical object in view—either to answer a question, which often leads to the giving of curious and valuable advice, or to request the performance of some act of justice or mercy at the hands of a feudal neighbour.

For instance, the great and puissant Lord of Champagne—to whom Bernard and his order will one day owe so much—was on one occasion guilty of a piece of ferocious cruelty, from which even the best of the middle-age knights were never quite free. One Humbert by name had been accused (falsely, Bernard says), and condemned to prove his innocence by a judicial combat. In this he failed ; and his suzerain not only confiscated his fief, and thus reduced his wife and children to destitution, but also incarcerated him, and, as a small addition to these penalties, put out his eyes. This occurred at Bar-sur-Aube, and Bernard was probably better acquainted with the facts than Theobald, the Count of Champagne. Perhaps, also, he did not think so highly of single combat, as a means of satisfying justice, as the count did.   He wrote him a letter, in which he pointed out, that whatever the crime of the man, his guiltless wife and children ought not to be made to suffer. Count Theobald took no notice of this letter, apparently. Bernard applied to Geoffrey, bishop of Chartres, to get him to use his influence with the count.   He wrote himself in a much sharper tone—telling him, that if he had asked for gold or silver, he did not doubt but he would have received it; that God could disinherit Theobald as easily, nay, far more easily, than Theobald could Humbert, and concluded with a prayer, that as he himself hoped to receive mercy from God, he would not hesitate to show mercy to others.   At last Bernard, by his importunity, brought the unwilling baron to examine the case himself, and, when satisfied of Humbert's innocence, to reinstate him by an act of grace.[1]

In such cases as this—and they are constant during the best period of the Middle Ages—there can be very little doubt what was the part played by the spiritual power.   It was the tradition of a divine morality and superior culture coming into conflict with, and strong enough to withstand, a vigorous barbarism.   It is just possible to imagine what might have been the result to Greek and Roman civilization, if such a restraining influence had been at work among their patricians and oligarchs.

On another occasion the Abbot of Mount Cornelius consults him about a grave scandal which had occurred in his monastery, through the incontinence of a certain brother.   Bernard is deeply shocked at the circumstance, and conjures the abbot,

[1] St. Bern. Op. vol. i, col. 50-1. Epist. 37 — 39.   It is Mabillon's opinion that the mutilation referred to in Epist. 39 ("In manu Barrensis propositi dudum facto duello, qui victus fuit, statim ex vestra jussione oculos amisit") relates to the Humbert of the other two epistles.   And this view is, at least, extremely probable.   But I see that M. d'Arbois de Jubainville (in his useful " Hist. des Ducs et Comtes de Champagne," vol. ii. p. 297, now in course of publication at Paris) considers this " une erreur évidente."   I have adopted Mabillon's view.

by "that blood which was shed for souls, that the danger of intimacy between men and women be not made light of." [1] As for the poor fallen brother, if he had spontaneously confessed his sin, there might be hope that he would recover, when he might have been allowed to remain in his monastery. But, inasmuch as the foulness of his crime had come to light through other means, the question was, what could be done with him, as it was to be feared the evil example might spread through the rest of the little flock. It would be well to relegate him to a distant house, where a sharper discipline would bring him to repentance, and whence in time he might return. Bernard will not offer to receive him in a Cistercian convent; it might not suit the Praemonstrants, to which order he belonged. If there is an absolute impossibility of getting him disposed of anywhere else, then, of necessity, he must be retained at home. But great care must be taken that all opportunity of his repeating or propagating his turpitude be entirely removed. Still this was a particular instance of a general evil. The fact was, that the mill where the lay brethren were compelled to meet the society of women was the cause of the mischief, and one of three courses must be followed—(1) "Either that no women be allowed to come near the mill; (2) or that the care of the mill be transferred to non-monastic persons; (3) or that the mill itself be entirely given up." All half measures or palliatives were useless.

Again, we find him writing long letters to one Ogerius, a regular canon, who had resigned the pastoral care of others to become a monk. Bernard had always a great objection to any one relinquishing a post of trust and power where he

---

[1] " Obsecramus per sanguinem illum qui pro animabus fusus est, ne tanti emptarum parvipendatur periculum, quod maxime ex virorum et feminarum cohabitatione **non** immerito timetur ab his qui, diu jam diu in schola Dei contra diaboli tentamenta luctati, propria experientia edocti dicere possunt cum Apostolo, *non enim ignoramus astutias ejus.*"—ST. BERN. *Op.* vol. i.; *Epist.* 79.

might do good. Even a pilgrimage to the Holy Land lost all
its beauty in his eyes, if a distinct dereliction of an established
duty and sphere of usefulness must be the price. Thus to the
Abbot of Saint John's, at Chartres, he says : "I am told you
intend to desert your country, and the religious house over
which God has placed you, in order to go to Jerusalem, to
devote yourself to God and live for yourself. It is, perhaps,
advantageous to one aiming at perfection to leave his country,
as it is said, 'Get thee out of thy country and from thy
kindred ;' but I cannot at all see on what grounds you must
needs forsake the care of souls entrusted to you ;"[1] and in
this tone he always writes. Much against his advice, William
of St. Thierry gave up his abbey. " Never mind," he says,
"what you or I may wish you to do in this case, but what
God wishes, that is what it is important for us to get persuaded
of. Remain, therefore, where you are. Strive to benefit those
you are placed over ; neither hesitate to bear rule when you
can do good."[2] And his advice to Ogerius is in the same
strain. He begins by excusing himself for not writing sooner ;
indeed he had written long before, but the want of a carrier
had caused a great delay. Ogerius had evidently written
rather a flattering letter to Bernard—and flattery was a thing
of which he was especially impatient. He always refuses it in
a half-angry, half-scoffing style. " Throughout your letter,"
he says, " you exalt me above myself, and mix a great deal of
praise withal. All this, as I am unconscious of deserving it,
I ascribe to your good nature, and forgive to your ignorance."[3]
As regards the main topic of the letter, viz. the renunciation

---

[1] "Sed qua ratione curam tibi creditam animarum exponere debeas, omnino non video."— St. Bern. *Epist.* 82.

[2] Ibid. Epist. 86.

[3] " . . . . propter latoris inopiam tardavi mittere, quod scribere non tardavi. . . . Praeterea per totam seriem literarum attolens me supra me, multum de me laudabilia intermisces ; quorum quia ipse mihi conscius non sum, et tuae haec benevolentiae ascribo, et ignosco ignorantiae."—Ibid. *Epist.* 87.

of the superiorship, he says : " Is it not true that your own ease
was more pleasing to you than the welfare of others ? I am
glad you enjoy your calm of rest, so that you do not enjoy
it *too much.* Every good thing which pleases so much that we
love it, even when it is not expedient or lawful, ceases for that
cause to be good. One thing you have done which I can
unreservedly praise, viz. that when you put off authority over
others, you did not therefore wish to escape authority yourself ;
you did not hesitate to seek a friendly discipline, to pass from
dominion to discipleship. You would not be your own
scholar. And rightly, for he who is his own disciple has a
fool for his master. What others feel I know not ; but with
myself I find from experience it is far easier to command
many than to rule myself.[1] . . . . I also praise you for
returning to your old monastery, instead of seeking a new one.
. . . And now, be simple among the brethren, devout
before God, subject to your superior, obedient to your elders,
kindly to your juniors, pleasing to the angels, useful in speech,
lowly in heart, gentle to all. Be careful lest, for having once
been placed in authority, you think yourself entitled to honour,
but rather show yourself more humble to all as one of a
number. And another danger may arise to you from this
quarter, of which I would wish to give you warning. We are
all of us so changeable, that what we wished for yesterday we

---

[1] " Amicam repetens disciplinam,
de magistro fieri denuo discipulus
non erubuisti . . . qui se sibi ma-
gistrum constituit, stulto se dis-
cipulum subdit . . . ego de me
expertus sum quod dico ; et facilius
imperare et securius possum praeesse
multis aliis, quam soli mihi." It is
odd to find Auguste Comte agreeing
almost literally with Saint Bernard,
in a view not very popular just now.
" However excessive may be the desire of command in our revolutionary
day, there can be no one who in his
secret mind has not often felt more or
less vividly how sweet it is to obey,
when he can have the rare privilege
of consigning the burdensome responsibility of his general self-
conduct to wise and trustworthy
guidance ; and probably the sense
of this is strongest in those who are
the best fitted to command."—*Posi-
tive Philosophy of Auguste Comte,*
Martineau's Translation, vol. ii.
p. 148.

refuse to-day, and what we care not for to-day we shall desire to-morrow. Now, if it should happen, through the devil's suggestions, that a regret for your lost power assault your mind, all that you have manfully despised you would then childishly long for. What was so unpleasant before would be invested with charms to you then : the height of place, the care of the house, the despatch of business, the obedience of the servants, your own liberty, your power over others, so that you will almost repent of having left what it was painful to keep. If this most evil temptation seduces you even for an hour, it will not be without grave injury to your soul."

There was no deficiency of clear practical advice here, and it is not surprising that the giver of it should have been often called upon for more. He concludes his letter in this odd fashion :—

"And now you have got all the wisdom of that most elegant and eloquent doctor, of whom you have begged, from such a distance, to be taught. Behold that expected and wished-for wise saying which you have so long been anxious to hear ! Here is the sum of my learning. You have got it all. What more do you want ? The fountain is dry, and do you seek for water in the dry land ? Like the widow in the Gospel, all that I had of my penury I have sent. You need not be ashamed or look downcast. You forced me to it. You asked for a sermon, and you have got a sermon. I say you have got a sermon, and one long enough too ; only it is mute, full of words, but void of sense. How can I excuse it ? I could say that labouring under a tertian fever, that full of the cares of my office, I wrote this ; whereas it is written, *write wisdom at leisure.*[1]

[1] St. Bern. *Epist.* 87. "Sapientiam scribe in otio." Saint Bernard quotes here, as he often does, from memory, and varies a little the words of the Vulgate, which are — " Sapientia scribae in tempore vacuitatis." E.V. "The wisdom of a learned man cometh by opportunity of leisure." —*Ecclesiasticus* xxxviii. 24.

"But, let the will supply the place of the deed; and, although it may be useless to you, it will help me to humility. A fool, while he speaketh not, is reputed wise: so, if I had been silent, I should have been called wise, but should not have been so. Now, some will laugh at me as foolish, others will deride, others will resent my presumption. But this will be to my advantage, seeing that humility, to which we are led by humiliation, is the groundwork of all spiritual life.[1] If you wish for humility, you must not avoid humiliation. If you cannot bear humiliation, you will never attain to humility. It is, therefore, good for me that my foolishness should be known, and be put to confusion by the wise—foolishness which is often praised by the ignorant. . . . *I will play and be more vile:* a good game, at which Michal is angry, but God well pleased; a good game, which is ridiculous to men, but most beautiful to angels; a good game, I say, by which we are a reproach to the rich and a contempt to the proud. For what else but playing do we appear to be doing to secular persons? What they seek after we avoid; what they avoid we search after. We are like the mountebanks and jesters, who, turning upside down, with legs aloft and head below, walk on their hands in an unnatural manner, and attract the eyes of all men. This is no childish game taken from the theatre, by feminine and filthy gestures and antics to provoke sensual desires and represent disgusting actions; but it is a pleasant, honourable, grave, worthy game, which is able to give delight to celestial witnesses. It was at this chaste and devout game that he played who said, 'We are made a spectacle to angels and men.' And at this game, in the meantime, we will play, that we may be made sport of, confounded, humiliated, until He come who putteth down the

---

[1] "Putasne parum hoc mihi conferat religionis emolumentum, cum humilitas, ad quam utique ducit humiliatio, totius sit spiritualis fabricae fundamentum."

mighty from their seats, and exalteth the humble and meek. May He fill us with joy, glorify us, and exalt us for ever."[1]

This must have been one of the first letters with which friend Ogerius was honoured by Bernard. Others which followed display a far deeper and more considerate tone, and evidently were dictated by an affectionate esteem. They are curious, as showing the internal and unrestrained aspect of monastic life ; the *human* element as distinct from the ascetic ; the portion of social and warm-blooded interests and feelings which survived amid the fasts, vigils, and manifold mortifications of cœnobite existence. They show that, in spite of the most cultivated development of an ecstatic enthusiasm, mother earth and her little cares and joys will never be quite forgotten. Friendly visits, interchange of books and opinions, amicable criticisms and mutual advice, form a pleasant change from the stately, formal, and even oppressive solemnity usual to monastic literature.

On one occasion Bernard informs his friend that so busy is he, that when he received his last letter, he could only find time to read it while at dinner.[2] Another time he tells him that epistolary correspondence during Lent is very undesirable ; and adduces reasons which give an insight into literary composition in those days.

"I ask you, where are peace and quietness if I am writing, and dictating, and despatching you letters ? But all this, you say, can be done in silence. It is strange if this be really your opinion. What a tumult invades the mind when in the act of composition—what a rushing multitude of words—what variety of language and diversity of expressions come upon one, so that what occurs is often rejected, and what escapes one is eagerly sought for. Now the harmony of the words ;

---

[1] St. Bern. Epist. 87.
[2] "Vix quippe illas tuas inter prandendum (nam illa hora mihi primum redditae sunt) perlegere potui."—Ibid. Epist. 88.

now the clearness of the expression ; now the depth of the
doctrine ; now the ordering of the diction, and what shall
follow, and what shall precede, are subjects successively of
most intense study, besides many other things which the
learned take note of in matters of this sort. And do you
call this quiet, and regard it as silence, because the tongue
speaks not ? . . . . As regards the book you ask for at the
present moment, I have not got it. For there is a certain
friend of ours who has kept it a long time now, with the
same eagerness with which you desire it. Still, lest your
kind request should seem to be slighted by me, I send you
another book of mine which I have lately brought out, 'On
the Praises of the Virgin ;' and inasmuch as I have not
another copy, I beg you will return it as soon as you can,
or, if you are likely to be coming this way tolerably soon, to
bring it yourself."

Again he says, in reference to the same book most probably :
"The book you want I have asked for from the man to whom
it is lent, but have not yet had it returned to me. You shall
have it as soon as possible ; but, though you may see it and
read it, I do not allow you to copy it. I did not give you
leave to copy the other one I lent you, although you did
so ; and what you gained by it, it is yours to discover. I
remark, also, that you sent it to the Abbot of St. Thierry—not
that I object to that. . . . I beg that you will not think it too
much trouble to seek an opportunity to go to him, and not to
allow any one either to read or copy the said opuscule, until he
and you have overlooked the whole of it, and have compared
and corrected together what requires correction ; so that in
the mouth of two witnesses every word may be established.
Then, in the last instance, I leave it to your joint opinion
whether it is advisable to publish it completely to the world,
or only to a few, or to here and there one, or to none at all.
And that little preface, too, whether it is fitting—or if another

more suitable can be found—I leave to be determined by you.

"I had all but forgotten to allude to the beginning of your letter, in which you complain that I taxed you with falsehood. I do not recollect ever having done so ; but if I ever did, you surely would not doubt but that it was in jest."[1]

About this opuscule, which causes so much anxiety and caution, we shall soon hear more, when the alternative of giving it to the world is adopted. To conclude with a gentle touch on Saint Norbert's little extravagances, sent in a letter to Geoffrey, bishop of Chartres.

"What you ask of me touching Norbert, viz. whether he be going to Jerusalem, I cannot tell you. I saw him, and spoke to him, a few days ago, and from that heavenly flute—I mean his mouth—I heard many things ; but on this point nothing at all. But when I spoke of Antichrist, and asked his opinion, he declared that he knew most certainly that he (Antichrist) would be manifested during the very generation which now is. When I pressed him to give me the reasons for his certitude, his answer was not of a kind to make me adopt his view as undoubted truth.[2] He finished by saying that he should not see death till he had witnessed a general persecution in the Church."

So could men pass pleasant and thoughtful days, even amid the turmoil and barbarism of the twelfth century.

---

[1] St. Bern. Epist. 88.

[2] "Audito quod respondit, non me illud pro certo credere debere putavi."—Ibid. *Epist.* 56.

CHAPTER VII.

(A.D. 1127. AETAT. 36.)

SUCH is the mode of life and thinking which Bernard's convent walls secure for him. Shut up within these he can pray, fast, read, write, just as he pleases. His life is a continuity of endeavour, an even flow of thought and actions regulated on principles. But all around him is a very different world. Confusion, discord, aimless turmoil have got possession of it: cruelty, **treachery,** and selfishness are the motives of most of the actors in it. They are perpetually tearing, and worrying, and devouring each other. Destruction of men, and man's work, and man's food is their usual occupation. They have been at it for some centuries now, and it does not seem at all likely to abate. It, doubtless, looked to spectators as quite fixed and unalterable—this feudal fighting, plundering, and slaying. It is probable that if Bernard ever thought at all on the subject, he regarded knights, villeins, tournaments, and private wars as part of the nature of things. His reading told him it had existed for five or six hundred years at least, under circumstances but little different from those before his eyes. It is very unlikely that he expected any great change—probably any change at all comparable to what has taken place : while the feudal castle, with its sombre keep, the savage brigands who dwelt in it, the plundered merchants who shuddered at it, and the novices who came to the abbey gates to avoid it all, appeared to him both the actual and the final and permanent phase of human society.

About this time Bernard came into collision with the feudal lord who enjoyed the title of the King of France. Though a king, he had a far less enviable position than Bernard. He did not fast much ; indeed, he was a prodigy of obesity. It is probable he said his prayers only occasionally ; in short, made no pretence of monastic austerity ; yet few monks of his day led a harder, more painful life. Although he was called a king, his nominal subjects were, many of them, far more powerful than he. Even the small territory which was especially called the royal domain was always on the point of being further reduced, and even extinguished, by the intrigues and rebellions of the numerous little knights and barons who held castles all over it. Even at the gates of Paris Burchard of Montmorency was a source of great trouble to him. The lords of Montcheri, the Troussels, could cut him off entirely from his good city of Orleans ; and except when surrounded by a strong force, he never attempted the passage thither from Paris. His life was a long tournament, a succession of sieges, forays, and general devastation. But there was this difference between Louis VI. and his enemies—that generally he was in the right, and they were in the wrong ; that he generally fought for the good cause of justice and mercy, they for their own selfish aggrandizement or plunder.

The growth and power of the feudal aristocracy had now reached their height. In the greater part of Europe the independence of the barons had produced a system of intolerable oppression to their dependents. Exactions and personal service of the most galling kind ground the plebeian vassal to the dust in poverty and misery. Almost every act and necessary of life was under a merciless tax. When the lord gave his daughter in marriage, the vassal paid something towards her dower. When the lord was taken prisoner, the vassal paid his ransom. When the young heir was made knight, the vassal paid for it. If the poor creature himself wished to marry, he must pay for it.[1] If he wished to grind his corn, he could only do so at his lord's mill. The distance might be great, yet he could go nowhere else under penalties. He had perhaps to wait several days before his turn came. The exactions and frauds of the lord's miller were very grievous; yet for all this oppression he must *pay* at the rate of one bushel in fifteen on the amount ground.[2] When the corn was at last turned into flour, the peasant might not bake it into bread except in the lord's oven. The peasant was taxed; his wife, his children, his home, his land, were all taxed. Besides this, there was the constant exaction of personal service—now to repair the castle and its outworks, now to thrash corn, now to carry wine, or to mount guard at night,

[1] " Lorsque que le seigneur mariait sa fille, le vassal payait une redevance ; lorsque qu'il était fait prisonnier, le vassal payait ; lorsque son fils était fait chevalier, le vassal payait encore. Lorsqu'un paysan mourait, le fils, pour pouvoir lui succéder, devait *finare*, comme on disait alors une certaine somme au seigneur. S'il se mariait, il devait faire un présent au seigneur afin d'obtenir son consentement, et il devait se garder de choisir une femme au dehors, c'est à dire, qui ne fût pas serve du même seigneur."—*Économie politique du Moyen Age*, par Louis Cibrario, *trad.* par Wolowsky, tom. i. p. 38. Paris, 1859.

[2] " Le paysan était ordinairement trop pauvre pour avoir dans sa chaumière un pressoir et un four. Le seigneur se chargeait d'en faire construire à ses frais près de son manoir, et tous les serfs avaient le droit de venir, moyennant certaine redevance. C'était d'abord un bienfait ; ce fut bientôt une servitude. Il fallut que le cultivateur amenât son grain, souvent de fort loin ; qu'il attendît son tour pendant plusieurs jours ; et que ne pouvant s'addresser à d'autres, il subît patiemment les fraudes et les vexations du meunier du seigneur. A Marnes . . . quand ils avaient inutilement attendu leur tour au moulin banal pendant un jour et une nuit,"—they might go elsewhere we are told. But "dans d'autres pays la coutume accordait trente-six heures, et même trois jours au meunier, et dans quelques-uns elle ne fixait rien à cet égard."—*Hist. des Classes ouvrières en France*, Levasseur, vol. i. p. 165. Paris, 1859.

or to shoe the horses. If the lord went into a village, food, lodging, and stabling must be found for him. In some countries it was the peasant's business to keep his lordship's dogs. In others the vassals must lend their horses, cows, and oxen to their suzerain when he wanted them. They were also prohibited from selling their wine as long as his remained unsold. Every bridge and castle exacted a toll ; and, with a grotesque tyranny, defects or deformities of body had to be paid for. In Provence players and minstrels were forced to dance and make merry before the lady of the castle : the pilgrim must sing a song ; the Moor had to throw up his turban, and paid five sous full weight ; the Jew was forced to put his stockings on his head, and recite a Paternoster in the dialect of the place.[1] Over and above all this came the perpetual devastation, plundering, and massacring caused by the baronial wars. The lord stripped his vassals to make war on his enemies, and his enemies stripped them still more to impoverish and paralyse him.

Such was the position of the bulk of the population. The feudal aristocracy was without any competent rival power to restrain and balance it. The Church alone was at all able, but only partially and on grand occasions, when all the resources of the spiritual arsenal were called out against some inveterate offender. After all, a sudden raid—the cattle carried off and the village fired—was a more rapid argument, or, at least, far more practical and evident in its

---

[1] " La puissance seigneuriale se manifestait encore dans les péages qu'on exigeait à chaque pont, à chaque château. Il est souvent fait mention du denier que le passant payait pour chaque difformité ou défectuosité qu'on découvrait sur son corps. Les histrions, les baladins, et menestrels devaient dans le péage de Provence *faire jeux, exercices et galantises, la dame du château présente.* Le pèlerin chantait une romance. Le Maure jetait en l'air son turban, et comptait cinq sous trebuchants à la porte du château. Le Juif devait mettre ses chausses sur la tête, et réciter un *pater* dans le jargon du pays." — *Économie politique de Moyen Âge,* par Louis Cibrario, *trad.* par Wolowsky, p. 40.

effects, than the spiritual thunders of the Church. The papacy, the Church in its entirety, made great and haughty pretensions ; but in detail, in the hands of isolated abbots and bishops, it must have often yielded to present and immediate violence. Thus the serfs and the clergy were drawn together by the feeling of a common weakness before a common enemy. And now, in France, in the centre of feudalism, another ally is going to join them, viz. the royal power. "King Louis VI.," says Suger, "took care of the interests of the Church, and, what had been for long unknown, was anxious for the peace of the labourers and of the poor." "Louis VI.," says Ordericus Vitalis, "claimed the assistance of the bishops all over France, to help to repress the rebels and brigands. Then the bishops instituted in France a 'popular community,' in order that the priests might accompany the king to battles and sieges, with their standards and all their parishioners."[1]

He wanted all the assistance that clergy or serfs could render him. The lords of the castles all round him made leagues among themselves, and even involved him in contests with our powerful and politic Henry I. But the historical significance of Louis VI.'s reign is in the gradual revival of the influence and extent of the kingly power, which he fostered and stimulated. The great barons began to recognise him as something more than a mere phantom of authority ;

---

[1] "Ludovicus itaque . . . jam adultus, illustris et animosus regni paterni defensor, ecclesiarum utilitatibus providebat, aratorum, laboratorum, et pauperum (quod diu insolitum fuerat) quieti studebat."— SUGERII *Vita Ludovici Crassi*, cap. i. col 1258, ed. Migne. "Ludovicus ad comprimendam tyrannidem praedonum et seditiosorum auxilium totam per Galliam deposcere coactus est episcoporum. Tunc ergo communitas in Francia popularis sta- tuta est a praesulibus, ut presbyteri comitarentur regi ad obsidionem vel pugnam cum vexillis et parochianis omnibus." — ORDERICUS VITALIS, lib. xi. cap. 34, vol. iv. p. 285, ed. Provost. . . . See especially D'Acherii Spicilegium, vol. iii. p. 481, a most curious charter of Louis VI., in which "confirmat privilegium quo servi Carnotensis ecclesiae habent in omni foro sæculari liberam potestatem testificandi."

and a growing respect for his office and person is manifested during his whole life. A curious incident illustrates this. The haughty and powerful counts of Anjou were, by right of inheritance, the seneschals of the kings of France. But the degradation of the monarchy had been such that they willingly neglected an office which to their minds carried with it more of ignominy than honour. Fulk V. formally reclaimed his ancestral rights, and was reinstated in his privilege of placing, on grand occasions, the dishes on the table of the king.[1]

Two of Louis's military undertakings will be related as examples of the rest. They show, with tolerable distinctness, the various methods and results of the feudal wars, and the natures of the men who conducted them.

The lords of the castle called Le Puiset, situated on the frontiers of La Beauce and the Orléannais, had been for many years the terror of their neighbours. The possessor, Hugo, at this date (A.D. 1112), was in no wise more peaceable than his ancestors. Suger, abbot of St. Denis, says he was much worse, and that those whom his father chastised with whips he chastised with scorpions. Perhaps Suger was prejudiced, inasmuch as he suffered manifold and numerous injuries at Hugo's hands. The village of Monarville, which belonged to the Abbey of St. Denis, was plundered and oppressed by him in a " manner which infidel Saracens could not have rivalled."[2] He would come with a number of others, and insist on being entertained, and " with open mouth consume the property of

---

[1] Henri Martin, Hist. de France, tom. iii. p. 276.

[2] " Monarvilla . . . quae sub jugo castri Merevillae conculcata non minus quam Sarracenorum depressione, mendicabat : cum ejusdem castri dominus quotiescunque vellet, in eadem hospitium cum quibuscumque vellet, raperet, rusticorum bona pleno ore devoraret, talliam et annonam tempore messis, pro consuetudine, asportaret. Lignaria sua bis aut ter in anno carrucarum villae dispendio aggregaret, porcorum, agnorum, anserum, gallinarum, importabiles quasque molestias, pro consuetudine tolleret."—SUGERIUS, *De rebus in administratione sua gestis,* cap. xi. col. 1218, ed. Migne.

the farmers." In the time of harvest he would carry off his
taille. Such was his want of humanity, that twice, and even
three times, in the year he would cut his wood and cart it,
and this, too, at the expense and trouble of the servants of
St. Denis; whilst his exactions in the way of pigs, lambs,
geese, and fowls were simply insupportable. The property
was becoming a solitude under his multiform tyranny. The
famous village of Thoury, again, he treated in the same
way; and to such a condition did he reduce it, that whereas
it formerly had afforded welcome food and lodgings to merchants, foreigners, and all kinds of travellers, it at last was
stripped of even its farm labourers. "If we (*i.e.* the monks of
St. Denis) tried to defend it, Hugo soon came and destroyed
everything; he carried off all he could, and levied a tax, first
for himself, secondly for his butler, thirdly for his steward.[1]
This went on for two years, and as all the churches which had
land in those parts were equally oppressed, we all took counsel
to decide how it was possible to throw off this intolerable
tyranny. Ives, Bishop of Chartres, the Bishop of Orleans, the
Archbishop of Sens, besides several other abbots and ourselves, went to King Louis, and with tears unfolded our
pitiable case. He, a man of noble industry, full of piety,
and an illustrious defender of the churches, promised to help
us, and made an oath that that wicked man should never
again destroy the goods of the Church."[2]

---

[1] " Tauriacus igitur famosa Beati
Dionysii villa, caput quidem aliarum,
et propria et specialis sedes Beati
Dionysii, peregrinis et mercatoribus
seu quibuscumque viatoribus alimenta cibariorum in media strata,
lassis etiam quietem quiete minis-
trans, intolerabilibus dominorum
praefati castri Puteoli angariis usque
adeo miserabiliter premebatur ut . . .
jam colonis pene destituta langueret
. . . annonam et talliam sibi primum,
deinde dapifero suo, deinde prae-
posito suo, rusticorum vectigalibus
ad castrum deferri cogeret."—SUGE-
RIUS, *De rebus in administratione
sua gestis,* cap. xii.

[2] " Qui ut vir erat nobilissimae
industriae, plenus pietate, ecclesiarum illustris defensor, auxiliari spo-
pondit; et quod ecclesias et ecclesiarum bona deinceps destrui a prae-
fato nequam nullo modo pateretur,
jurejurando firmavit."—Ibid.

In the meantime Hugo had involved himself in a quarrel with Theobald, Count of Blois, and was wasting the lands of the latter, up to the gates of Chartres, with fire and sword.[1] Young Theobald, in spite of his wide possessions, which extended over Blois, Chartres, Sancerre, and Meaux, and the vigorous race he sprang from (he was grandson of the Conqueror of England), did not feel himself strong enough to oppose Hugo single-handed, and did not dare to approach the latter's castle of Le Puiset nearer than within eight or ten miles.   But now he came to King Louis, asking for the same thing as the bishop and abbots had just asked for, with this difference, that, as a great feudal lord, he could offer to the king most valuable co-operation.   The king summoned Hugo to appear before him, as his suzerain, and to confront his accusers, Theobald and the clergy, whom he had despoiled. Of course he did not come, and immediately the king and the count marched to assail the terrible Le Puiset.   They led a large army of horse and foot, and at once commenced the storming of the castle.   The glittering of the armour and the helmets, which seemed to strike fire under the repeated blows —the crushing and piercing of the shields—the clouds of arrows which rose from both sides—formed a sight to fill the spectator with wonder.   Then, as the besiegers forced their way through the outer gateway into the inner court, the defenders poured such a hail of darts and missiles from their towers and bastions that it was almost intolerable even to the bravest, and they nearly succeeded in driving out their assailants.   But the king's troops made a desperate effort.   They filled some carts with their broken shields, and beams, and planks, and fragments of doors, and all the dry wood they could collect, and smearing the whole

---

[1] " Terram . . . usque Carnotum depopulans rapinis et incendiis exponebat."—SUGERII *Vita Ludovici Grossi*, cap. xviii. col. 1289, ed. Migne.

with grease, they pushed them to the door of the keep, and set them blazing. The defenders were excommunicate and utterly devilish,[1] so that the plan of burning them alive was highly desirable, if it could only be accomplished. In the meantime Count Theobald was assaulting the castle from the other side, which looked towards Chartres. He urged his men to mount the steep incline and scale the palisade, which was here the only obstacle. But as soon as they reached the summit of the slope, they fell over and rolled to the bottom, either badly wounded or killed. The cause of this was, that knights mounted on swift horses were constantly moving about on the upper works of the castle, and as soon as any of the enemy made the attempt to reach them they were sent tumbling into the ditch. Hugo and his friends were getting the best of it, when a strange circumstance changed the face of matters. A bold priest who was present, with no protection to his uncovered head, rapidly ascended to the foot of the palisade, holding a plank before him by way of shield. Here he placed himself out of reach of the enemy's swords or missiles, by crouching beneath the loopholes, and began loosening the stakes. When he found he could do so without molestation, he beckoned to the others to come and help him. A crowd, with axes and bars, now followed the priest's example, and in a short time a breach was made. At the same moment the king's forces on the opposite side had effected an entrance, and the Castle of Puiset was taken. Hugo was sent off to a dungeon at Château Landon ; and the king ordered all the furniture of the castle to be sold, and the castle itself to be burnt.[2]

But, while the ruins were still smoking, the allies had quarrelled. Count Theobald, wishing to turn his success to advantage, determined to erect a castle at a place called

---

[1] " Erant enim excommunicati et omnino diabolici."—SUGERII *Vita Lud. Grossi.*
[2] Ibid.

Allonnes. To do this without his suzerain's permission was a breach of feudal law. Louis refused to allow the building to continue. Theobald offered to settle the matter by a single combat between a representative of himself and the king. The duel does not appear to have ever taken place. A good deal of confused fighting between the king and the count followed, generally to the detriment of the latter. But he gradually succeeded in detaching several of Louis's most valuable allies from him; and seizing the occasion of his absence in Flanders, the count, with his confederates, Henry I. and Hugo of Puiset (who had recovered his liberty), prepared to strike a decisive blow at his sovereign and recent ally.

Hugo had been released from his captivity at Château Landon in the following manner :—On the death of his uncle Eudes, Count of Corbeil, Hugo was declared his heir.[1] He consented to relinquish his new inheritance to the king in return for his freedom and the restitution of the domain of Le Puiset, with this condition, that the castle should not be rebuilt without Louis's express consent. This engagement he kept as long as it seemed expedient. But the king's absence in Flanders promised to be a good opportunity for breaking his word. Louis had left his good Suger behind him in a stronghold at Thoury. Hugo thought the place might be taken by a *coup de main*, if by any artifice Suger could be induced to leave it. He accordingly came to the unsuspecting ecclesiastic, and begged of him to use his great influence with Louis to his (Hugo's) advantage. Suger fell into the snare laid for him, and left Thoury to find the king. The cunning Louis

---

[1] " Eudes, Comte de Corbeil, vint à mourir. Il ne laissait point d'enfants, Hugues du Puiset alors prisonnier à Château Landon était son neveu et son héritier. . . . Hugues obtint du roi la liberté et la restitution du château du Puiset, mais il prit l'engagement de ne point rétablir les fortifications de ce château, et il fit au roi l'abandon du Comté de Corbeil."—*Hist. des Comtes de Champagne*, par d'Arbois de Jubainville, vol. ii. p. 202.

smiled bitterly at Suger's simplicity when he heard of his errand, and, with much anger, bade him return and repair his error. Suger, wise too late, hastened back, expecting to see across the wide plain the smoking tower of his priory in the distance.[1] Towards nightfall he reached it, and found that Hugo's soldiers and his own men had had a hard day's fighting, and were now on both sides resting from their exertions. The soldier-prior deceived the enemy, who mistook him for one of his own party. Suger made signals to his friends in the castle, the door was opened, and a sudden dash through the town—not without danger—brought him back to the position he had so imprudently left.

Soon after a general and fierce engagement took place at Le Puiset. Louis fought like a gladiator at the head of his men, seeking a conflict with Count Theobald, who had declared his wish for a personal contest. But presently the king fell into an ambuscade which Randolph of Beaugency had prepared for him ; he was utterly routed, and his army being dispersed in all directions, fled in all haste to the protection of Thoury. Here he collected his scattered troops, and in a short time, on the same battle-ground, met his enemies again, and with better fortune : Count Theobald was wounded, and begged for a truce and leave to retire to Chartres. "The king, who was gentle and merciful beyond human belief," gave him per-

---

[1] "Et dum ipse Stampensi via exercitum colligens, nos rectiori et breviori Tauriacum dirigimur; hoc unum multo et frequenti intuitu a longe assumentes, necdum occupatae munitionis argumentum, quod tristega turris in eadem munitione longa planitie supereminens, apparebat, quae capta munitione illico igne hoste solveretur Et quia hostes totam viciniam rapiendo, devastando occupabant, neminem occurrentium donis etiam aut promissis nobiscum ducere poteramus. . . . Jam sole in vesperum declinante, cum quia hostes nostros tota die impugnantes expugnare non valerent, fatigati parum substitissent, nos ac si essemus de eorum consortio, speculata opportunitate, non sine magno periculo per medium villae irruentes ; quia quibus innueramus in propugnaculis nostrates portam citissime Domino annuente intravimus."—SUGER. *Vita Ludov. Gross.* cap. xx.

mission. As regards Hugo, the king entirely confiscated his property, and demolished Le Puiset level with the ground.[1]

The next incident in Louis's reign that will be adverted to occurred at an interval of fifteen years from the last. It took place in Flanders ; and perhaps no event since the capture of Jerusalem made a more resounding echo in Europe. This occurrence was the murder of Charles the Good, Count of Flanders, in the Church of St. Donatian, at Bruges, on the 2d of March, 1127.

The County of Flanders was in a very different state of material prosperity from the rest of Europe. Ever since the times of the illustrious Bras de Fer the inhabitants, through either good fortune or their own merit, had been ruled by a series of energetic and able princes. An industrious population was developed in the self-governed towns, and the powers of mind and body of the people at least were devoted to other purposes than those of mutual destruction. A race of hardy fishermen became in time the source of a widespread, opulent commerce. The coasts of England, of France, and of distant Spain, were well known to these intrepid mariners, so that even the haughty Norman Conqueror of Britain was glad of their assistance both in men and ships. But it was to her vigorous artisans, her weavers of woollen and linen cloths, that Flanders owed her prosperity and power. These, in their numbers and unanimity, formed a strong middle-class element, and a valuable counterpoise to the feudal aristocracy around them. The result was, that nowhere in Europe were life and property so safe. "Whatever may be the case in other countries, and whatever wars may there break out, from of old with us in Flanders it has been established by our counts, and is now observed as a law, that no one shall presume to

---

[1] Suger. Vita Ludov. Gross.

plunder or steal, or take another captive, or in any way despoil him."[1]

It happened that in the reign of Baldwin the Pious one Balderannus was castellan of Bruges. He had a wife named Dedda or Duva, who loved one of his knights (Erembaldus), and hated her husband. At last the woman told her paramour that he should hold her husband's place as castellan and viscount, if she ever became a widow. At this period war broke out with the Emperor Henry III., and a military expedition took the castellan and his knight Erembaldus to the banks of the Scheldt. Boats on the river operated in concert with the forces on shore. In one of the boats were the husband and his betrayer. Night descended on the dreary waste of mud and water, and in the morning the chatellaine of Bruges was a widow, as she had hoped to be. Erembaldus returned to claim her hand, and to seize her husband's power and offices.[2]

From this guilty couple sprang a family which soon came to be reckoned among the most powerful in Flanders. They were related by marriage with the rich and noble houses of the country. One of them, Hacket, was castellan of Bruges; another, Bertolf, was provost of the Chapter of the same place. But a reverse was at hand.

---

[1] " Antiquo et comitibus terrae nostrae statutum, et hactenus quasi pro lege observatum est, ut quantacunque inter quoslibet homines guerra emergeret, nemo in Flandria quidquam praedari, vel aliquem capere aut exspoliare praesumeret."—GUALTERUS, *De Vita et Martyrio B. Caroli Boni*, pars v.—This is the first of those two most remarkable narratives which we possess concerning the murder of Charles the Good. They resemble, for their graphic portraiture of events, the vividness of Froissart or Herodotus rather than the usual blank dullness of the chroniclers. Walter was Canon of De Térouane ; Galbert a notary of Bruges. The little works are to be found both in the *Acta Sanctorum Martii*, tom. i. die 2, p. 152, and also in Migne, *Patrologia*, tom. clxvi. col. 874.

[2] Erembaldus drowned his master. " Facto quoque noctis silentio, dum castellanus ad mingendum in ora stetisset navis, ille Erembaldus retro accurrens, longe a navi projectum dominum in profundum torrentis aquosi praecipitavit."— GALBERT, cap. xv.

A niece of the provost's had married a gentleman, who, on challenging another to fight a duel, was told that the husband of a serf was not fit to do battle with a noble, and even by the law of Flanders was considered ignoble himself. This deadly insult aroused the united animosity of the provost's kindred. An inquiry took place before Charles, Count of Flanders. The servile origin of this haughty family was a point which had been already discussed, though their long possession of power and wealth made the investigation difficult and obscure. But Charles in time succeeded in proving —to his own satisfaction at least—that these rich and puissant subjects, to whose aid he owed not a little when he obtained the County of Flanders, were serfs by origin, and belonged to himself. Bertolf scornfully replied, " Let him inquire as much as he will, we are and always will remain free ; and there lives not the man upon earth who is able to make us slaves."[1]

It chanced that at this juncture Count Charles had occasion to pass over into France for a short time. " His presence, ever painful to the workers of iniquity, and even a sort of intolerable prison to them," no longer acting as a check, the provost and his nephews planned and executed a scheme of genuine feudal barbarism, such as was happening daily in neighbouring countries, but was comparatively rare in Flanders. Bertolf and his relations had enemies named Thancmar, who stood well with the count. Now that their protector was absent, the nephews of the provost determined to attack them. The astute provost himself was careful not to appear as partaker in their proceedings. He

---

[1] There is a slight discrepancy between Walter and Galbert at this point. The former says the provost's nephew received the insult from his adversary in Count Charles's court of justice, when he was told that a free man was not going to answer the interrogations of a serf.— Walter, cap. xv. Galbert's statement is followed in the text.

even hypocritically lamented that such bloodshed and destruction should take place. Yet clandestinely he was assisting his nephews to the utmost of his power. "He himself went down to the carpenters who were working in the choir of the brethren, and ordered their tools—that is, their axes—to be carried to the scene of action, that with them the tower, the orchards, and the houses of their enemies might be destroyed. He sent, also, from house to house in the suburbs to collect more axes, which were at once taken thither." So equipped by the aid of their relative, they (the "nephews") soon accomplished their work of destruction on the houses and lands of the Thancmars. They carried off all the moveables, and what they could not carry off they destroyed. Some of their enemies they hanged; but the majority they killed with the sword. At last they returned by night to Bruges, a troop of five hundred knights and a numerous body of foot soldiers. The provost received them with open arms. He took them into the cloister and refectory of the brethren, and refreshed the whole of them with a diverse assortment of victuals and drinks, "and was merry and elated over it." Flanders was shocked and amazed at such a spectacle. "From the beginning of the kingdom rapine has never been permitted by any one of our counts, for the reason that great wars and death would be the consequence."[1]

[1] "Captata, cum in Franciam forte perrexisset, comitis absentia (omnibus enim iniquitatis operariis semper gravis erat, et quasi carcer quidam intolerabilis ejus praesentia) copiosam congregant et validam militum manum . . . quosdam suspendunt; plerosque in ferro trucidant." —WALTER, cap. xix. Galbert, as usual, adds several further details: . . . "ipse praepositus descendit ad carpentarios qui in claustro fratrum operabantur, et jussit ferramenta eorum, scilicet secures, illuc deferri, quibus detruncarent turrem et pomaria et domos inimicorum suorum. . . . Cumque in nocte rediissent nepotes ejus cum quingentis militibus armigeris et peditibus infinitis, induxit eos in claustrum et fratrum refectorium, in quo refecit universos . . . et super hoc laetus et gloriosus erat."—GALBERT, cap. ii.

Presently Count Charles returned to Flanders, and stayed at Ypres. The rustics and others who had suffered in the late raid, to the number of two hundred, came to him under the cover of night, and, falling at his feet, "implored his paternal and accustomed aid." They begged that their goods, their cattle, and their silver might be restored to them. When he heard their complaints, he was deeply moved ; and calling his councillors together, he asked them what stern justice demanded as a retribution for such a crime. Several declared that it was not the first time the inhabitants of Bruges had misbehaved themselves ; that they had suffered much both in property and person at the hands of those haughty burghers. But there was such a discrepancy of opinion as to the course to be pursued, that no conclusion could be arrived at, save this—that the count should himself visit the scene of destruction, and, from personal inspection on the spot, estimate the amount of punishment demanded by the wicked deed.[1]

The next day the whole cavalcade went out to behold the ruin and destruction which Bertolf's "five hundred knights and numerous foot" had brought about. Charles gazed on the prospect before him with tears in his eyes. The crime was evident. What should be the penalty for it? Well, the provost's nephew has a castle, as his enemy Thancmar had. There it stands, a terror and a torment to the country round, full, probably even now, of ill-gotten plunder. "Let it be fired," was a verdict which was soon pronounced by Charles's advisers with prompt unanimity. As the afternoon sun of the last day in February was nearing the horizon, the Count of Flanders and his company had turned their backs on the

---

[1] " Audierunt rustici comitem venisse apud Ipram, ad quem . . . usque ad ducentos transierunt, pedibusque ipsius convoluti, obsecrantes paternum et consuetum ab eo auxilium."—GALBERT, cap. ii. "Tandem in hoc omnium convenit sententia, ut comes ipse partes illas praesentialiter visitaret, et quae gesta fuerant, visu et auditu certius exploraret."—WALTER, cap. xx.

smoking ruins, and were making their way to Bruges and to supper.[1]

Count Charles had finished his evening meal when emissaries from the provost came, requesting an audience. They begged that the count would be pleased to turn away his wrath and receive Bertolf and his nephew Burchard into his favour again. The good Charles replied that he was quite willing to act justly and mercifully by them, if they were ready at the same time to lay aside their lawless practices. Nay, he promised to give Burchard a better house than the one he had just lost. Another house, but not in the same place ; not while he was Count of Flanders should Burchard hold another property in that quarter. Not again should he be neighbour of Thancmar, and disturb the public peace with his plunders and murders. The spokesmen whom Bertolf had sent were partly cognisant of the intended treason, and did not insist very much on the terms of reconciliation ; and when the servants were going to fill their cups, they begged the count that he would order some better wine. Having drunk it, as usually happens with topers, they wanted more, and asked for a parting bumper, after which they would retire to bed. At Charles's order, all present had their cups well filled, whereupon they took their leave and departed.[2]

---

[1] "At illi consilium dederunt ut sine dilatione domum Burchardi incendio destrueret, eo quod rapinam in rusticos comitis exercuisset. . . . Descendit super hoc consultus consul, et incendit domum et funditus mansionem ejus destruxit."—GALBERT, cap. ii. "Munitionem ipsius Burchardi . . . evertit, et funditus destruxit, ac deinde . . . Brugas eadem die, heu ! nunquam reversurus, perrexit."—WALTER, cap. xxi.

[2] "Postquam comes coenaverat, ascenderunt coram eo intercessores ex parte praepositi. . . . At consul si lites et rapinas postponere deinceps voluissent, meliorem do

mum restituere Burchardo se debere promisit. In loco tamen in quo domus combusta est, jurabat, se comitatum obtinente, amplius Burchardum nullam possessionem obtenturum, eo quod usque tunc juxta Thancmarum manens, nunquam nisi lites et seditiones in hostes et in cives cum rapina et caede ageret. Qui vero intercessores fuere partim conscii traditionis, non multum super reconciliandis vexabant comitem, et quando propinatum ibant ministri, rogabant comitem ut de vino meliore afferri juberet. Quod cum ebibissent, sicut potores solent, rogabant semel sibi propinari et abundanter

H

When they returned and informed the provost and his nephew that they had not succeeded in winning the count's promise of favour or forgiveness, Bertolf and Burchard at once proceeded to mature their plans for revenge. They shut themselves in a room, the door of which the provost himself guarded, and swore over their clasped hands mutual fidelity in a scheme to slay the count. The conspirators were six in number, besides the provost, viz. his brother Guelricus. his nephews Burchard and Robert, his relative Isaac, William of Werwyck, and Ingrasnus of Esne. After an anxious debate, each of them went to his own place. Isaac, when he got home, made pretence of going to bed, but he only waited the silence and obscurity of the night to remount his horse and hasten back to the town which he had left shortly before. On his way he called at Burchard's house, and assembling those whom he wanted, they all proceeded to another house belonging to a knight named Walter, where they carefully extinguished all the fires, which they feared might betray them and their doings. Thus, in the dark and cold of a March night, did they complete their plans for the count's murder in the morning. They selected the men they thought fit for the work, and promised them great rewards if it was accomplished. To the knights they gave four marks, to their attendants two. Isaac, having thus animated his friends by example and advice, retired, and reached home a little before dawn.[1]

It was a foggy, dark morning, so that one could not see farther than a spear's length off. Burchard took measures to ascertain when the count would leave his house and enter the church, as he was accustomed to do every morning. Charles had

---

adhuc, ut posteriore licentia et ultima a consule accepta quasi dormitum abirent : et jussu comitis abundanter propinatum est omnibus illis qui aderant, donec accepta licentia ultima, ipsi abiissent."—GALBERT, cap. ii.

[1] Ibid. cap. iii.

passed a disturbed night; and his chaplains related that, when
he had retired to rest, an anxious wakefulness took possession
of him; that his mind appeared confused and agitated, and
that in his sleepless meditation he turned from side to side, sat
up in bed, then sank back, as if weary of himself. Towards morning he slept, and arose a little later than was his wont, washed,
and prepared himself for the day's work by his usual exercises
of charity and devotion. He never failed to begin the day by
the relief of the poor, which he did by giving them food with
his own hands, and never would allow the assistance of any
servants in this office, which he moreover performed barefoot. He had lately added to this custom another, of giving
to five poor persons every morning new clothes and shoes.
He then proceeded to the Church of St. Donatian, ascended
the tribune, and before an altar dedicated to the Mother of
God prostrated himself in prayer, and, with his book of hours
before him, proceeded to sing the seven penitential psalms.[1]

He had got through the first three, and was singing the
fourth—the fiftieth Psalm—when Burchard, attended by his
six accomplices, suddenly came behind him, and pricked the
back of his neck with a dagger. The count immediately

---

[1] "Igitur cum dies obvenisset
obscura valde et nebulosa, ita ut
hastae longitudine nullus a se dis-
cernere posset rem aliquam, clanculo
servos aliquot misit Burchardus in
curtem comitis praecavere exitum
ejus ad ecclesiam. Surrexerat quidem
comes multo mane, et distribuerat
pauperibus, sicut consueverat. . . .
Sed sicut referebant capellani ejus,
nocte cum in lectum se compossu-
isset ad dormiendum, quadam vigi-
lantiae sollicitudine laborabat, mente
quidem confusa et turbata, ita ut
multiplici rerum meditatione pul-
satus, modo in altero cubans latere,
modo residens in stratu totus langui-
dus sibi ipsi videretur."—GALBERT.

Walter says he "groaned" in bed
longer than usual, "cum gloriosus
princeps paulo diutius solito in
stratu suo gemuisset," &c.

I have been profuse, perhaps redundant, in quotations from these
two interesting narratives by Walter
and Galbert. I trust that the
above extracts will suffice to give
a notion of their picturesque power
and value. As all the remainder of
this chapter rests on their authority,
I content myself from this point
with a general reference to them.
BOLLAND, *Acta Sanct. Martii*, tom. i.
die 2, p. 152, and Migne, *Patrologia*,
tom. clxvi.

turned round, as the murderer wished, and exposed his uncovered head to the full sweep of the heavy sword already
raised to strike him. The blow descended, cleft his skull in
twain, and scattered his brains on the pavement of the church.
The ruthless assassins mangled and hacked at his lifeless
corpse, till they had chopped off his head and almost his
right arm.

Their chief object being thus attained, the murderers sought
for the remainder of their open or supposed enemies. They
caught Thancmar, dragged him down the steps by his heels,
and thought to have despatched him in the doorway of the
church, but he lived for some time after. His two sons,
Walter and Gilbert, when they heard of the count's death,
took horse and rode fast out of the town; but the traitors were
after them, and before they had reached a place of safety,
succeeded in overtaking and slaughtering both. Burchard and
Isaac, with drawn and still bloody swords, rushed about the
cathedral, and amid loud cries and clashing of arms sought
under the benches and in the cupboards for Walter of Locres, a
great friend of the slain count, shouting out, " Walter, Walter !"
In this search they came again on Thancmar, who still breathed,
though mortally wounded. This time they did not leave their
work unfinished. Before his death the priests of the church
had time to hear his confession and administer the last sacrament to him. A woman also, a nun, was seen lying over the
dying man : it was the Abbess of Aurigny, to whom he gave
his ring to take to his wife in token of his death ; in token
also of farewell and love to her and his children, whose tragic
end he knew not of till he had passed beyond the grave.

Walter of Locres in the meanwhile was safely hidden in an
upper part of the church. A priest had covered him with his
cloak, and those who sought his life had not yet discovered
him. But the terrible suspense, the noise of their weapons,
and the shouting of his name, had quite confused his reason.

He came out from his concealment, and at one desperate
bound precipitated himself into the body of the church in the
midst of his enemies — "ran below the choir, calling with
piteous cries on God and the saints." Burchard and Isaac
pressed upon him closely, brandishing their gory swords. They
were tall and powerful men, with such expression of ferocity and
rage in their visages that no one could look on them without
terror. Burchard seized his victim by the hair of his head,
and, holding him at arm's length, prepared to deal him a mortal
blow. Here some priests came forward, and begged that he
at least might be killed outside the church. Burchard granted
their request, and the poor creature was led forth. As he
walked to his doom, he cried, "God have mercy on me!" As
soon as he was in the churchyard, he was struck down with
swords and staves, and half buried under a shower of stones.

Some succeeded, however, in making good their escape.
Gervase, the count's chamberlain, fled on horseback to his
kinsfolk in Flanders. John, the count's body-servant, whom
he liked above all his other domestics, hastened all the morning through by-ways till he reached Ypres about midday.
The town was full of merchants from the surrounding country,
who had come to one of the fairs, which, under the protection
of the good count, could be safely held in the cathedral of
St. Peter. It was here that Count Charles had bought of the
Lombard traders for twenty-one marks his wonderful silver
goblet, which, through the skill of the artist, robbed the spectators of the draught which it contained. Into this busy crowd
of buyers and sellers the scared and exhausted John suddenly
burst. The news he brought had soon traversed the astonished
multitude. In a moment the bargaining and chaffering were
over, and the packing up of bales and the lading of beasts
occupied all the market-place. When ready, they started,
whether by day or by night, hastening every man to his own
country, and spreading far and wide the disgrace of Flanders.

The news, it was thought, flew over the world with miraculous celerity. The count was murdered on Wednesday morning, and the event was known in London, we are told, by the sunrise of the second day ; and towards evening of the same day the inhabitants of Laon, in the opposite direction, also knew it. Galbert says he had these facts in the one case from students of his town, who were at that time studying at Laon ; in the other, from merchants of Bruges who were on business in London.

But a scene was occurring about the possession of the body of the slaughtered count highly characteristic of the age. For several hours after the deed the murderers were too busy, and the rest too fearful, to take any notice of the mangled corpse, which lay on the spot where it fell, undisturbed. The elder Frumold got leave of the provost to wrap it in a linen cloth, and place it on a bier. But these attentions alarmed the traitors extremely. They saw that the dead body of the count was likely to be more dangerous to them than his living mind had been. They saw an incipient saintship rising before them, and away from them, into heaven. They saw the calm, sorrowful martyr's face burning into their very souls with the light of its gentle eyes. And then the miracles, and the people cured of "infirmities" at his tomb. The body must be got away if possible. With this end a strong watch was placed round and in the church, and a message sent to the abbot of Ghent that he should come and fetch the body and bury it at Ghent ; and another message, with a present of four hundred marks, to friend Walter of Ulaerslo, adjuring him by the fidelity he had sworn to the provost and his nephews, to come at once to his assistance with all the force he had. But Walter kept the money and did not come. The abbot of Ghent rode all night, and appeared early on Thursday morning at the castle gates, asking for the body which had been promised to him. The inhabitants of Bruges were on the alert, and inferred no good omen from this early visit of the abbot; and it soon got reported that his object was, with help from the traitors, to carry off the body secretly. And now the provost held a council with his friends, to decide how it could be managed. He had a bier made, such as could be carried on horseback. This was brought to the church door. But the people were more and more excited at the dread of losing the martyr's bones. "Suffer not," they cried, "lord provost, the body of our father and glorious martyr to be taken from us: for if this be done, his castle and buildings will some day be destroyed without mercy. But if he remain, our enemies will have some pity on us when they attack this castle, and will not utterly destroy this church, in which the body of the blessed count is reverentially buried." On hearing these words and clamours the provost and the abbot made haste. They were about to remove the body from the bier in the church to the one which was waiting at the door, when the canons of the church ran up, and, violently replacing the body, asked the provost for what reason he had ordered this? Then, in presence of the thronging crowd, one of the elders amongst them addressed the provost: "My lord provost, if you had wished to act justly in this matter, not without the consent and counsel of the brethren, would you have surrendered so precious a martyr —such a ruler of the country—such a treasure to our Church —whom the Divine mercy and providence have granted to us. There is no reason why he should be taken away from us, among whom chiefly he grew and lived, and among whom he was betrayed for righteousness' sake. Indeed, if he be removed, we fear for the destruction of this stronghold and this church. God will forgive us and be merciful to us, if we have him to intercede for us. Without him God will, without mercy, punish the sin committed among us." Hereupon the provost and the rest kindled into anger, and ordered the body at once to be carried off. Then the canons, with loud cries, rushed to the church doors, saying that, as long as they lived, the body should not go, that they would die sooner. They seized for weapons the tables, benches, candlesticks, and even sacred vessels, of the church, and fought valiantly. They rang the bells to summon the citizens to their assistance, who came in troops, well armed, and with drawn swords, standing round the body, dared any one to touch it.

But the tumult, both in and outside the church, was stayed presently in a remarkable manner. A poor, paralysed cripple, whose legs had never supported him, and who crawled painfully along by the help of a wooden frame, was in the midst of the excited, almost ferocious, crowd. He had crept under the bier, partly for devotion, and partly, perhaps, for safety. Suddenly the sinews of his legs were loosed, and limbs whose use he had never had before grew strong, and he stood up. The miracle calmed all present. The provost and his accomplices retired to the count's palace. The abbot of Ghent went home again, "glad to have escaped." The canons and the people were careful to avail themselves of the opportunity to secure their martyr's bones. Masons and labourers who could work quickly were sought for, and ordered to build a tomb with the despatch the occasion demanded. The day following it was ready. A mass for Charles's soul was said, and Frumold scattered alms to the poor. " But his tears fell faster than his halfpence." The body was carried to, and enshrined in, the tribune where "he won the martyr's palm."

"On the 7th of March God unsheathed the sword of divine vengeance against the enemies of His Church, and moved the heart of a certain knight named Gervasius to execute punishment." Gervasius had been the count's chamberlain, and his most attached and trusted friend. He forthwith advanced on the murderers, who had shut themselves up in the castle of Bruges. "Our citizens rejoiced in their hearts when they heard that God had begun to avenge so quickly, but publicly they said nothing, on account of the traitors, who as yet went backwards and forwards amongst them in security and confidence." But the citizens of Bruges, however much they might approve of an offer to punish the count's assassins, were not disposed to allow an armed knight and his company to enter their town without some understanding. They sent, therefore, privately to Gervasius, and made "agreement with regard to mutual faith, amity, and security." They, moreover, swore to aid in avenging the count, and on the following day to admit Gervasius and his army into their suburbs, and to receive them "as brothers within their fortifications." The chronicler says that the return of the delegates who concluded this alliance was welcomed with more joy than he was able to express.

A regular siege now commenced. The men of Bruges were soon joined by a large force—or, rather, multitude—which came from Ghent. They came boasting "that they were men renowned in battle, and possessed of warlike science, which would demolish the besieged." They collected all "their archers, and ingenious workers, and bold plunderers, and cutthroats, and thieves, and fellows ready for all the crimes of war, and loaded thirty waggons full of weapons for them." They arrived horse and foot, hoping to acquire a large booty if they reduced the castle. On reaching the gates of the town they essayed to enter by force. But the whole body of the citizens of Bruges resisted them ; and it nearly came to blows, when the wiser on either side interfered, and determined conditions of joint action. The men of Ghent, anxious to show their superior skill, at once set about the manufacture of ladders to scale the walls. These ladders were about sixty feet in length, and twelve in breadth. They were furnished on each side and in front with planking, to protect those on them from the missiles of the besieged. On the top was placed a second ladder, of the same length, but less broad, so arranged, that when the larger one was erected against the wall, this should fall over on the other side, and thus facilitate descent into the stronghold. On the 18th of March they advanced to the attack. Stones and arrows flew in volleys from both parties ; but those who brought up the ladders were protected by shields and breastplates. Numbers followed to look on, and see how the ladders could be placed against the walls, as from their size, and the greenness of the wood they were made of, their weight was enormous. Shouts and cheers rent the air as they approached. But, in the meantime, some bold and ardent young men got lighter ladders, "such as ten men could carry," and determined to be quicker than the others. One after another they ran up. But, as soon as they reached the top, they were at once struck down by those within, so that the small ladders were given up. Others, again, strove to undermine the walls by means of mallets and iron tools. But, although they demolished a good deal, they were obliged to desist without accomplishing their purpose. Night fell upon the combatants as the heavy ladders were placed in position, amid showers of great stones, which caused much mischief to the men of Ghent. "Whoever was struck by a stone from above, however great might be his strength and courage, was at once exposed to certain ruin. Prostrated and crushed, he soon expired."

The partial success with which the besieged had repelled the attack of the men of Ghent made them a little presumptuous and careless. The watchmen deserted their posts on the walls, and went to warm themselves at a fire in the count's house, being driven in by a bitterly cold wind. The courtyard of the castle was thus left unguarded. The men of Bruges saw this, and promptly took advantage of it. They crept up, by the help of small ladders, without noise or clamour, till a sufficient number was collected to begin the attack. They then detached some of their body to the work of forcing the gates of the castle, against which the traitors had heaped quantities of mud and stones. One gate they found without this obstruction, and secured only by a strong lock. This they soon burst open, and immediately the surging multitude rushed in, "some to fight, some to plunder whatever they could find, others to enter the church, and carry off the body of Count Charles to Ghent."

The traitors in the castle were still ignorant that the court-yard was in possession of their enemies. The noise and tumult soon revealed to them the loss they had sustained. Some yielded at once; others, hoping for no quarter, flung themselves from the walls, and were dashed to pieces; but others, seizing their arms, stood at the doorways of the castle, and prepared to offer a stout resistance. The invaders attacked them with such vigour with swords and axes, that they drove them, through the castle, to the passage which connected it with the Church of St. Donatian, and along which Charles had passed on the morning of his murder. In this narrow passage, which was arched and built of stone, a fearful conflict ensued. Fighting desperately, sword in hand, neither party would retreat, but "remained as immovable as the walls." The ferocious Burchard, driven to madness, fought like a wild boar at bay. His strength was prodigious, and with the murderous blows of his sword he felled his foes as fast as they approached him. At last a rush forward cleared the passage, and the traitors retired to the church. At this point the citizens suspended the attack, and betook themselves to plunder, running through and about the castle of the count, the house of the provost, the dormitory and cloister of the monks. All who were in the attack did the same, hoping to find the treasure of Charles, and to get the furniture of the houses within the walls. In the castle they seized pillows, carpets, linen, cups, kettles; also chains, iron bars, handcuffs, fetters, thongs, collars—in a word, every sort of iron instrument applied to captives; the iron doors of the count's treasure-house, the leaden pipes which carried the water from the roof. In the house of the provost they took beds, lockers, chairs, clothes, vases, and all the other furniture. In the cellars they found an "infinite quantity" of corn, meat, wine, and beer. In the dormitory of the monks they came upon such an abundance of rare and costly garments, that it took them the remainder of the day, till nightfall, in journeys backwards and forwards, to carry off their booty.

Meanwhile the traitors, driven into the church, fortified themselves as they best could in the tower. They even ventured to annoy the plunderers of the castle by casting great stones down upon them as they moved about beneath with their stolen goods. By this means they killed several. The captors of the castle immediately directed their arrows against the windows of the tower, so that not a head could peer out of a window without a thousand arrows being at once shot at it; and at last the tower, stuck all over with arrows, presented a hairy appearance.

The alliance between the men of Bruges and the men of Ghent was far from cordial. They were ever ready to quarrel about the body of the count, and were once on the point of coming to blows. The men of Ghent asserted that they had a right to the body, as through their ladders and instruments they had frightened the besieged, and made them fly from the castle. To which their allies of Bruges replied that they, forsooth, had done nothing with their machines, that they had done nothing throughout the siege but plunder, and cost a great deal to keep. Again the leaders interfered, and calmed the tumult when it was getting dangerous.

A combined attack was then made on the church. The assailants burst open the door which looked towards the choir, and drove the traitors from the nave up into the tribune. A terrific and revolting struggle here took place. Stones, arrows, javelins, were showered down upon the assailants, till not only were numbers wounded and killed, but the whole choir was full of stones, and the very pavement could no longer be seen. Nothing of its sacred character was left to the church, which resembled in its desecration the deformity of a prison rather than a house of prayer.

At this juncture Louis VI. made his appearance. He sent his greeting from Arras to the princes and barons of the siege, promised them his aid and approbation in avenging his nephew, Count Charles, and concluded by saying, "I wish and order you to appear before me without delay, and in common council to elect a useful count, whom you shall agree to consider your peer and a ruler over the land and its inhabitants. For the country cannot long remain without a count, and escape dangers greater even than those which now threaten it."

The election of a new count was a long and troublesome business. While King Louis and his barons were getting through it, news came that the provost Bertolf had been captured at Yprès. He had escaped from Bruges some time before, by the help of Walter, the butler, to whom he gave four hundred marks, "trusting more in Walter than any man on earth," who, nevertheless, took him to a desert place and there left him. He afterwards fled to Furnes, where his wife was, and again from thence, on the night of Good Friday, he continued his flight. Of his own accord he travelled barefoot, in order to obtain pardon of God for his sins. When he was taken, the soles of his feet were torn and lacerated from contact with the stones. His sufferings must have been great, as he had lived all his life in the utmost luxury, and dreaded, it was said, the sting of a flea as if it were a javelin. William the Bastard, of Yprès, was especially anxious to secure him, and disclaim all cognisance of, or partnership in, his crime, although no one doubted that William, on the count's murder, not only had sent messages of approval and promises of support, but had actually, through the provost's nephews, received five hundred pounds of English money out of Charles's treasure. However, he now sought to prove, by his readiness to punish and torture his accomplice, that he had no connexion with him.

The clamour and tumult of the men of Ypres round the wretched captive were, in the chronicler's opinion, without a parallel. The whole neighbourhood assembled to see him, dancing and shouting before and behind, pulling him with ropes, first this way, then that. He had no garments on but his breeches, and was exposed to a constant shower of mud and stones. With motionless eyes and features he bore his agony. Presently one of his persecutors, striking him on the head with a stick, said, "Oh, proudest of men, why do you disdain to speak to the princes and to us who have power to slay you?" He answered nothing. The market-place was by this time reached, where he was to meet his death. He was attached to a fork-shaped gibbet, having been denuded of the scanty clothing that still remained to him. He hung suspended from the instrument of torture by his neck and wrists, by which means he underwent a gradual suffocation. At the commencement he supported himself a little by resting his toes on a part of the gibbet. This prolonged his misery, to which the missiles and injuries he received from the crowd added not a little. The treacherous William the Bastard, of Ypres, approached, and hypocritically begged him to reveal his accomplices, besides those in open rebellion. He answered, "You know them as well as I do." William, maddened with rage, told the people to recommence their tormentings. They got fish-hooks and pulled bits of his flesh off with them, they beat him with cudgels, they made holes in him with stakes. They pushed his feet from the meagre support they had found, and, twisting round his neck the entrails of a dog as his eyes rolled in the last agonies of death, they held up a dog's face to his, to show their opinion of him and his doings.

It happened that on the very day on which the provost was put to death a single combat had been appointed to come off between a nephew of his (by marriage), named Guido, and a knight named Herman. As soon, therefore, as the provost's sufferings were over. the people flocked to the place of encounter. At the first shock Guido unhorsed Herman, and as often as the latter attempted to rise, thrust him down with his lance. Presently, by a dexterous movement, Herman got near enough to Guido's horse to strike his sword in his belly and disembowel him. This brought down Guido, who then drew his sword and met his enemy on more equal terms. They fought long and stoutly, exchanging terrific blows, till fatigued with the exertion and the weight of their armour, they cast aside their shields and weapons, closed, and wrestled body to body. Guido again got the best of it, and threw his adversary, and fell upon him. Seated upon the prostrate knight, he bruised and mangled his eyes and face with his iron gauntlets. Herman seemed to endure this sullenly, and allowed Guido to get confident of victory. But at the same time he gently slid his hands down to the lower end of Guido's corselet, and seizing him by a tender part of the body, with one supreme, intense effort cast him off. Guido, torn and ruptured in the most shocking manner, fell powerless, and owned himself vanquished. The bastard, William, "who wished to do all things for his own good fame in this war," ordered Guido to be gibbeted beside the lifeless body of the provost.

In fact, the work of the count's avengers was nearly completed. Burchard and Isaac had both fled, and were now both captured. The former lived through a day and night of torture on the wheel. The latter, with that sudden transition from hellish wickedness to Christian piety and resignation not unusual in the Middle Ages, thanked his persecutors for the pains they inflicted on so grievous a sinner. When he reached the place where he was to be executed, he saluted the gibbet, and kissed the rope, which he placed round his own neck, and, begging the people to pray God for him, he cheerfully met his fate.

Those who were still shut up in the tower were also convinced of the hopelessness of further resistance. They offered to surrender and come out one by one through the window which looked towards the provost's house. Such as were too corpulent to come through that window let themselves down by ropes from a larger one. They were thrust into a small prison, where they were so cramped that they could not all sit down at one time. Three or four at least of their number were obliged to keep standing. The darkness, heat, and the stench half poisoned them. They hoped, as an extreme boon, that they might be permitted to die in the same manner as the common thieves.

King Louis and the new count, William the Norman, had returned to Bruges from Oudenarde; the first on the 4th of May, the latter on the day following. William, as count-regnant, took up his residence in Charles's palace, and dined there. The king came to meet him; but, as the house was "full of people, and servants, and soldiers," the count descended to him in the courtyard of the castle, "being careful to have his doors locked meanwhile." They then decided on the punishment which the imprisoned traitors should receive. It was agreed that they should be cast down from the high tower of the palace. The king and count sent the executioners to the prison, who called forth, first of all, Wilfric Knop, brother of the provost. They told the prisoners, with cruel mendacity, that the king was going to be very merciful to them. On hearing this, they were all ready to come forth. But only Wilfric at that time was led out. He was taken through the interior of the castle up to the top of the tower. There, fastening his hands behind his back, they let him contemplate the prospect of death, and then over the parapet he was whirled, " having on nothing but his shirt and breeches." Crushed and mangled, he soon expired, " pitied by no one." The second whom they led forth was a knight named Walter. His hands were tied in front, instead of behind him, and they were just going to pitch him over, when he begged so hard to be allowed to say one more prayer, that they granted him a few minutes' grace. When he had done, he was sent over after Wilfric. Another knight, named Eric, in his fall came down upon a wooden flight of stairs, and wrenched off one step, " which was fastened with five nails." It was noticed that, though he had fallen from such a great height, he yet sat up and made the sign of the cross. Some women who saw him offered to go and tend him, but a soldier from above sent a great stone down amongst them, and stopped their interference. And so it went on till the whole number, *i.e.* two dozen and four, were dashed to pieces.

William the Norman soon got into fierce discord with his subjects, who, at last, openly rebelled, and elected young Thierry of Alsace, cousin-german of Charles the Good, to be their count. A disastrous period for Flanders of civil war and irregular fighting then followed. " At last, on Saturday, July 27th, the Lord, in His providence, deigned to put an end to our persecutions. At the siege of Alost the Count William, as he was attacking the enemy, was thrown from his horse, and, as he strove to rise and defend himself, a foot soldier ran him through with a lance." The death of his Norman rival left Thierry without a competitor : from this time he began a long and prosperous reign of forty years.

CHAPTER VIII.

(A.D. 1127.   AETAT. 36.)

QUARREL WITH THE BISHOP OF PARIS—APOLOGY—CLUNY—EXTRACTS.

SUCH, in its harsh and repulsive reality, was the secular world with which Bernard was now at frequent intervals to be brought into collision.   Near men like these, or differing only by greater brutality and barbarism, his life was to be spent.   The Church he served had to do battle with this exuberant animalism, and tame it, and drill it, by what means she could, into moderation and reflection—a huge and all but overwhelming task, which tried the extreme energies of many a century of churchmen and aspiring monks.   In the great ages of the Church it was no question of "priestly influence" exerted for worldly and selfish interests.   These came with the fall of the Church's authority before the rising tide of modern thought and knowledge.   In the fourteenth and fifteenth centuries the leaders of the ecclesiastical power had lost faith in spiritual wealth if accompanied by earthly poverty; they believed rather in broad lands and gold pieces.   Hence the blindness which hid from them the signs of the changes which were coming upon the earth; and they imagined, in their presumptuous weakness, to strike at thought and knowledge with their feeble crosiers; to excommunicate truth and reason, even as they would a burglarious baron; that is, they abdicated, and were unfit for, their intellectual leadership.   But it was not so when Saint Bernard, when the great popes and bishops of the twelfth and thirteenth centuries, stood forth the champions of law, morality, and religion, against the anarchy and violence of their times.   Doubtless there were always some bad exceptions—bishops who thought of the temporalities, abbots who devoted to the revenues of their abbeys more attention than they gave to their spiritual office as shepherds of souls; but these men were the exception in the vigorous period of the Church's development.   It is as demonstrable as anything historical can be, that the aspiring and noble characters of the twelfth and thirteenth centuries found the Church not a hindrance, but a help ; that the good and true generally were welcomed and protected in it ; that in ages of cruelty, violence, and injustice, men turned to their "mother," as they were glad to call her, in loving hope, mostly fulfilled, of justice, mercy, and forgiveness.

The slight dispute which about this time occurred between Bernard—or, rather, the Cistercian order—and King Louis VI., is not a little obscure in itself, and only worthy of notice as the first passage of Bernard from his monastic seclusion to intercourse and conflict with that outer world which he had long ago forsaken.   It arose in this manner.   Louis VI., whose whole life showed his respect and sympathy for the Church, for some cause but ill-defined, had a disagreement with Stephen, Bishop of Paris, and, shortly after, with Henry, Archbishop of Sens.   Bernard would lead us to suppose that his enmity arose entirely from the religious conversions and reformation which, taking place in these prelates about this time, caused them to abandon the king's court, and to strive after a life and conversation more worthy of Christian bishops than they had hitherto displayed.   "King Louis," says Bernard to Pope Honorius, "persecutes not so much bishops, as the zeal for justice, the observance of piety, and even the habit of

religion which he finds in them."[1]   This appears a strange
subject of quarrel for a sensible and worthy man, such as
certainly was Louis, to adopt.   An anonymous letter from
some dependant of the Bishop of Paris to the latter points to
a more probable reason.   The writer and the bishop have
evidently already suffered a good deal from the king's wrath.
He exhorts his superior to keep up his spirits, and to stand
firmly by the liberties and privileges of his see.   He then tells
him what he in his own person has suffered for the bishop's
cause.   "How the king and queen have plundered him, and
ordered his vines to be uprooted, and his friends and relations
have given them ten livres to refrain ; and all this has been
done at the instigation of the dean and archdeacons—nay,
through the nocturnal tale-bearing of the succentor G—."[2]
This letter makes it probable that there were some venal
clerks about Louis, who advised him to take measures with
regard to the taxation of ecclesiastical persons, which the
Bishop of Paris thought himself justified or strong enough to
resist.   However, the result was that he and the Archbishop
of Sens placed the kingdom under interdict, and fled to
Citeaux, to watch the effect of their measure.

Then came forth a voice from that asylum of poverty and
religion, which fell on the ears of men with a sudden and
strange emphasis of authority and power.

"To the illustrious King Louis—Stephen, Abbot of Citeaux,
and the whole assembly of the abbots and brethren of Citeaux,
send health, safety, and peace in Christ Jesus.

---

[1] "Rex Ludovicus non tam episcopos quam in episcopis justitiæ
persequitur zelum."—St. Bern.
Epist. 49.

[2] "Sciatis autem me in omnibus
et per omnia vobiscum perseverare,
nec pro damnis quae mihi et hospiti-
bus meis pro vobis contigerunt, a
proposito meo pedem retrahere . . .

mei parentes et amici regi et reginae,
vineas meas exstirpari jubentibus,
decem libras dederunt, et hoc totum
decani et archidiaconorum instiga-
tione, imo G— succentoris nocturna
susurratione, peractum est." — *In
Mabil. notis ad St. Bern. Epist.* 45 ;
also in D'Achery's *Spicilegium*, vol.
iii. p. 491.

"The King of heaven and earth has given you a kingdom in this world, and will give one in that which is to come, if you study to rule justly and wisely over what you have already received. This is what we wish for you, what we pray for you—that you may reign faithfully below and happily above. But wherefore do you now so rudely repel those prayers of ours, which, if you remember, you once asked for with so much humility? For with what confidence could we now lift our hands to the Church's Spouse, whose bride you have, as we think, so recklessly grieved without a cause? Momentous charges are brought against you before the Bridegroom, her Lord, when the Church finds you an enemy whom she ought to have found a friend. Bethink you, whom do you offend by this? Not the Bishop of Paris, but the Lord of Paradise, and that terrible One who cuts off the spirit of princes. He it is who says to the bishops, 'Whoso despiseth you despiseth Me.'

"These things, and in this manner, we have been careful to impart to you—boldly, yet lovingly withal—advising and urging in the name of our mutual friendship and brotherhood, which you condescended to join, but are now ready to seriously wound—that as soon as may be you desist from this evil. If it should be otherwise—if you should judge us worthy not to be heard, but to be despised—us, your brethren and friends, who daily pray for you, your sins, and your kingdom—then be it known unto you that, mean as we are, we cannot be wanting in our duty to God's Church, or that minister of it, the venerable Bishop of Paris, our friend and father. He has requested of us letters to the pope by right of his brotherhood with us. But we have judged it fitting, first of all, to address you by these presents, especially as the said bishop offers to abide by the decision of justice, if, as a preliminary, his property be restored to him. Equity itself would seem to demand this, as he has been unjustly deprived of it. In the meantime we have deferred yielding to his request of writing to the pope. If it please God to make you incline an ear to our prayers, and to make your peace with the bishop, or rather with God, we are prepared, for this end, to undergo any fatigue, or to meet you wherever you please to appoint. If it is not as we hope, then we must listen to the demand of our friend, and obey the priest of God. Farewell!"[1]

This vigorous epistle and the measures taken by the bishops of the province of Sens had nearly induced Louis to restore the stolen property, now the whole subject of dispute, when, to the consternation of all, the king produced letters from Pope Honorius, raising the interdict, and putting the militant churchmen in a most painful, almost ludicrous, position before the world. Bernard and Hugh of Pontigny wrote a short, but very significant, letter to the pope, upon his conduct on this occasion. "Great is the necessity which draws us from our cloisters into the world. We testify that we have seen. We have seen it, and speak it with sadness, that the honour of the Church has received no slight wound in the time of Honorius."[2]

This bold pun, levelled at the supreme head of the Western Church by the abbot of an obscure monastery but just founded, showed men how little of a respecter of persons Bernard was, and gave evidence of that stamp of character which was destined before long to transfer the papacy virtually from Rome to Clairvaux.

We now reach one of the memorable events in Bernard's life, one by which he was emphatically marked off as a leader and apostle in his generation, viz. his controversy with the monks of Cluny, of which the chief monument survives in his "Apology to the Abbot William of St. Thierry."

[1] St. Bern. Epist. 45.

[2] Tristes vidimus, tristes et loquimur: honorem ecclesiae Honorii tempore non minime laesum."— Ibid. *Epist.* 46.

Pre-eminent in power, grandeur, and moral authority was
the great Burgundian Abbey of Cluny. Dating its foundation
as far back as the beginning of the tenth century, A.D. 909, it
had grown less in wealth and splendour, though these were
enormous, than in religious renown, as the foremost training
school of great churchmen in Europe. It had had for abbots
a series of illustrious men, several of whom the Church had
judged worthy of the extreme mark of respect in her power to
bestow—canonization. Saint Odo, Saint Mayeul, Saint Odilo,
Saint Hugh, had raised the estate and reputation of Cluny to
the second rank among the monasteries of the West. It had
given to the papacy one of the greatest governing minds which
ever adorned the pontifical or any throne—the great Hildebrand. Urban II. and Paschal II., two successors not unworthy
of him, were also Cluniac monks. Cluny became itself almost
a small kingdom, and its abbot an elective king. He coined
money for the use of the broad territories which belonged to
him. He could summon a Chapter of three thousand monks;
and, to show that his munificence was equal to his power, in
one year seventeen thousand poor persons were relieved at the
gates of Cluny alone.[1] Distant potentates, such as our William
the Conqueror, besought Saint Hugh to take the religious
affairs of their realms entirely under his supervision.

At the commencement of the twelfth century Cluny's
influence and importance rose higher still. Several popes
successively tried to surpass each other in their favours and
liberalities to the great abbey. Louis VI. called it the
"noblest member of his kingdom." Rich and powerful from
its lands and dependencies, richer still from the great men it

---

[1] ". . . ut non aliud dicam quam
quod contigit hoc ipso anno; illi,
qui pauperes recensuerint, testati
sunt septemdecim millia fuisse,
quibus et in Christi nomine ducenti
quinquaginta baccones divisi sunt."
—UDALRICUS, *Antiquiores Consue-
tudines Cluniacensis Monasterii*, lib.
iii. cap. xi. D'Achery's *Spicilegium*
vol. i. p. 692.

had nurtured and given to the Church, Cluny was, after Rome, the foremost place in Christendom.

But Cluny was destined to show, in an extreme form, some of those evils incident to monastic rule which Saint Stephen's wisdom effectually opposed in his general Chapter and Charta Charitatis.

Pontius de Melgueil, sprung from a noble and opulent family of Auvergne, and godson of Pope Paschal II. (himself a Cluniac), was elected to be ruler of the great Abbey of Cluny in the year 1109. The first years of his government were not discreditable either to his character or office. He had, besides his high rank and connexions, many graces of manner and education which were quite becoming in an abbot of Cluny. The exceptional favour with which it had become a habit of the popes to treat Cluny was not likely to be discontinued now that one of its monks had become pope, and the godson of that pope was abbot of Cluny. Paschal II. sent to his friend Pontius his own dalmatic. His successor, Calixtus II., paid Cluny a visit, and was so satisfied with his reception, that before leaving the abbey he determined to find, if possible, an omission in the numerous privileges and donations his predecessors had heaped on it, and to confer further immunities on the favoured monastery. He took his own ring from his finger and placed it on that of Pontius, and declared solemnly that for the future, always and everywhere, the abbot of Cluny should exercise the functions of a Roman cardinal. He asserted, more emphatically than ever, his freedom from episcopal jurisdiction, and granted this supreme mark of confidence, of permitting the Cluniacs to celebrate mass with closed doors, even when an interdict was weighing on all the surrounding country.[1]

But these honours and dignities seemed to have turned Pontius's head. At the Council of Rheims, holden in the

---

[1] Histoire de l'Abbaye de Cluny, par M. P. Lorain, p. 80. Paris, 1845.

year 1119, the Archbishop of Lyons declared, on behalf of
his suffragans, that the conduct of the abbot of Cluny was
unendurable. The Bishop of Macon in particular, through
the mouth of his metropolitan, complained of the violation of
rights, of the injury and wrong he suffered in his churches
and his tithes, at the hand of Pontius. Numbers of others,
bishops, monks, and clerks, loudly re-echoed the charge, and
accused the Cluniacs of extortion and outrage. Still, even
then such was the authority and repute of Cluny, that Pontius
succeeded in quashing any further proceedings by a bold
denial of his alleged crimes, and a declaration that Cluny
was subject solely to the pope, who might, if he liked, take
the matter in hand.[1] Pontius, more intoxicated than ever by
this triumph, then disputed with the abbot of Monte Casino
for the monastic supremacy of Christendom. Such was his
pride that he scorned to take only the second place, and
wished to arrogate to himself the title of Abbot of Abbots,
generally accorded to the successors of Saint Benedict. In
this he failed, and was fain to satisfy his vanity with the
designation of Archabbot. But the waywardness, prodigality,
and luxury of Pontius had worked such scandal in the Church,
that on going to Rome he was induced, voluntarily or otherwise, to resign his abbacy, and undertake a pilgrimage to
Jerusalem. He even took an oath that he would never return
from the Holy Land.[2]

When Pontius was well away, the monks of Cluny elected
another abbot, who dying almost forthwith, they were again
called to choose a head; and in this instance they selected the

[1] Ordericus Vitalis, lib. xii. vol. iv.
p. 385; ed. Le Prevost. Pontius
treated his opponents, even when
represented by the Archbishop of
Lyons, with quiet disdain. "Tandem silentio facto, Cluniacensis
abbas cum grandi conventu monachorum surrexit, brevique responso
et modesta voce et tranquilla locu-
tione querulosos impetitores com-
pressit. Cluniacensis ecclesia soli
Romanae ecclesiae subdita est," &c.
Loc. cit.
[2] Hist. de l'Abbaye de Cluny.
Lorain.

most known and illustrious of all the abbots of Cluny, Pierre Maurice de Montboisier, also from the Auvergne country, one of the noblest and most genial natures to be met with in this or in any time. (A.D. 1122.) He is generally known as Peter the Venerable.

Peter soon found that his large abbey had been made a very poor one by mismanagement. Its resources were enormous, and with economy and attention a more prosperous state of things was returning, when, lo! Pontius, at the head of an armed force, invaded the abbey. He had grown tired of his Eastern life, had forgotten his oath, had loitered in the neighbourhood of Ravenna—where he had established a small monastery—and from thence had stolen across to Cluny at an opportune season of the Abbot Peter's absence. With a body of partisans collected in his wanderings, he took possession. Having forced open the gates, and seized all the valuables he found, he compelled those of the monks who had not fled to swear fidelity to him. He laid hands on the sacred things ; he seized the golden crosses, tablets, candlesticks, censers, and numerous other vessels of great weight. In fact, he spared nothing in the devastation of what had once been his own monastery. The gold and silver plate he melted down to make money for the pay of his hirelings. He invited the robbers and gentlemen of the neighbourhood to the war, and laid all the country round under contribution—sacking, plundering, and destroying. This state of things lasted from the beginning of Lent till the end of October.[1]

At last the fame or infamy of these proceedings reached

---

[1] "Explorata absentia mea"— Peter the Venerable is speaking— "fingens se Cluniacum nolle venire, paulatim tamen appropinquabat . . . cum promiscua armatorum multitudine ; ipsis quoque mulieribus irruentibus, claustrum ingressus est. . . . Convertit statim manum ad sacra . . . circumpositas monasterii villas et castra invadit, ac sibi barbarico more religiosa loca subdere moliens, ignibus et ferro quae potest cuncta consumit."—PETRUS VEN. *De Miraculis*, lib. ii. cap. xii.

Rome. Honorius II., the successor of Calixtus II., despatched
the legate Peter to pronounce a terrible anathema on Pontius
and the Pontians, as his partisans were called. Both sides
were then summoned to Rome, and Pontius, the "usurper, the
sacrilegious person, the schismatic, the excommunicate," was
deposed from all ecclesiastical honours and functions, and
ordered to restore—not a very likely thing to be done—all
that had been taken away unjustly from Cluny. And so at
length was this scandal extinguished.[1]

But the disgust, or the sorrow, which it caused wherever
the news of it came, was deep and lasting ; and of all places
where the evil tidings could be carried, we may be sure in
none would they be less welcome than at Clairvaux. Bernard
had no reason especially to love the Cluniacs. They had
seduced and detained his young cousin, Robert ; they were
very sorry specimens of monks in his opinion, although very
powerful ecclesiastics. But Robert had been restored by this
time, and if they chose to break Saint Benedict's rule, it was no
concern of his. Still, a feeling the very reverse of friendly was
growing up between the two orders. While the Cistercians, by
their own conduct, showed that they considered the Cluniacs
to be lax, the latter were apt to think the austerity of the new
monks was not free from affectation. The leaders on neither
side said anything, but the jealousy had been growing secretly
among their followers, till at last William of St. Thierry wrote
to Bernard to say that it was time for him to speak out, that
the Cistercians were looked upon as the detractors of Cluny,
and that a scandal in the Church was the result. The evil as
well as the good emotions in Bernard were ready to respond
to this appeal. It was made just after the disgraceful scenes
lately enacted by Pontius. It came when laxity in observance
of the rule had produced its ultimate and most bitter fruit.
It was an unequalled opportunity, for contrasting the worldly

[1] Petrus Ven. De Miraculis, lib. ii. cap. xii.

grandeur of Cluny with the primitive poverty of Citeaux; it was an occasion to humble rather contemptuous rivals, and to exalt long-tried friends, which might never come again.

That Bernard hesitated at the last is evident. He wrote his Apology, as he called it, and sent it to William of St. Thierry and Ogerius. He begged them to read it through, to correct it, to examine it together, and then, after all, whether it should be shown to few or many, or any or none, he left entirely to their judgment. Their verdict was favourable, and about the year A.D. 1127 this piece of vigorous controversy was sent forth to the world.[1]

"Who," he asks, "ever heard me publicly denouncing or privately depreciating that order? Whom did I ever see belonging to it without joy, or receive without honour, speak to without reverence, admonish without humility? I have said, and still say, it is a holy mode of life, honourable, adorned by chastity, distinguished by prudence, founded by the fathers, pre-ordained by the Holy Ghost, not a little profitable to the salvation of souls. Do I condemn or despise that which I thus extol? I can remember the times when I have been a guest in houses of that order; and may the Lord return such kindness to His servants as they have shown me in illness, and may He repay them for the honour beyond my deserts which they have offered to me. I commended myself to their prayers; I was present at their collations often; concerning the Scriptures and the salvation of souls I have held discourse with many, publicly in their Chapters, privately in their cells. Did I ever, in any open or secret manner, try to dissuade any one from entering that order, or exhort any one to leave them and come to us? Have I not rather done the reverse—checked many who wished to

---

[1] In the letters to Ogerius, quoted in a former chapter, several allusions to the Apology are made. The treatise itself, from which the above extracts are selected, is to be found in St. Bern Op vol. i. col. 526.

come, refused those who had come, and were knocking to
be admitted?   Did I not send back brother Nicholas to
St. Nicholas's ; and two others belonging to you (William
of St. Thierry), were they not returned?   Were there not,
besides these, two abbots, whose names I shall not mention,
but whom you know well (how intimate I was with them
is also known to you) : did they not wish to migrate to another
order, and was not my advice the cause of their not forsaking their sees?   Wherefore, then, am I supposed or said
to condemn the Order of Cluny, when I exhort my friends to
remain in its service, when I restore its fugitive monks, when
I ask for and receive its prayers for myself with such anxious
devotion?"

After dwelling on the advantage to the Church of a variety
of orders and forms of religious life, he proceeds to reprove
"some of his own order for their hastiness in judging others."
Of such, he says, they are not of his order, although "they
may live in a regular—monastic—manner, who by their proud
speech and conduct make themselves sons of Babylon, that is,
of confusion, even of darkness, and of hell itself, where order
is not and eternal horror abides."   But, replied the critical
Cistercians, "how can they be said to keep the rule who wear
leathern garments ; who, when in good health, eat meat and
fat ; who allow themselves three and four dishes in the day,
which the rule forbids? whereas manual labour, which it commands, they neglect ; and many things besides, at their discretion, they alter, add, or take away."   This may be true; but
what does the Word of God say, with which certainly the rule
of the holy Benedict will not clash?   "The kingdom of God
is within you."   This is, not externally, in the food or clothing
of the body, but in the virtues of the inner man.   "Thus," he
proceeds, his wrath against his own monks waxing hotter, "you
calumniate your brethren concerning corporeal observances,
and the greater things of the law, its spiritual ordinances, you

leave undone—straining at a gnat and swallowing a camel. Great is your error. Great care is taken that the body be clothed according to the rule, but the soul is not provided with the heavenly vesture which the same rule prescribes. A man without a tunic or a cowl would not be considered a monk; are piety and humility less necessary? We in our tunics and our pride have a horror of leathern garments, as if humbleness in skins were not far preferable to pride in tunics. . . . . Again, with our bellies full of beans, and our minds of pride, we condemn those who are full of meat, as if it were not better to eat a little fat on occasion than to be gorged even to belching upon windy vegetables."

Passing on to the topic of manual labour, he says to his Cistercians: "In that you subdue your bodies by much and manifold labour, and by regular mortifications depress your earthly frames, you do well. But your pride in this excellence takes it all away. Who is the better, the humble man or the tired man? Who observes the rule most?"

Bernard then says that he hopes the above strictures on his own monks will show he is not animated by any ill-will to the Cluniacs. Still, the force of truth will not allow him to stop here. He has fairly earned, by the blame he has given his own side, a right to make a remark or two on the other.

"I can never believe that the holy fathers, when they tempered the rule to suit the weak as well as the strong, ever intended thereby to introduce the vanities—the superfluities which we now see in most monasteries. I am astonished to see among monks such intemperance in eating, in drinking, in clothes, in bed-covering, in horse-trappings, in buildings, insomuch that where their indulgences are most carefully, extravagantly, voluptuously sought after, there the rule is said to be best kept, there religion is said most to flourish. So economy is now thought avarice, soberness austerity, silence sulkiness. On the other hand, laxity is called discretion, extravagance liberality, talkativeness affability, silly laughter a happy wit; pomp and luxury in horses and clothing respectability; superfluous attention to the bedding is called cleanliness; and when we countenance each other in these little trifles, that forsooth is charity."

He then specifies in greater detail some of the changes he has here merely indicated generally. The excess of diet especially irritates him. At meals, he says, "No man asks his neighbour for the heavenly bread. No man gives it. There is no conversation concerning the Scriptures, none concerning the salvation of souls; but small talk, laughter, and idle words fill the air. At dinner the palate and ears are equally tickled—the one with dainties, the other with gossip and news, which together quite prevent all moderation in feeding. In the meantime dish after dish is set on the table; and, to make up for the small privation of meat, a double supply is provided of well-grown fish. When you have eaten enough of the first, if you taste the second course, you will seem to yourself hardly to have touched the former: such is the art of the cooks, that after four or five dishes have been devoured, the first does not seem to be in the way of the last, nor does satiety invade the appetite. . . . Who could say, to speak of nothing else, in how many forms eggs are cooked and worked up? with what care they are turned in and out, made hard or soft, or chopped fine; now fried, now roasted, now stuffed; now they are served mixed with other things, now by themselves. Even the external appearance of the dishes is such that the eye, as well as the taste, is charmed. And when even the stomach complains that it is full, curiosity is still alive." A Cluniac dinner must have been the opposite of an uninviting repast, if only a portion of this is true.

So much for the eating; the drinking is thus described:—
"What shall I say about water drinking, when even wine and

water are despised? We all of us, it appears, directly we become monks, are afflicted with weak stomachs, and the important advice of the Apostle to use wine we, in a praiseworthy manner, endeavour to follow; but, for some unexplained reason, the condition of a *little* is usually omitted. And would that we were content with one wine. It is shameful to relate, but it is more shameful to do. . . . You may see, during one meal, a cup half full three or four times carried backwards and forwards, in order that out of several wines—smelt rather than tasted, and not so much drunk as sipped—by a quick and accomplished judgment one, and the most potent, may be selected. Have we not heard that in some monasteries it is observed as a custom, on great festivals, to mix the wines with honey, and to powder them with the dust of spices? Shall we say that this also is for our stomach's sake and our often infirmities? I should say it was that a greater quantity, and that more pleasantly, might be drunk. But, with his veins swelling and throbbing in his head, under the influence of wine, what can a man do on rising from table except sleep? And if you force a man thus gorged to rise to vigils, you will get rather a sigh than a song from him.

"A ridiculous story which I have heard from several, and which they declared they knew for certain, I cannot omit here. They say that strong, hearty young men are accustomed to forsake conventual discipline and place themselves in the infirmary, and there to regale themselves to their hearts' content on those viands which the rule allows to the utterly prostrate and weak for the recovery of their strength. . . . In order to distinguish between the sick and the healthy, the former are made to carry sticks in their hands. A most necessary arrangement: as neither pallor nor leanness disfigures their cheeks, the sustaining staff is required to indicate that they are invalids. Shall we laugh or weep over such absurdities?"

The clothing is next dwelt upon. It seems that the monasteries contained a "dandiacal body," as more modern societies
have also done.

"Not only have we lost the spirit of the old monasteries,
but even its outward appearance. For this habit of ours,
which of old was the sign of humility, by the monks of our
day is turned into a source of pride. We can hardly find in a
whole province wherewithal we condescend to be clothed.
The monk and the knight cut their garments, the one his
cowl, the other his cloak, from the same piece. No secular
person, however great, whether king or emperor, would be
disgusted at our vestments if they were only cut and fitted to
his requirements. But, say you, religion is in the heart, not in
the garments. True: but you, when you are about to buy
a cowl, rush over the towns, visit the markets, examine the
fairs, dive into the houses of the merchants, turn over all their
goods, undo their bundles of cloth, feel it with your fingers,
hold it to your eyes, or to the rays of the sun, and if anything
coarse or faded appears, you reject it. But if you are pleased
with any object of unusual beauty or brightness, you at once
buy it, whatever the price. I ask you, Does this come from
the heart, or your simplicity?

"I wonder that our abbots allow these things, unless it
arises from the fact that no one is apt to blame any error with
confidence if he cannot trust in his own freedom from the
same; and it is a right human quality to forgive without much
anger those self-indulgences in others for which we ourselves
have the strongest inclination. How is the light of the world
overshadowed! Those whose lives should have been the way
of life to us, by the example they give of pride, become blind
leaders of the blind. What a specimen of humility is that, to
march with such pomp and retinue, to be surrounded with
such an escort of hairy men, so that one abbot has about
him people enough for two bishops. I lie not when I say,

K

I have seen an abbot with sixty horses after him, and even more. Would you not think, as you see them pass, that they were not fathers of monasteries, but lords of castles—not shepherds of souls, but princes of provinces? Then there is the baggage, containing table-cloths, and cups and basins, and candlesticks, and well-filled wallets—not with the coverlets, but the ornaments of the beds. My lord abbot can never go more than four leagues from his home without taking all his furniture with him, as if he were going to the wars, or about to cross a desert where necessaries cannot be had. Is it quite impossible to wash one's hands in, and drink from, the same vessel? Will not your candle burn anywhere but in that gold or silver candlestick of yours, which you carry with you? Is sleep impossible except upon a variegated mattress, or under a foreign coverlet? Could not one servant harness the mule, wait at dinner, and make the bed? If such a multitude of men and horses is indispensable, why not at least carry with us our necessaries, and thus avoid the severe burden we are to our hosts?"

He thus finishes his invective, by an attack on the architecture of the Cluniacs:—" But these are small matters. I pass on to greater ones, which seem less only because they are more common. I will not speak of the immense height of the churches, of their immoderate length, of their superfluous breadth, costly polishing, and strange designs, which, while they attract the eyes of the worshipper, hinder the soul's devotion, and somehow remind me of the old Jewish ritual. However, let all this pass; we will suppose it is done, as we are told, for the glory of God. But, a monk myself, I do ask other monks (the question and reproach were addressed by a pagan to pagans),[1] 'Tell me, O ye professors of poverty, what does gold do in a holy place?' The case of bishops and monks is not the same. We know that they, as debtors to the

---

[1] " Dicite, Pontifices, in sancto quid facit aurum?"—PERS. *Sat.* ii. v. 69.

wise and foolish, when they cannot rouse the sense of religion
in the carnal multitude by spiritual means, must do so by
ornaments that appeal to the senses.   But among us, who
have gone out from among the people; among us, who have
forsaken whatever things are fair and costly for Christ's sake;
who have regarded all things beautiful to the eye, soft to the
ear, agreeable to the smell, sweet to the taste, pleasant to the
touch—all things, in a word, which can gratify the body—as
dross and dung, that we might gain Christ, of whom among
us, I ask, can devotion be excited by such means?

" Or, to speak plainly, is it not avarice—that is, the worship
of idols—which does all this? from which we do not expect
spiritual fruit, but worldly benefit. . . . . So carefully is the
money laid out, that it returns multiplied many times.   It is
spent that it may be increased, and plenty is born of profusion.
By the sight of wonderful and costly vanities men are prompted
to give, rather than to pray.   Some beautiful picture of a saint
is exhibited—and the brighter the colours the greater the holiness attributed to it; men run, eager to kiss; they are invited
to give, and the beautiful is more admired than the sacred is
revered.   In the churches are suspended, not *coronæ*, but wheels
studded with gems, and surrounded by lights, which are scarcely
brighter than the precious stones which are near them.   Instead
of candlesticks, we behold great trees of brass, fashioned with
wonderful skill, and glittering as much through their jewels as
their lights.   What do you suppose is the object of all this?
The repentance of the contrite, or the admiration of the gazers?
O vanity of vanities! but not more vain than foolish.   The
church's walls are resplendent, but the poor are not there. . . .
The curious find wherewith to amuse themselves; the wretched
find no stay for them in their misery.   Why, at least, do we not
reverence the images of the saints, with which the very pavement we walk on is covered.   Often an angel's mouth is spit
into, and the face of some saint trodden on by the passers-

K 2

by. . . . . But if we cannot do without the images, why can we not spare the brilliant colours? What has all this to do with monks, with professors of poverty, with men of spiritual minds?

"Again, in the cloisters, what is the meaning of those ridiculous monsters, of that deformed beauty, that beautiful deformity, before the very eyes of the brethren when reading? What are disgusting monkeys there for (or satyrs?), or ferocious lions, or monstrous centaurs, or spotted tigers, or fighting soldiers, or huntsmen sounding the bugle? You may see there one head with many bodies, or one body with numerous heads. Here is a quadruped with a serpent's tail; there is a fish with a beast's head; there a creature, in front a horse, behind a goat; another has horns at one end, and a horse's tail at the other. In fact, such an endless variety of forms appears everywhere, that it is more pleasant to read in the stonework than in books, and to spend the day in admiring these oddities than in meditating on the law of God. Good God! if we are not ashamed of these absurdities, why do we not grieve at the cost of them?"[1]

[1] "Caeterum in claustris coram legentibus fratribus quid facit illa ridicula monstruositas, mira quaedam deformis formositas, ac formosa deformitas? Quid ibi immundae simiae? quid feri leones? quid monstruosi centauri? quid semihomines? quid maculosae tigrides? quid milites pugnantes? quid venatores tubicinantes? Videas sub uno capite multa corpora, et rursus in uno corpore capita multa. Cernitur hinc in quadrupede cauda serpentis; illinc in pisce caput quadrupedis. Ibi bestia praefert equum, capram trahens retro dimidiam; hic cornutum animal equum gestat posterius. Tam multa denique tamque mira diversarum formarum ubique varietas apparet, ut magis legere libeat in marmoribus quam in codicibus, totumque diem occupare singula ista mirando, quam in lege Dei meditando. Proh Deo! si non pudet ineptiarum, cur vel non piget expensarum?"

"The more I have examined the subject, the more dangerous have I found it to dogmatize respecting the character of the art which is likely at a given period to be most useful to the cause of religion. One great fact first meets me. . . . I never met with a Christian whose heart was thoroughly set upon the world to come, and, so far as human judgment could pronounce, perfect and right before God, who cared about art at all."—*Stones of Venice*, vol. ii. p. 103.

"'May the devil fly away with the

Fine Arts,' exclaimed confidentially once, in my hearing, one of our most distinguished public men; a sentiment that often recurs to me. I perceive too well how true it is in our case. A public man, intent on any real business, does, I suppose, find the Fine Arts rather imaginary . . . feels them to be a pretentious nothingness; a confused superfluity and nuisance, purchased with cost; what he, in brief language, denominates a bore." — *Latter-day Pamphlets,* "Jesuitism," p. 34. This is not very remote from Saint Bernard—" Proh Deo ! si non pudet ineptiarum, cur vel non piget expensarum ?" And does not the history of religion bear witness to the same thing? Early Christians, English Puritans, Cistercian mediæval monks, and modern reformers of an earnest type, agree on one point, however much they may differ on others, viz. that people who *are* filled with practical sincerity are apt to pass by Art with indifference, or reject it with anger. It is a fact not undeserving of notice in these days.

LITERARY COMPOSITIONS—THE TRACTATE ON HUMILITY AND PRIDE—
THE COUNCIL OF TROYES—ILLNESS—THE FAIRS OF CHAMPAGNE—
THE KNIGHTS TEMPLARS—BERNARD'S ADDRESS TO THEM.

IN spite of a certain degree of polemical warmth manifested
in this controversy with the monks of Cluny, the half-dozen
years preceding the death of Pope Honorius, in 1130, were
the most peaceful and monastic which Bernard was destined
to know. Although the Cistercians felt, and Bernard also
must have felt, that their order contained no man who could
be compared with him for force of character and intellect ; yet
his growing ascendancy had not, up to this time, burdened him
with those unending responsibilities of fame and power, from
which he afterwards strove in vain to escape. During these
years he found leisure for literary composition, and was evidently not devoid of a natural human pleasure and interest in
his effusions. While protesting that they are quite unworthy
of his friends' attention, he recapitulates the names and scope
of his writings with a coy bashfulness which does not mean to
be taken too literally. To Peter, cardinal deacon and legate,
he writes,—" As regards those works of mine which you ask
for, they are few in number, and contain nothing which I
consider worthy to interest you. Still, as I would rather you
thought ill of my genius than of my desire to oblige you,
please send a line by the bearer of this, to signify which of my

writings you would like, and also whither I am to send them.
I make this request that I may be able to recover any that are
lent, which I will then forward to any place you name.   But
that you may know what your choice is, here is a list :—

" (1) A little book on Humility.

" (2) Four Homilies on the Praises of the Virgin.

"(3) An Apology to a certain friend of mine, in which I
have discoursed concerning the Cluniac and Cistercian observances of the Rule.

" (4) A few Letters to various friends.

" (5) Sermons ;—which some of the brethren here have
taken down as I delivered them, and still keep by them.

" Would that I might venture to hope that my rustic productions may prove of the least service to you."[1]

The "little book on Humility" is placed first, and it is
probably the first thing of any importance which Bernard ever
wrote.   The full title, as we have it, is "De Gradibus Humi-
litatis et Superbiae ;" and, in truth, pride and humility are
equally discussed.   Whether it be owing to the qualities of
the subject, or to Bernard's mode of treating it, or any other
cause, it is quite certain that he has succeeded in being far
more interesting when discoursing of the vice than of the
virtue.   Some of the forms of pride, as shown in the monkish
life, are described not only forcibly, but with even a sly
humour and comic perception of character about them.

" The first degree of pride," says Bernard, " is curiosity ;
and curiosity may be known by the following signs.   If you
see a monk, of whom you had better hopes at one time, begin,
whether he be standing, or walking, or sitting, to cast his eyes
about, to hold his head up, and to keep his ears on the watch,
then you may recognise by these motions of the outward man
the change that has taken place within.   *A naughty person
winketh with his eyes, speaketh with his feet, and teacheth with*

[1] St. Bern. Op. vol. i. col. 37.   Epist. xviii.

his fingers ;[1] the unwonted movement of his body reveals the new disease which has fallen on his soul." Nevertheless there are two reasons for lifting the eyes to which no blame attaches, viz. either to ask for help, or to give it. If, with due regard to time and place, "you lift your eyes, through your own or your brother's necessity, you are deserving of praise rather than censure. If you do so for any other cause, I would say that you imitate Dinah, Eve, nay, Satan himself, rather than Christ and David."

The third degree of pride is " thoughtless mirth." " It is characteristic of the proud to seek after joyful things and to avoid sad ones. Now these are the signs by which you may recognise in yourself or others this third step in pride. A monk given up to this vice you will rarely or never see groaning or weeping. You would suppose he had either forgotten who he was, or else had been washed clean of his sins. Buffoonery is in his gestures, hilarity in his face, vanity in his gait. Ever eager for his joke, he is ready and prompt to laugh. He cannot keep his countenance, he cannot restrain his thoughtless mirth. Even as a bladder blown out with wind, if squeezed, when pricked makes a hissing noise as it collapses, and the air, rushing out, from want of a free vent, gives divers sounds ; so, with the monk who has filled his heart with vain and wanton thoughts, the wind of vanity, by reason of the discipline of silence, not finding another exit, is driven off in laughter through the narrow passage of his jaws. Often in shame he hides his face, closes his lips, and grinds his teeth ; he laughs involuntarily, he giggles when he would not, and even when he stops his mouth with his fists, he can still be heard snorting through his nostrils."

The fifth degree of pride is " singularity." " A monk who has reached it is more pleased with himself for one fast kept

---

[1] Prov. vi. 12, 13.

while others are dining, than for a week's abstinence in company with others. A little private prayer of his own he likes better than the entire psalmody of a whole night. At dinner-time he often casts his eyes about the table, so that if he see any one eat less than himself he may lament his discomfiture, and at once diminish his own portion, fearing more the loss of glory than the pains of hunger. If he meet any one haggard and cadaverous in an unusual degree, he has no peace, he feels undone; and as he cannot see his own face as it appears to others, he looks at his hands and arms, he feels his ribs, he touches his shoulders and loins, and accordingly as he judges his own emaciation to be satisfactory or not, he draws inferences as regards the pallor of his cheeks. He keeps awake in bed, he sleeps in the choir. While others are singing all night at their vigils, he is dozing; but, after the vigils, when the rest have gone to repose in the cloisters, he remains alone in the church."

The ninth degree shows that even mediæval monasteries had their Tartuffes. "Some there are who, when chidden for a manifest fault, knowing very well that, if they defend themselves, they will not be believed, take a more subtle line, and answer artfully with a deceiving confession. The countenance is cast down, the body is prostrated. If they can, they squeeze out a few tears, their voice is broken with sighs, their words are mingled with groans. A monk of this sort not only will not excuse himself, he will exaggerate the fault, he will add to it something impossible or incredible, to make you doubt even that which you think you are sure of: the absurdity of one part of the confession throws uncertainty on all of it."[1]

---

[1] See the matchless scene in the third act of Molière's "Tartuffe," where Tartuffe conceals his half-discovered guilt by a deceitful confession of general wickedness :—

"Oui, mon frère, je suis un méchant, un coupable,
Un malheureux pécheur, tout plein d'iniquité,
Le plus grand scélérat qui jamais ait été.
Chaque instant de ma vie est chargé de souillures ;

And so at his leisure did Bernard draw these little portraits.

But the period of quiet and retirement for Bernard was drawing to a close. Much against his will, he was becoming indispensable to his contemporaries. The council that was about to assemble at Troyes in the commencement of the year 1128 was the means of bringing out this fact very clearly. Bernard had promised the Legate Matthew, under whose presidency the council was to meet, that he would be present. Shortly before the meeting he fell ill—so ill that he had no hope of being able to attend. He wrote, therefore, the following letter to excuse himself:—

" To the Legate Matthew.

" My heart is ready to obey, but not my body. Burnt up by the heat and exhausted by the sweats of a raging fever, my weak flesh is unable to answer the call of my willing spirit. I was anxious to come, but my desire has been frustrated by the above-mentioned cause. Whether it be a sufficient one, I leave those of my friends to judge who, taking no excuse, are daily devising plans to draw me, a monk involved in a network of duty and obedience, from my cloister into cities. And let them note that I have not artfully discovered this impediment, but have painfully endured it. If I were to say to them, '*I have taken off my coat, how shall I put it on ? I have washed my feet, how shall I defile them ?*' they would doubtless be offended. Now they must be offended, or reconciled, with God's judgment, by which it happens that, though I would, I cannot leave home.

Elle n'est qu'un amas de crimes et d'ordures ;
   *   *   *   *   *   *
Non, non ; vous vous laissez tromper à l'apparence :

Je ne suis rien moins, hélas, que ce qu'on pense.
Tout le monde me prend pour un homme de bien ;
Mais la vérité pure est que je ne vaux rien.
       Le Tartuffe, Act iii. Scene 6.

" But, they reply, the business is most important—the
necessity is urgent. If so, they must seek some one who is
fit for great and important business. I do not think—I know
that I am not such an one. Indeed, whether the matter be
large or small, I have nothing to do with it. I ask, Is it
difficult or easy, this affair with which you are so anxious to
burden me, and disturb my beloved silence? If easy, it can
be done without me. If difficult, it cannot be done by me,
unless I am thought able to do what no one else can, and one
to whom impossibilities should be referred. If this be so, what
an error has God committed in my solitary case—placing a
candle under a bushel, which could have given light upon
a candlestick; or, to speak more plainly, trying to make a
monk of me, and wishing to hide in His tabernacle, in the
days of evil-doers, a man who is necessary to the world, without
whom even bishops cannot get through their own business.

" And this is what my friends have brought about, that I am
now apparently speaking in a disturbed manner to a man, of
whom I always think with serenity and joy. But you know,
father, that I am not unduly moved, but ever ready to obey
your commands. I trust to your indulgence where you consider
it needed."[1]

He went to the council nevertheless.

Troyes was a place of considerable importance in the twelfth
century. Under the government of the able Counts of Champagne it had become the seat of two annual fairs, which would
bear comparison with any in Europe. In the Middle Ages
fairs were a prominent, if not the sole, means of commercial
traffic on a large scale. The regular action of modern trade
was not needed, and would have been impossible in that wild
feudal time. The merchant was essentially a huckster, going
where he could, or found safest, paying his way cautiously,
hopeful of gain, but having more reason to fear loss. In time

[1] St. Bern. Op. vol. i. col. 38. Epist. xxi.

some baron wiser than his fellows—in advance of his age in
this respect—saw that more might be made by favouring
merchants than by plundering them : saw that one was an
accidental and precarious source of revenue, tending naturally
to destroy itself ; that the other was of an accumulative and
perennial nature, quite worthy of care and attention.   No
barons had perceived this fact more distinctly than the Counts
of Champagne ; and Count Theobald, the reigning count, saw
it as distinctly as any.   His fairs had a reputation with the
commercial world of that day, which it was worth his while not
to lose.   Traders might expect good treatment who came to
his fairs, as far as he could give it ; and he took pains to make
it a reality.   Soldiers, and escorts of a proper strength, were
appointed to attend the caravans of merchants travelling
towards Troyes and the other towns of his dominions where
fairs were held, viz. Lagny and Provins.   These escorts were
commanded by knights, who had received the charge as a fief,
and who also found an interest in effectually performing their
duty.   And so it came about that Champagne had six fairs in
the year, of which two took place at Troyes ; that troops of
Levantines, of Armenians, of Flemings, of Italians, of Germans
and Provençals, with their various wares, costumes, and lan-
guages, went by or near the ascetics at Clairvaux, who, most
likely, regarded them all as worldly and profane persons.
However, it was in this busy, commercial Troyes that the
council was appointed to meet.   The buyers and sellers had
not long completed their bargains when the solemn and
emaciated monks and bishops made their entrance.   The
second fair at Troyes began on All Souls' Day, the 2nd of
November, and the fathers of the council met on the 14th of
January.[1]

[1] See in the Bibliothèque de
l'Amateur Champenois the historical
notice prefixed to the fabliau called
"La bourse pleine de Sens, ou ce
qu'on apprenait aux foires de Troyes
et de Champagne au XIII. siècle."—

The memory of the Council of Troyes survives solely in consequence of the part it took in founding the Order of the Knights Templars. The advantage of uniting piety and prowess in the Eastern Wars had made itself felt. The two strongest impulses which the age knew—the impulse to fight, and the impulse to fast and pray—could not continue to remain separated, since the Crusades had begun. At home in Europe there was not much reason for uniting the two at once; the motive was, perhaps, the other way; but out in Palestine the plan of becoming knight and monk at the same time must have appeared most natural. The Knights Hospitallers had been incorporated in the year 1113. And in the year 1118 Hugo de Paganis and some others made vows, " like regular canons, to live in chastity, obedience, and poverty, and, for the remission of their sins, to keep the roads and passes free of robbers and assailants, and to watch over the safety of the pilgrims as much as they could." This was the origin of the Knights Templars. But their institution did not thrive immediately. In ten years' time their number had only increased to nine. It is probable that Hugo thought a more public recognition of his order in Europe might contribute to its success. He addressed himself to Bernard, and his plan received the solemn sanction of the Council of Troyes. It was

---

The power, or rather influence, of the Theobalds extended beyond their domain. "Garin fils de Salo, Vicomte de Sens, dévalise des changeurs de Vézelay *sur le chemin du roi* entre Sens et Bray. Le Comte de Champagne écrit à l'abbé de St. Denis, et obtient prompte justice," p. 36. Credit was well understood even in those turbulent times. " L'acheteur n'est pas obligé de verser de beaux deniers au moment de la livraison; il peut contracter l'engagement de payer à la foire prochaine. Son engagement est revêtu du sceau des foires; l'intérêt ne peut s'élever à plus de quinze pour cent par an—c'est à dire, à deux et demi par foire. [There was an interval of forty days between each of the six fairs.] Les gardes veillent au remboursement des obligations et poursuivent les débiteurs par leurs nombreux sergents. Ils vont même jusqu'à interdire l'entrée de l'église aux chanoines qui ne font pas honneur à leur billet, et ne craignent pas les distances pour atteindre les mauvais clients."—Ibid. p. 41.

decreed that the Templars should wear white mantles. In their monastic character they belonged to the order of Saint Augustine.[1]

Bernard's share in this matter does not appear to have extended beyond a general furtherance and approbation of the new order. The rule of the Templars, which it is often said he drew up, was the work of a later period. But his relations with Hugh, the first Grand Master of the Temple, were of the most friendly nature; and, at the latter's request, he wrote a tractate in praise of the " new warfare," which is highly characteristic both of the times and of Bernard himself. His " Exhortation to the Knights of the Temple " was composed probably four or five years after the Council of Troyes; but it is more convenient to consider it in this connexion than in any other.

He begins by contrasting the secular with the monastic warfare.

" You always run a risk, you worldly soldier, of either killing your adversary's body, and your own soul in consequence, or of being killed yourself, both body and soul. If, while wishing to kill another, you are killed yourself, you die a homicide. If you vanquish and kill your enemy, you live a homicide. But what an astounding error, what madness is it, oh, knights, to fight at such cost and trouble for no wages except those of death or sin ! You deck out your horses with silken trappings; you wear flaunting cloaks over your steel breastplates; you paint your shields, your spears, and your saddles; your spurs and bridles shine with gold and silver and gems; and in this gay pomp, with an amazing and incredible madness, you rush upon death. Have you not found from experience that these things are especially needed by a soldier, viz. that he be bold,

---

[1] Mabillon has proved that the rule of the Templars, commonly ascribed to Bernard, bears evident traces of a later authorship. See his " Admonitio in Opusculum Sextum."—ST. BERN. *Op.* vol. i. col. 541

yet vigilant, as regards his own safety, quick in his movements, and prompt to strike? You, on the contrary, cultivate long hair, which gets in your eyes; your feet are entangled in the folds of your flowing robes; your delicate hands are buried in your ample and spreading sleeves. In addition to all this, your reasons for fighting are light and frivolous, viz. the impulses of an irrational anger, or a desire of vain glory, or the wish to obtain some earthly possession. Certainly, for such causes as these it is not safe either to slay or to be slain.

"But Christ's soldiers can fight in safety the battles of their Lord; fearing no sin from killing an enemy; dreading no danger from their own death. Seeing that for Christ's sake death must be suffered or inflicted, it brings with it no sin, but rather earns much glory. In the one case Christ is benefited, in the other Christ is gained—Christ, who willingly accepts an enemy's death for revenge, and, more willingly still, grants Himself to the soldier for consolation. Christ's soldier can securely kill, can more securely die: when he dies, it profits him; when he slays, it profits Christ. Not without just cause is he girded with a sword. When he kills a malefactor, he is not a slayer of men, but a slayer of evil, and plainly an avenger of Christ against those who do amiss. But when he is killed, he has not perished, he has reached his goal. The Christian exults in the death of a pagan, because Christ is glorified. In the death of the Christian the King's bountifulness is shown, when the soldier is led forth to his reward. The just will rejoice over the first, when he sees the punishment of the wicked. Of the latter men will say, ' *Verily there is a reward for the righteous: doubtless there is a God that judgeth the earth.*'"

Bernard reaches this point in his bloodthirsty enthusiasm before he even remembers that he is a Christian pastor and preacher of the Gospel of peace. He here makes a sudden halt, then moves again, though gently and with greatly diminished spirit.

"Not that even the pagans ought to be slain, if they could by any other means be prevented from molesting and oppressing the faithful. As it is, it is better that they should be killed than that the rod of the wicked should rest upon the lot of the righteous, lest the righteous put forth their hands unto iniquity."

The Templars are thus described :—

"Never is an idle word, or a useless deed, or immoderate laughter, or a murmur, even if only whispered, allowed to go unpunished among them. Draughts and dice they detest. Hunting they hold in abomination ; and take no pleasure in the absurd pastime of hawking. Soothsayers, jesters, and story-tellers, ribald songs and stage plays, they eschew as insane follies. They cut close their hair, knowing, as the Apostle says, that 'it is a shame for a man to have long hair.' They never dress gaily, and wash but seldom. Shaggy by reason of their uncombed hair, they are also begrimed with dust, and swarthy from the weight of their armour and the heat of the sun."

Further on he has a few remarks which show that, after all, those who remained at home had no reason to regret the departure of the Crusaders.

"But the most joyful and salutary result to be perceived is, that in such a multitude of men who flock to the East there are few besides scoundrels, vagabonds, thieves, murderers, perjurers, and adulterers, from whose emigration a double good is observed to flow, the cause of a twofold joy. Indeed, they give as much delight to those whom they leave as to those whom they go to assist. Both rejoice,—those whom they defend and those whom they no longer oppress. Egypt is glad at their departure ; yet Mount Zion and the daughters of Judah shall be joyful over the succour they will bring : the one for losing its most cruel spoilers, the other at receiving its most faithful defenders."[1]

On the whole this exhortation must be set down as one of Bernard's weakest compositions. It sprang much more from his rhetorical imagination than from his deep and fervent soul. He wrote it in the early morning of his influence and rising fame. In after years, when sorrow, disappointment, and sickness had subdued and saddened him, when the men and things of this world had passed from a romantic dream to a painful reality, it is at least probable that, if he had written anything at all on the subject, it would have been in a different strain.

And now the time for his commencing his enlarged experience is close at hand.

---

[1] St. Bern. Op. vol. i. col. 549.

BOOK II.

BOOK II.

CHAPTER I.

DEATH OF POPE HONORIUS II.—THE SCHISM—INNOCENT II. AND ANA-
CLETUS II.—PROGRESS OF INNOCENT THROUGH FRANCE—CLUNY—
CLAIRVAUX—COUNCIL AT RHEIMS—ENLARGEMENT OF THE MONAS-
TERY AT CLAIRVAUX.

POPE HONORIUS II. died February 14, 1130. As the factions
and party spirit of Rome had so often penetrated into the
Sacred College, and produced the most scandalous results, the
cardinals had agreed that the election of a new pope should
be confided to eight of their number, chosen with the express
object of avoiding confusion and disputes.[1] But although
William, Bishop of Praeneste, made them bind themselves
under pain of an anathema to respect this convention, although
the ambitious and intriguing Peter Leonis declared that he
fully adhered to it, and would rather be plunged in the depths
of the sea than be the cause of strife and bitterness, it became

---

[1] " Convenientibus cardinalibus in ecclesia St. Andreae Apostoli, statutum est ab eis, octo personis, duobus episcopis, G. Praenestino, et C. Sabinensi, tribus cardinalibus presbyteris, P. Pisano, P. Rufo, et Petro Leonis, tribus cardinalibus diaconis, Gregorio scilicet Angeli, Jonathae, Americo cancellario, electionem pontificis committi, ita ut si committeret dominum Papam Hono-rium, qui tunc in articulo mortis positus erat, ab hac vita transire, persona quae ab eis communiter eligeretur, vel a parte sanioris consilii, ab omnibus pro domino et Romano pontifice susciperetur."— HENRICI LUCENSIS EPISCOPI *Epist. ad Magdeburgensem Archiepiscopum ;* MANSI, *Conc.* xxi. 432 ; also in MIGNE, *Patrologia,* tom. clxxix. col. 40.

evident that neither party intended to observe the conditions
longer than their apparent interest required.   Peter Leonis
found that he had made a hasty bargain.   Through his
wealth—he was the grandson of a Jewish usurer—he was at
the head of the strongest party in Rome and in the conclave,
but in the committee just appointed his friends were in the
minority.   He showed, even before the death of Honorius,
that he did not mean to stand by the agreement.   A report
was spread that the pope was no more.   Peter appeared at
the head of a troop of friends and mercenaries, and, if the
dying pontiff had not been dragged to a window and shown
to the people, it is probable that he would even then have
made a bold attempt to mount the chair of St. Peter.[1]   When
Honorius did die, those of the cardinals who were determined
that, whoever was pope, Peter Leonis should be excluded,
hastily assembled, and on the same evening proclaimed
Cardinal Gregory, of St. Angelo, supreme pontiff of the
Christian world, under the name of Innocent II.   The party
of Peter forthwith went through the form of election with
their pope, dressed him in the proper pontificals, and declared
that he, under the title of Anacletus II., was the authentic
Vicar of Christ.[2]

Rome now contained two armies of ferocious partisans, who
soon intermixed their spiritual threats and curses with worldly
devastation and bloodshed.   Anacletus began the attack by
laying siege to the Church of St. Peter : bursting open the
doors, and making a forcible entrance into the sanctuary, he
carried off the gold crucifix, and all the treasure in gold and

---

[1] "Quod nisi dominus Papa
Honorius, quem credebant jam
mortuum, se ad fenestram populo
ostendisset, cum fratrum et propin-
quorum, ac muneribus et obsequiis
conductorum turba ministrorum,
praeco Antichristi, supra quod dicitur Deus, ante tempus se ex-
tulisset."—HEN. LUC. *Epist.*

[2] . . . "Congregatis quos potue-
runt, proh dolor ! cum episcopo
Portuensi, rubea cappa illum vestie-
runt."—Ibid.

silver and precious stones. He was so well satisfied with his success, that he assailed and despoiled the churches of the capital, one after another.[1] Through his ill-gotten gains he bought over the powerful, while he constrained the weak to take his side. Innocent II. was driven to great straits. His friends, the family of Frangipani, could with difficulty protect his person. He determined to fly from the turbulent city. Two galleys, containing himself and his few faithful adherents, dropped down the Tiber, and landed him safely at Pisa. Again taking ship, he sailed for St. Gilles, in Provence, and began his journey into France.

Innocent's bold trust in the allegiance of the nations of Northern Europe was fully justified by the event. He received at once a mark of respect from the Abbey of Cluny, which augured well. Sixty horses and mules, with everything which could be wanted by a pope in distress, were despatched to meet him, and escort him to Cluny.[2] Inasmuch as Anacletus had been a monk of Cluny, this recognition of the right of Innocent produced a strong presumption in his favour. The pope tarried eleven days at the great Burgundian abbey. During this time he consecrated the new church, which had been forty years building, and was the pride and wonder, not of Cluny or Burgundy only, but of the Christian world.[3]

[1] As usual, the remote writers and chroniclers knew more than those on the spot. The bishops and cardinals of Innocent's party, who thought it a duty to blacken the character of Anacletus, say simply that he plundered the churches. Arnold, of Bonnevaux, in the diocese of Chartres, tells us, "cum calices frangere, et crucifixos aureos membratim dividere, ipsi profani Christiani vel timerent, vel erubescerent; Judaeos aiunt esse quaesitos, qui sacra vasa et imagines Deo dicatas audacter comminuerent."— ST. BERN. *Op.* vol. ii. col. 1092.

[2] "Cluniacenses, ut ejus adventum cognoverunt, sexaginta equos seu mulos cum omni apparatu congruo papae et cardinalibus clericis destinaverunt, et usque ad suam basilicam favorabiliter conduxerunt."— ORDERICUS VITALIS, lib. xiii. cap. 11, ed. Prevost.

[3] "The pride of Burgundy was the great Abbey church of Cluny, which, with its narthex or antechurch, measured 580 feet in length, or considerably more than any other church erected in France in any age. Its nave was throughout 37 feet 6 inches in width, and it had double

Still the French bishops had not decided which pope they would choose, and yet the necessity of a decision was daily becoming more apparent. A papal schism in those days did not mean a far-off, imaginary evil, which could be avoided when convenient, but a very present and palpable inconvenience thrust into common life. " In most abbeys two abbots arose ; in the bishoprics two prelates contended for the see, of which one adhered to Anacletus, the other favoured Innocent. In a schism of this kind one has reason to fear, and yet a difficulty to escape, being cursed, for each pope attacks his adversary with all his might, and anathematizes him and his partisans most fatally. Thus each being prevented from accomplishing his purpose seeks, by his imprecations, to enlist God on his side against his rival."[1] To prevent, therefore, or mitigate, so formidable an evil, the ever-vigilant Louis VI., in concert with his bishops, convened a council at Etampes, for the purpose of fully discussing the respective claims of the hostile popes. To this council Bernard was invited, "in a special

side aisles, making the total internal width 120 feet ; and the whole internal area covered by it was upwards of 70,000 feet. Nor do even these colossal dimensions convey an adequate idea of its magnificence. The style throughout was solid and grand, and it must have possessed a degree of massive magnificence which we so frequently miss among the more elegant beauties of subsequent erections."— FERGUSSON's *Handbook of Architecture*, p. 653.

" Sixty-eight massive columns supported this wonderful fabric, into which light was admitted by three hundred narrow windows."— *Hist. de l'Abbaye de Cluny*, par M. LORAIN, p. 69.

The destruction under the Republic and the Empire of the glorious

old abbey was the work of many years, beginning in 1793, and terminating in 1811. When the great tower fell, it shook the whole neighbourhood : "On se souvient encore à Cluny de l'effroyable bruit qui secoua la ville à la chute de la plus grande tour."—Ibid. p. 278.

[1] " Nam in plerisque coenobiis duo abbates surrexerunt, et in episcopiis duo praesules de pontificatu certaverunt, quorum unus adhaerebat Petro Anacleto, alter vero favebat Gregorio Innocentio. In ejusmodi schismate anathema formidandum est, quod difficulter a quibusdam praecaveri potest, dum unus alium summopere impugnet, contrariumque sibi cum fautoribus suis feraliter anathematizet."—ORDERICUS VITALIS, lib. xiii. cap. 11.

manner," by the king and the chief bishops. He confessed afterwards that he went in fear and trembling. On the road, however, he had a vision, in which he saw a large church, with the people all singing harmoniously in praise of God. This raised his spirits. Fasting and prayer preceded the opening of the council, which at once began its deliberations by unanimously agreeing that a "business which concerned God should be entrusted to the man of God," and that his judgment should decide the views of the assembly. He examined the whole question of the double election; the respective merits of the competitors; the life and character of the first elected; and when he opened his mouth, the Holy Ghost was supposed to speak through it. Without hesitation or reserve he pronounced Innocent the legitimate pope, and the only one whom they could accept as such. Acclamations received this opinion, and amid praises to God, and vows of obedience to Innocent, the council broke up.[1]

Louis VI. forthwith sent Suger to Cluny to greet his newly-

---

[1] It is quite clear that Innocent owed his warm welcome from the French clergy to his supposed moral superiority over Anacletus. Even Bernard is forced to admit that Innocent's election was a little hurried and indecorous.

"Nam etsi quid minus forte solemniter, minusve ordinabiliter processit in ea [*i.e.* the election of Innocent] quae praecessit, ut hostes unitatis contendunt; numquid tamen praesumi altera debuit, nisi sane priore prius discussa ratione, cassata judicio?"—*Epist.* 126, vol. i. col. 134.

Of Anacletus he says, "Si vera sunt quae ubique divulgat opinio, nec unius dignus est viculi potestate.

Domini papae Innocentii et innocens vita, et integra fama, et electio canonica praedicatur. Priora duo nec hostes diffitentur; tertium

calumniam habuit, sed per Christianissimum Lotharium nuper falsi calumniatores in suo sunt mendacio deprehensi."—*Epist.* 127.

Suger says plainly that at the Council of Étampes the question of the regularity of election was secondary to that of the personal character of the two popes.

"Rex . . . concilium archiepiscoporum, episcoporum, abbatum, et religiosorum virorum Stampis convocat, et eorum consilio magis de persona quam de electione investigans (fit enim saepe ut Romanorum tumultuantium quibuscunque molestiis Ecclesiae electio minus ordinarie fieri valeat) ejus assensum electioni consilio virorum praebet, et deinceps manu tenere promittit."—SUGERIUS, *Ludovici Vita.*

recognised spiritual chief, and escort him on his way northward.
The pope came to Saint-Benoit-sur-Loire, and was there met
by the king, queen, and royal children.   Louis bowed "his
often crowned head" as if before the sepulchre of St. Peter,
fell on the ground at the feet of the pontiff, and promised
affection and devoted service both to him and to the Church
From thence the pope moved on to Chartres, where came also
the Norman Henry I. of England, with an immense retinue
of bishops and nobles.   Henry was undecided as to which
pope would suit him best.   His own clergy had a leaning
towards Anacletus ; that might be a reason for him to choose
Innocent.   He hesitated.   His own bishops had nearly persuaded him to acknowledge Anacletus, when Bernard appeared
before him.   The two foremost men then in Europe were in
the presence of each other—the wisest soldier-statesman of
his age, and the greatest monk out of all the cloisters of
Christendom.   These two were thus brought for once face to
face—the old knight and the young priest, the man of action
and the man of meditation ; there they were urging and disputing.   The enthusiast convinced the man of the world.
"Are you afraid,"[1] said Bernard, "of incurring sin if you
acknowledge Innocent ?   Bethink you how to answer for
your *other* sins to God ; that one I will take and account for."
Henry yielded to the supremacy of Innocent.

Having thus received the friendship of the two western
sovereigns, Innocent determined to sound the disposition of
the German emperor.   He accordingly left Chartres and proceeded to the monastery of Morigny, near Étampes.   Here
the goodly company of pope, bishops, and cardinals, with the
chief of them all, Bernard, remained three days.   Here they

---

[1] "Quid times ? ait.   Times peccatum incurrere, si obedias Innocentio ?   Cogita" inquit " quomodo
de aliis peccatis tuis respondeas Deo;
istud mihi relinque, in me sit hoc
peccatum."—St. Bern. *Op.* vol. ii.
col. 1094.

met a man by whose fame, misfortunes, and errors all Europe
had for many years been amused or scandalized, viz. Peter
Abelard; on whom the anathema of the Church had already
once fallen, and before long was to fall again, the second time
directed by one of the guests that night at Morigny—the Abbot
of Clairvaux.   They then proceeded to Liège; and it was a
time of anxious deliberation in the councils of the pope, for
they were going to meet the owner of that imperial crown, of
which former possessors had wrought such trouble and injury
to the Church.   But Lotharius had been the acknowledged
chief of the papal party before he was emperor, and this,
coupled with the mildness of his character, might permit hopes
of a cordial, or at least friendly, reception.   Innocent discussed
his affairs in the presence of his cardinals as usual, but a secret
conference with his now inseparable adviser, Bernard, always
preceded any plan of definite action.   Lotharius received the
pontiff with due honour, but, to the amazement of all, he
appeared to think that this was a good opportunity to renew
the question of investitures which had been settled eight years
before, between Henry V. and Calixtus II., at the Concordat
of Worms.   There was something quite horrible in such a
suggestion at such a moment, when the schism had nearly
paralyzed the papacy for offensive war.   In bidding for the
favour of a German emperor the rival popes would possibly
think less of the immunities of the Church at large, and more
of their own chance of being rulers of it, than a single independent pope might do.[1]   This, doubtless, was what the unam-

<hr>

[1] " Et honorifice quidem sus-
ceptus est [papa], sed velociter ob-
nubilata est illa serenitas.   Siquidem importune idem rex institit,
tempus habere se reputans oppor-
tunum, episcoporum sibi restitui
investituras, quas ab ejus praede-
cessore imperatore Henrico per
maximos quidem labores et multa
pericula Romana ecclesia vindicarat.
Ad quod verbum expavere et ex-
palluere Romani, gravius sese apud
Leodium arbitrati periculum offen-
disse, quam declinaverint Romae.
Nec consilium suppetebat, donec
murum se opposuit abbas sanctus."
—St. Bern. Op. vol. ii. col. 1094.

bitious Lotharius dimly felt ; and, had he had a little of the spirit of his Franconian predecessors, Innocent, Bernard, and Anacletus would, one and all of them, have passed some anxious and sorrowful years. The Romans shuddered and turned pale, and wished themselves in Rome again, where the small and domestic dangers they knew well had not the vague terror about them which was inspired in the barbarian north. Again Bernard came to the rescue, and placed himself as a wall of strength before the frightened Italians. He boldly faced the emperor in his demands, and with great freedom of speech reduced him to humble acquiescence in the claims of Innocent. Lotharius, on foot, went through the crowd towards the pope on his white palfrey. With one hand he took the rein, in the other he held a wand—a symbol of protection to his acknowledged lord. When Innocent got down from his horse, the emperor was there to assist him ; and thus, before all men, in that age of forms and ceremonies, proclaimed his submission.[1]

Having succeeded in this important conference, the pope returned towards St. Denis, where he purposed to pass the few remaining days of Lent, and celebrate Easter. Suger and his monks met him with a grand procession, chanting hymns of jubilee over his happy return to them. Maunday Thursday was observed in the Roman fashion, and a sumptuous donative, called a " Presbytery," was given to the clergy. But on the Vigil of the most holy Resurrection, to show it due honour, Innocent passed the night in prayer. At early dawn he and his attendants proceeded to the Church of the Holy Martyrs— St. Denis and his companions—and there they made preparations, as they do at Rome, and adorned themselves with many wonderful ornaments. They placed on the pope's head the phrygium, or helmet-shaped cap circled with gold, and led him forth sitting on a white palfrey richly caparisoned. Then,

[1] Sugerius, Vita Ludovici Grossi.

proceeding in front, two abreast, on horseback, they struck up a joyous chant. The barons and noble feudatories of the abbey, acting as grooms, on foot attended the pontiff, and led his horse by the rein. Some in advance cast money among the thronging crowd to clear a way. But the king's road was strewn with willows, and rich hangings were carried along the side on a line of posts. Troops of knights and crowds of people pressed to see the procession ; but, strangest of all, even the wretched, persecuted Jews of Paris came forward, and offered to the head man of their persecutors a copy of their law covered by a veil. "May God Almighty take away the veil which is on your hearts!" was the reply of Innocent. At last he came to the Church of the Holy Martyrs, which glittered with golden coronas and stones far more precious than gold. Suger and the pope offered up a mass, and then the whole company retired to the cloister to a magnificent feast.[1]

[1] Sugerius, ibid. The history of the Jews in the Middle Ages contains perhaps the heaviest catalogue of crimes which can be laid at the door of men "calling themselves Christians." One way of celebrating Easter was this :—"A Toulouse il fut établi que le Dimanche de Pâque un Chrétien donnerait un soufflet à un Juif sous la porche de la cathédrale. Adhémar de Chabannais raconte qu'en 1018 le Vicomte de Rocheouart étant venu faire ses Pâques à Toulouse, le clergé toulaisain *délégua par civilité* à Hugues, chaplain de ce seigneur, l'office de souffleter le Juif ; Hugues s'en acquitta si rudement, *qu'il fit sauter d'un coup de poing les yeux et la cervelle du patient.*"—*Histoire de France*, par HENRI MARTIN, tom. iii. p. 53. The Jews were always being accused of insulting and mutilating the Host, and the most preposterous fables were propagated and believed to their injury in consequence. A Jew in Paris, it is related, had received in pledge a Christian woman's best clothes. Easter was drawing near, and the usurer refused to give up the articles unless the woman promised to bring to him the Host, which she was about to receive at Holy Communion. Refusing at first, she finally consented. The fact became known that a Jew had got possession of the consecrated bread ; it was instantly spread abroad that he had thrown it into a cauldron of boiling water, and that, ever since, the infant Jesus had been swimming about on the surface, beneath which nothing would cause Him to sink. Crowds beset the Jew's house. People pretended to have seen the Infant. The wretched Hebrews were seized, and in abject fear confessed all they were ordered. The supposed culprit was condemned to be burnt alive. The poor creature regretted not having his thalmud with him,

Innocent visited many of the French towns after this, but his sojourn at Clairvaux is the only one which will need notice here. There he was met by a tattered flock "of Christ's poor," preceded by a cross, without noise or tumult. The pope and bishops were moved to tears at the sight of so much austerity. They marvelled at the self-restraint which made the monks receive this unwonted visit in solemn silence. Every eye was fixed on the ground, no prying curiosity watched and followed the movements of the brilliant cavalcade : with closed lids, the monks were seen of all, and saw no one. The plain unornamented church, the simple bare walls of the monastery, offered nothing to the Romans either to admire or wish for.[1] The hard fare of the monks appeared more wonderful still. If by chance a fish was to be had, it was placed before the pope alone.

Innocent had consumed more than a year in his politic and profitable visits to the French churches, when he began to think of going southward. Indeed there was a danger, if he stayed too long, that he would tire the hospitality of his hosts. A pope with all his following of bishops and courtiers, especially a pope cut off from his Italian revenues, was necessarily a most expensive guest.[2] Before setting out, however, on his

thinking it would save him. They brought him his thalmud, and burnt both him and it together.—See G. B. DEPPING's interesting work, *Les Juifs dans le Moyen Age*, p. 123, from which the above story is taken.

[1] "Nihil in ecclesia illa vidit Romanus quod cuperet."—ST. BERN. *Op.* vol. ii. col. 1094. The visit of a pope seems to have been anything but desirable or welcome in these times. Suger, as usual, speaks out plainly. Referring to Pope Paschal's progress in France in the year 1107, he says of his coming to St. Denis : "Qui gloriose et satis episcopaliter

receptus, hoc unum memorabile et Romanis insolitum, et posteris, reliquit exemplum, quod nec aurum, nec argentum, nec pretiosas monasterii margeritas, quod multum timebatur, non tantum non affectabat, sed nec respicere dignabatur."—SUGERIUS, *Vita Ludov. Gros.*

[2] "Deinde praefatus Papa toto illo anno Franciam peragravit, et immensam gravedinem ecclesiis Galliarum ingessit, utpote qui Romanos officiales cum multis clientibus secum habuit, et de redditibus apostolicae sedis in Italia nihil adipisci potuit."—ORDERICUS VITALIS, lib. xiii cap. 11.

return south, it was arranged that a grand council should be holden at Rheims; Louis VI. wished it—wished the pope to consecrate his young son Louis, under circumstances of peculiar solemnity—for the active and politic king of France was at this moment bowed down with sorrow by a domestic bereavement. Shortly before, as his eldest son Philip, a "rosy-cheeked, pleasant youth" of sixteen years, was riding in the suburbs of Paris, a "diabolical pig" ran between his horse's legs, and threw horse and rider heavily on the ground. Before night the prince expired.[1] Louis was inconsolable from grief; indeed, Suger and others of his friends feared he might sink under the shock; so they persuaded him to proceed to Rheims, and preside at the consecration of his second son, Louis.

The council was well attended. Thirteen archbishops, two hundred and sixty-three bishops, besides a large number of abbots, clerks, and monks, assembled at Rheims towards the middle of October, 1131. The king entered—followed by Rudolf of Vermandois and a crowd of barons—ascended the dais where the pope sat, kissed his feet, and took his seat beside him. Louis then made a prayer for his lost son, which brought tears to the eyes of all present. Whereupon the pope, turning towards the king, began thus :—

"It behoves you, most excellent king, who rule over the most noble nation of the Franks, to lift up your eyes to the Majesty of that Highest King, by whom kings reign, and to adore and submit to His will in all things. He governs all things, for He created them; and as He knows all things in the universe of the world, He neither does nor permits anything unjust, although injustice is often wrought. The good

---

[1] "Regis enim Ludovici filius, floridus et amoenus puer, Philippus, bonorum spes timorque malorum, cum quadam die per civitatis Parisiensis suburbium equitaret, obvio porco diabolico offensus equus, gravissime cecidit, sessoremque suum nobilissimum puerum silice consternatum, mole ponderis sui conculcatum contrivit."—SUGERIUS, *Vita Lud. Gros.*

and merciful Lord is wont to console His faithful servants with prosperity, and to instruct them through adversity. For as we read in Holy Scripture, which is His letter from heaven directed to us on earth by the Holy Spirit, He smiteth and healeth and chasteneth every son He loveth. And why? Lest man, who, made in the image of God, through the transgression of sin has fallen into the shadows of this mortal life, should mistake for his country the land of his exile. For we are all strangers and sojourners, as our fathers were; nor have we here an abiding city, but we seek that which is to come. To that city your child, full of purity and innocence, has departed. David, the model and exemplar of kings, while his son lay sick wept most bitterly, but when he was told that his child was dead, he arose from the sackcloth and ashes. changed his garments, washed his hands, and called his household to a feast. The holy man knew how great would be his sin if he withstood the Divine ordinances even in thought. Lay aside, therefore, this sadness of mind. God, who has taken to Himself one of your sons, has left you others to reign after you. To us strangers, driven from our sees, you owed and you gave consolation. You received us with honour, and loaded us with benefits. May God repay you for it in that city of which glorious things are spoken, in which life knows no death, eternity no failing, joy no end."

The speech of Innocent appeared to have a soothing effect on the wounded spirit of the French king. The pope, when he had finished speaking, rose, and reciting the Lord's prayer in an undertone, absolved the soul of the deceased youth. Preparations were then made for the ceremony of consecration, which was to take place on the morrow.

The sun rose on the morning of the solemnity with a splendour which surpassed his wonted brightness. At the doorway of the cathedral the king and his knights awaited the arrival of the pope. When he came, they all entered the church.

The little prince was presented at the altar, and "consecrated with the oil with which St. Remigius, who had received it from an angel's hand, had anointed Clovis on his conversion. Louis was so comforted through the performance of this rite, that he returned home with his queen, his son, and his court, and again gave his attention to the public business of his kingdom.

The Council of Rheims, moreover, passed the usual decrees, which, from constant repetition, had settled almost into received formulas. Simony is forbidden, as a matter of course. Monks may not learn or practise either medicine or law. "Neglecting the cure of souls, promising health for hateful money, they make themselves healers of human bodies. The unchaste eye is the forerunner of the unchaste heart, and religious men may not handle things which modesty is ashamed even to mention." Tournaments are interdicted. "We entirely forbid those detestable fairs or holidays at which knights are wont to meet by agreement, and where, in order to show their strength and bravery, they rashly encounter each other ; where often arise death to their bodies and danger to their souls. If any one should die at any of these meetings, although, if he can ask for it, the last sacrament shall not be withheld from him, still, he shall not receive ecclesiastical burial." The last decree is a most animated condemnation of incendiaries, who would seem to have been not a small class of offenders. They are to repair, to the best of their ability, the injury they have done, and do a year's penance either in Spain or the Holy Land.[1]

Innocent, after the rising of the council, began his journey towards the south without further delay. He again visited Cluny. Whether the obligation he had been under to Peter and the Cluniacs had faded from his mind through the more

---

[1] What is known of the Council of Rheims besides the canons will be found brought together in the tenth volume of Labbe's Collectio Conciliorum. Paris: 1671.

brilliant services of Bernard and the Cistercians, or that the austere poverty of Clairvaux became more distinct when contrasted with the sumptuous Cluny, it is not easy to say. But it is certain that during this second sojourn at Cluny he granted immunities and favours to the Cistercians, which incensed the Cluniacs to the highest pitch. Even the gentle abbot of Cluny, by nature the meekest of men, was forced to utter a cry of complaint and injustice. In a letter directed to Abbot Stephen, bearing date from Cluny, Feb. 18, 1132, Innocent, besides confirming the Cistercian freedom with regard to episcopal interference, proceeds to order their complete immunity from tithes. "Let no one presume to ask or receive tithes of any of the brethren of your congregation." This was a blow—if not a very severe one, still one to be felt—at the revenues of Cluny, the monks of which had taken their tithes of their poorer brethren of Citeaux without scruple. "Your devoted congregation," writes Peter to Innocent, "begs that your newly adopted children shall not expel their elders from your fatherly love." So great a resistance did Peter's subjects make to the papal command, that the long favoured and indulged Cluny had to be threatened with an interdict, to bring it to submission. But the warm, deep heart of Peter could never harbour resentment or enmity, whatever the provocation ; and not long after, he was rejoicing and congratulating Bernard on the fact, that not even the dispute concerning the tithes had been sufficient to impair their friendship.

From this Innocent continued his journey into Italy, still accompanied by the Abbot of Clairvaux. Bernard, entirely convinced that the cause of Innocent was the cause of right, justice, and religion, set no bounds to his passionate advocacy of it. Kings, dukes, private persons, bishops, and monks, were caressed or threatened in long discourses or laconic notes, to induce them to acknowledge or assist the pope of Bernard. This is a letter to the King of England, Henry I :—

" To Henry, the illustrious King of the English, Bernard, called
the Abbot of Clairvaux, wishes honour, safety, and peace.

" To wish to give you instruction, especially in those matters
which concern propriety of conduct, is what would occur only
to a very foolish person, or to one entirely unacquainted with
your character. A simple account is therefore all that is needed,
and this in few words, as many are superfluous to one who
apprehends all things with ease. We are then at the entrance
of the city ; Salvation is in the gates ; Justice is with us. But
that is a food not palatable to Roman soldiers. Therefore
by righteousness we appease God ; by warfare we terrify our
enemies. We are only deficient in every necessary. What
remains to be done, in order that you may complete the work
which you began by that magnificent and honourable reception
of our Lord Pope Innocent, you know best."[1]

It appears that the crafty Norman did not find it convenient
to understand the hint which Bernard conveyed to him. He
sent no money by which " our Lord Pope Innocent" could be
relieved from his painful condition of indigence. The pope,
nevertheless, through the help of the Emperor Lotharius, succeeded in entering Rome. But Anacletus was still too strong
for him in his own capital. Indeed, he also had been able to
attach to his cause one powerful adherent ; who, moreover, was
not too far off to give valuable assistance when it might be
needed. This was the Norman, Roger Duke of Sicily, who
saw distinctly that Innocent, favoured and supported by two
kings and an emperor, would appreciate his adhesion much
less than Anacletus, who had hitherto depended on the Roman
populace and his own wealth only. Roger therefore professed
himself satisfied that Anacletus was the lawful pope, and Innocent a schismatical usurper. This view of the claims of the
rival pontiffs required for its durability that Anacletus should,

[1] St. Bern. Epist. 138.

M 2

in his turn, recognise Roger as King of Italy. Innocent felt that it was wise to retire in time. The help of the German emperor was distant and doubtful ; Roger was present and unscrupulous. Pope Innocent therefore withdrew to Pisa, and there remained till the termination of the schism. A comparative calm came over Europe in consequence. Each portion of Europe was satisfied with its own pope, and waited the time when his rival should be removed.

But Bernard still kept up a vigorous agitation. To the Pisans, among whom Innocent was residing, he wrote :—" Pisa is chosen to take the place of Rome, and, out of all the cities of the earth, is selected for the dignity of the apostolic see. O Pisans ! O Pisans ! the Lord has dealt liberally with you, and we are made to rejoice."[1] To the Milanese, who were showing signs of insubordination, he says :—" The Church of Rome is clement, but she is powerful. Do not abuse her clemency, lest you be crushed by her power. The plenitude of authority over all the churches of the world, by a singular prerogative, is given to the apostolic see. He, therefore, who resists this authority, resists the ordinance of God. The pope could, if he judged it fit, create new bishoprics where none existed before. Of those which exist, he can either raise them or degrade them, according to his good pleasure. He can summon ecclesiastical persons, however high their rank, from the ends of the earth to his presence—not once, or twice, but as often as he sees fit ; and he is easily able to punish disobedience, if any think proper to withstand him."[2] In a word, everybody had better display a becoming haste in obeying Innocent. Bernard's zeal at this period was abundantly warm ; but it may be doubted whether the flames of party spirit and theological bitterness did not contribute much to its heat. His language is vehement, not to say violent : Anacletus is

[1] St. Bern. Epist. 130.   [2] Ibid. Epist. 131.

Antichrist ; he is the Beast of Prophecy ; and his name, Leo, is the occasion of many a venomous pun.

The Milanese at last received the right pope, and thus caused great rejoicing. Bernard came to visit them. When his arrival was expected, the whole population went out to meet him as far as the seventh milestone. Nobles and common people, on horse, on foot, as if they had been going to migrate from their city, all proceeded to welcome with an incredible reverence the man of God. They kissed his feet, and eagerly sought to pick even the hairs from his garments. Signs and wonders of all kinds marked his sojourn in the city of St. Ambrose.[1]

But Bernard began to feel that his absence from home could not be prolonged without grave disadvantage both to himself and his flock at Clairvaux. During the four years which had elapsed since the death of Honorius II. he could only have given them a few hasty visits, snatched from the turmoil of business and travelling. It is supposed he returned at the beginning of the year 1135. His long-expected advent was the cause of the deepest joy to his friends and monks. And not only to them. Such was the renown for superhuman holiness which by this time had filled all Europe with his name, that, wherever he passed, even the shepherds came from their hills, and the rustics from their fields, if it might only be to behold him afar off, and implore his blessing. When they had caught sight of him, they returned to their huts, conversing and rejoicing with one another that they had seen the saint of God. When he reached Langres, he was met by a company from Clairvaux, who, with embraces and tears of gladness, led him home. The whole convent was assembled to receive its abbot —the "beloved father," as a contemporary calls him. There was no tumult, or weak, undisciplined demonstrativeness in their joy, but a great gravity, through which shone the deep glow of intense love. The measure and propriety of their

---

[1] St. Bern. Op. vol. ii. col. 1096.

words and actions were a proof that their efforts towards self-subjection had not been fruitless. And they restrained, we are told, their very affections, lest a reign of self-indulgence might offend the "maturity of religion." During the abbot's long absence the devil, it was noticed, had been able to effect little or nothing. There were no discussions or disputes awaiting Bernard's return ; no hatreds nursed up against the day of reckoning and adjustment. Old and young, rich and poor, the high and the low, the knight and the serf, were all living in amity and Christian brotherhood. Bernard, we are told, was moved to great humbleness by this proof of God's favour. The fact that the work of his hands seemed to prosper filled him with a certain reverential awe, not with vain-glory and self-conceit. In fact, his humility generally strikes his biographer, Arnold of Bonnevaux, as the most remarkable of his many wonderful gifts. Some marvelled, he says, at Bernard's doctrine, others at his holy life, others at his miracles. Although Arnold admits all these to be worthy of the highest admiration, for himself, he considers the humility Bernard ever manifested to be the most wonderful of all.[1] "When he was a chosen vessel, and announced the name of Christ before nations and kings ; when the princes of this world bowed down to him, and the bishops of all lands awaited his bidding ; when even the holy see revered his advice, and made him a sort of general legate for all the world ; when, greatest of all, his words and actions were confirmed by miracles ; he was never puffed up, but, in all humility, considered himself the minister, not the author, of mighty works ; and when every one thought him the greatest, in his own judgment he was the least. Whatsoever

---

[1] " Plurima in eum probabilia et laude digna concurrunt. Alii namque doctrinam, alii mores, alii mirantur miracula, ... hoc sublimius duco, hoc propensius praedico, quod cum esset vas electionis, etc. etc. . . nunquam excessit, nunquam supra se in mirabilibus ambulavit."—St. Bern, *Op.* vol. ii. col. 1102.

he did, he ascribed to God. He said, and felt, that he could neither wish nor perform any good thing without the inspiration of God.[1]

Bernard had left Clairvaux to the care of hands he could well confide in during his long absence in Italy. His kinsman Geoffrey was prior, and his brother Gerard cellarer. These two took upon them the working routine of the monastery, and did all in their power to increase the leisure of their abbot, which they were well persuaded would not be lost to the interests of the Church. But, after all the turmoil and agitation of the schism, Bernard wanted not leisure only, but rest, reflection, and solitude. He retired to a little hut, or bower, near the abbey, where he could write, think, and dream. Melancholy, lingering, retrospective glances at bygone days were unknown to either Bernard or his age. Still it is hardly possible that he can have fallen back on this repose and seclusion without remembering the fact and circumstances—now fifteen years past—of his similar retreat once before. What a change had those fifteen years been witnesses of! He was then a young abbot of an unknown order; he was now the acknowledged chief of the most active minds in Europe. Over all those broad realms of France and Germany he was respected and feared. Even the Britons, entirely divided from the whole world, had lately been showing they knew of him and revered him. And the changed life he had recently led! Years of solitude and patient endeavour after holiness and peace followed by world-wide activity and command. And now a little haven of shelter again showed in the midst of that tempestuous sea; quiet hours, and loved faces, and the sound of old voices, known from childhood, were to be his again for a season. As he sat in his beautiful vale, looking out on the landscape (still visible to us), he cannot have

---

[1] St. Bern. Op. vol. ii. col. 1102.

wanted material for thought, and even for meditation. But his meditations were destined to be soon interrupted.

Godfrey the prior, and several others, had come to the conclusion that the buildings at Clairvaux were quite inadequate to the daily growing requirements of the monastery. Regretful as they were to disturb the reflections of the abbot, they felt that an important step must be taken one way or another; that they must either enlarge Clairvaux, or else make it understood they did not mean to admit any fresh members. Bernard was in the heavens, says Arnold of Bonnevaux, and they compelled him to come down and listen to their sublunary business. They pointed out to him the narrowness and inconvenience of the existing site as quite unfit for the expanding necessities of the order.[1]   Numbers were coming, for whom there was really no room; and even the abbey church soon would be insufficient to hold the monks alone, to say nothing of visitors. They said that they had well considered the matter, and had discovered lower down the valley an open plain, very convenient from the position of the river, and altogether roomy enough for all the needs and probable increase of the monastery.   There was space for fields, sheds, shrubberies, and vineyards.   And as for the neighbouring wood, if it seemed to require some sort of fence, the abundance of stones would render the construction of stone walls, where wanted, a matter of ease. Bernard listened to these suggestions, and replied that he did not agree with them. "You see," he observed, "that our present stone buildings have been erected at great cost and labour. If we sacrifice all this, worldly people may have a bad opinion of us; may say that we are light and fickle; or else say that too much riches, which we

---

[1] "Hic [Godfridus] ergo atque alii plures viri providi et de communi utilitate solliciti virum Dei, cujus conversatio in coelis erat, ali-quando descendere compellebant, et indicabant ei quae domus necessitas exigebat."—St. BERN. *Op.* vol. ii. col. 1103.

are far from possessing, have made us mad. Now you, good friends, know well enough that we have not the money, and, to use the words of the Gospel, 'He that intendeth to build a tower, must sit down first and count the cost : otherwise it will afterwards be said of him, This man began to build, but was not able to finish.'" "True," they replied ; "if the buildings of the monastery were complete, and God were pleased not to send any more sojourners to us, such an opinion might hold. But now we see our flock increase daily, and they who come must either be sent away, or a habitation in which to receive them must be found. We cannot doubt that He who provides dwellers will provide houses for them also. But God forbid that, through fear of the expense, we run the risk of rejecting what He sends us." Bernard was delighted with the faith they showed, and in time gave his consent to their plan. Many prayers were offered, and even some revelations were vouchsafed as a preliminary encouragement. There was great rejoicing at Clairvaux when the decision was generally known.[1]

Theobald, Count of Chartres, soon heard of the scheme, and at once gave a handsome contribution towards it, with the promise of more. Theobald was not at this time the ambitious war-loving knight he had been some years back, when he fought with Louis VI. for the castle of Le Puiset. Fifteen years before he sailed for England from the coasts of Normandy with his uncle, Henry I. In another ship which sailed with them were Henry's two sons and Theobald's own sister, Matilda of Blois. The ship was called " The White Ship." It never reached England, and Theobald lost a sister, a brother-in-law, and four first cousins in one day. He had been a grave man ever since, very fond of monks and religious persons, and had replaced his old taste for fighting by a spirit of gentle Christian benevolence. He was exactly the friend Bernard wanted now he was doubtful about "the cost of it."

---

[1] St. Bern. Op. vol. ii. col. 1103.

The bishops of those parts also, and the men of renown, and the merchants, joyfully, and without being pressed, gave liberally to the work of God.[1]   The resources were thus abundant.   Labourers were hired, and the monks themselves fell vigorously to work.   Some cut timber, others squared the stones, others built the walls.   The river was divided into a number of channels, and these were led to the various mills. The fullers and millers, the tanners and carpenters, and other artificers erected the machines and fittings required in their several trades, and the obedient water, brought by subterranean pipes throughout the offices, afforded a plentiful and gushing spring wherever it was wanted.   At last, having fulfilled its various duties, it retired to its original bed, and swelled to its ancient size.   The walls were completed with unexpected celerity, enclosing the whole extent of the spacious monastery.   The abbey rose from the earth, and, as if animated by a spirit of life, the new church seemed to grow and increase.

---

[1] "Audierunt episcopi regionum, et viri inclyti, et negotiatores terrae, et hilari animo, sine exactore, ultro ad opus Dei copiosa contulere suffragia."—St. Bern. *Op.* vol. ii. col. 1104.

CHAPTER II.

WILLIAM, COUNT OF AQUITAINE, STILL FAVOURS ANACLETUS —
BERNARD'S TRIUMPH OVER HIM—SERMONS ON THE CANTICLES.

BERNARD could hardly have begun to solace himself with the
hope of a little peace and retirement, when he was again called
away from Clairvaux to overcome and control the enemies of
the Church.

Innocent, in his progress through France, had not deemed
it necessary to visit the south-western provinces of that country.
The wide district which extends from the Loire to the Pyrenees,
in the more urgent circumstances of the Church at the commencement of the schism, had been either forgotten or neglected, as comparatively of less importance. But when, through
the vigorous efforts of Bernard and others, order and allegiance
to Innocent had been established in the north, the condition
of Aquitaine began to attract attention. The office of legate
in those parts had, during the pontificates of Calixtus II. and
Honorius II., been discharged by Gerard, Bishop of Angoulême.
On the death of the latter pope, Gerard wrote to Innocent in
terms of submission and allegiance, at the same time inti-
mating that he should expect his position as legate to be confirmed by the new pope. Gerard's administration had been
notorious for its corrupt and worldly character, and Innocent
refused to reinstate him. He at once transferred his obedience
to Anacletus. He induced the weak Count of Poitiers,

William X., to share his views, and acknowledge Anacletus. With the count's connivance, or even assistance, he drove from his see William, Bishop of Poitiers, who favoured the cause of Innocent. A new bishop was hastily thrust into the vacant see—"a man ambitious and noble, but of degenerate faith," which probably meant only that he was a mail-clad knight, who was willing to be called bishop, and take the episcopal revenues. The intruder had powerful family connexions, who were brought over by this elevation of their relative to the cause of Anacletus. He was consecrated with due formality, though his " cursed head was not so much anointed as defiled by the imposition of their profane hands." [1]   The see of Limoges also suffered in the same manner. Ramnulf, Abbot of Dorat, was intruded upon it, "whom the Divine vengeance was not long in overtaking." As he was riding one day along an even road, he fell from his horse, "a single stone, placed there for this very purpose," struck his head, fractured his skull, and killed him.

Pope Innocent had made the learned and pious Geoffrey, Bishop of Chartres, his legate in Aquitaine. Geoffrey, when he heard of these proceedings, at once determined to "postpone all other business, and avert, if possible, the danger which was threatening the Church." He and Bernard were intimate friends. Like nearly all his contemporaries, he appears to have thought that the Abbot of Clairvaux could accomplish what nobody else could. He begged, he intreated him to be his companion and helper in the difficult enterprise, in which both felt an equally vivid interest. Bernard replied that he was about to found a colony of monks in Brittany ; that this would necessitate his going to Nantes ; but that when he had done so in a satisfactory manner, he would be willing and

---

[1] " Profanas ei imponentes manus, exsecrabile caput ejus non tam unx- erunt quam contaminaverunt."— St. Bern. *Op.* vol. ii. col. 1105.

able to proceed southward into Aquitaine. They started on the journey together.[1]

After Bernard had settled his new abbey, and relieved a lady of the district from most distressing visits which she received from a demon,[2] he and Geoffrey proceeded to the dominions of the Count of Poitiers. They sent word that the Abbot of Clairvaux and the Bishop of Chartres had come to him on business of the Church and that they wished much to discuss with him a subject of great importance. He was persuaded not to decline the proposed conference. They all met at Parthenay. Bernard and Geoffrey dwelt on the division of the Church, and continuance of the schism. They said that, north of the Alps at least, Aquitaine alone remained a marked spot of disunion and disobedience. They insisted on the unity of the Church, and pointed out that whatever is outside of the Church,—as it were outside of the ark,—by the judgment of God, must of necessity perish. They bade him reflect on the fate of Dathan and Abiram, whom the earth swallowed up alive for the sin of schism ; and showed him that God's vengeance on such crimes had never been wanting. The count heard them very patiently, and replied that, as regarded the acknowledging of Pope Innocent, he had no objection whatever ; they might be satisfied on that point. He was willing to renounce Anacletus ; but as for the restitution of the bishops whom he had expelled from their sees, he declared that nothing in the world should induce him to receive them again. Their cause might be good, and he gave his allegiance to it ; but the men themselves were hateful to him. They had offended him beyond forgiveness, and should never more be friends of his.

[1] St. Bern. Op. vol. ii. col. 1105.

[2] "Erat autem in regione illa misera mulier, quae a quodam petulante diabolo vexabatur. . . . Abutebatur ergo ea, etiam in eodem lectulo cubante marito." — *Ibid.* Bernard relieved her by lending her his pastoral staff to place in the bed. The demon threatened awful revenge when Bernard should be gone, but he was utterly defeated.

As the count appeared likely to be firm in what he said, Bernard broke off a discussion which was useless. He and those who might lawfully do so entered a church to celebrate mass, leaving the count standing outside at the door, which, as an excommunicated person, he might not pass through. Bernard went through the rite—the overwhelming miracle, as it was thought—of consecrating the elements. Then rising into an ecstasy of enthusiasm and command, he came forth with flaming eyes and a countenance of fire, bearing the Host before him. Not with soft words of supplication, but in loud tones of anger and menace, he addressed the count. "We have beseeched you, and us you have despised : an assembled multitude of God's servants have implored you, and them you have despised. Behold the Virgin's Son, the Head and Lord of that Church which you persecute, comes towards you. Your Judge is here, at whose name every knee shall bow, whether in heaven, on earth, or in hell. Your Judge is here, into whose hands your soul will fall. Will you spurn Him also ; will you despise Him as you have His servants?"[1] A silence as of death reigned over the assembled and terrified multitude, who, amid prayers and tears, waited in expectation of a miracle from heaven. The count, when he saw the awful zeal of Bernard, in whose hands he verily believed at that moment was his Judge and Lord, stiffened and paralyzed in every limb, fell insensible to the ground. Raised up by his attendant knights, he could neither speak nor see, and again fell with his face on the grass, foaming at the mouth. Bernard came close to him, and pushing the prostrate man with his foot, told him to stand up and hear

---

[1] "Rogavimus te, et sprevisti nos. Supplicavit tibi in altero quem jam tecum habuimus conventu servorum Dei ante te adunata multitudo, et contempsisti. Ecce ad te processit Filius Virginis qui est caput et Dominus Ecclesiae quam tu persequeris. Adest judex tuus, in cujus nomine omne genu curvatur coelestium, terrestrium, et infernorum. Adest judex tuus, in cujus manus illa anima tua deveniet. Nunquid et ipsum spernes ? nunquid et ipsum sicut servos ejus contemnes ?"—St. Bern. *Op.* vol. ii. col. 1107.

the judgment of God. "Here," he said, "is the Bishop of Poitiers, whom you have driven from his church. Go and be reconciled to him with the kiss of peace. Lead him back to his see, whence you have expelled him. Give glory to God instead of contumely, and throughout your dominions restore that unity which has fled from it." The count heard, although he neither dared nor was able to speak; but he went at once and received the bishop with a kiss; and with the same hand by which he had abjured him, he now led him back to his church amidst general rejoicing. Soon he and Bernard were in friendly converse, and the latter urged him for the future to avoid such impious doings, lest at last he should tire out God's patience by his misdeeds.[1]

Such was the force of belief in the old times. The infinite, the supernatural, can never be altogether excluded from men's minds. Men think of them deeply and wisely, or meanly and foolishly, according as their horizon is wide or narrow, their vision far-reaching or weak; but still they think of them. In these rough, strong, mediæval knights a fearful conflict was ever going on. The ferocious appetites and instincts which they inherited from their fathers who conquered Rome were still, in scarcely diminished intensity, working in their own breasts. But in the midst of these appetites and passions had been dropped the leaven of the Christian creed. Part of that creed (at least, as propounded by the Church) they could, and did, thoroughly assimilate. The God of wrath and vengeance was perfectly comprehensible to them; they only forgot Him in the moments of their own vengeance and wrath. These moments often recurred in the lives of even the best of them; but the intervals of remission were as often filled with the bitterest reaction and remorse. The dormant religious awe would wake up in vengeful tyranny, and the fire of the Divine anger seemed to run along the ground. Then came repentance

---

[1] St. Bern. Op. vol. ii. col. 1107.

in sackcloth and ashes ; then the agony of soul which brought
their stiff, iron-clad knees to the ground, or even their "faces
on the grass, foaming at the mouth." So they passed through
life, which for them was a narrow pathway, now skirting the
gates of hell, now rising towards the plains of heaven.

Meanwhile, Bernard was again at Clairvaux, striving to shut
out the world, and to be left with his own thoughts alone for a
season. For a season he succeeded, and the first twenty-six
sermons on the Canticles were the result.

In the "auditorium," or talking-room of the monastery—
sometimes in the morning, sometimes in the afternoon—
Bernard, surrounded by his white-cowled monks, delivered his
spiritual discourses—a very solemn business to all concerned.
Sermons must always, in their essence, resemble that for ever
memorable one, addressed in the prison cell at Athens to a
party of mourning friends, concerning that "journey" which
the speaker was about to make.[1] Sooner or later the journey
has to be made by all, and those who best realize that fact
are ever the least reluctant to hear discourse, "sermo," in
reference to it. To Bernard's hearers, whose lives were one
long, painful toil and endeavour after holiness and peace, the
address from the father abbot—who was believed to know
every incident of the Pilgrim's Progress they were attempting
to perform—came as a sweet pause of rest and reflection in the
midst of the labour of the steep ascent. Bernard preached
often, oftener than was usual among the Cistercians. He
scarcely allowed a day to pass without saying some words to
his monks. For this he gives several good reasons. "If I
address you," he says, "more frequently than is customary in
our order, I do not do so from presumption, but at the
expressed wish of the venerable abbots, my brethren, who
order me to do that which they would not generally permit to
themselves ; for they know that a different system and other

[1] Plat. Phaedon, cap. 5.

necessities are imposed on me. I should not, indeed, be speaking to you now, if I could be working with you. That would be perhaps more useful to you, and more acceptable to me. But such labour is denied me for my sins, by the multiplied infirmity of this burdensome body—of which ye are well aware—and also by the want of time. Please God that speaking, and not doing, I may be worthy to be found, if only the least, in the kingdom of heaven." [1]

The hour of the sermon varied, from early morning to approaching sunset. When Bernard was at home and well enough to preach, the assembly of grown, silent men would noiselessly gather in the auditorium, whether from the night's vigils and psalmody, or the day's labour in the hot fields. A strange company it must have been : the old, stooping monk, whose mortifications were nearly over—the young beginner, destined perhaps to pass half a century in painful self-denial —the lord of wide lands, and the peasant who had worked on them—one after another came in with soft glide and took their places, waiting for the man whose thoughts and conversation they verily believed came from another world. To them, in the year 1135, Bernard thus spoke :—

" Different things, my brethren, ought to be said to you, from what are said to men yet in the world, or, at least, the manner of saying them should be different. For he who adheres to the apostle's rule, feeds the latter with milk, not with meat. But the spiritual require a stronger fare, as the same apostle teaches also by his example, when he says— 'Which things also we speak, not in the words which man's wisdom teacheth, but which the Holy Ghost teacheth ; comparing spiritual things with spiritual :' and again—'Howbeit we speak wisdom among them which are perfect,' such as I firmly trust you are ; unless perchance you have for this long

---

[1] In Psal. Qui habitat, Sermo X., St. Bern. Op. vol. i. col. 856.

N

time devoted yourselves to heavenly studies, exercised your
senses, and meditated day and night on the law of God, in
vain.   Open your mouths, therefore, not for milk, but for
bread.   With Solomon there is bread, and that full beautiful
and savoury; I mean the book which is entitled the Song of
Songs; let it be brought forth and broken."

These are the words with which he begins the first sermon
of the series.   Bernard's mystical views on a mystical book of
the Old Testament would probably have but feeble attractions
for modern readers.   But his sermons on the Canticles are
extremely free and discursive, running off frequently into
long disquisitions and contemplations, which have little or no
connexion with the spiritual raptures of the Hebrew king.
Thus in the fifth sermon he discourses on spirits as follows:—

SERMON

*On the Four Orders of Spirits: that is, the Spirit of God,
of Angels, of Man, and of Beasts.*

" Four kinds of spirits are known to you: the animal, our
own, the angelic, and the divine.   To all of these a body
is necessary, either on account of itself, or on account of
another, or on account of both; excepting that One to whom
every creature, whether corporeal or spiritual, justly confesses and says, 'Thou art my God; Thou hast need of
none of my goods.'   Now the first spirit, that is of animals,
it is plain, is in such need of a body, that it cannot even
exist without it; for when the animal dies, that spirit ceases
at once both to vivify and to live.   But we live after the
body; still to us no access to those things by which we
live, happily, is open, except through the body.   He had
perceived this who said, 'The invisible things of God are
clearly seen, being understood by the things that are made;'
for, indeed, those things that are made, that is bodily and

visible things, except they be perceived by the instrumentality
of the body, come not within our knowledge. The spiritual
creature, therefore, which we are, must necessarily have a body,
without which it certainly will not gain that instruction which
is the only means whereby it may attain to those things by the
knowledge of which it is made blessed. If any one object to
me the case of regenerate little children, that leaving the body
without a knowledge of corporeal things, they are believed,
nevertheless, to pass to a blessed life, I answer briefly that
grace, not nature, confers this upon them. But for that, what
have I to do with God's miracles, I who am discussing things
natural ?

" Again, that celestial spirits have need of bodies is proved
by that true and plainly Divine sentence, 'Are they not all
ministering spirits, sent forth to minister unto them who shall be
heirs of salvation ? ' But how can they, without bodies, fulfil
their ministry, especially among those who have bodies ? In a
word, it belongs only to bodies to move about from one place
to another—a thing which, by undoubted and known authority,
angels are shown frequently to do. And so it came to pass
that they were seen of the fathers, and entered in unto them,
and ate with them, and washed their feet. Thus, both higher
and lower spirits require bodies of their own ; but only in
order that they may render assistance, not receive it. For
the animal, through the debt it owes of service, affords help
only to needs arising from temporal and corporeal necessities ;
therefore the spirit which is in it passes away with time, and
dies with the body. The servant, indeed, abideth not in the
house for ever, although those who use him well apply all the
profit of this temporal servitude to the gaining of things
eternal. But the angel is careful and quick in the freedom
of the spirit to discharge his office of compassion, showing
himself to mortal men, his fellow-citizens and joint heirs of
heavenly bliss, a prompt and ready minister of good things to

come. Both the animal, then, that he may serve us from obligation, and the angel that he may assist us from pity, have need of their bodies in order to afford us help. For I do not see how they themselves are benefited by them as regards the gain of eternity. The irrational spirit, although it lays hold of corporeal things by means of its body, yet is never so far assisted by its body, that, through the corporeal and sensible things which it perceives by it, it can progress and attain to spiritual and intelligible things. Nevertheless, for the attainment of these things, the animal, it is known, by its corporeal and temporal obedience, helps those who, using this world as though they used it not, transfer all use of temporal things to the profit of things eternal.

" Moreover, the heavenly spirit, without help from the body, or the perception of those things which are felt through the body, simply by the vivacity and kinship of its nature to them, is able to apprehend the highest things and penetrate the deepest. Was not this the apostle's meaning when, after saying, 'The invisible things of God are clearly seen, being understood by the things that are made,' he adds immediately, 'by the creature of the world'? Surely because they are not so by the creature of heaven.[1] For what the spirit, inhabitant of earth, and clothed in flesh, strives painfully, and by slow degrees, to attain, that the dweller in the heavens, by his natural subtlety and sublimity, can swiftly and easily reach, without help from body or member, and uninstructed by the perception of any corporeal thing. Why should such a spirit search out spiritual meanings among bodies, while he can read in the book of life without contradiction, and understand without difficulty? Why, in the sweat of his brow, should

[1] St. Paul had a very different meaning when he wrote ἀπὸ κτίσεως κόσμου (from the time of the creation).—See Alford and Jowett, in loc. St. Bernard was misled into this fanciful argument by the Vulgate, which has " a creatura mundi."

he labour to thrash grain, make wine, press oil, who has abundance of all ready to his hand? Who would beg his food from door to door, having plenty in his own house? Who would dig a well, and seek for veins of water in the bowels of the earth, if a living spring of limpid waters gushed up for him spontaneously? Therefore neither the brutish nor the angelical spirit, in the acquirement of those things which render a spiritual creature blessed, are helped by their bodies : the first, from natural stolidity, not being equal to it ; the latter, by his pre-eminence of exceeding glory, not requiring it.

" But the spirit of man, which holds a certain mean between the highest and the lowest places, must necessarily have a body for both purposes, to help others and to be helped itself. For, to say nothing of the other members of the body or of their duties, how, I ask, could you instruct a hearer if you had not a tongue, or comprehend without ears the words of an instructor ?

" Hence it is clear that every created spirit, whether to help or to be helped, has need of a body. What if some animals, as far as the use of them is concerned, are found to be inconvenient and ill suited to human needs ? They are good to look at, if not to use ; more profitable to the hearts of those who gaze on them than to the bodies of those who use them. Although they be hurtful, although they be pernicious to human safety in this world, still their bodies do not lack that which worketh together for good to those who, according to the purpose, are called saints. For although they be not killed for food, nor apt to render service, yet verily they exercise the wit, agreeably to that benefit of common discipline which presides over all methods of putting things in use, by which ' the invisible things of God are clearly seen, being understood by the things that are made.' For the devil and his satellites, having always a malignant intention, are ever anxious

to work mischief; but God forbid they should succeed against
the followers of good, of whom it is said, 'And who is he
that will harm you if ye be followers of that which is good?'
Yea, rather they assist, though unwilling, and work together for
good to the good.

"On the other hand, whether the angelic bodies be natural
to the spirits themselves, as men's bodies are to them; whether
the animal bodies be, like men, immortal, although they are
not men; whether they can change and alter their bodies in
form and appearance when they wish to appear, densifying
and solidifying them as they choose, naturally being of such
subtle and impalpable substance as to be imperceptible to our
senses, or whether, abiding in their simple spiritual state, they
put on bodily forms when they want them, casting them aside
again when they have served their purpose, suffering them to
dissolve into the material from which they—the bodily forms
—were taken; these are points on which I would rather not
speak.   The fathers appear to have held diverse opinions
respecting them.   I do not see clearly which I ought to teach,
and confess I do not know.   I, moreover, do not think that a
knowledge of these subtleties will assist you much in your
progress.   But bear this in mind, that no spirit can by itself
reach unto our minds; that is, supposing it to have no assistance from our body or its own.   No spirit can so mix with,
and be poured into us, that we become in consequence either
learned or good.   No angel, no soul, can comprehend me;
none can I comprehend in this manner.   Even angels themselves do not thus seize each other's thoughts,—*i.e.* without
bodily organs.   This prerogative is reserved for the highest
and unbounded Spirit, who alone, when He imparts knowledge
either to angel or man, does not need that we should have
ears to hear, or that He should have a mouth to speak.
By Himself He is poured in; by Himself He is made manifest.
Pure Himself, He is understood by the pure.   He alone needs

nothing ; alone sufficient to Himself and to all by His sole
omnipotent will.

" Yet He works things immense and numerous by means of
the subject creature, be it corporeal or spiritual : but as commanding, not as entreating. To give an example. He has at
this moment taken my tongue to do His work—that is, to teach
you ; whereas He could doubtless have done it far more easily
and sweetly Himself. This, therefore, is condescension, not
indigence. In your progress He is seeking my merit, not
assistance for Himself. This it behoves every man who
worketh good to become convinced of, lest he should glory in
himself of the Lord's goods, and not in the Lord. It is
possible for a bad man or a bad angel to do good unwillingly ; and it is clear that the good which is done by such a
one is not done for him, seeing that no good can be of service
to one unwilling to work it. Therefore the dispensation alone
is entrusted to him. But, I know not how, we feel the good
done by an evil minister to be more grateful and pleasant ; and
that is the reason why God often does good to the just by
the medium of evil men, not that He needs their assistance in
doing good.

" As regards those beings which are void of sense or reason,
who can doubt that God needs them much less ? but when
they concur in the performance of a good work, then it appears
how all things serve Him who can justly say, ' The world is
Mine, and the fulness thereof.' Assuredly, seeing that He
knows the means best adapted to ends, He does not in the
service of His creatures seek efficacy, but suitability. Supposing, in the next place, that the greater part of the Divine
work is carried on by means of corporeal agents,—as, for
example, in the case of rain falling to quicken the seeds, or to
increase the crops, or to ripen the fruit,—I would ask, what
need of a body has He to whom the universe of bodies in
heaven and earth yields an instant obedience ? Clearly He

would find a body of His own superfluous, to whom no body is alien.   But if I tried to embrace in the present sermon all that occurs to me on this head, it would exceed its proper limits and, may be, the strength of some ; therefore I reserve for another occasion what remains unsaid on this."

The next sermon contains also some passages well worth quoting. The following paragraphs, taken from the conclusion, are all that can be given here :—

"But I must not pass over in silence those spiritual feet of God, which, in the first place, it behoves the penitent to kiss in a spiritual manner.   I well know your curiosity, which does not willingly allow anything obscure to pass by it ; nor indeed is it a contemptible thing to know what are those feet which the Scripture so frequently mentions in connexion with God. Sometimes He is mentioned as standing on them, as 'We will worship in the place where Thy feet have stood ;' sometimes as walking, as 'I will dwell in them and will walk in them;' sometimes even as running, as 'He rejoiceth as a strong man to run a race.'   If it appear right to the apostle to call the head of Christ God, it appears to me as not unnatural to consider His feet as representing man ; one of which I shall name mercy, and the other judgment.   Those two words are known to you, and the Scripture makes mention of them in many places.

On these two feet, fitly moving under one Divine head, Christ, born of a woman, He who was invisible under the law, then made Emmanuel [God with us], was seen on the earth, and conversed with men.   Of a truth, He even now passes amongst us, relieving and healing those oppressed by the devil ; but spiritually and invisibly.   With these feet, I say, He walks through devout minds, incessantly purifying and searching the hearts and reins of the faithful.

"Happy is that mind in which the Lord Jesus has placed

both of these feet. You may recognise that mind by these two signs, which it must necessarily bear as the marks of the Divine footprints. These are hope and fear; the first representing the image of judgment, the other of mercy. Justly doth the Lord take pleasure in them that fear Him, in those that hope in His mercy; seeing that fear is the beginning of wisdom, of which also hope is the incease, and charity the consummation. These things being so, in this first kiss which is received at the feet is not a little fruit; only be careful that you are not robbed of either kiss. If you are pricked by the pain of sin and the fear of judgment, you have pressed your lips on the foot of judgment and truth. If you temper this fear and pain by regarding the Divine goodness, and by the hope of forgiveness, you may know that you have embraced the foot of mercy. It profits not to kiss one without the other, because the dwelling on judgment only casts you into the abyss of desperation, while a deceitful trust in mercy generates the worst kind of security.

" To me also, wretched one, it has been given sometimes to sit beside the feet of the Lord Jesus, and with all devotion to embrace first one, then the other, as far as His loving-kindness condescended to permit me. But if ever, forgetful of mercy, through the stings of conscience I have dwelt too long on the thought of judgment, at once cast down with incredible fear and confusion, enveloped in dark shadows of horror, breathless from out of the deeps I cried, 'Who knoweth the power of Thy wrath? and through fear of Thee who can reckon Thy displeasure?' If it has chanced that I have then clung too closely to the foot of mercy, after forsaking the other, such carelessness and indifference have come upon me, that my prayers have grown cold, my work has been neglected, my speech has been less cautious, my laughter more ready, and the whole state of both my outer and inner man less firm. Learning then from experience, not judgment alone, nor mercy alone, but mercy and judgment together, will I sing unto Thee, O Lord : I will never forget those justifications; they both shall be my song in the house of my pilgrimage, until mercy being exalted above judgment, then misery shall cease, and my glory shall sing to Thee for ever, and not be silent."

A little while after this sermon, Bernard delivered others, " On the Three Spiritual Ointments : that is to say, Contrition, Devotion, and Compassion." The subject was pursued through three sermons: the second is given here.

SERMON

On Two Things [i.e. the mode and the result] pertaining to Human Redemption.

"I said at the conclusion of my last sermon, and I do not mind repeating it, that I wish all of you to be partakers of the sacred anointing ; of that one, viz., in which a holy devotion remembers the goodness of God with joy and thanksgiving. For this it is good to do, both because it lightens the labours of this present life, which become more tolerable to us whilst we exult in praise of God ; and also because nothing so fitly images in this world a certain condition of the celestial habitations, as they who are swift to praise God. As the Scripture saith, 'Blessed are they that dwell in Thy house, O Lord : they will be alway praising Thee.' It is of this ointment especially that I believe the prophet spake : 'Behold how good and joyful a thing it is for brethren to dwell together in unity ! it is like ointment upon the head.' This cannot refer to the former ointment ; for that, although it be good, is not pleasant also, because the remembrance of sins bringeth bitterness, not joy. Nor do they who make it live together, when each one laments and deplores his own particular sins. But those who are steadfast in thanksgiving behold and think of God alone, and by this very fact live together in unity. What they do is good, for they most rightly give glory to Him whose it is ; and it is pleasant also, for it gives them joy.

" Therefore I exhort you, my friends, to leave for a season the painful and anxious remembrance of your ways, to strike away into the softer parts of memory, and dwell on the loving-kindness of God, that you who are confounded in yourselves may recover by gazing on Him. I wish you to experience that which the holy prophet advised, saying, ' Delight thou in the Lord, and He shall give thee thy heart's desire.' Now grief over sin is necessary, if it be not constant ; it must be broken by the more joyful remembrance of the Divine goodness, lest the heart grow hardened through sadness, and from despair perish more exceedingly. Let us mix honey with our worm-wood, in order that the wholesome bitter, tempered by the added sweetness, may be swallowed, and give us health. Listen how God softens the bitterness of a contrite heart, how He recalls the faint-hearted from the pit of despair, how through the honey of pleasant and faithful promises He consoles the sorrowful and establishes the weak. He says by the prophet, ' I will bridle thy mouth with My praises, lest thou perish.' This means, lest by the sight of thy wickedness thou be too much cast down, and even like an unbridled horse thou rush head-long and perish desperately. With the bridle, He says, of My indulgence will I restrain thee, and will raise thee up with My praises ; thou who art confounded with thine own evil shalt breathe again in My good, and shalt surely find My mercy is greater than thy sin. If Cain had been so restrained, he would never have said in despair, ' My sin is too great for me to be forgiven.'[1] God forbid ! God forbid ! for His loving-kindness is greater than any iniquity. Wherefore the just man, not throughout, but only in the beginning of his discourse is a self-accuser, while he is wont to close with the praises of God. See, thus doeth the righteous man : ' I thought,' he says, ' on

[1] Vulgate.

my ways, and I turned my feet to Thy testimonies.' That is, having found sorrow and misery in his own ways, he took delight in the way of God's testimonies, as in all manner of riches. Follow ye the example of the just ; if ye think of yourselves in humility, think also of the Lord in His mercy and goodness. Now this becomes easy to the mind, if we preserve a frequent, nay a constant, recollection of the Divine kindness. Otherwise, how shall we obey the saying of the apostle, "In everything give thanks," if those things for which thanks are due vanish from the mind? I would not have you deserve the reproach earned by the Jews, of whom it is declared that they forgat His works, and the wonders that He had showed them.

"But seeing that the good which the kind and merciful Lord ceases not to shower on mortals cannot all be remembered by man—for who can utter the mighty acts of the Lord? who can show forth all His praise?—let that which is chief and greatest—the work, namely, of our redemption—never fade from the memory of the redeemed. In this work there are two points which in a special manner I will offer to your attention, and this as briefly as may be, being mindful of that saying, 'Give instruction to a wise man, and he will be yet wiser.' These two things, then, are the manner and the fruit, or result, of our redemption. Now the manner is the emptying out or humbling of God; the fruit thereof is our being filled with Him. To dwell on the last is a seed-plot of holy hope ; to think of the former an incentive to the highest love. Both are necessary to our progress, that hope without love should not grow sordid, nor love wax cold, hoping for no return.

"But indeed we expect such a return for our love as He whom we love has promised us : 'Good measure, pressed down, and shaken together, and running over, shall men give into your bosom.' That measure I hear will be without measure. But I would fain know of what is that measure to consist, or rather that immensity which is promised in return. Eye hath not seen, O God, besides Thee, the things that Thou hast prepared for them that love Thee. Tell us, then, Thou who preparest, what Thou preparest. We believe, we trust, it will be such as Thou dost promise. ' We shall be filled with the good things of Thy house.' But which good things, and of what kind? Is it with corn, wine, and oil, with gold and silver, or precious stones? But these we see and know, we see and despise them. That we seek which eye hath not seen, nor ear heard, neither hath it entered into the heart of man to conceive. This pleases, this is sweet, this delights us to inquire concerning it, whatever it may be. And they all shall be taught of God; and He will be all in all. As I understand, the fulness which we expect from God will not be except of God.

" But who can grasp the magnitude of delight comprehended in that short word, God will be all in all? Not to speak of the body, I perceive three things in the soul—reason, will, memory; and these three make up the soul. How much each of these in this present world lacks of completion and perfectness is felt by every one who walketh in the Spirit. Wherefore is this, except because God is not yet all in all? Therefore it is that our reason falters in judgment, that our will is feeble and distracted, that our memory confounds us by its forgetfulness. We are subjected unwillingly to this threefold weakness, but hope abides. For He who fills with good things the desires of the soul, He himself will be to the reason the fulness of light; to the will the abundance of peace; to the memory the unbroken smoothness of eternity. O truth! O charity! O eternity! O blessed and blessing trinity! to thee my miserable trinity miserably groans, while it is in exile from thee. Departing from thee, in what errors, griefs, and fears is it involved! Alas, for what a trinity have we exchanged thee

away.   My heart is disturbed, and hence my grief; my strength
has forsaken me, and hence my fear ; the light of my eyes is
not with me, and hence my error.   O trinity of my soul! what
a changed trinity dost thou show me in mine exile?

"'But why art thou cast down, O my soul? and why art
thou disquieted within me?   Hope thou in God, for I shall
yet praise Him': that is, when error shall have left my mind,
sorrow my will, fears my memory, and serenity, sweetness, and
eternal peace shall have come in their stead.   The first of these
things will be done by the God of truth, the second by the
God of charity, the third by the God of omnipotence, that God
may be all in all : the reason receiving light inextinguishable,
the will peace imperturbable, the memory cleaving to a fountain which shall never fail.   You may judge for yourselves
whether you would rightly assign the first to the Son, the second
to the Holy Ghost, and the last to the Father; in such a manner, however, that you take away nothing of any of them, either
from the Father, or the Son, or the Holy Ghost.

"As regards the manner of our redemption, which, if you
remember, we defined as the emptying out or humbling of God,
there are three points I commend to your notice.   It was not a
simple or moderate humbling, but He humbled Himself even to
taking flesh, even to death, to death on the cross.   Who can
measure the humility, gentleness, and condescension which
moved the Lord of Majesty to put on flesh, to be punished
with death, to be disgraced by the cross ?   But some one may
say, could not the Creator repair His work without that difficulty?
He could ; but He chose to do it with His own injury, rather
than that the foulest and most odious vice of ingratitude should
again find its place in man.   He took upon Him much fatigue,
that He might hold man His debtor to much love, and that the
difficulty of redemption might remind man of thanksgiving,
whom an easier condition had made less devout.   For what
was created and ungrateful man wont to say? 'I was made

indeed free of charge, but with no labour or effort to my Maker.' 'He spake the word and I was made, as all things were.' 'Nothing is great, if it only costs a word.' Thus human wickedness, attenuating the benefit of creation, found food for ingratitude where it ought to have discovered a source of love, and that to make an excuse for sin. But the mouth of the evil speaker is stopped. It is clearer than daylight now, O man, what an outlay He has made for you. From the Lord He became a servant; from rich He became poor; from the Word, flesh; from the Son of God, the Son of man. Remember now, that though you were made from nothing, you were not redeemed for nothing. In six days He made all things, and you among them; but for thirty whole years He wrought at your salvation in the midst of the earth. What did He not endure in His labours? Necessities of the flesh, temptations of the enemy,—did He not gather and heap all these on Himself by the ignominy of the cross, by the horror of His death? Not without necessity indeed. Thus, thus, Thou, Lord, shalt save both man and beast. 'How excellent is Thy mercy, O God.' Meditate on these things, dwell upon them. Draw refreshment from these spices for your inward parts, long tormented by the reek of your sins, that you may abound also in these ointments, not less sweet than salutary. Still, do not suppose that you yet possess those best of all which are praised in the breast of the Spouse. These cannot be spoken of now, the sermon must be finished. What has been said concerning the other ointments, keep it in your memory, try in your life; and concerning these which are to follow, help me with your prayers, that it be given to me to speak something which shall be worthy of these delights of the Spouse, and able to build up your souls to a love of the Bridegroom, our Lord Jesus Christ. Amen."[1]

[1] St. Bern. Op. vol. i. col. 1294.

CHAPTER III.

(A.D. 1136.   AETAT. 45.)

CONVERTS AT CLAIRVAUX—FREEDOM OF SPEECH IN THE MIDDLE
AGES—LETTERS TO POPE INNOCENT II. AND OTHERS—DEATH OF
LOUIS VI.

IT was partly to hear such sermons as these that men came to
Clairvaux.   The whole fact and its circumstances are difficult
to realize now.   Far off, indeed, is the entire meaning and
motive of monkery from modern European thought.   Self-
mortification has few practisers, or even admirers, at the
present day, when it is justly thought that, in a world so full of
work waiting to be done, a man can employ himself in a more
profitable manner than by diminishing his sleep and food,
singing all night and holding his tongue all day.   The modern
man, as a general rule, is occupied in a long, vigorous life-
struggle with external nature, subjecting and compelling the
elements to yield a prompt obedience to his will.   Thought, as
such, thought which does not at least promise to aid in this
great object, is not very favourably regarded ; speculation
which leads to no very tangible result is rather impatiently dis-
missed, as being, probably, idleness with a fine name.   There
can be little doubt of the fact, whatever inferences it may
suffice to sustain, that the tendency of the modern mind is to
give a marked approval to the practical as opposed to the
speculative.   But if the philosopher is warned of the existence
of this tendency—if the thinker, whose views, though they be

derided as chimerical to-day, may to-morrow make their weight
felt in trade and politics—if these are reminded of the hurry
mankind have got into just now, what treatment may the monk
expect to receive? In truth, the treatment he deserves, as a
useless loiterer, a relic of the old time, superfluous or obstructive in the new. The raft which served well down the
river is of small avail when we get to the ocean. The social
contrivances of the twelfth century are not a little out of place
in the nineteenth.

But this "conquest of nature," this "practical science," are
modern, and the Middle Ages had no suspicion of them
Dominion over nature, except it was miraculous, was not
dreamed of then. There was, indeed, much more urgent
work to do—viz. acquiring dominion over man. It must be
remembered that although then men were called Christians,
their remove from the savage was of the shortest. Work was
not their pleasure, but their detestation; not to make, but to
destroy, was their delight. Not self-control nor humanity were
their characteristics, but ferocity, lawlessness, and revenge.
To tame these fierce natures was a long and difficult task, and
no little debt of gratitude is owing to those who did it, whatever were the means they found it necessary to employ. Even
in those times men were born "who were a law unto themselves," men in whom the carnivorous instinct did not pre-
dominate; and these men gradually transferred the law and
harmony they found in their own minds and hearts into the
confused world around them. First of all they renounced the
world, as they said; they drew a sharp line of demarcation
between themselves and the outer darkness; they lived apart,
—that is, they lived in monasteries; they saw men's passions
consuming them like the flames of hell, they extinguished in
themselves the simplest instincts of human nature; excess
begetting excess, according to the law of reaction. Asceticism
is not needed nor appreciated now, because daily life offers no

revolting wickedness to recoil from.   In the twelfth century it was the only kind of protest which told with sufficient force. The era for work, as now understood, had not yet come.   In the higher, or perhaps highest, sense the work done by the Bernards, the Brunos, and the Norberts, was as important as the world has seen.

The way in which the small nucleus of law and order which survived in the monasteries attracted to itself individuals from the feudal confusion around is curious to observe.   These man-slaying barons were drawn into the monastic life very often as by a force they could not resist.   They hovered near the abbey half knowing, half dreading, their fate, retired from it, and then returned, as a moth to a candle, with increased haste.   Many are the histories preserved of such "conversions;" of a party of knights riding to a tournament, to a fair, and putting up over-night at the welcome and opportune monastery.   In the morning they leave, having spent a quieter night than is usual with them ; by some of the company the solemnity, order, and peace of the convent have not been witnessed in vain ; the psalm-singing, the ceremonies, and the music of the frequent bells, have sent strange emotions of gentleness and awe into one or two, who perhaps noticed some old companion or enemy in arms now shouting Gregorian chants instead of battle-cries.   The barbarian, yet childishly simple, mind is struck : first of all it believes—intensely and utterly believes—that all those monks are going to heaven. That point is certain ; whereas the barbarian mind is conscious of no such certainty as regards itself; anticipates, perhaps with good reason, the opposite of heaven.   In the next place, the monastery is as pleasant, taken altogether, as the castle ; the choir is not worse than the camp, or it may be the dungeon. Such reflections often made, often interrupted, at last get a permanent hold ; and a visit then to any monastery of which the abbot, like Bernard, is a "fisher of men," suffices to consummate what they have begun.   Thus, on one occasion, fifteen young German nobles, on their way from the schools of Paris, stopped for the night at Morimond.   In their company was Otho, son of Leopold, Margrave of Austria.   After being received with the usual forms of monastic hospitality, they retired to bed, but not to rest.   The Abbot Walter, a worthy disciple of Bernard, had made a deep impression on them; the psalms the monks were singing when they arrived still rang in their ears; the bell which called the community to matins summoned them also from their sleepless beds.   They found they had all had the same reflections and the same unrest; they sent for the Abbot Walter, and begged leave to become his monks.[1]

More remarkable still was the conversion of Henry of France, son of Louis VI.   Henry came one day to Clairvaux to speak with Bernard on some secular business.   Seeing the monks assembled, he commended himself to their prayers. Bernard said to him: "I trust in the Lord that you will not die in the state in which you now are, but rather that you will soon test by your own experience what these prayers which you have just asked for can effect for you."   A little while afterwards, on the very same day, Henry astounded the whole convent by declaring his intention of becoming a monk.   His suite and companions were beyond measure astonished at so sudden a change: one especially, Andrew of Paris, surpassed all the rest in his indignant disgust; he declared that Prince Henry was drunk, that he was mad, and expressed his vexation in language from which blasphemy was not excluded.[2]   Henry

---

[1] Histoire de l'Abbaye de Morimond, par l'Abbé Dubois, p. 61. Paris, 1852.

[2] " Quod [*i.e.* his conversion] eodem postmodum die non absque multorum admiratione completum est, et de tanti juvenis conversione coenobium omni exultatione reple-tum. Lugentibus autem sociis, et familia tota, ac si mortuum illum cernerent, ejulante, prae caeteris Andreas quidam Parisiensis Henricum ebrium, Henricum vociferabatur in-sanum, nec conviciis nec blasphemiis parcens."—St. Bern. *Op.* vol, ii co!. 1136.

was grieved to see the violence of his friend, and implored
Bernard to take steps to procure his conversion also. "Leave
him alone," said Bernard ; "his soul is bitter now : but be not
troubled over much about him, for he is certainly yours."
Andrew heard these words of the abbot as he was standing by,
and heard them with scorn, for he was of a most unspiritual
turn of mind.   He thought within himself, "Now I know you
are a false prophet ; I know the word you have spoken will
never come to pass ; I will publish it everywhere, before the
king and his court, that your falsehood may be known to all."
Andrew, in after years, confessed that these were his reflections.
The next day he left, imprecating curses on a monastery in
which he had lost his master, and wishing that the valley and
all its inhabitants might be utterly destroyed.   His departure
astonished and even pained those who had heard Bernard's
confident predictions ; they expected to see his boldness and
blasphemy receive an open and stunning confutation on the
spot.   But God did not suffer "their little faith" to be tempted
long.   During the very next night Andrew was quite conquered :
he seemed to be drawn and forced by the Spirit of God to
return to the abbey ; he could not wait for the dawn ; before
daybreak he arose and flew to Clairvaux.   The monks likened
his conversion to that of St. Paul.[1]   From which it may be
inferred that his zeal as an ascetic equalled his vehemence as
a soldier.

Peace, doubtless, and great calm there were within the gates
of Clairvaux, for many who sought them like Prince Henry ;
but they were for the monks far more than for the great abbot,

---

[1] "Sed non diu pusillanimitatem
eorum et fidem modicam tentari pas-
sus est Deus.   Illa tantum die pro-
cedens et repellens quodammodo
gratiam Dei, nocte proxima victus
et quasi vinctus trahente se et vim
faciente Spiritu Dei, diem expectare
non potuit ; sed exsurgens ante dilu-
culum, velociterque rediens ad monasterium, alterum nobis Saulum vel
magis de Saulo altero Paulum alterum exhibebat."—St. Bern. *Op.*
vol. ii. col. 1136.

whose commanding personality had attracted them to a religious life. Although Bernard might descant on the heavenly joys in his sermons on the Canticles, and almost give his hearers a foretaste of divine peace in his mellifluous eloquence, yet peace and rest were never long to be his in this world; he might truly have said that on him rested the "care of all the churches." And not only churchmen, but all persons of distinction in Europe, seem to have thought that Bernard's time, attention, and influence were, or ought to be, at their disposal. Bishops in England, the Queen of Jerusalem, the Kings of France, Italy, and Britain, abbots and ecclesiastics without number, write to and receive letters from him. On a certain occasion Theobald, Archbishop of Canterbury, was prevented by a "tempest of wars"[1] from going to Rome to answer an unjust accusation: he prevailed on Bernard to excuse him to the Pope. Robert, Bishop of London, suffered much from an intruder into his see, who withheld from him certain lands and pledges belonging to his church: a single hint from Bernard placed the matter before the Pope, and doubtless had the desired effect. When Robert Pullen, the distinguished English scholastic, prolonged his stay at Paris according to Bernard's advice, Robert's diocesan, the Bishop of Rochester, was very wroth, and even rude to the Abbot of Clairvaux. "You are very hard upon me," writes the humble great man; "but what have I done amiss? I thought his sojourn in Paris necessary because of the sound learning which is in him, and I think so still. . . . . I beg and advise you to allow Master Robert to dwell some time longer at Paris."[2] But it is in his corre-

---

[1] Viz. the civil wars during King Stephen's reign, which might well be called by St. Bernard a "tempest of wars." Theobald was unjustly treated by Innocent, and his history amply justifies the complaints which the Abbot of Clairvaux thought himself called upon to address to the Pope in a letter which will be read in the next page.—BISHOP GODWIN, *De Praesulibus Angliae Commentarius.*

[2] Pullen was a worthy representative of English learning at this period, and one who has received more justice from foreigners than

spondence with the Pope that his manly, vehement spirit is best displayed. It is indeed, in a general way, a most notice-able fact—the freedom of speech and censure practised by the great churchmen of the Middle Ages, as compared with the dumb, unbroken submission of subsequent times. A prominent bishop or abbot, in the good period, if he sees an abuse or an injustice, never hesitates to denounce it with all his power, to call all men to witness against it, and to do what he can to get it removed. Even the mild and gentle Peter of Cluny does not refrain from strong language to the Pope on occasion. As for Bernard, he writes to Innocent in this manner :—

" I speak boldly because I love faithfully ; nor is that love sincere where any uncertainty keeps up suspicion. The com-plaints of my Lord of Treves are not confined to him alone, but are common to many others, and chiefly to those who have a sincere affection for your person. There is but one voice among our faithful bishops, which declares that justice is vanishing from the Church ; that the power of the keys is gone ; that episcopal authority is dwindling away ; that a bishop can no longer redress wrongs, nor chastise iniquity, however great, even in his own diocese ; and the blame of all this they lay on you and the Roman Court. What they ordain aright, you annul; what they justly abolish, that you re-establish. All the worthless contentious fellows, whether from the people or the clergy, or even monks expelled from their monasteries, run off to you, and return boasting that they have found protection,

from his own countrymen. He left England during the civil wars just mentioned, and had the honour of Bernard's friendship. On returning to his native country he devoted himself to the restoration of learning, which had suffered severely during the recent troubles. At Oxford he not only contributed the example of his zeal and acquirements to the cause of letters, but even assisted it largely at his own personal expense. His fame was wide-spread, and Inno-cent II. made him a cardinal—being the first Englishman, probably, who attained to that dignity in the Church. Of his writings, the " Sen-tentiarum Libri Octo " are the most noteworthy. They probably sug-gested to Peter Lombard the plan of his more renowned " Sentences."

when they ought to have found retribution. Your friends are confounded, the faithful are insulted, the bishops are brought into contempt and disgrace ; and while their righteous judgments are despised, your authority also is not a little injured.

"Yet it is these men who care for your honour, who faithfully, but I fear unsuccessfully, labour for your peace and exaltation. Why do you diminish your own power? The church of St. Gengulfus, at Toul, deplores her desolation, nor is there any one to comfort her. St. Paul, at Verdun, complains that he is exposed to violence, the archbishop being no longer able to defend him from the rudeness of the monks, who, as if forsooth they were not bold enough without it, are encouraged by apostolic support. . . . . God's favour is not so won. For these and similar things 'the anger of the Lord is not yet turned away, but His arm is stretched out still,' and that rod spoken of by Jeremiah, which watches over our sins. Of a truth, God is angry with schismatics ; but He is far from well pleased with Catholics. The church at Metz, as you well know, is in great jeopardy, through the dissension between the bishop and the clerks. I suppose you know what it will please you to decide on that subject ; but peace is not there, nor is there room to hope it will be there for some time to come. It seems to me that in all these cases the metropolitan, who knows all the points in dispute, who is a faithful and esteemed servant of the Church, can bring matters to a happy conclusion better than anybody else. Otherwise you will have to see what is to be done with those bishoprics,—that is to say, those of Metz and Toul. For, to say the truth, they appear to be without bishops now : would that they were also without tyrants as well. Many wonder, many are scandalized, when such men as these bishops are defended, supported, honoured, protected ; men whose lives and morals are infamous to a pitch that would disgrace, I do not say bishops, but any laymen you please. I am ashamed to write this, nor ought you to have ever heard it. Granted that, while no one accused them, they could not be deposed, I ask, Ought those whom general rumour denounces to be the special objects of favour and promotion from the holy see?

"I should fear the charge of presumption for writing this, if I forgot to whom I was writing, or were myself unknown to him.   But I know your inborn gentleness ; and the affection I bear to you, which prompts me to this, is known to you. . . . Again, to return to the Archbishop of Treves, that you may know how to receive both his messenger and his message. I declare to you that he holds a great place in that country, is a firm and a faithful friend to you and the Church of God, by no means a favourer of turbulent, evil-minded persons, of whom he is often enough sorely tempted.   Nor will he now lack insult from the same quarter, if you pay no regard to him.   I wished in conclusion to commend the messenger who carries this.   But his own merits sufficiently do that, besides an especial love and devotion to yourself, at least as I firmly believe ; otherwise I should never have made him the bearer of such intimate and familiar remarks."[1]

The admirers of Ultramontanism may see, by this letter, what one who yielded to none in devotion to religion thought of the first encroachments of that gigantic centralization which has ended by making popery and catholicism interchangeable terms.   They may trace, if they choose, from this point, the gradual suffocation of liberty under the Roman despot, through the unblushing venality of the great schism, the pagan profligacy of the Borgias, the desperate Machiavellism of the sixteenth century, even to the pitiful senility of the nineteenth.

Henry, Archbishop of Sens, also fell under the lash of Bernard's anger :—"I admit I have often interceded, in consequence of your conduct, in favour of many persons, and I had

[1] St. Bern. Epist. 178.

determined to do so no **more, by** reason of your hateful cruelty.
But charity prevails.   I wish to retain your friends for you
This you disdain.   I should be glad to reconcile to you your
enemies.   You will not suffer it.   **You are** determined not to
have peace ; **you** seek, you summon, your confusion, your
destruction, yea, your deposition.   **You** multiply your accusers ;
you diminish your defenders.   You excite against yourself old
dissensions that have been allayed.   You provoke your adver-
saries ; you offend your friends.   Your own self-will is your **law.**
All you do is for your ambition, never from the fear of God.
Which of your enemies does not laugh ?   Which of your friends
does not weep?   How have you dared to despoil a man, I
do not say uncondemned, but not even **accused ?   How many**
will be scandalized at this?   How many tongues **will scoff?**
How many hearts will swell with anger?   **Do you think that**
justice has vanished from the whole **world, even as it has from**
your heart, that a man can thus be deprived of his archdeaconry?
. . . . . Do not, do not do this thing, which all will wonder
at, none will praise.   I have written more clearly and boldly
than you may like to **hear,** but perhaps not unwisely for you,
if you are willing to mend." [1]

In striking contrast to these fiery effusions are those tokens
of love and tenderness which Bernard, from time to time, found
leisure to send to **absent friends.   Then** the thunder-clouds
and lightnings have passed away from his mind, and a serene
deep heaven of affection is laid bare.   **Here is a good** letter
to a man he had never seen :—

"Although your face is unknown to me, you are not.   Fame
has told me of you, nor is it a small or vulgar part of you which
I rejoice to possess through her means.   For, to confess the
truth, most beloved brother, such is the picture formed of you
in my mind, that even though I be occupied with many things,
the serene thought of you will **so lay** hold of me and win me to

[1] St. Bern. Epist. 182.

itself, that I willingly dwell upon it, and find a sweet rest therein.   But then the more I welcome you in mental vision, the more I desire your bodily presence.   But when will that be?   This at least is certain, that if we meet not before, we shall do so in the city of our God; that is, if we have not here an abiding city, but are seeking for that other one.   There, there shall we see face to face, and our hearts shall rejoice. In the meantime, these things which I hear of you shall still be my delight, and for the remainder, *i.e.* the sight of you in the body, I shall hope and expect it in the day of the Lord, that my joy may be full.   Please to add, dearest father, to those good things which are constantly coming to us from you, your prayers for us, and those of your monks." [1]

In some editions this little drop of love and friendship is directed to the Abbot of St. Alban's, in others to the Abbot of St. Albin, in Anjou.   One could wish it had been to the English house that this little epistle was written.   In that wild, stormy time, across the broad countries and the rough seas, under the influence of a truly "Catholic faith" in the good and true, two separated human hearts shoot a bright, warm ray of kindness across the dark.

This also to a young abbot, a disciple and friend, is characteristic and good :—

"The letter you have sent is redolent of your love to me, and has stirred up mine towards you.   I cannot write an answer such as I am moved to do.   But I will not waste time on excuses, seeing that I am writing to one who is wise.   You know the load I groan under, and my sighing is not hid from you.   And you, at least, will not estimate by the shortness of a letter an affection which no words could ever declare.   The number and importunity of my occupations may indeed be a cause that I write little, but never that I love little.   One action may interfere with, and even exclude, another, but it

[1] St. Bern. Epist. 204.

can never prevent the flow of feeling. As a mother loves her only son, even so did I love you, when you clave to my side, and rejoiced my heart. And now I will love you when far from me, lest I should appear to have loved my own comfort in you, and not you yourself. You were indeed necessary to me. And from this fact it may be plainly seen how sincerely I love you. At this very time, indeed, I should not have been without you, if I had sought my own interest. But now you see, forgetting my own advantage, I have not envied you your gains, seeing I have so placed you that in time you may be set over all the goods of your Lord.

"And now be careful to be found a wise and faithful servant, and communicate the heavenly bread to your fellow-servants without envy or idleness. Do not take up the vain excuse of your rawness or inexperience, which you may imagine or assume. For sterile modesty is never pleasing, nor that humility laudable, which passes the bounds of reason. Attend to your work ; drive out bashfulness by a sense of duty, and act as a master. You are young, yet you are a debtor ; you may know you were a debtor from the day you were bound. Will youth be an excuse to a creditor for the loss of his profits ? Does the usurer expect no interest at the beginning of his loan ? But I am not sufficient for these things, say you. As if your offering were not accepted from what you have, and not from what you have not. Be prepared to answer for the single talent committed to your charge, and take no thought for the rest. 'If thou hast much, give plenteously ; if thou hast little, do thy diligence gladly to give of that little.' For he that is unjust in the least is unjust also in much. Give all, as assuredly you shall pay to the uttermost farthing ; but of a truth out of what you have, not out of what you have not.

"Take heed to give to your words the voice of power. What is that, do you ask ? It is, that your works harmonize with your words, or rather your words with your works ; that you be careful to *do* before you teach. It is a most beautiful and salutary order of things that you should first bear the burden you place on others, and learn from yourself how men should be ruled. Otherwise the wise man will mock you, as that lazy one to whom it is labour to lift his hand to his mouth. The Apostle also will reprove you, saying, 'Thou which teachest another, teachest thou not thyself?' . . . . That speech, also, which is full of life and power is an example of work, as it makes easy what it speaks persuasively, while it shows that can be done which it advises. Understand, therefore, to the quieting of your conscience, that in these two commandments, *i.e.* of precept and example, the whole of your duty resides. You, however, if you be wise, will add yet a third, namely a zeal for prayer, to complete that treble repetition of the Gospel concerning feeding the sheep. You will then know that no sacrament of that trinity is in any wise broken by you, if you feed them by word, by example, and by the fruit of holy prayers. Now abideth speech, example, prayer, these three; but the greatest of these is prayer. For although, as it has been said, the strength of speech is work, yet prayer wins grace and efficacy for both work and speech.

"Alas! I am carried, I am torn away, I may not go on. Yet one word more; it is this: I entreat you to relieve me as soon as may be from an anxious care, and to declare clearly what you mean by the wound you complain of, among other things, 'from one of whom you did not expect such a thing,' for that has given me great concern."[1]

Shall we not say that this, whether monk or not, was a broad, strong, and good man? Here is "culture" in the highest sense. Monasticism, as practised by Bernard, was temporary, caducous, and charged with germs of evil, which in time overcame the good. But that it had a soul of goodness is very manifest, or Bernard could not have grown up to the

---

[1] St. Bern. Epist. 201.

height he did **under its shelter.** The drill, the stoicism, the
order, the association, and the solitude, driven to an excess
of caricature by the old monks, yet still realized by them,
are too valuable **to** be lost for ever. We have not so much
good that **we** can afford to throw **much away** because it
is old.

In writing some hundreds of letters such as the above did
Bernard spend his leisure time at Clairvaux. He will **soon**
have to leave his fair valley again, though he can **never do so**
without a pang of regret. But Anacletus, at Rome, and Roger
of Sicily are still troublesome, and he must go to Italy again.
It seems understood that he alone can put things straight when
they **go wrong.**

But the melancholy condition of **Louis VI. of France must**
be **noticed before** Bernard starts **on his journey across the**
Alps.

In spite **of** all his campaigning and jousting, Louis had
grown so fat that he could hardly move about. He sorely
grieved over his lost activity, and gave vent to his feelings in
moral reflections such as these :—" Alas, how miserable is the
lot of man, who rarely, or never, has knowledge and the ability
to carry it into effect **at the same time. As a young man, I**
was strong but ignorant ; as an old man, I am wise but weak.
Verily, if I had ever been strong, and, at the same time, wise,
most completely would I have conquered many **kingdoms."**
Still his fightings **and** disputes **with** the **King of** England
and Count Theobald continued as before. Exhausted and
unwieldy from his excessive corpulence, and nearly confined to
his bed by **a** wound in the leg, **he** nevertheless attacked Theobald with **much** of his old vigour. He burnt the town of
Bonneval, " except the cloister **of the** monks, which he protected." On another occasion **he** destroyed Château Renard,
sending a party of his men for **the** purpose, as he was too
unwell to **go** himself. But his **last** expedition was near at

hand, the last castle he was to burn was near being burned.[1]
With a most noble army " he attacked the Château of Saint
Brisson on the Loire, to punish the rapacity of its owner in
plundering merchants." He " dissolved it by fire, and compelled both the lord and the tower to capitulate."

The exertion he made on this occasion brought on an attack
of diarrhœa, to which he was not unfrequently subject. He
soon became greatly alarmed about himself, and reflected on
the state of his soul with much anxiety. He prayed and
confessed with earnestness. He had but one strong wish, and
that was to be carried to the shrine of St. Denis, and, before
the sacred relics, to lay aside all regal state, and replace it by
the frock and cowl of a Benedictine monk. His friend and
minister Suger, abbot as he was, was apt, in courts and camps,
occasionally to discard a good deal of his ecclesiastical character. But in this instance his pride as a monk was roused
within him. After narrating the above facts concerning his
dying friend and king, he says with quite an air of triumph,
" Let the detractors of monastic poverty see from this how
not only archbishops, but even kings themselves, prefer to
things temporal the life eternal, and in all confidence fly to
the one shelter of the monastic rule."

Still Louis continued too ill to carry out his wish. His
doctors prescribed for him potions and powders so nauseous
and bitter, that scarcely would a hale, hearty man have been
able to endure them.[2] Still none of these evils ruffled the
evenness of his temper; he was accessible, kind, and bene-
volent to all, as if he suffered no pain or inconvenience.

---

[1] Suger is rather negligent of
dates. Louis's illness and last expedition, mentioned above, must have
preceded his death by four or five
years; but from his biographer's
language it might be inferred that
he was not long ill.

[2] " Cum autem de die in diem

gravi diarrhœa turbaretur, motus
tantis et tam molestis medicorum
potionibus, diversorum et amarissi-
morum pulverum susceptionibus ad
restringendum infestabatur, ut nec
ipsi incolumes et virtuosi sustinere
praevalerent."—SUGER, *Vita Lud.
Gross.*

Presently his disease grew suddenly worse, and, "scorning to die suddenly or meanly," he summoned many bishops and abbots and religious persons to his presence. Laying aside all ceremony, through reverence of God and his holy angels, he begged that he might confess himself at once, and be fortified in his death with the viaticum of the Lord's body and blood. While they were making their preparations, to the astonishment of all, the king dressed himself, and proceeded forth from his room to meet the Eucharist, of which he most devoutly partook. Then, before a great assemblage of clergy and laity, he abdicated his kingdom, confessed that he had reigned in sin, and placed on the finger of his son Louis the ring of investiture. He made him also swear that he would defend the Church, the poor, and the orphan, give every one his due, apprehend no one in his court, unless for the cause of actual misdemeanour. He then made a grand distribution of all his goods to the poor, his gold and silver and "desirable cups;" his cloaks and cushions, and every movable he was possessed of, he gave away, for the love of God, to the churches, the poor, and the needy, not sparing his own clothes, even to his shirt.[1] Being thus denuded of all earthly attractions, humbly on his bended knees, before the body and blood of our Lord Jesus Christ, he broke forth into this confession of the true and Catholic faith, not as an illiterate layman might have been expected to do, but more like a learned theologian.

"I Louis, a sinner, acknowledge one true God, the Father, the Son, and the Holy Ghost. I confess that one person out of this holy Trinity, namely the only-begotten, consubstantial,

---

[1] "Ubi etiam aurum et argentum et vasa concupiscibilia et pallia et palliatas culcitras, et omne mobile quod possidebat, et quo ei serviebatur, ecclesiis et pauperibus et egenis, pro amore Dei, distribuens, nec chlamydibus, nec regiis indumentis usque camisiam pepercit."— SUGER, *Vita.* The affectionate detail with which household property is often dwelt on must strike the reader, even in the quotations already given in this work.

co-eternal Son of God the Father, took flesh of the most holy Virgin Mary, was crucified, dead, and buried; that the third day He arose again from the dead, ascended into heaven, and sitteth on the right hand of the Father, to judge the quick and the dead at the great last judgment. And this Eucharist of His most holy body I believe to be the same that He took in the Virgin's womb, and which He gave to His disciples that they might be bound and united to Him, and might dwell in Him. This His most sacred blood I confess, with my heart and my lips, and most firmly believe to be the same that flowed from His side, while He hung upon the tree. And I hope that by this most comfortable viaticum my soul in its departure will be safe and invincibly protected from every power of the air."

So spake Louis, and received the sacrament. He rallied awhile after this, and, in spite of the heavenward direction of his thoughts, took advantage of the respite to marry his son to the rich heiress of Guienne, the young Eleanor, daughter of that Count William whom Bernard had frightened so thoroughly not long ago, and who was destined to play a notable, if not honourable, part in English and French history. But Louis was soon ill at Paris of his old malady. This time there was to be no reprieve; he made haste to confess and communicate, and desired forthwith to be carried to the shrine of St. Denis. But it was too late; he must die where he was. Ordering a carpet to be placed upon the ground, and ashes to be sprinkled thereon in the form of a cross, the failing king was laid on this monastic death-bed, where he soon gave up the ghost, in the act of making the sign of his faith.

CHAPTER IV.

THIRD JOURNEY TO ITALY—END OF THE SCHISM—LETTERS HOME—
DISPUTE WITH PETER OF CLUNY CONCERNING THE ELECTION OF A
BISHOP OF LANGRES.

IN the meanwhile the affairs of the papacy had not improved;
the schism existed still, a vexation and a scandal to the
orthodox believer. Innocent II., though supported by the
most powerful potentates of Europe, was still at Pisa, an exile
from his see. Anacletus II., who had no protector but the adventurous chief of the marauding invaders of Southern Italy,
was still supreme in the Eternal City. Of late matters had
taken a worse aspect than ever. Roger, who had a pope all to
himself, did not hesitate to make him of use; and Anacletus
had to pay dearly for the aid which kept him at Rome. Roger
encroached on the Church's lands; and when a Norman had
once encroached on lands, the probability was great against
his ever retiring from them. Presently came more sombre
news still. The monastery of Monte Casino, the head and
type of western monachism, declared for Anacletus, deposed
its abbot Senioretus, and thrust one Rainaldus, a creature of
the anti-pope, into his place. Unspeakably horrible must such
an event have appeared to northern and orthodox Europe.
That the abbot of abbots, the successor of the great Benedict,
the universal father of monks, should turn a schismatic and an
opponent of catholic unity, must have seemed a calamity, one

P

of those fiery trials which are destined to try the faith even of the elect.[1] Clairvaux and Canticles and everything must be left in such an extremity as this. In the spring of the year 1137 Bernard, accompanied by his brother Gerard, set out for Italy. The devil, we are told, had a particular objection to this journey. He foresaw and hated what was to come of it. Therefore, when Bernard was passing through the Alps, the demon broke the wheel of the carriage in which the abbot travelled, in order to hinder him as much as possible, or even pitch him over a precipice. The saint took a saintly and yet a fearful vengeance on his enemy. Careless and contemptuous of the intended injury, he ordered Satan himself to become a wheel, and replace the broken one. The fallen angel obeyed the words of the holy man ; the carriage moved on as before ; and the worsted and rotatory fiend, amid scorn and laughter, carried Bernard in safety to his destination.[2]

Innocent had left Pisa, so Bernard followed him to Viterbo. Here brother Gerard fell ill—so ill that no hope seemed left. Bernard himself tells us how the possible loss of his friend, companion, and relation in a strange land almost overcame him. He thought, too, of his dismal and solitary return home, when Gerard's friends—and they numbered all who knew him— would ask for his lost brother, and he should have to reply that he was left in a distant country, he who, like all of them, ought

---

[1] "Laborabant Campania et Apulia sub Anacleto, Rogerio Siculo non solum favente, sed eo velut pietatis quaesito t tulo (is hominum mos est) ecclesiae terras sacrilege occupante. Quin etiam magnum illud praeclarumque occidui monachatus caput, Casinus Mons, Romanae ecclesiae pars non contemnenda, unde tot veri pontifices prodierunt, tunc a vero pontifice deficiens, Rogerii metu an amore quis definiat? ad Anacletum proterve

declinaverat, et Senioreto abbate de medio facto, substitutum Rainaldum sibi praefecerat." — *Manricus ad annum* 1137, *apud S. Bernardi Acta*, § xxiv.

[2] Manricus admits that this story rests on tradition, rather than "veterum testimoniis." A twelfth-century miracle would hardly be so wanting in dignity as this is. Even in the concoction of spurious miracles a progressive decline may be noticed in the Roman Church.

to sleep in the cemetery at Clairvaux. With sobs and tears Bernard prayed, "Wait, O Lord, until our return. When I have restored him to his own, then shalt Thou have him if Thou wilt, and I will not gainsay."[1]   And Gerard recovered.

Bernard now proceeded to Rome. The pope and his cardinals imparted their plans to him. He did not take much notice of them ; he was not for employing force, or increasing the anger of his opponents by a voluntary profession of hostility ; he felt his way in conversation, and by inquiries, and tried to discover the number and zeal of Anacletus's party. He found that a fear of losing everthing if they forsook him was the chief cause that his clerical friends still adhered to Anacletus. Some pretended their oaths of allegiance, others their relationship to him.[2]   Bernard quietly undermined them all, and before very long it was manifest to every one that Anacletus was being rapidly deserted.[3]

Roger of Sicily was still an opponent. With great show of fairness he said he would hear each side defend its own cause, *i.e.* Bernard for Innocent, while Peter of Pisa was to speak for Anacletus. This Peter was a renowned rhetorician, full of canon law and subtlety ; and the artful Roger expected that his champion, in a public dialectic contest, would easily worst and annihilate the good rustic abbot of the north.[4]   Peter

[1] "Expecta, inquam, Domine usque ad reditum. Restitutum amicis tolle jam eum, si vis, et non causabor." —*Sermo in Cantica*, 26.

[2] "Nec in curribus, nec in equis spem ponens, sed colloquia quorumdam suscipiens, sciscitatur quae sit eorum facultas, qui fautorum animi. . . . . Intelligit ex secretis clerum qui cum Petro erat, de statu suo sollicitum, scire quidem peccatum, sed non audere reverti. . . . . . Caeteri juramento fidelitatis excusabant perfidiam."—ST. BERN. *Op.* vol. ii. col. 1109.

[3] Ibid.

[4] "Aiebat autem se dissensionis hujus, quae jamdiu induruerat, velle scire originem : et cognita veritate, aut corrigere errorem, aut sancire sententiam. Mittebat autem in dolo, quia audierat Petrum Pisanum eloquentissimum esse, et in legum et canonum scientia nulli secundum ; putabatque si eloquentiae ejus in publico consistorio audientia praeberetur, declamationibus rhetoricis simplicitatem abbatis posse obrui, et silentium ei vi verborum et pondere rationum imponi."—ST. BERN. *Op.* vol. ii. col. 1109.

started off on his rhetoric, his canons, and his legal quibbles, and doubtless satisfied himself and his friends. It was now Bernard's turn. He said :—" I know, Peter, that you are a wise and learned man, and would that a better cause and a more honest business engaged your attention, for it is my opinion that no eloquence could withstand yours, if you had truth and reason on your side. As for myself, a rustic, more used to the hoe and the mattock than to public declamations, if it were not that the faith required it, I should preserve the silence prescribed by my rule. Now charity compels me to speak, seeing that the Lord's vesture, which neither the heathen nor the Jew presumed to rend, that vesture Peter, the son of Leo, protected by King Roger, tears and divides. There is one faith, one Lord, one baptism ; neither do we know two Lords, two faiths, two baptisms. To begin from antiquity, there was but one ark at the time of the Flood. In this ark eight souls were saved ; all the rest, as many as were outside the ark, perished. No one will deny that this ark was a type of the Church. Lately another ark has been built ; and as there are now two, one must be false, and must sink in the depths of the sea. If the ark which Peter rules be of God, it follows that in which Innocent is must perish. Therefore the Eastern Church will perish, and the Western also. France, Germany, Spain, England, and the barbarous countries, will perish in the waters. The monastic orders of the Camaldoli, the Carthusians, the Cluniacs, the Cistercians, the Premonstrants, and innumerable other congregations of servants and handmaidens of the Lord : it is inevitable that they all go to the bottom of the sea. The bishops and abbots and princes of the Church, with millstones fastened to their necks, will plunge headlong in the depths of the sea. Alone, out of all the lords of the earth, that Roger will enter the ark of Peter, and while all the rest perish, he alone will be saved. God forbid that the religion of the whole world should perish, and that the ambition of Peter, whose life has been such as is known to all, should obtain the kingdom of heaven."

At these words the assembly could not contain themselves any longer, and expressed their abomination of the character and cause of Peter Leonis. Bernard took his late adversary in the dispute by the hand, and raising him up said, " If you will trust in me, we will enter a safe ark;" and he persuaded him to go to Rome, and be reconciled to Innocent.[1]

Roger was not to be converted so. Those lands which he had occupied in the neighbourhood of Beneventum and Monte Casino, he knew very well, would have to be relinquished along with Anacletus. However, the latter soon solved the difficulty to the general satisfaction by dying. The phantom anti-pope, Victor, who succeeded him for a few days, soon renounced of his own accord the empty honour. And so ended the schism. Bernard left Rome within five days after finishing his work.

How he felt during these long wanderings may be seen by these letters :—

" Brother Bernard to the most dear brethren the monks of Clairvaux, the lay brethren, and the novices : may they ever rejoice in the Lord.

" Judge from yourselves what my sufferings are. If my absence is painful to you, let no one doubt that it is more painful to me. For the loss you experience in my single absence is not to be compared with mine, when I am deprived of all of you. As many as there are of you, so many cares do I feel ; from each one I grieve to be separated ; for each do I fear dangers. This double pang will not leave me, until I am restored to my own bowels. I do not doubt that you feel the same for me ; but I am only one. You have a single, I a multiplex, reason for sadness. And not only because I must live for a time separated from you, without whom a kingdom would

[1] St. Bern. Op. vol. ii. col. 1110.

seem a bondage to me, is my mind troubled, but because I am compelled to live in a way which utterly destroys my dearly loved peace, and which indeed perhaps hardly agrees with my monastic vows."[1]

This was written during his first absence. What follows he wrote during the last journey, which has just been narrated. It is addressed to the same :—

"My soul is sad until I return, and will not be comforted till I be with you. What consolation have I in an evil time, or in the place of my pilgrimage? Is it not you in the Lord? The sweet thought of you is indeed with me wherever I go. But this makes me feel our separation the more. Alas for me, that my sojourn is not only prolonged, but increased, and as it were piled up. And, truly, according to the prophet, they who have separated me from you, even though only in the body, 'have added to the pain of my wounds.' The exile we share in common, is sufficiently hard to bear of itself, that while we dwell in this body, we are absent from the Lord.[2] Besides this grief I have the special one, which almost makes me impatient, that I am compelled to live without you. Long is the trial, and tedious to remain so long subject to vanity which occupieth all things, to be caged in the dismal prison of this impure body, to be still tied by the chains of death and the bonds of sin, and for so long a time to be away from Christ. Against these evils one resource alone is granted me, verily from above, that instead of the face of glory, which is hidden as yet, I am allowed in the meantime to behold the holy temple of God, which temple ye are. From this temple the passage seemed easy to that glorious one for which the prophet sighed, when he said, 'One thing have I desired of the Lord, that I will seek after; that I may dwell in the house of

---

[1] St. Bern. Epist 143.

[2] " Est commune exsilium ipsumque molestum satis, quod quamdiu sumus in hoc corpore, peregrinamur a Domino."—ST. BERN. *Epist.* 144.

the Lord all the days of my life, to behold the beauty of the Lord, and to enquire in His temple.'

"What am I saying? how often has that joy been taken from me? This is the third time, if I mistake not, that my loved ones have been torn from me. My little ones are weaned before their time; those whom I have begotten in the Gospel I am not suffered to bring up. I am obliged to forsake my own business and look after other people's, and hardly know which I feel most painful—to leave the one, or to be involved in the other. Is all my life, kind Jesus, destined to flow away thus in sorrow, and my years in sighs? It is better, Lord, for me to die than to live, but not so unless it be among brothers, friends, and my heart's darlings. It is sweeter, gentler, and safer to die so surrounded. It is but just, Lord, that I should be refreshed, before I depart and be no more. If it is well pleasing to my Lord that the eyes of a father who is not worthy to be called a father should be closed by the hands of his children—that they should see his last moments, console him in the hour of death, raise his spirit by their prayers, if thou judgest it worthy, to the fellowship of the blessed, and bury his poor body beside the bodies of poor men—this, if I have ever found favour in Thy sight, I wish to obtain through the merits and prayers of those same brethren with an exceeding great desire. Nevertheless, not my will, but thine, be done; I wish neither to live for myself nor to die for myself.[1]

"Yielding to the earnest entreaty of the Emperor, the command of the Pope, the prayers of the Church and the princes, sorrowfully, reluctantly, weak and suffering as I am, and, to say

---

[1] "Si placet Domino meo, ut oculi patris qualiscunque, qui non sum dignus vocari pater, claudantur manibus filiorum, ut extrema videant, exitum consolentur, spiritum suis desideriis levent ad consortium si dignum judicas beatorum, cum pauperum corporibus pauperis corpus sepeliant; hoc prorsus si inveni gratiam in oculis tuis, precibus et meritis eorumdem fratrum meorum obtinere toto affectu desidero. Verumtamen non mea voluntas sed tua fiat. Nec mihi vivere volo nec mori."—ST. BERN. *Epist.* 144.

the truth, carrying about a pale and fearful image of death, I am dragged off into Apulia. Pray for the peace of the Church ; pray for my safety, that I may see you again, and live with you and die with you ; and so live that ye may obtain your prayer. I have dictated this letter in a short space of time, amid tears and sobs, being very ill, as our dear brother Baldwin, who has taken down my words, can bear witness. Pray for him also, as for my only consolation, and one in whom my spirit hath much rest. Pray for the Lord Pope, who has for me and all of you a faithful affection ; pray for our lord the Chancellor, who has been a mother to me, and for those who are with him, viz. my Lords Luke and Chrysogonus, and Master Yvo, who have shown themselves brothers to me. Brothers Bruno and Gerard, who are with me, salute you, and beg to be remembered in your prayers."

This is evidently the letter of a man who wishes, rather than hopes, to see loved and absent faces before he dies.

Again, this absence in Italy not only caused the regret and sorrow above depicted, but it also kept Bernard from attending to his duties in the annual Chapter at Citeaux. The month of September must pass by this year without seeing Bernard wend his way to Citeaux. An abbot who, without legitimate excuse, did not attend the General Chapter, lay under heavy pains and penalties. Beside the infliction of penance by fasting, he was forbidden to stand in his stall in church, and was prohibited from celebrating mass, till forgiven by the Chapter. The discipline at this time at Citeaux was vigorous and sound, and all the renown and influence of Bernard did not dispense him from a literal obedience to the rule of his order. While therefore he is in Italy, balancing and righting the great ark of the Church, he is compelled humbly to make his excuses to his brother abbots in the following strain :—

" To the Abbots assembled at Citeaux,—In great weakness of body and anxiety of mind, as God knows, I have dictated this letter to you ; I, a miserable man, born unto trouble, but still your brother. Would that that Spirit in which you are now assembled would become an intercessor with you for me, impressing on your minds the misfortunes I endure, and representing to your brotherly hearts a sad and supplicating image of me, such as I really am. This I do not wish in order to create in you a new feeling of mercy, for I know how you all abound in that virtue ; but for this reason it is that I so pray, that you may be able to realize in all its depth how great is my need of pity. I am quite sure if it were so even as I wish, forthwith tears from the treasure-house of pity would break forth—sobs, and sighs, and groans would so assail the heavens, that God would hear, and relent towards me, and say, ' I have restored thee to thy brethren ; thou shalt not die among strangers, but among thine own people.' So numerous are my sorrows and afflictions, that I am often weary of life. I speak as a man, owing to my weakness. I wish to be respited till I return to you, that I die not except among you. For the rest, brethren, make good your ways and your desires, holding and establishing that which is right, honourable, and salutary ; above all things anxious to preserve the unity of the Spirit, in the bond of peace, and the God of peace shall be with you."[1]

With such feelings of longing regret and gentle hope did Bernard revert in thought to the fair valley and its inhabitants. He wishes rather than expects to see them all again. He speaks in the languid tone of a man who has just accomplished a great work, which has called out all his energies. The stimulus was gone, and immediately life was dull and empty to him. For Bernard belonged to that class whom action ceaseless and vehement refreshes and soothes ; not work, but idleness, exhausts them. So when this long, irritating schism was at last suppressed, and the spasm of effort had ceased, Bernard

---

[1] St. Bern. Epist. 145.

was in low spirits; he thought he should probably die. An event soon occurred to restore him to his former vigour.

It happened that, while he was still at Rome, the Archbishop of Lyons, Robert the Dean of Langres, and the Canon Olricus also came thither: the latter in order to beg permission for themselves and the Chapter of Langres to elect a bishop to that see; for they had received an order from the Pope in no wise to presume to do so without the advice of religious persons. They tried to persuade Bernard to urge their suit with the Pope. He replied, "God forbid that I should support your request, unless I knew for certain that you intended to elect a good and proper person." They answered that their intention should be guided entirely by Bernard, that they would not do anything which he did not advise, and gave a solemn promise to that effect. But Bernard had by this time seen far too much of the world, to trust implicitly to fair promises. He very much doubted the sincerity of their promises. So the Archbishop of Lyons came forward and added his word to theirs. The Chancellor was brought in to witness the agreement, and Bernard, not yet completely satisfied, sought the Pope, and made him a party to the conditions. The fitness of a large number of possible candidates was then discussed, and it was settled that only two were eligible persons, either of whom would be a satisfactory choice. The Pope ordained everything that Bernard proposed, and the petitioners, apparently contented, gave their assent. They then went off home, leaving the city a little before Bernard. He made but small tarrying there, as on the sixth day after the final submission of Anacletus's party to Innocent he set out on his journey.[1]

But as he was crossing the Alps, he heard that the day was near at hand when "a man" was to be consecrated Bishop of

---

[1] These facts, and those which follow, till we come to Peter of Cluny's counter-statement, rest entirely on Bernard's authority. The long letter in which they are laid before the Pope is the 164th.

Langres.   Of this "man" he had heard very bad reports,
so bad that he would not repeat what he had heard.   However,
he was soon met by a number of religious persons, who had
come to meet and salute him, and these earnestly begged that
he would diverge from his road, go to Lyons, and prevent the
accomplishment of a "nefarious business."   Bernard was
reluctant to lengthen his journey, as he was ill, and wanted to
hasten home; and in fact he did not entirely give credence to
the rumours in circulation.   He thought it impossible that the
Archbishop could have forgotten his solemn promise, and the
command of the Pope as well.   However, he yielded to the
representations of his friends, and struck off to Lyons.   There,
even as he had heard, so he saw.   "A solemnity not joyful,
but melancholy, was being prepared."   The Dean and the
greater part of the Canons were offering a vain resistance.

Bernard was amazed.   What was he to do?   He conferred
with the Archbishop on these proceedings, none of which were
denied by that prelate, who shifted all the blame of them to
the son of the Duke of Burgundy.   The latter having changed his
mind on the subject of the election, the Archbishop had feared
he would disturb the public peace if he were resisted.   But now
that Bernard was arrived, he declared his willingness to be guided
solely by his will.   "Nay," said Bernard, "not mine, but God's
will be done, which may perhaps be known in this wise.
Leave the matter to be decided by the council of religious
persons which at your bidding have assembled here, or will
shortly do so.   If, after the invocation of the Holy Spirit, you
are still inspired to continue the work you have begun, so do;
if the contrary takes place, then obey the Apostle, who says,
'Lay hands suddenly on no man.'"   This advice the Archbishop seemed to accept.   In the meanwhile "the man" who
was to have been consecrated came to Lyons.   But instead of
going to the palace, he hid himself at an inn.   He came on
Friday evening, and went away on Saturday morning—a retreat

which at least showed his disinclination for a contest with
Bernard, whether from conscious guilt, as the Abbot declares, or
other motives, it is impossible to say.

Bernard appears at this position of affairs to have moved on
to Clairvaux, hoping for the best from his slippery Archbishop.
But "the man," who had hastened away from Lyons, went to
seek the king, and had actually obtained the investiture of the
temporalities of the see of Langres.   Then the time and the
place of his consecration were suddenly changed, for all the
promises to Bernard about taking the counsel of religious persons were forgotten when he had turned his back upon Lyons.
So great was the speed used, that when Bernard heard of the
resumption of the procedings, he had only four days in which
to enter his protest.

Such was the account of this transaction which Bernard,
in a long letter, laid before the Pope.   This first letter was
rapidly followed up by others, his wrath and indignation waxing even hotter ; indeed, during the whole course of his life
he never used more excited and unmeasured language than
he did in this matter.   Two things are evident : (1) that his
appeal to Rome in the first instance was taken but little
notice of; (2) that he was determined no one of whom he did
not completely approve should sit in the see of Langres.   He
declares that "a multitude of saints will be put to confusion,
if this yoke be thrust on them ; that they will bear it as they
would bear compulsion to bend the knee to Baal, or, in the
words of the prophet, to make a covenant with death, and
with hell to conclude an agreement."   He says gold and silver
have prevented his appeal to law, reason, and equity from
being heard ; and asserts, at last, that if his opponents do not
desist from their wicked and audacious attempt, his life will
end in sorrow, and his years in groaning.[1]

[1] St. Bern. Epist. 166, 167.

After such a torrent of strong language and sentiments, it is not a little surprising to find, in a letter of Peter of Cluny, a simple and dispassionate narrative of what took place, giving a totally different impression of the whole business. Peter's letter is addressed to Bernard, and tells him how, as he was lately coming from Poitou, he was met by the Canons of the church of Langres, who told him that they, with the consent of everybody who was concerned in the matter, had canonically elected one of his monks to the bishopric. They now only wanted and asked for Peter's sanction to the removal of his monk. He hesitated for a time, he says, not wishing to lose the services of the monk in question; but at last yielded to the importunity of the petitioners. They forthwith went to seek the king, whose court was then at Le Puy, and begged and obtained his confirmation of the election. The monk who had been chosen was seen and approved of by Louis VII., who with his own hands solemnly invested him with the regalia in the usual manner.

Matters had reached this stage when Peter heard that certain persons belonging to Lyons had, by means of he knew not what sort of rumours, aroused Bernard's opposition to the harmonious agreement which all parties had come to. His first wish was to have a conference with Bernard on the subject; but, as this was impossible, he wrote. He then says that he does not wonder that evil reports should be displeasing to a good man, but adds, with a slight sarcasm very rare with him, that it should have been noticed that even as it was possible for these reports to be true, so it was possible for them to be false. And this point, he thinks, *i.e.* their truth or falsehood, ought to have been ascertained before they were denounced publicly to the Pope. He reminds Bernard that this monk was a monk of Cluny, and a son of the Abbot Peter, whom he— Bernard—so loved. He reminds him that the persons who had instilled these prejudices into his ear were such implacable enemies of Cluny, that they could not restrain either their tongues or their hands from sacrilege and violence against that monastery. He adds, "Therefore it was unworthy of you or of any good man to believe such manifest foes of ours, to give credence to such declared enemies of Cluny."[1]

Peter then goes on to say that, hearing these rumours, he examined the inculpated monk himself; that he begged, he advised, he adjured, him to tell the truth; promising to keep his secrets if he had any; that he—Peter—did not wish to expose, but heal, the wounds of his soul. The monk replied he was guiltless, that if he lied to his Abbot Peter, he should lie unto God, and that he was ready to clear himself by oath of the charges brought against him.[2]

"I know very well," Peter continues, "from whom these reports have sprung, and why and how they have been disseminated. In the freedom of conversation I could have explained the whole matter to you, and have clearly shown what a black cloud of falsehood, rising from a pit of darkness, has tried to obscure the bright surface of your mind; and this I will do when I can. . . . . I beg you will not think I thus defend my monk because I wish him to be made a bishop.

[1] Petri Cluniacensis, Epist. lib. i., Epist. 29. Nothing could be more just and more deserved than this rebuke. But the relations between Peter and Bernard throughout their lives give rise to contrasts little favourable to the latter. Peter nearly always is gentle, conciliating, and careful not to give offence, even when, as here, sorely provoked. Bernard too often made return by harsh and even violent language and conduct.

[2] This emphatic testimony of Peter bears hard upon Bernard. He was far more calm, and he had far better means of knowing the truth, than the Abbot of Clairvaux, who did not pretend to any knowledge of "the man" in question, except at second hand. It is absurd to suppose, as Bernard represents, that the bad character of the monk was universally notorious, and also to conceive that Peter could be ignorant of such a fact. But Bernard rarely postponed action for the sake of inquiry. The "enemies of Cluny," to whom Peter alludes, had secured his partisanship, and he was troubled by no scruples when once the ardour of battle came upon him. He doubtless thought that whatever might be the truth as regarded the worth of a Cluniac monk, a Cistercian monk was sure to be much better.

It is no new thing for a Cluniac monk to be made a bishop. Bishops, archbishops, patriarchs, and, what is above all, supreme pontiffs of the Church, have been taken from Cluny. And is it very improper that a wise and educated Cluniac should now be elected to the bishopric of Langres? Do you fear that, as a Cluniac, he will not love the Cistercians? Discard such a thought. A monk will love monks. The Bishop of Langres, if he has been a monk, will love Cistercians and all monks, because he will know that love is gain and hatred loss. Neither will a monk of ours dare to differ from us, when he sees us loving you."

This firm yet kindly letter seems to have had no effect on Bernard. He had made up his mind, and nothing could make him change it. He now wrote to the " Bishops and Cardinals of the Roman court." He reminds them, as he had reminded the Pope, of his services to them—how faithful he had been to them "in the evil time," and how "the strength of his body was nearly consumed in the cause." He says he does not recall these facts in a boastful spirit, but simply because he stands in need of a return of good offices. He says if he had done what it was his duty to do, still he considered himself, in the words of the Lord, an unprofitable servant. But did he deserve stripes for doing his duty? "Coming back from Italy I found tribulation and trouble. I called on the name of the Lord, and it availed not. I appealed to you, and it availed not. Indeed, the great ones of the earth are lifted up, the Archbishop of Lyons and the Abbot of Cluny. They, trusting in their goods, and boasting themselves in the multitude of their riches, have drawn themselves nigh, and stood against me. And not only against me, but against a number of the servants of God, against you, against themselves, against God, and against all justice and honour. And they have placed a man over our heads, whom, O shame! the good loathe, and the wicked laugh to scorn." Then comes his peroration :—" What dost thou want, O Rome, mistress of the world, placed over the universe as a wrathful avenger and a merciful judge? Dost thou wish that, while the wicked waxes proud, the poor may be consumed, and that 'poor' one, who for thy service, when he had not gold to give, spared not his own blood? Does it appear fitting to thee, to sit in peace thyself, and to be careless of my affliction, to exclude from consolation thy companions in sorrow? If I have found grace in your eyes, Bishops and Cardinals of Rome, snatch one who is helpless from the hands of a stronger than he, a poor man from those who despise him. If not, then I shall labour and groan, and tears shall be my bread day and night. But to you I will cite this verse, 'Whoso withholdeth pity from his friend, hath forsaken the fear of the Almighty.' And this, 'All my friends have departed from me.' And this one also, 'My kinsmen stood afar off, and they also that sought after my life laid snares for me.' "[1]

The Pope, the Cardinals, and the Bishops yielded. The Archbishop of Lyons yielded; the good Peter of Cluny yielded. Bernard caused the Cluniac monk to be deposed from his see, another election to be made, and a monk of Clairvaux, a kinsman of his own, to be placed in his room. His name was Godfrey; he had been prior of Clairvaux during Bernard's absence in Italy, and was one of those who on his return urged and carried out the removal and enlargement of the monastic buildings at Clairvaux.

[1] St. Bern. Epist. 168.

DEATH OF BERNARD'S BROTHER GERARD—FUNERAL SERMON ON THE
DEATH OF GERARD—VISIT OF ST. MALACHY TO CLAIRVAUX.

THIS very exciting business about the bishopric of Langres,
and its successful issue in Bernard's favour—if such an issue
can be called successful—were followed by an event well fitted
to sadden and sober him, if he needed such chastening. His
brother Gerard, who had been ill when they were in Italy the
year previous, had become ill again; so ill that this was to be
the last time, for he was dying. It was the custom among the
Cistercians, when a monk was very ill, or approaching death,
to proceed thus :[1]—The bell was rung, and the religious
hastened into the choir. They then went in procession to the
infirmary, the abbot first, followed by priests, who carried a
cross, a light in a lantern, and holy water. The sacristan was
in his place bearing the oil and a piece of flax or a towel, with
which to wipe it away. The rite of extreme unction was
then performed.[2] They all then left the sick man, went to the
church, and presently returned with a cross, a light, and holy
water, with which the patient was sprinkled. The priest then
said to him, "Behold, brother, the body of the Lord Jesus

---

[1] Usus antiquiores ordinis Cisterciensis. Nomasticon Cisterciense,
Paris, 1664. Pars iv. cap. 94, 95.
Also Migne's Patrologia, tom. clxvi.
col. 1471.

[2] " . . . . procedant eo ordine
quo stant in choro, sacerdotibus
sequentibus abbatem post crucem et
lumen in absconsa et aquam benedictam. . . . . Sacrista vero pergens
in ordine suo ferat oleum et stupas
vel pannum ad detergendum unctu-
ram. . . . . Et sic unctionis impleat
officium."—*loc. cit.*

Q

Christ which we bring to thee. Dost thou believe that in it are our salvation, resurrection, and life?"[1] On his answering, "I believe," he was bidden to repeat the *Confiteor.* The priest next administered the holy viaticum, saying, "The body of our Lord Jesus Christ preserve thee unto everlasting life;" and they all left him. But when his end visibly drew near, he was placed on the floor on a serge cloth, under which had been spread some straw over a cross of ashes which had been blessed. The bell was rung four times, and wherever the community might be, they must hasten to the infirmary as quickly as possible. They there knelt around the sick brother and answered the prayers recited by the celebrant. The seven penitential Psalms were said, and, unless he was actually dying, the monks again retired, leaving him a lighted candle, the cross, and holy water.[2]

That all the proper forms and ceremonies were observed at the death-bed of the brother of Bernard we cannot doubt. When at last the lamp of life was extinguished, the funeral service was performed by the bereaved abbot, who, however, of all present appeared the least moved at the burial of the dead. The grief of others broke forth in sobs and tears. The infinite sorrow of Bernard made him only preternaturally calm. He went through the routine of duty as usual, and part of that duty was his exposition of the Song of Songs, which he had resumed since his return from Italy. At the appointed time

---

[1] "Cum ad infirmum veniunt, qui fert aquam aspergat eum. Sacerdos vero dicat ei, 'Ecce, frater, corpus Domini nostri Jesu Christi quod tibi deferimus ; credis hoc illud esse in quo est salus, vita, et resurrectio nostra?'"—*loc. cit.*

[2] "Cum aliquis morti penitus appropinquaverit, ponatur ad terram super sagum, supposito prius cinere in modum crucis et aliqua matta vel straminis aliquanto. . . . . . Dicta itaque Litania, si adhuc vixerit, dicantur septem Psalmi Poenitentiales : quod si nondum obierit, discedant, relinquentes ibi crucem et aquam benedictam." — Ibid. See also "Regulations of the Cistercian Congregation of our Lady of La Trappe, Primitive Observance ; drawn up by the General Chapter." London: Richardson and Son, 1854. Book viii. cap. 5.

he ascended the pulpit, as he was wont, and began the
following

SERMON.

" As the tents of Kedar, as the curtains of Solomon."
SOL. SONG, i. 5.[1]

"We must begin from this point, because it was here that
the preceding sermon was brought to a close. You are waiting
to hear what these words mean, and how they are connected
with the previous clause, since a comparison is made between
them. Perhaps both members of the comparison, viz. 'As
the tents of Kedar, as the curtains of Solomon,' refer only to
the first words, 'I am black.' It may be, however, that the
simile is extended to both clauses, and each is compared with
each. The former sense is the more simple, the latter the
more obscure. Let us try both, beginning with the latter,
which seems the more difficult. There is no difficulty, however, in the first comparison, 'I am black as the tents of
Kedar,' but only in the last. For Kedar, which is interpreted
to mean 'darkness' or 'gloom,' may be compared with blackness justly enough; but the curtains of Solomon are not so
easily likened to beauty. Moreover, who does not see that
'tents' fit harmoniously with the comparison? For what is
the meaning of 'tents,' except our bodies, in which we sojourn
for a time. Nor have we an abiding city, but we seek one to
come. In our bodies, as under tents, we carry on warfare.
Truly, we are violent to take the kingdom. Indeed, the
life of man here on earth is a warfare; and as long as
we do battle in this body, we are absent from the Lord, *i.e.*
from the light. For the Lord is light; and so far as any
one is not in Him, so far he is in darkness, *i.e.* in Kedar.
Let each one then acknowledge the sorrowful exclamation as
his own : 'Woe is me that my sojourn is prolonged ! I have
dwelt with those who dwell in Kedar. My soul hath long

---

[1] St. Bern. Op. vol. i. col. 1353.

Q 2

sojourned in a strange land.'[1]   Therefore this habitation of the
body is not the mansion of the citizen, nor the house of the
native, but either the soldier's tent or the traveller's inn.   This
body, I say, is a tent, and a tent of Kedar, because, by its
interference, it prevents the soul from beholding the infinite
light, nor does it allow her to see the light at all, except
through a glass darkly, and not face to face.

   " Do you not see whence blackness comes to the Church
—whence a certain rust cleaves to even the fairest souls?
Doubtless, it comes from the tents of Kedar, from the practice
of laborious warfare, from the long continuance of a painful
sojourn, from the straits of our grievous exile, from our
feeble cumbersome bodies; for the corruptible body presseth
down the soul, and the earthy tabernacle weigheth down the
mind that museth upon many things.   Therefore the souls'
desire to be loosed, that being freed from the body they may
fly into the embraces of Christ.   Wherefore one of the miserable ones said, groaning : ' Oh, wretched man that I am, who
shall deliver me from the body of this death !'   For a soul of
this kind knoweth that, while in the tents of Kedar, she cannot
be entirely free from spot or wrinkle, nor from some stains of
blackness, and wishes to go forth and to put them off.   And
here we have the reason why the spouse calls herself black as
the tents of Kedar.   But now, how is she beautiful as the
curtains of Solomon?   Behind these curtains I feel that an
indescribable holiness and sublimity are veiled, which I dare
not presume to touch, save at the command of Him who
shrouded and sealed the mystery.   For I have read, He that
is a searcher of Majesty shall be overwhelmed with the glory.
I pass on therefore.   It will devolve on you, meanwhile, to
obtain grace by your prayers, that we may the more readily,

---

[1] In such cases as this, to trans-
late the Vulgate is preferable to
inserting the English version, which
is really different.   See Psalm cxix.
5, 6, Vulgatae editionis.

because more confidently, recur to a subject which needs attentive minds; and it may be that the pious knocker at the door will discover what the bold explorer seeks in vain.

"But I must desist; my grief and the calamity I have suffered command it. How long shall I dissemble? how long shall I conceal the fire which is within me, scorching my sorrowful breast and consuming my vitals? The more I repress its flames, the more fiercely it burns and rages. What have I to do with this canticle, who am steeped in bitterness? The sharpness of grief paralyses my will, and the indignation of the Lord has drunk up my spirit. My very heart left me, when he was taken away through whom my meditations in God were made free. But I did violence to my mind, and have dissembled until now, lest it should appear that faith was overcome of feeling. While others wept, I, as ye may have observed, followed his body to the grave with unmoistened eyes; I stood by his tomb, and dropped no tear till the burial of the dead was over. Clad in my priestly robes, I pronounced with my lips the usual prayers; with my own hands, in the wonted manner, I cast the earthy mould on the body of my beloved, soon itself to be dissolved to earth. Those who watched me wept, and wondered why I wept not also, for their pity was less for him than for me—for me who had lost him. Would not even a heart of steel be moved, to see me the survivor of Gerard? The loss was a general one, but it was not thought of in comparison with my calamity. And I resisted my affliction with all the resources of faith which I could summon—striving even against myself not to be disturbed vainly by the law of Nature, by the debt which all must pay, by the rule of our condition here, by the command of the powerful One, by the judgment of the Just, by the scourge of the Terrible, by the will of the Lord. By means of such thoughts I overcame myself for that time and afterwards, so as not to indulge in much weeping, though sorely troubled and sorrowful. I could not command my grief, though I could control my tears! As it is written, 'I was afflicted, and I kept silence.' But the suppressed anguish struck deeper root within, and has become more bitter, as I perceive, from not being allowed a vent. I own I am conquered. Let it go forth, as I cannot endure it within. Let it go forth before the eyes of my children, who, knowing my affliction, will bear more leniently with my complaint, and give me a sweeter consolation.

" You know, my children, the reasonableness of my sorrow —you know the lamentable wound I have received. You appreciate what a friend has left me in this walk of life which I have chosen—how prompt to labour, how gentle in manner! Who was so necessary to me? To whom was I equally dear? He was my brother by blood, but more than brother by religion. Deplore my misfortune, I beseech you, who know these things. I was weak in body, and he sustained me; downcast in spirit, and he comforted me; slow and negligent, and he stimulated me; careless and forgetful, and he admonished me. Whither hast thou been torn from me, whither hast thou been carried from my arms, O thou man of one mind with me, thou man after my own heart? We loved each other in life: how are we separated in death! O most bitter separation, which nothing could have accomplished but death! For when wouldest thou have deserted me in life? Truly, a horrible divorce, altogether the work of death. Who would not have had pity on the sweet bond of our mutual love but death, the enemy of all sweetness? Well has raging death done his work; for, by taking one, he has stricken two. Is not this death to me also? Yea, verily, more to me than to Gerard—to me to whom life is preserved far gloomier than any death. I live that I may die living; and shall I call that life? How much more merciful, O stern death, hadst thou deprived me of the use, than of the fruit, of life. For life without fruit is a more grievous death. Again, a double ruin is prepared for the unfruitful tree—the axe and the fire. Hating, therefore, the labours of my hands, thou hast removed from me the friend through whose zeal chiefly they bore fruit, if they ever did. Better would it have been for me, O Gerard! to have lost my life than thy presence, who wert the anxious instigator of my studies in the Lord, my faithful helper, my careful examiner. Why, I ask, have we loved, only to lose one another? Hard lot! But I am to be pitied, not he; for if thou, dear brother, hast lost dear ones, they are replaced by dearer still: but what consolation awaits wretched me, deprived of thee, my only comfort? Equally pleasing to both was the companionship of our bodies by reason of the unison of our minds; but the separation has wounded only me. The joys of life were shared between us; its sadness and gloom are mine alone. God's wrathful displeasure goeth over me, and His indignation lieth hard upon me. The delights we derived from each other's society and conversation I only have lost, whilst thou hast exchanged them for others, and in the exchange great has been thy gain.

"In place of us, dearest brother, whom thou hast not with thee to-day, what an exceeding multitude of joys and blessings is thine! Instead of me thou hast Christ; nor canst thou feel thy absence from thy brethren here, now that thou rejoicest in choruses of angels. Nothing, therefore, can make thee deplore the loss of our society, seeing that the Lord of majesty and the hosts of heaven vouchsafe to thee their presence. But what have I in thy stead? What would I not give to know what thou now thinkest of thy Bernard, tottering amid cares and afflictions, and bereaved of thee, the staff of my weakness; if, indeed, it be permitted to one who is plunged into the abyss of light, and absorbed in the great ocean of eternal felicity, still to think of the miserable inhabitants of the earth. It may be that though thou knewest us in the flesh, thou knowest us no more; and since thou hast entered into the power of the Lord, thou

rememberest only His justice, forgetful of us.   Moreover, he
that is joined unto the Lord is one spirit, and is entirely
changed into one holy feeling; neither can he think of or
wish for aught but God and the things which God thinks
and wishes, being full of God.   But God is Love, and the
more closely a man is united to God, the fuller he is of love.
Further, God is without passions, but not without sympathy, for
His nature is always to have mercy and to spare.   Therefore
thou must needs be merciful, since thou art joined to the
Merciful One, although misery now be far from thee.   Thou
canst compassionate others, although thou sufferest not thyself.
Thy love is not weakened, but changed.   Nor because thou
hast put on God hast thou laid aside all care for us, for
'He also careth for us.'   Thou hast discarded thine infirmities,
but not thy affections.   'Charity never faileth:' thou wilt not
forget me at the last.

   "I fancy I hear my brother saying to me, 'Can a woman
forget her sucking child, that she should not have compassion
on the son of her womb?   Yea, they may forget, yet will I not
forget thee.'   Truly it were lamentable if he did.   Thou
knowest, Gerard, where I am, where I lie, where thou leftest
me.   No one is by, to stretch forth a hand to me.   I look, as
I have been wont to do in every emergency, to Gerard, and
he is not there.   Then do I groan as one that hath no help.
Whom shall I consult in doubtful matters?   To whom shall I
trust in trial and misfortune?   Who will bear my burdens?
Who will protect me from harm?   Did not Gerard's eyes prevent my steps?   Alas, my cares and anxieties entered more
deeply into Gerard's breast than into my own, ravaged it more
freely, wrung it more acutely.   His wise and gentle speech
saved me from secular conversation, and gave me to the silence
which I loved.   The Lord had given him a learned tongue, so
that he knew when it was proper to speak.   By the prudence of
his answers, and the grace given him from above, he so satisfied

both our own people and strangers, that scarcely any one
needed me who had previously seen Gerard. He hastened to
meet the visitors, placing himself in the way lest they should
disturb my leisure. Such as he could not dispose of himself,
those he brought into me ; the rest he sent away. O diligent
man ! O faithful friend ! He humoured the feelings of his
friend, and was not wanting to the duties of charity. Who ever
left him empty-handed ? If the applicant were rich, he got
counsel ; if poor, help. He who plunged himself in cares that
I might be spared them, did not seek his own advantage ; for
he expected, such was his humility, more profit from my leisure
than from his own. Yet sometimes he would ask to be discharged, that he might yield his place to another who would
fulfil its duties better. But where was such an one to be
found ? Nor did he remain in his office, as many do, kept
there by a feeling of pride and insolence, but solely from an
impulse of charity. He laboured indeed more abundantly than
all, and received less than any other ; so that often when he
was serving out necessaries to others, he himself was lacking in
many things : for example, in food and raiment.

"When he felt his end was approaching, he exclaimed :
'Thou knowest, O God, that as far as I was concerned, I have
ever wished for peace and retirement to devote myself to Thee.
But I have been kept immersed in cares and outward activity
by fear of Thee, by the will of the community, by zeal to obey,
above all things by the love of him who is both my abbot
and my brother.' And this was true. I thank thee, my
brother, for the fruit—if there be any—of all my studies in the
Lord. To thee I owe it, if I have advanced myself, if I have
contributed to others' advancement. Thou wast oppressed
with business, while I, through thy means, sat enjoying my holiday, or spent my time more devoutly in the worship of God,
or more usefully in teaching my spiritual sons. How could I
fail to be peaceful within, when I knew that thou wast abroad

acting the part of my right hand, the light of my eyes, my heart, my tongue? and truly an unwearied hand, a single eye, a head of counsel, a tongue talking of judgment, even as it is written, 'The mouth of the righteous speaketh wisdom, and his tongue talketh of judgment.'

"But why do I dwell so long on his outward activity, as if Gerard had been deficient in inward culture, and devoid of spiritual gifts? All those of a spiritual mind who knew him know how redolent his words were of the Spirit. His companions know how free his heart and mind were from fleshly thoughts, and how they glowed with a spiritual fervour. Who more strict than he in the preservation of discipline—who more stern in the chastening of his body—who more rapt or more sublime in contemplation—who more subtle in discourse? How often in discussion with him have I learnt things I knew not before; and I, who came to teach, have gone away taught! Nor is it wonderful that this should have occurred to me, when even great and wise men testify that the same thing has happened to themselves. He had not a deep knowledge of literature, but he had that sense which is the ground and origin of literature; he had the illumination of the Spirit: and not only in the greatest things, but also in the least, was he surpassing great. What—to give some examples—what did there exist in the matter of either building, or lands, or gardens, or waters, or any one of the arts of husbandry, which had escaped the sagacity of Gerard? He easily took the post of master among masons, smiths, gardeners, shoemakers, and weavers; and while all regarded him as wiser than any, in his own eyes only he knew nothing. Would that many—albeit less wise than he—were not more exposed to the curse pronounced against those 'who are wise in their own eyes.' I am speaking to men who know these things, who know also more and greater things than these concerning him. But I refrain from further allusion, for he is my flesh, my

brother.   This I can safely add, that to me he was useful in all
things, and beyond every one else : he was useful in great
things and in small, in public and in private, at home and
abroad.   It was fitting that I should depend for everything on
him who was everything to me.   He left me but little besides
the name and honour of superintendent, for he did the work.
I was called abbot, but he monopolised the abbot's cares.
Justly did my spirit repose on him, through whom I could
delight in the Lord, preach more freely, pray more confidently.
Through thee, O brother mine, have I enjoyed a quiet mind, a
grateful rest ; through thee my speech has had more power, my
prayer more unction, my reading has been more frequent, my
affection more fervent.

"Alas ! thou art gone, and with thee all these things as well.
With thee all my delights and joys have flown away.   Already
cares rush down upon me, troubles assail me from either side,
difficulties from every quarter have found me alone.   Now thou
art absent, I groan unassisted under my load ; I must lay it
down or be crushed, since thy strong shoulders are withdrawn.
Will it be granted me to die soon after thee ? for I desire not
to die in thy stead, nor to rob thee of thy glory on high.
To survive thee is labour and grief.   I shall, whilst I live, live
in bitterness.   I shall live in sorrow ; and be this my consolation, that I be stricken down with grieving.   I will not spare
myself, but will assist the chastening hand of the Lord ; for
the hand of the Lord hath touched me.   Me it hath touched
and smitten, not him whom it hath called unto rest.   I was
slain when he was cut off.   For who could call him killed whom
the Lord has planted in life ?   But the portals of life to him
were death to me ; and I would say that I died with that death,
not he who fell asleep in the Lord.   Flow forth, ye tears, long
since ready to gush out ! flow forth, since he who would have
stayed your flow has been taken away !   Let the sluices of my
wretched heart be opened ! let the fountains of waters burst

forth, if they, peradventure, suffice to wash out the stains of sin by which I have deserved the anger of God ! When the Lord shall be appeased toward me, then perhaps I may be worthy to receive consolation, if only I cease not to grieve ; for they who mourn, the same shall be comforted. Wherefore let every holy man bear with me, and in the spirit of lenity, which is of the Holy Spirit, endure my lamentation. Let my grief be estimated by human affection, not by custom. We daily see the dead mourning their dead ; their sorrow is great, but it availeth nothing. We blame not the feeling, except it exceed just bounds, but the cause of it. The feeling is natural ; such disturbance is the penalty of sin ; the cause is vanity and wickedness. For, if I mistake not, in such cases men deplore only the injuries to their carnal glory, the trials of this transitory life. Lamentable, pitiable, are they who lament thus. Do I even so ? My feeling is the same, the cause is different, the intention is dissimilar. No complaint have I concerning the things of this world ; it is in matters which of a truth belong to God that I deplore the loss of a faithful helpmate, a profitable counsellor. I weep for Gerard—Gerard, my brother in the flesh, but nearest of all in the spirit and scheme of life. My soul clave to his, and identity of mind, not of blood, made us one. The relationship by the flesh was not wanting, but the fellowship of spirit, the harmony of mind, the agreement of manners, did more to achieve our union. When we, therefore, were of one mind, one heart, the sword which pierced through his soul pierced mine also, and, separating us, placed one part in heaven and left the other in the mire of earth. I am that wretched portion lying in the dust, with the best part of me cut off ; and it is said to me, 'Weep not.' My bowels are torn out, and I am told, 'Feel not.' I feel, I feel, because I have not the fortitude of stones, and my flesh is not brass. Truly, I feel and grieve, and my grief is ever in my sight. He who striketh cannot reproach me with hardness and insensibility, as He did those of whom He says, 'I have stricken them, and they have not grieved.' I have confessed my emotion, and denied it not. Does any one say it is carnal? I deny not that it is human—I deny not that I am a man. If this sufficeth not, I deny not that it is carnal; for I also am carnal, sold to sin, made over to death, exposed to pains and tribulations. I am not, I confess, insensible to punishment. I shudder at the thought of death, whether my own or of those belonging to me. He was my Gerard, truly mine. Was he not mine, who was my brother by blood, my son by profession, my father by his care for me, who was closest to me in affection, concordant in spirit? and he has departed from me. I feel it. I am wounded, yea, deeply wounded.

"Forgive me, my children; nay, if children, sympathise with your father's trial. Pity me, pity me, you, at least, my friends, who surely know how severely I am chastened of the Lord for my sins. He hath smitten me with the rod of His indignation, justly for my misdeeds, heavily according to my strength. Would any one say it was a light thing for me to survive Gerard, except one who knew not what Gerard was to me? I do not contradict the words of the Holy One. I do not find fault with the judgment by which every man receives according to his merits: he the crown which he had won—I the punishment I deserved. Because I feel the blow, do I therefore dispute the sentence? One is human, the other impious. It is human, it is inevitable, to yearn towards our dear ones; pleasantly when they are near, painfully when they are away. Social converse, especially among friends, is no idle thing; and the intensity of their attachment may be measured by their horror of separation, by their grief when parted. I grieve for thee, beloved Gerard, not because thou needest pity, but because thou art taken away. And therefore, perhaps, I should rather grieve for myself, who am drinking the cup of bitterness. I only am to be pitied, for I only drink

it.   Hence I alone endure what lovers are wont to endure
in common when they lose each other.

   "God grant that I may not have lost thee, but only have
sent thee before me! God grant that at some future time,
even though remote, I may follow thee whithersoever thou art
gone! For there is no doubt that thou art gone to those
whom, towards the middle of thy last night upon earth, thou
invitedst to join in praise, when, to the astonishment of all
present, with a voice and countenance of exultation, thou didst
break forth into that Psalm of David, 'Praise the Lord of
heaven, praise Him in the height.' Already, my brother, the
dark midnight was becoming day to thee, and the night was
made bright as the day. That night was all brightness to
thee in thy heavenly joys. I was summoned to the miracle,
to see a man exulting in death, nay, heaping scorn upon death.
'O death, where is thy sting? O grave, where is thy victory?'
No longer is there a sting, but joyfulness. A man dies singing,
and sings dying. O mother of mourning, thou art pressed
into the service of gladness! O enemy of glory, thou art
made a handmaid of glory! thou gate of hell art become an
entrance to the kingdom! thou pitfall of perdition art turned
to a means of salvation!—and all this by a sinful man. And
justly too, for thou rashly hast usurped dominion over the
innocent and just! Thou art dead, O death, and pierced by the
hook thou hast imprudently swallowed, which saith, in the
words of the prophet, 'O death, I will be thy death! O hell,
I will be thy bite.' Pierced, I say, by that hook, to the faithful
who go through the midst of thee thou offerest a broad and
pleasant pathway into life. Gerard fears thee not, thou ghastly
form! Gerard passes through thy jaws into his own country,
not only fearless, but singing songs of praise and rejoicing.
When, after the summons, I had reached his side, and he, with
a clear voice, in my hearing, had finished the last words of the
Psalm, looking up into heaven he said, 'Father, into Thy hands I

commend my spirit!' and repeating the passage, he said again
and again, 'Father, Father!' Then turning to me with a
brightening countenance, he said, 'How gracious of God to be
the Father of men! what a glory to men to be the sons of God,
to be the heirs of God; for if children, then heirs!' Thus did
he sing for whom we mourn. He hath, I confess, almost turned
my grief into rejoicing. While I gaze on his glory, my own
misery almost vanishes away.

"But the sharp sting of sorrow recalls me to myself, and a
piercing anguish awakens me from that serene vision as from
a gentle slumber. I will not weep, then, but for myself, for
reason forbids us to weep for him. I think he would say now
to us, if occasion offered, 'Weep not for me, but weep for
yourselves.' David justly mourned over his parricidal son,
whom he, nevertheless, knew to be for ever shut in the womb
of death by the greatness of his sin. Justly did he likewise
mourn over Saul and Jonathan, for whom also no hope remained after their death. They will indeed rise again, but not
unto life; or only unto such a life, that alive in death they may
die the more wretchedly; although with regard to Jonathan
our judgment may well hesitate a little. I have not these
reasons for grief, but I have reasons! I grieve over my own
wound, over the loss to this monastery, over the needs of the
poor, to whom Gerard was a father! I mourn over the universal state of our order and the monastic profession, which, from
thy zeal and example, Gerard, drew no little support. Lastly,
I mourn, if not over thee, yet on account of thee. Hence I
am greatly moved, because I love so vehemently; and let no
one, to trouble me, assert that it is not right so to be affected,
when the gentle Samuel and the pious David gave vent to
their mourning; the one over a reprobate king, the other over
a parricidal son,—and this without injury to their faith, not in
contempt of the judgment of Heaven. Holy David said, 'O
my son Absalom, my son, my son Absalom!' and, behold, a

greater than Absalom is here. The Saviour also, when He
beheld the city of Jerusalem, and foresaw its approaching ruin,
'wept over it.' And shall not I feel my own desolation?
shall not I mourn my recent grevious wound? He wept from
compassion; shall not I from suffering? And verily, at the
tomb of Lazarus, He neither rebuked the weepers nor forbade
them; He even wept with those that wept. 'And Jesus wept,'
it is written. Those tears, truly, were evidence of His human
nature, not signs of distrust. Soon after the dead came forth
at His word, lest His sorrow should appear to throw doubt
upon His faith.

"Neither is this our weeping a mark of unbelief, but rather
of our condition; nor, because I groan when smitten, do I
arraign the striker. I appeal to His mercy. I would fain
appease His wrath. My words are charged with grief, but
not with murmuring. Have I not proclaimed the sentence
as full of justice, by which the one who deserved it was
punished, the other who merited it received a crown? And
I say the same still. The good and righteous Lord hath
done all things well! I will sing to Thee, O Lord, of mercy
and judgment. Mercy which Thou showedst to Thy servant
Gerard shall sing. The judgment which we even now bear
shall sing also. Thou shalt be praised as good in one, as just
in the other. Does praise belong only to goodness? There
is praise also for justice. 'Righteous art Thou, O Lord, and
upright are Thy judgments.' Thou gavest Gerard; Thou hast
taken him away. And if we mourn for his being taken, we
forget not that he was given; and we render thanks that we
deserved to have him, and wish not to lament him more than
is expedient.

"I call to mind, O Lord, the covenant I made with Thee,
and the mercy Thou hadst on me, that Thou mayest be justified
in Thy saying, and clear when Thou art judged. When last
year we were at Viterbo, on the business of the Church,

Gerard fell sick ; and as his illness increased, and his calling
seemed at hand, I grieved to lose the companion of my wanderings, to leave him in a strange land, and not to restore
him to those who had entrusted him to my care,—for he was
loved by all, and deserved to be loved. Then, turning myself
to prayer with tears and groans, 'Wait,' I said, 'O Lord, until
our return. After he has been restored to his friends, Thou
shalt take him if Thou wilt, and I will not complain.' Thou
heardest my prayer, O God. He grew strong again. We
finished the work Thou gavest us to do ; we returned with
joy and gladness, bearing with us the sheaves of peace. And
then I nearly forgat my agreement, but Thou didst not. I am
ashamed of these sobs, which accuse me of prevarication.
What more can I say ? Thou hast sought again what was
entrusted to us ; Thou hast received Thine own. These tears
put an end to my words. Do thou, O Lord, vouchsafe an
end and a measure to my tears."

Thus spoke the sorrowful Bernard on the death of his
brother : assuredly among funeral sermons one of the most
remarkable on record. Evidently the monk in those days did
not cease to be a man—even a loving and impassioned man.

The year following this great affliction Bernard made the
acquaintance of a man whose fortunes and character excited
his interest, and ultimately his warm affection. This was
Archbishop Malachy, Primate of Ireland, who, on his way to
Rome, put up at Clairvaux, and tarried there a while. Malachy
was a man whose apostolic zeal and sanctity might bear comparison with Bernard's own. Indeed, his long and heroic
struggle against the barbarism of his countrymen, if not beyond
the power of the Abbot of Clairvaux to imitate, was at least
such as circumstances never allowed the latter to show he was
equal to. Bernard evidently regarded him with an admiration
mingled with wonder. He constantly refers to the "bar-
barians" from amidst whom he sprang, and places Malachy's

virtues in startling contrast with the social condition of his nation. He speaks of the Irish as utter savages, much as a modern philosopher might of Polynesian islanders. He clearly felt that the Frenchmen, Germans, and Italians with whom he came in contact were quite civilized compared with Malachy's countrymen.[1] So much the stronger and more genuine were his regard and reverence for his illustrious guest. Bernard survived him by several years, and wrote his life,—a curious record both of the man and his nation ; one of the pleasantest and most interesting of Bernard's works, in which, though never thinking of it, he has put an image of his own beautiful and ardent soul.

Malachy had reached only his thirtieth year when he was consecrated Bishop of Connaught. His previous life had not been very remarkable, although of course he had performed several miracles.[2] But when he began to discharge the duties of his sacred calling, " the man of God discovered that he had not been appointed to rule over men, but over beasts. He had never met with such—so insolent in manners, so deadly in their rites, so unbelieving in religion, so rebellious against discipline, so filthy in their lives. They were Christians in name, but pagans in reality.[3] They would not pay tithes, nor

---

[1] " Malachias noster, ortus Hibernia de populo barbaro, ibi educatus, ibi litteras edoctus est. Caeterum de natali barbarie traxit nihil, non magis quam de sale materno pisces maris." — *Op.* St. Bern. vol. i. col. 659.

[2] His commencement in this line was the miraculous escape of a man whom he had accidentally felled with an axe. " Quadam die cum in securi ipse secaret, casu ex operariis unus, illo vibrante in aera securim, locum incaute occupavit quo ictus destinabatur ; et cecidit super spinam dorsi ejus, tanto utique impetu quanto

ille conatu impingere valuit. Corruit ille : accurrere omnes, putantes aut percussum ad mortem aut mortuum. Et tunica quidem scissa a summo usque deorsum ; homo vero illaesus inventus est : tam modice et summatim perstricta cute, ut vix in superficie vestigium appareret."— Ibid. col. 665.

[3] " Nusquam adhuc tales expertus fuerat in quantacunque barbarie ; nusquam repererat sic protervos ad mores, sic ferales ad ritus [does this point to any remains of Druidical sacrifices ?], sic ad fidem impios, ad leges barbaros, cervicosos ad dis-

give the 'first-fruits,' nor enter the bonds of wedlock, nor make confession; they would neither ask for nor perform penance. There were very few priests; but even those few were too many, and had very little occupation. What was Malachy to do? He stood an intrepid pastor in the midst of wolves, full of arguments by which to turn the wolves into sheep. Some he admonished publicly; some he rebuked privately; with others he shed tears. He passed whole nights sleepless, extending his hands in prayer; and when they would not come to church, he ran after them through the streets, and searched through the city whom he could win to Christ."

While Malachy was exhibiting such a worthy pattern of a Christian bishop, it chanced that Archbishop Celsus fell sick. Knowing that he was about to die, "he made as it were a testament," in which he appointed Malachy his successor, as he saw no one more worthy to be Primate of Ireland. But among the numerous vices of the Irish which Bernard holds up to reprobation was one which especially excited his indignation, viz. their habit of regarding the episcopal office in the light of hereditary property, which ought not to be suffered to go out of the family. Any one who did not belong to the favoured clan was not permitted to be made bishop; and for several generations, extending over a period of two hundred years, this iniquitous custom had prevailed. We may well believe Bernard's assertion, that the worst results flowed from it. Not only did ecclesiastical discipline and religious purity suffer, but relapses into paganism were not unknown. Among other evils was the shameless creation of new bishoprics, according to the pleasure of the metropolitan. They were multiplied to such an extent, that nearly every church had a bishop of its own.[1]

<hr>

ciplinam, spurcos ad vitam. Christiani nomine, re pagani," &c.—*Op.* St. BERN. vol. i. col. 666.

[1] "Verum mos pessimus inoleverat quorumdam diabolica ambitione potentum, sedem sanctam obtentum iri haereditaria successione. Nec enim patiebantur episcopari nisi qui essent de tribu et familia sua. Nec parum processerat exsecranda suc-

Celsus hoped that Malachy would put an end to these evils, and therefore wished him to succeed himself as metropolitan. But one Maurice by name, "of the wicked seed" who had held the see for two hundred years, stepped in and kept out Malachy. This lasted five years, when Maurice died, and was succeeded by another of the same kin called Nigellus.[1] But Malachy had by this time won over a large portion of the population, and one of the petty kings of the country, to his side. These determined to install him in his see of Armagh. The scheme was as determinedly opposed by the other party, who resolved to attack the archbishop and his adherents when they least expected it. Malachy became aware of the plot, and entering a church which was close by, "lifted up his hands, and prayed unto the Lord." And, behold, clouds and thick darkness forthwith turned day into night. Lightning-flashes and thunder-peals quickly followed, accompanied by terrific blasts of wind. The last day, or rather night, seemed to have arrived, and all the elements appeared to threaten death.[2] "Now that you may know, reader," remarks Bernard, "that Malachy's prayer did all this," take the following facts. The storm destroyed those only who sought after his soul ; the dark

---

cessio, decursis jam in hac malitia quasi generationibus quindecim. [This must be a mistake : Bernard further on says that the custom had existed for two hundred years.] . . . . inde illa ubique, pro mansuetudine Christiana, sæva subintroducta barbaries, imo paganismus quidam inductus sub nomine Christiano. Nam (quod inauditum est ab ipso Christianitatis initio) sine ordine, sine ratione mutabantur et multiplicabantur episcopi pro libitu metropolitani, ita ut unus episcopatus uno non esset contentus, sed singulae pene ecclesiae singulos haberent episcopos."—*Op.* St. Bern. vol. i. col. 667.

[1] Bernard can seldom resist a pun : "Nigellus quidam—immo vere nigerrimus—sedem praeripuit."

[2] "Res innotuit Malachiae, et intrans ecclesiam (erat enim prope) elevatis manibus oravit ad Dominum. Et ecce nubes et caligo, sed et tenebrosa aqua in nubibus aeris, diem verterunt in noctem : fulgura quoque et tonitrua et horribiles spiritus procellarum diem ultimum minitantur, vicinamque elementa intentant omnia mortem."—*Op.* St. Bern. vol. i. col. 669. Bernard here enters into competition—it can hardly be unconsciously—with Virgil : Æn. i. 81–92.

whirlwind overwhelmed only those who had prepared works
of darkness.   The prince and all who favoured the impious
intruder and schismatic were killed by the lightning, and were
partners in death as they had been in crime.   On the day
after the half-charred, putrid bodies were discovered dispersed
about, some even sticking in the branches of trees, just as the
wind had blown them.   As for Malachy and his friends, though
quite close to this devastation, they suffered no hurt whatever.
" In this event," continues Bernard, " we have a recent instance
of the truth of that saying, ' The prayer of the humble pierceth
the clouds ;' indeed it is a modern example of the old miracles
which covered Egypt with darkness, while in Israel it remained
light.   As the Scripture saith, ' All the children of Israel had
light in their dwellings.'   It brings to my mind also the history
of Elijah, who, at one time, brought clouds and rain from the
ends of the earth ; at another, invoked fire from heaven on the
blasphemers.   In a similar manner God was glorified in his
servant Malachy."[1]

   After this signal proof of his sanctity and fitness for the archiepiscopal office, Malachy found no opposition to his entrance
into Armagh.   A man who really can confute and destroy
his enemies with fire from heaven by simply "holding up
his hands," is not one whom others will oppose on trivial
grounds.   Still it would appear that the electric fluid was not
always equally at his command ; for Nigellus, the intruder, the
schismatic, the cause of all the grief and mischief, by some un-
accountable means contrived to escape the lightning, and get
away unhurt.   And, worse still, he had carried away with him
certain priceless relics which were of more importance to him

---

[1] " Et ut scias, lector, quod oratio
Malachiae concusserit elementa, solos intercepit tempestas qui quaerebant animam ejus ; solos turbo tene-
brosus involvit qui paraverant opera
tenebrarum. . . . Quorum sequenti
die inventa sunt corpora semiusta
et putrida, haerentia ramis arborum,
ubi quemque spiritus elevans allisis-
set." — *Op.* St. Bern. vol. i.
col. 669.

than the city of Armagh itself.   They consisted of a text of the
Gospels which had belonged to St. Patrick, and a pastoral staff,
covered with gold and adorned with the most costly jewels,
which was called Jesus' staff, because the belief was, that the
Lord Himself had held it in His hands, and even had made it.
Nothing could exceed the veneration with which these treasures
were regarded, and to such a degree was the feeling about
them carried, that whoever had them in his possession was
thought to be really and legally Archbishop of Armagh.   This
incident rouses Bernard's intense disgust.   He liked saints
and their relics as much as any one, in moderation, but this
childish devotion to a book and stick provokes him almost to
the use of intemperate language.   He calls the people who
could be so deceived "stupid" and "foolish," and Nigellus a
vagabond, another Satan going to and fro in the earth, and
walking up and down in it.   It was certainly enough to ruffle
even a saintly temper.   Nigellus was safe away, beyond the
reach of either thunder or lightning, showing off his relics,
which procured for him the most honourable reception wherever he went.   In fact, he was still considered archbishop, and
Malachy an intruder, who had thus reaped but a barren victory
after all.   He had the town, but his rival kept the office.[1]

Still Malachy bore up manfully against this and other trials.
He rushed unarmed among his enemies, and quelled them by
his bold innocency when they were just prepared to strike

---

[1] "Porro Nigellus videns sibi im-
minere fugam, tulit secum insignia
quaedam sedis illius, textum scilicet
Evangeliorum qui fuit beati Patricii,
baculumque auro tectum, et gemmis
pretiosissimis adornatum, quem no-
minant baculum Jesu, eo quod ipse
Dominus, ut fert opinio, cum suis
manibus tenuerit, atque formaverit.
. . . . Nempe notissima sunt cele-
berrimaque in populis atque in ea
reverentia apud omnes, ut qui illa
habere visus fuerit, ipsum habeat
episcopum populus stultus et insi-
piens.   Ibat homo gyrovagus, et
alter Satanas circuibat terram et
perambulabat eam, insignia sacra
circumferens ; quae ubique osten-
tans, ubique eorum gratia recepta-
batur, concilians sibi per haec ani-
mos omnium, et a Malachia quosque
potuissit avertens."—*Op.* St. Bern.
vol. i. col. 669.

him.   He introduced order and propriety in the city of
Armagh,—not, however, without constant risk to his life.
He was now no longer openly attacked; but neither time
nor place secured him from the danger of assassination.   A
body-guard of armed men was appointed to protect him day
and night; "but he trusted more in the Lord."

Nigellus, however, was a source of anxiety to him.   That
unprincipled person had still got in his possession those powerful relics, by which he seduced many, persuading them that he
ought to be considered primate.   But Malachy had acquired
an ascendancy among the population which his adversary
found it impossible to withstand.   He presently submitted
himself, and restored the relics to their rightful owner.

And now Malachy thought he would go abroad—would go to
Rome, and ask the Pope to give him the pallium.   He crossed
the Channel, and went to York.   There he met one Wallen,
"at that time the prior of regular canons at Kirkham, but now
a monk and the father of monks of our order in the Monastery
of Mailros."   Wallen noticed that, although Malachy had
several companions, he had but few horses for them; so he
offered them his own, if they would accept it.   "I would," said
he, "give it with far greater pleasure if it were a better one, and
not quite so rough."[1]   "I, on the contrary," said Malachy,
"receive him the more willingly the worse you speak of him.
Nothing can be bad to me which is given with such rare
good feeling."   Then to his own people, "Saddle him for me;
he will be comfortable enough, and will last a long while."
He then got on, and truly at first found him rough enough.   But

---

[1] "Obtulit ei suum [equum], quo
ipse vehebatur, hoc solum dolere se
inquiens, quod esset *runcinus* dure
portans."—*Op.* ST. BERN. vol. i.
col. 673.
  "He rode upon a rowncy as he could."
                        Chaucer.

"Quidam vocem ab Teutonico
Ross, equus, deducunt, non impro-
babili conjectura.   Nam nostri olim
Rous, pro *Roncin*, dicebant."—DU-
CANGE, *sub voce* Runcinus.

afterwards a wonderful change came over him, and he became the most soft and easy-going palfrey conceivable, lasting longer than his new master. He was still good when Malachy died. But one of the strangest facts about him has yet to be told, viz. that from nearly black he became white, and in a short time few could be compared to him for whiteness.

Malachy then proceeded on his way to Clairvaux. Touching his visit there Bernard enthusiastically says, "To me also in this life was it given to see this man ; in his look and word I was restored, and rejoiced as in all manner of riches. And, sinner as I was, I found grace in his sight from that time forth even to his death. For he deigned to turn aside to visit Clairvaux ; and when he saw the brethren he was pricked to the heart, and they were not a little edified by his presence and discourse. Thus accepting the place and ourselves, and becoming very dear unto us, he bade us farewell, and, departing, crossed over the Alps."

At that time Innocent II., of happy memory, was Pope. He received Malachy kindly, and politely condoled with him on the length of his journey. And first of all, with many tears, the Bishop begged a favour which was very near his heart, viz. that by the permission and blessing of his Holiness he might be allowed to live and die at Clairvaux. Innocent thought proper to refuse this request. Malachy then spent a month in Rome, examining and frequenting the holy places for the sake of prayer. When he was about to depart, the Pope made him legate for the whole of Ireland. Malachy then besought the Pope to confirm the constitution of the new metropolitan see which Celsus had established, and to grant the use of the pallium both to that and to Armagh. The confirmation asked for was granted at once. "As regards the pallium," said the Pope, "that is a more solemn matter. You must summon a general council of the bishops, clergy, and chief men of the country ; and then, on the wish and approbation of all, you will send honourable persons to ask for the pallium, and it shall be given to you." Then taking the mitre from his own head he placed it on Malachy's. He gave him also the stole and maniple which he himself was in the habit of using. And so, with the kiss of peace and his blessing, he sent him off on his long journey.

At this point we bid farewell to Malachy for a time. His remaining adventures will be told in his second visit to Clairvaux, nine years after this date.

BOOK III.

BOOK III.

———

CHAPTER I.

LETTER OF WILLIAM OF ST. THIERRY TO BERNARD AND THE BISHOP
OF CHARTRES—ALARM ABOUT THE HERESIES OF PETER ABELARD.

TOWARDS the end of the year 1139 Bernard and Geoffrey,
Bishop of Chartres, received the following letter from William
of St. Thierry :—

"I am confounded before you, my lords and fathers, when I,
a person of no consideration, am compelled to address you on
a subject of great and general importance, through your silence
and that of others to whom it belonged to speak.   For seeing,
as I do, that faith which is the hope of all dangerously and
greviously injured, no man gainsaying or resisting—the faith
which Christ consecrated by the shedding of His blood, for
which apostles and martyrs have fought even unto death,
which holy doctors, by their severe and manifold labours,
have transmitted to these wretched times sound, complete, and
incorrupt—I wither and pine away, and for very anxiety of
heart and sorrow of spirit I am driven to speak in defence
of that, for which, if it were necessary and fitting, I would lay
down my life.   Nor is the danger concerning minor points
only but threatens faith in the Blessed Trinity, in the person
of the Mediator, in the Holy Spirit, in the grace of God, in

the mystery of our common Redemption.   Peter Abelard is
again teaching novelties, again writing about them.   His books
pass the seas, cross the Alps; his new notions and dogmas
about the faith are carried through kingdom and province;
they are preached before many and as freely defended, insomuch that they are reported even to have influence at the
court of Rome.   I tell you it is with danger to the Church,
no less than to yourselves, that you keep silence.   We seem
to reckon it a small matter, that that faith is corrupted for
which we have denied ourselves to ourselves : lest we should
offend men, we do not fear to offend God.   I tell you this
evil has grown, and is growing, and, if it be not stopped,
will become a serpent for which a charmer will scarce be found.
The reason I speak thus you shall now hear.

"I lately fell by accident upon one of the works of that
person, which bore the title, 'The Theology of Peter Abelard;'
—I acknowledge I was struck, and felt a curiosity to read the
book.   There were two treatises containing almost the same
things, except that one embraced a little more than the other.
I have marked those passages which moved me to anger, and
have annexed my reasons for being incensed.   And I have
sent the whole to you.   You must judge whether I have
been in the right or not.   Being vehemently disconcerted by
innovations of expression in matters of faith, by new discoveries of unheard-of senses, and having no one near me to
refer to, I have chosen you, before all others, whom I could
call to the defence of God's cause and that of the whole
Latin Church.   For that man fears and dreads you.   Shut your
eyes, and whom will he care for?   And if he can say what he
does say now, what will he not say when he fears no one?
Most of our great masters of ecclesiastical learning being
dead, this domestic enemy, rushing in upon the deserted
commonwealth of the Church, has assumed to himself a very
singular office in her : doing in the Holy Scriptures what

he was wont to do in dialectics—that is, palming off his own discoveries, his annual crop of novelties. He, forsooth, is a critic of the faith, not a disciple; a reformer, not a learner.

" Here are the positions maintained in his work, which I have thought fit to bring under your notice :—(1) That he defines faith as being the estimation of things not seen. (2) That the names of Father, Son, and Holy Ghost, according to him, are improperly applied to God, and that this is a description of the fulness of the Highest Good. (3) That the Father is full Power, the Son a certain Power, the Holy Spirit no Power. (4) Of the Holy Spirit, that He is not of the substance of the Father and of the Son, as the Son is of the substance of the Father. (5) That the Holy Spirit is the soul of the world. (6) That by free will, without the assistance of grace, we can will and act rightly. (7) That Christ did not take flesh and suffer, that He might deliver us from subjection to Satan. (8) That Christ, God and man, is not the third person in the Trinity.[1] (9) That, in the Sacrament of the Altar, the form of the former substance remains in the air. (10) That diabolical suggestions are made to men through physic. (11) That from Adam we do not contract the fault of original sin, but its punishment. (12) That there is no sin, except in consenting unto sin, and in the contempt of God. (13) That sin is not committed by concupiscence and delectation and ignorance, and what is thus committed is not sin, but nature.

" These few points, collected from his works, I judged expedient first to show you, in order to stimulate you, and to excuse myself lest I should appear excited without a reason. I shall amplify what I now send, caring little if I offend you in speech, if I do not in doctrine. God is witness that I loved him, and wished to love him; but in such a cause as this no one shall

---

[1] " Quod Christus, Deus et homo, non est tertia persona in Trinitate."

ever be either my friend or neighbour. Nor can this evil be rectified by private warning and reproof, he himself having made it so public. There are, as I hear, other works of his, of which the names are *Sic et non, Scito te ipsum,* of which I fear the monstrous names only too well indicate the monstrous doctrines. But, as it is said, they fear the light, and even when sought for they cannot be found."[1]

Bernard at once replied that he highly approved of what William had done ; that as for going deeply into so difficult a question, he could not do so yet, not before Easter (*i.e.* of 1140) ; and that he would be exceedingly glad to have some earnest consultation with William on the subject, if they could meet. Meanwhile Lent, in which they now are, is the season for prayer. Bernard confesses ingenuously that he has, however, as yet no knowledge of the matter, though we cannot suppose that the name of so notorious a person as Abelard was unknown to him. For more than a quarter of a century before this date, Europe had been ringing with his fame, or even his infamy, it might be in Bernard's eyes. His meaning, therefore, is, that the special details of Abelard's heresy were strange to him ; and it is quite consonant with the Abbot of Clairvaux's character, to suppose that he would not readily travel out of his way to seek such, if some practical object did not bring them before him. That object had now arrived and in a form which, of all others, was most calculated to rouse the whole force of energy within him, viz. the welfare of the Church and the Christian, faith. Abelard's delinquencies were soon mastered, and the voice of the most admired and authoritative man in Europe was calling on Pope, Bishops, and Cardinals, to stay the progress of a second Arius and Nestorius.

But this great duel between two such lofty men, who stand out like mountain peaks above the plain of their contem-

[1] Op. St. Bern. vol. i. col. 302 ; Epist. 326.

poraries, representing, as it does, the shock and conflict of two great currents of human thought, requires for its adequate delineation that a sketch of the life and fortunes of Abelard up to this time be here inserted. Leaving Bernard, therefore, occupied with his Lenten observances, we advert to Master Peter, as he was then called.

CHAPTER II.

A.D. 1079.

MASTER PETER, surnamed Abelard,[1] was at this time sixty-one years old—Bernard's senior, therefore, by twelve years. His career had been a strange union of the extremes of good and evil fortune; no man of his day had been so admired, loved, execrated, and condemned.[2]

Abelard began his adventurous life early, for he left his father's roof in Brittany, in search of "fame and name," when

---

[1] "Petrus qui Abaelardus, a plerisque Bajolardus dicitur . . . . cui simul afflicto et indignanti per jocum Magister Firricul ait: quid canis plenus nisi lardum Baiare consuevit? Baiare autem linguere est. Exinde Bajolardus appellari cepit. Quod nomen, tanquam ex defectu quodam, cum abdicaret, sub litteratura non dissimili Habelardum se nominari fecit, quasi qui haberet artium apud se summam et adipem."—DUCANGE, *sub voce* Baiare.

[2] *Historia Calamitatum*, Epist. i. Op. Abelard, 4to. Paris, 1616. Also MIGNE's *Patrologia*, tom. 178. This letter, written by Abelard himself, is by far the most important extant authority for the facts of his life. But while its interest as a piece of autobiography has been generally admitted, it is not too much to say that its real character and meaning have as often been misunderstood. It is the great arsenal whence the enemies of Abelard have drawn their means of attacking him. The confessions in it have been paraded as conclusive against the man who could make such concerning himself. But these are not the reluctant admissions of a depraved man, but the exaggerated self-accusations of a broken-hearted one. It would be as fair to take the "Confessions" of St. Augustine or the "Grace Abounding" of Bunyan as unqualified sources of biography, as to found a life of Abelard entirely on the rhetorical and melancholy recital which he wrote in the evening of his chequered life.

about twenty years old. His family were noble, and lords of the Castle of Le Pallet, near Nantes, both at this period and probably for many generations after this. The names of his father and mother were Berengarius and Lucia. His father, though a knight, had also a knowledge and love of literature, which he was anxious to impart to his son. Rarely have a parent's wishes found such welcome from a child. The young Peter had no sooner tasted the delights of knowledge, than all other pursuits appeared worthless and insipid to him. He relinquished his birthright as eldest son; he discarded all thought of the profession of arms and knighthood; he devoted himself with an undivided mind to study and philosophy. It is supposed he came to Paris about the close of the eleventh century.[1]

The only living branch of knowledge then existing—*i.e.* unconnected with Theology—was Dialectics, and for Dialectics Abelard had the same spontaneous, victorious aptitude that Pascal had for geometry, and Mozart for music. Natural acuteness and suppleness of mind, coupled with a bold aggressive spirit, now qualified him to contend for the foremost rank among scholastic disputants. It was not long before he tested his powers. His adversary was a man whom we have met before in a very different occupation from what we find him engaged in now. William of Champeaux as yet did not know Bernard—did not know or expect anything of the bishopric of Châlons. At this date he was only Archdeacon of Paris, and Lecturer on Logic in the cloister of Notre Dame. Abelard, who at first was his pupil, soon became his rival, and before long his vanquisher. The point in discussion was the question of Universals. William of Champeaux was a realist of the most decided type. Abelard pressed him so hard that he was

---

[1] *Vie d'Abélard*, par M. Charles de Rémusat, vol. i. p. 8. This luminous and thoughtful work has nearly exhausted the subject of Abelard's history and philosophy.

compelled to abandon, or at least greatly modify, the views he had taught for years. From this defeat his reputation never recovered ; and Abelard, although he had made many enemies by his haughtiness and success, could walk the schools without a rival.[1]

But before he had got so far, he had been compelled to leave Paris twice—the first time in consequence of impaired health, caused by the overwork and excitement of his ambitious career ; the second time he returned to Brittany to bid farewell to his "dear mother Lucia," who, following her husband's example, was preparing to adopt a monastic life.[2]

Up to this time Abelard had confined his attention to the human sciences of the Trivium,—that is, Grammar, Rhetoric, and Dialectics. In an evil hour for his peace, if not for his fame, he was seized with a desire to become master of Theology. For this purpose he repaired to Laon, where the aged Anselm lectured on Holy Writ. "I betook myself to the old man," says Abelard, "who had a great name, rather through use and routine than from genius or knowledge. He was that sort of man that if any one went to him, being uncertain, he returned more uncertain still. He was wonderful to hear, but at once failed if you questioned him. He had an extraordinary flow of words, but was void of reason and contemptible in sense. When he lit a fire, he filled his house with smoke, he did not illuminate it with light."[3]   With these far

[1] The little I have to say on Abelard as a philosopher I reserve to the next chapter ; but as regards the philosophical merits of this discussion with William of Champeaux, the reader is referred to "Ouvrages inédits d'Abelard," Paris, 1836, ed. Cousin, intro. p. cxvi., and Rémusat, vol. i. p. 19.

[2] Dean Milman (*Lat. Christ.*, vol. iii. p. 360) unaccountably says that "a domestic affliction, the death of his beloved mother, sent him back to Brittany.' All that Abelard has told is contained in these words :—"Dum vero haec agerentur, charissima mihi mater Lucia repatriare me compulit. Quae, videlicet post conversionem Berengarii patris mei ad professionem monasticam, idem facere disponebat."—*Hist. Calamitatum.*

[3] "Cum ignem accenderet, domum suam fumo implebat, non luce illustrabat."—*Ibid.*

from reverential feelings he listened to Anselm: with what result may easily be imagined. "I did not long remain idle under his shade," says Abelard. He ceased to attend the lectures. The favourite pupils of the teacher resented this as an insult to their master, and before long Anselm was prejudiced by them against him.

It occurred that on a certain day, when the students were joking among themselves, one of them, with a sinister motive, asked him what he thought of the divinity lectures? He, who as yet had studied nothing but natural sciences, replied that nothing could be more profitable than the reading and study of the Scriptures, in which we learn how to save our souls; but that, for his part, he could not sufficiently wonder how to educated men the text of the sacred writers, together with their glosses, were not enough for their comprehension, or that they should require any further master. This remark was received with general scorn and derision, and he was asked whether he could or dared attempt such a thing himself. In that age of authority and tradition, the very supposition that any one should think for himself appeared absurd. Abelard was always willing, and even anxious, to think for himself: hence the constant collision he was coming into with his age. He said he should like nothing better than to make the experiment they defied him to attempt. With scoffs and ridicule they accepted the offer, and agreed that he should expound the obscure prophecy of Ezekiel. He said he was quite ready to begin on the following day. This last proposition appeared to sober them; they seemed to feel that it might be possible to carry a joke too far. They begged that in so grave a matter he would proceed cautiously, and give more time to a study of which he was, as yet, ignorant. Abelard's pride and vanity were roused at this remark, and he replied that it was not his custom to do things from painful practice, but from spontaneous genius; and added, that if they did not come when he wished them, they might stay away, and he should take no further notice of them. To the first lecture very few came. They regarded it as preposterous that any one could pretend to understand the Scriptures without more preliminary study.[1] Yet those who were present were so delighted, that they urged him to turn his lecture into a commentary. This was the commencement of his ill-starred theological career. Before long he was as open a rival to Anselm as he had been to William of Champeaux, and had excited the enmity, not only of the old professor, but also of his most influential pupils. He was forced to leave Laon.

He returned to Paris. And now commenced the one short period of brilliant fame, the clear interval of unalloyed prosperity and gratified ambition, which he was destined to know in life. Paris was already the most renowned school in Europe. Students from England, Germany, Italy, and Southern Gaul flocked to imbibe the scholastic and theological lore which it afforded them. This crowd of learners was now startled by the appearance of a teacher among them who, for power to kindle enthusiasm, and make men rejoice that they were permitted to be his disciples, had not been equalled since the days of the Athenian sages. No pale pedant or emaciated bookworm was he. Noble by birth and haughty in carriage, gifted with vast powers and fully conscious of them, singularly handsome, and enhancing this advantage by a costly and scrupulous attention to dress, Abelard taught, with vigorous, daring originality, almost the whole sum of human science then known or cared for: that is, he taught philosophy as it was then understood, and he taught theology. He was admired, followed, waylaid, obstructed by passionate adherents, and by many who were not adherents. His success was complete;

---

[1] "Et primae quidem lectioni nostrae pauci tunc interfuere, quod ridiculum omnibus videretur, me adhuc quasi penitus sacrae lectionis expertem, id tam propere aggredi." —*Hist. Calam.*

his rivals were silenced; he grew rich; his head was nearly turned.[1]

But now came a great change upon Abelard. Up to this time his books and his studies, his ambition and his efforts to gratify it, had entirely absorbed his thoughts and energies. But the pinnacle was reached, the pressure was removed, his efforts were relaxed. The strong impulses which had been hitherto directed to a single end were now let loose to wander as they pleased. His victory was too much for him. The sleeping volcano of his adult passions burst forth. Pleasure, sensual and animal, was a novelty and a marvel to him: he became suddenly conscious of a fierce, fiery thirst for it. He drank deeply, wildly. He then grew fastidious and particular. He required some delicacy of romance, some flavour of emotion, to remove the crudity of his lust. He seduced Heloise.[2]

---

[1] M. de Rémusat has given an imaginative picture of Abelard at this period which is not necessarily untruthful, although it is without historical evidence of its truth. "On voyait souvent passer un homme au front large, au regard vif et fier, à la démarche noble, dont la beauté conservait encore l'éclat de la jeunesse, en prenant les traits plus marqués et les couleurs plus brunes de la pleine virilité. Son costume grave et pourtant soigné," &c., vol. i. p. 43. One sentence of Heloise is as graphic as anything: "Quis, te rogo, in publicum procedentem conspicere non festinabat, ac discedentem collo erecto, oculis directis non insectabatur."—Epist. ii., *Quae est Heloissae ad Petrum deprecatoria.*

[2] There are two assertions here which require proof: 1. That Abelard ever led a licentious life at all, considering his assertion to the contrary, "Quia igitur scortorum immunditiam semper abhorrebam."

(*Hist. Calam.*) 2. That this period of incontinence must have *preceded* his connexion with Heloise, and was not contemporary with it. As regards the first point, Abelard's statement is more than counterbalanced by the explicit account of his irregularities sent to him in a letter by Fulk, Prior of Deuil: "Haec corporis particula quam omnipotentis Dei judicio et beneficio perdidisti, quantum tibi nocuerat ac nocere quamdiu permansit, non desistebat, melius tuarum diminutio rerum quam mea possit monstrare oratio, docet. Quidquid . . . . acquirere poteras in voraginem fornicariae consumptionis demergere non cessabas. Avara meretricum rapacitas cuncta tibi rapuerat . . . qui nihil, ut dicitur, praeter pannos ex tanto quaestu habebas."—Ab. *Op.* p. 219. It is difficult to suppose that these assertions are entirely without foundation. Abelard's conduct, at the commencement, to Heloise was in no wise that of a

It is not probable that the depth of soul and mind of this wonderful woman were all seen by him when he first planned and perpetrated this enormity. She was the niece of a canon of Paris named Fulbert. It is supposed that Abelard was also a canon at this time. He might thus have facilities of access and intimacy from an early period of her life. Heloise was not beautiful,[1] but her intellectual and literary pre-eminence were truly marvellous in that age. Her name was already famous throughout the kingdom for her unequalled powers and cultivation of mind. The story is well known. Abelard got himself received into her uncle's house as her tutor. He was thus thrown into the closest relations with perhaps the only woman then in the world who could thoroughly appreciate and do justice to his own vast powers of mind. He corrupted and defiled her ; but the most burning passion and devotion that ever swelled under woman's breast were already kindled towards him. Abelard, the doctor, the world-famed scholar and philosopher, in the pride of manhood and renown, sought the young girl's heart. She fell willingly, knowingly, self-abasingly at his feet, and never wished to rise again. Through long years of shame, sorrow, and remorse, the unutterable ecstasy of those days of sin never faded from her memory, as she

novice in gallantry, but rather such as might be expected from a hardened offender. Still—to go on to the second point—I do not think he was ever base enough to lead the life above described *after* he had become acquainted with his future wife. Even if he had had the inclination, the various agitating vicissitudes of his courtship and marriage would not have allowed him the requisite leisure.

[1] It is strange that modern historians persist in seeing more beauty in Heloise than Abelard himself did. Dean Milman says she " was no less distinguished for her *surpassing beauty* than for her wonderful talents and knowledge." Abelard's words are very different : " Quae cum per faciem non esset *infima* per abundantiam litterarum erat suprema." M. de Rémusat and Mr. G. H. Lewes (Hist. of Philosophy, p. 295) both say more of her personal charms than their authority warrants. Bayle had to complain of the same assumption in his day, and he exposed it with his usual acuteness. After quoting the words of Abelard just given, he says, " Est ce ainsi qu'on parle d'une fille parfaitement belle?"

walked through life with ever-reverted glances on the glory of her girlish love.

Abelard's genius drooped and withered under this storm of passion. The delights of intellect and the treasures of knowledge, for which he had hitherto lived, grew black and tarnished to the fevered vision of his distempered mind. His books, his philosophy, his lectures, his pupils, were neglected. He spoke to his admiring audience of disciples as before, but with only a fraction of his soul. The rest was with Heloise. This could not last. His scholars saw the change, and mourned over it. All Paris saw it. The last person who saw it was the most interested to see it. At last the uncle Fulbert saw it, and the lovers were separated. They soon met again, and contrived a plan for Heloise to escape. One night, during Fulbert's absence, Abelard gained access to the house, and carried off his mistress. He sent her into Brittany, where she remained under the care of his sister Dionysia. She there gave birth to a son, whom she named Astrolabius.[1]

Meanwhile her lover, in Paris, was left exposed to the passionate resentment of Fulbert. Abelard says he became almost mad with rage. Nothing but fear prevented his revenge from taking the form of personal violence on Abelard's person, who, however, declares he kept himself prepared not only to resist, but even to assail, his foe, if he deemed it advisable. In time, prudence, contrition, or less worthy motives, induced him to offer terms of reconciliation to Fulbert. He freely acknowledged the enormity of his crime, and showed his

---

[1] " Quadam itaque nocte avunculo ejus absente, sicut nos condixeramus, eam de domo avunculi furtim sustuli, et in patriam meam sine mora transmisi; ubi apud sororem meam tamdiu conversata est donec pareret masculum quem Astrolabium nominavit."—*Hist. Calam.* Madame Guizot says, " Il l'enleva *déguisée* en *religieuse*, et la *conduisit* en Bretagne chez sa sœur" (*Essai Historique sur Abélard et Héloise,* p. 27); statements which Abelard's words in no wise bear out. Dean Milman has fallen into the same error (*Lat. Christ.,* vol. iii. p. 363), perhaps through reliance on Mdme. Guizot.

readiness to atone for it in any way Fulbert might choose; he was willing even to marry Heloise on the condition that the marriage should be kept secret.[1] Fulbert accepted, or appeared to accept, the satisfaction, and Abelard went into Brittany to fetch his bride.

There is a tradition that in that portion of the wild and rugged Armorica which is tempered and softened by the wooded banks of the Maine and Loire the lovers passed a short season of dreamy, absorbing happiness. But a difficulty of the most unexpected kind now arose. Heloise would not hear of Abelard's scheme of marriage. She declared that such a wrong should never be done to the world and the Church through her—that Abelard, who was created for all mankind, should not be sacrificed by bondage to a single woman. She drew arguments from antiquity, sacred and profane, to enforce her opposition. Even their love would suffer from the chains of wedlock, and no longer be the free passion of two unfettered souls. As his mistress, his *amica*, she would be happier in herself, and less burdensome to him, than if she were his wife. What if they could meet but rarely? Time and absence would only add to the intensity of their delight, when the wished-for moments came.[2] Abelard refused to be convinced.

---

[1] Abelard's words are, "Atque ut amplius cum mitigarem supra quam sperare poterat, obtuli me ei satisfacere, eam scilicet quam corruperam mihi matrimonio copulando: dummodo id secreto fieret, *ne famae detrimentum* incurrerem. Assensit ille," etc.—*Hist. Calamitat.* Fulbert was evidently playing with Abelard, as the latter afterwards saw. What he offered as a reparation—a secret marriage—was no reparation if the secresy was preserved. From the very nature of the case it was necessary that the satisfaction should be as public as the scandal had been. Fulbert saw this, and acted accordingly.

[2] Heloise's arguments against marriage with Abelard might afford material for a small dissertation. The ground she takes up is not a little remarkable. The marriage is represented not as illegal or sinful, but as disgraceful and lowering to herself as well as to him. "Quaerebat etiam quam de me gloriam habitura esset; cum me ingloriosum efficeret, *et se et me pariter humiliaret*. . . . . Detestabatur vehementer hoc matrimonium quod mihi per omnia probrosum esset atque onerosum."—

When Heloise saw the firmness of his resolution, she yielded, but added, with the darkest misgivings : " Nothing more remains for us, but that a misery as great as the love which preceded it consummate the ruin of us both." " Wherein," says Abelard, " the entire world has recognised that she was not wanting in the spirit of prophecy."

They returned, therefore, to Paris, the little Astrolabius being left in the care of Dionysia. " After a few days, we passed the

---

Hist. Calam. Abelard by no means considered wedlock entirely forbidden to churchmen. " Utrum clerici matrimonium contrahere possint quaeri solet. Sacerdotes qui non fecerunt, possunt. Si vero aliquis in ecclesia, quae votum suscepit, fuerit, qui non votum fecerit, potest ducere, sed in ecclesia illa officium non exercebit, quod est parochiam non tenebit."—*Epitome Theolog. Christ.*, cap. 31. But although the marriage of priests may not have been as yet strictly illegal, it is certain that both they and their wives were regarded most unfavourably. The following is part of a long address which a renowned prince and saint of the Church thought himself justified in making to the concubines of clerics. " Interea et vos alloquor, O lepores clericorum, pulpamenta diaboli, projectio paradisi, virus mentium, gladius animarum, aconita bibentium, toxica convivarum, materia peccandi, occasio pereundi. Vos, inquam, alloquor gynecaea hostis antiqui, upupae, ululae, noctuae, lupae, sanguisugae. . Venite itaque, audite me, scorta, prostibula, savia, volutabra porcorum pinguium . cubilia spirituum immundorum, nymphae, sirenae, lamiae, dianae," etc. etc.—*St. Petri Damiani Opusc.*, xviii., contra clericos intemperantes. The notion these men had of holy matrimony is partly shown in these words of the same writer :—" Ah scelus ! Manus quae deputatae fuerant ad ordinandas in coelestis mensae ferculo vitales epulas angelorum, tractare non metuunt obscoenitates et spurca contagia mulierum. Ii qui inter illa terribilia sacramenta choris admiscentur angelicis mox tanquam de coelo ruentes ad foemineae foeditatis relabuntur amplexus, et velut sues immundae coenosis vermigenae luxuriae volutabris immerguntur."—*Ibid.* Absurd bombast as all this is, yet coming from such a quarter, from a man whose party had won a great victory in the Church shortly before, it is not without significance; it shows what a woman who married a churchman was possibly exposed to. So far from " his career of advancement in the Church " being the main point of her objections, it is not dwelt upon at all.—See *Lat. Christ.* vol. iii. p. 363. The only words in which the Church is alluded to are these : " Quaerebat:—Heloisa . . . . quantas ab ea mundus poenas exigere deberet, si tantam ei lucernam auferret, quantae maledictiones, quanta *damna ecclesiae*, quantae philosophorum lacrymae, hoc matrimonium essent secuturae." The rest of her objections, which fill two quarto pages, refer to considerations of a totally different kind.

night in a certain church, celebrating in prayer and secresy the vigils of our marriage. At early dawn, in the presence of her uncle and a few common friends, we were united with the nuptial blessing."

But Fulbert broke his promise, and divulged the marriage. Whereupon Heloise vehemently denied it. Her uncle heaped upon her reproaches and contempt. Abelard, mortified and angry, removed her from his house, and placed her in the convent of Argenteuil, where she had been educated at a former period. She took the dress but not the vows of a nun. The distance from Paris is but a few miles. A few miles are but a small impediment to the meeting of ardent lovers. The swift feet of passion often carried Abelard to Argenteuil. His nun-wife, we may be quite sure, received him with no religious austerity or placid calmness of manner. She, in whose breast the fire of love burnt clear and radiant through years of fasting, vigils, solitude, and separation, would know how to welcome her worshipped lord when he came to the convent gate. The nuns of Argenteuil had not a reputation for excessive severity, and the married lovers availed themselves fully of the freedom afforded them by the hospitable convent. Abelard's passion and vainglory had now reached a point at which prudence and sobriety are utterly forgotten. But the fall was at hand, a mighty Nemesis was about to overtake him.

The revengeful nature of Fulbert had never really forgiven the wrong which had been done him by Abelard. Of late, circumstances had tended to kindle afresh all the fury of his resentment. Heloise's retreat to Argenteuil he interpreted as a deeply-laid scheme to rid Abelard of all encumbrance that might arise from his secret marriage. He invented, or accepted, a horrible and grotesque mode of revenge. In the dead of night he and others burst in upon the sleeping husband of his niece, and inflicted by an atrocious mutilation the utmost that could be devised by a barbarian's imagination.[1]

When the light of morning returned to the wretched man, it found the whole city agitated and confounded at the crime of the preceding night. The bishop, the canons, the clerics, above all the women[2] and students, were loud and vehement in their expression of indignation. Abelard lay in agony of mind and body, which all the condolences of friends and sympathisers only intensified. This sudden fall in mid-career utterly crushed him. So bright and victorious yesterday, so mean, miserable, and despised to-day. In the deepest gloom and confusion he sought a refuge in the abbey of St. Denis, while Heloise became a nun in reality as well as in appearance at Argenteuil.[3]

[1] Two of his assailants were captured, of whom one was his own faithless servant—and "oculis et genitalibus privati sunt." — *Hist. Calam.* p. 17.

[2] Abelard has not mentioned the fact of the women's lamentations. Fulk, Prior of Deuil, relates it in the letter already quoted. "Quid singularum feminarum referam planctum, quae sic, hoc audito, lacrymis more foemineo ora rigarunt propter te militem suum, quem amiserant, ac si singulae virum suum aut amicum sorte belli reperissent extinctum."— AB. *Op.* Epist. xvi. p. 221.

[3] It appears that in the first instance he was highly dissatisfied with the efforts made to punish his enemies, and even thought of going to Rome for the purpose of bringing his griefs before the Pope. Fulk, of Deuil, strongly urged him not to go on a useless errand : "You have not money," he says, "and what can you hope to do at Rome without money ?" "Quotquot enim nostris temporibus ad illam sedem sine pondere pecuniae accesserunt, perdita causa, confusi et reprobi abscesserunt." Every student of history who has felt under obligations to M. l'Abbé Migne for his cheap and portable editions of the Mediæval writers must be filled with disgust to find that a long passage of Fulk's letter —containing the last quotation and several facts—has been excised on the pretence that it would cause scandal to "Catholic ears." Such folly is surprising in a man of learning. Does he suppose the corruption of the court of Rome at this period is a rare secret, which Fulk's letter would reveal to the world ? He had better begin then by expurgating St. Bernard's works, and no longer allow the crushing charges in the "De Consideratione" to pervert the public mind. I cannot think that the faith of modern Romanists is so fragile that it is liable to injury from the words of Romanists written seven hundred years ago. This is the note in which M. l'Abbé Migne shows us how he views his duty as an editor :— "Pergit Fulco Abaelardum, quin Roman petat iis rationum momentis

He found the monks of St. Denis worldly and dissolute, and told them so in very plain terms, and before long he had made himself "odious and burdensome beyond measure to every one."[1]   Pleased as they had been at first to have him as one of their monks, they now openly rejoiced when, through the importunity of Abelard's scholars, who wished him to renew his teaching, a pretext for getting rid of him was offered.   He removed to the priory of Maisoncelle, and before long had gathered round him such a concourse of hearers, that neither food nor shelter could be procured for the thronging multitude. He still held out that double attraction to the more ardent minds of his day which had received such applause at Paris, viz. Dialectics and Divinity.   His divinity was what would now be called a philosophy of religion.   It was not a soul-moving call to repentance and sacrifice, but a scientific examination and corroboration of the grounds of belief.   "It happened that I first of all applied myself to discuss the basis of our faith, by the aid of analogies drawn from human reason, and composed a treatise on the 'Divine Trinity and Unity' for my pupils, who wanted and asked for human and philosophical reasons, and such as could be understood as well as spoken. They said that the pronouncing of words which the intellect could not follow was useless, nor was it possible for anything to be believed unless first understood.   It was ridiculous for a man to preach to others that which neither he himself nor they could intellectually grasp."[2]   Those were solemn and signifi-

absterrere quae non sine maximo scandalo catholicae aures exciperent, siquidem Romanam curiam talibus lacessit injuriis quales haeretici, immo impiissimi nostrae aetatis homines usurpare consueverant. Hunc igitur locum ut sanctae ecclesiae, ita lectoribus nostris molestissimum, expungere non dubitavimus."—*Patrologia*, tom. clxxviii. col. 375.
    [1] Abelard's accusations against the monks of St. Denis would be willingly denied, were they not supported by St. Bernard's authority.— *Epist.* 78.
    [2] "Accidit autem mihi ut ad ipsum fidei nostrae fundamentum humanae rationis similitudinibus disserendum primo me applicarem, et quemdam Theologiae tractatum de Unitate et Trinitate divina scholaribus nostris componerem, qui

cant words at the beginning of the twelfth century. The deep sleep of ages, which fell on the intellect of Europe with the fall of Rome, is apparently passing away. Through this long period, during which the human mind has lain still in the similitude of death, occasional starts and turns, signs that the giant was not dead, but sleeping, have not been entirely wanting. There have been Gotteschalc and Scotus Erigena, Berengarius and Roscelinus. The light of free reason had appeared in scattered stars more than once during these six hundred years. But the sacred fire could not spread then. It was soon and easily extinguished by a little violence to the original kindler of it. But now a change is preparing; "words which the mind cannot follow" are pronounced useless. Numbers of men, young men, are asking for "human and philosophical reasons," declaring they wish to understand as well as to believe. These poor scholars, following their Abelard into desolate places, are the unconscious parents of a good deal.

Meanwhile, his enemies were on the watch. William of Champeaux and Anselm of Laon had left successors who were only too willing to carry on the rivalry against Abelard which had been waged by their masters. And now this work on the Trinity exposed him to their attacks in a way they had hardly hoped for. A gathering, "which they called a council, was got together at Soissons;" the papal legate Conan presided; and Abelard was summoned to appear. He and a few faithful disciples narrowly escaped stoning by the ignorant populace, who had been led to believe that he maintained there were three Gods. But, even so, Abelard had friends. He preached to the people, and expounded his views, and his

humanas et philosophicas rationes requirebant, et plus quae intelligi quam quae dici possent efflagitabant; dicentes quidem verborum superfluam esse prolationem, quam intelligentia non sequeretur, nec credi posse aliquid nisi primitus intellectum, et ridiculosum esse aliquem aliis praedicare quod nec ipse nec illi quos doceret intellectu capere possent."— AB. *Op.* p. 20.

enemies trembled lest his great name, influence, and powers
might be too much for them. They were careful to avoid a
discussion in which they knew well who would fare best, they
or the greatest disputant in Europe. They at last prevailed
upon the legate to condemn the book without further inquiry.
" On being called, I presented myself before the council, and,
without any discussion or examination, they compelled me to
burn it with my own hand. And so it was burnt amid general
silence. One of my adversaries, in an undertone, murmured
that he had found it asserted in that book that God the Father
alone was Almighty. The legate said he could hardly believe
it ; even in a child such error was incredible, seeing that the
common faith holds and professes 'three Almighties.'" Hereupon a certain Terricus, a professor in the schools, burst out
laughing, and, quoting St. Athanasius, whispered : " And yet not
three Almighties, but one Almighty." His bishop reproved
him for his rude behaviour, but Terricus boldly continued, saying in the words of Daniel : "Are ye such fools, ye sons of
Israel, that without examination or knowledge of the truth ye
have condemned a daughter of Israel? Return again to the
place of judgment : for they have borne false witness against
her." Archbishop Rodolph, of Rheims, came to the rescue
of the zealous but incautious legate, and, slightly changing the
words, said : "Truly, my lord, the Father is Almighty, the Son
Almighty, and the Holy Ghost Almighty. And now," he went
on to say, " it were good if that brother"—pointing to Abelard
—"were to explain his faith before us all, so that it may be
approved, condemned, or corrected, as may be necessary."
When he arose to expound his faith in his own words, his
judges said there was no necessity for anything beyond his
recital of the Athanasian creed, "a thing which any boy could
do." To complete his humiliation by a practical sarcasm, they
placed a copy of the creed before him, hinting thereby that
the document was doubtless new to him, and that he could not

be expected to know it without. "I read amid sobs and sighs and tears, as well as I could," and then, "like a convicted criminal, I was given over to the Abbot of St. Medard, to be kept in close custody at his monastery." [1]

Abelard declared that the mental anguish he felt at this condemnation far outweighed the physical pain he had endured in Paris. The excess of his grief drove him into impatience, even into profanity. In the words of St. Anthony, he exclaimed : "Good Jesus ! where wast Thou then?" His former punishment he acknowledged had been partly due to his own fault, but the conduct which had led to this disgrace had been purely meritorious. However, this misery also became lighter in time. The abbot and monks of St. Medard were kind to him, although the prior occasionally lectured him with some severity. He, by degrees, grew more gentle and submissive. He got to dread the convent whip, and generally improved. He was then restored to his own monastery of St. Denis. [2]

He soon again aroused the hatred of his brother monks. It occurred to him to doubt, from the perusal of Bede, whether St. Dionysius the Areopagite really was the founder of their abbey, and patron saint of the kingdom. There was something revolting at that day in a monk's seeking to degrade the character of a saint to whom his convent was dedicated. They rebuked him, they threatened him they would tell the king, whose very crown was injured by him, they whipped him for such a horrible opinion. Abelard was in despair. His enemies

---

[1] I have very much condensed Abelard's graphic and sarcastic account of the council, which can be read in the Hist. Calam. pp. 20—24.

[2] St. Medard appears at this time to have become a sort of general penitentiary under the superintendence of the vigorous Gosvinus, who did not hesitate, when occasion offered, to break a lance in argument, even with Abelard himself. "Mittebantur illuc indocti ut erudirentur, dissoluti ut corrigerentur, cervicosi ut domarentur." —*Dom Bouquet*, tom. xiv. p. 445. It was after a dispute with Gosvinus that Abelard "pavefactus rhinoceros ille quietius dies illas transigebat, patientior disciplinae, timidior flagellorum."—*Ibid.*

and his troubles pursued him like his shadow. He fled away
by night from St. Denis into the lands of Count Theobald, the
old friend of Bernard.   His persecutor, the Abbot Adam, presently died, and the liberal and statesmanlike Suger, who succeeded him, gave Abelard free permission to seek any refuge
he liked, provided he did not become the subject of any other
monastery.

Abelard was now past forty.   He had tried many modes of
life, and none had succeeded with him.   In utter disgust and
abhorrence of men and their ways, he plunged into the deepest
solitude, and became a hermit on the banks of the Ardusson,
not far from Troyes.   He built an oratory of reeds and stubble.
But men like Abelard can no more live without society than a
flame without oxygen gas.   His eager admirers soon knew of
his retreat, soon sought for him, and found him ; and we are
nowhere told that he sent them empty away.   Before long he
had again peopled the wilderness.   They rebuilt his church
for him, which he dedicated to the Paraclete.   This also nearly
involved him in fresh disaster.   It was regarded as a dangerous
innovation to dedicate a church to one Person of the Trinity,
except that Person was Christ.   Custom had ruled that to the
entire Trinity or to the Son alone could a dedication be made.
He was thus again the centre of admiration and animosity.
Gloom and distrust settled on his mind.   Like Rousseau,
whom he resembled in many ways, he fancied he was persecuted by men who scarcely knew of his existence.   He was
quite convinced at this period that Bernard was a strenuous
enemy of his, which is not far short of impossible.   He at last
meditated a flight from Christian countries altogether, and
taking up his abode with the infidels.   He would pay them
tribute, he thought, and obtain peace and quietness among the
enemies of Christ.   He says he expected to meet with good
treatment from them, as they would regard him, by reason of
the charge of heresy, as offering probable hopes of conversion

to their faith. These reflections show that he must have carried this thought almost to the verge of a determination.[1]

In this condition of irritation and anxiety he passes some years in the flat, dreary country of Champagne. At last a deliverance seemed to be brought to him. On the bleak and savage coasts of Brittany, on a promontory to the south of Vannes, there was a monastery called St. Gildas de Rhuys. The shore is covered with large masses of pointed granite rocks; the surrounding country is full of sombre and marvellous monuments of Druidical architecture or worship. To be the abbot of this lonely convent Abelard was now invited. He accepted the offer, and at once undertook his new charge. Painful, even insupportable, must have been his life near Troyes, to cause him to look on such a change as a happy one. Amid a semi-barbarous race, whose language was unintelligible to him, without friends, without sympathy, the careworn Abelard assumed the command of a poor monastery of dissolute, unscrupulous monks. He could hear the melancholy plash of the Atlantic waves; the cold ocean stretched out beyond, and seemed to say that he could fly no more, that here he must rest and suffer.[2] Night and day he was tormented by the wickedness of his new subjects. They were shameless. They kept concubines in the abbey, and lived surrounded by their illegitimate offspring. He found the lands of the monastery were completely in the power of a neighbouring petty tyrant, and the monks expected their abbot to furnish

---

[1] "Saepe autem (Deus scit) in tantam lapsus sum desperationem, ut Christianorum finibus excessis, ad gentes transire disponerem, atque ibi quiete sub quacunque tributi pactione inter inimicos Christi Christiane vivere."—*Hist. Calam.* p. 33.

[2] "Terra quippe barbara, et terrae lingua mihi incognita erat [a strange assertion, considering he was born not many miles distant]. sic ego ab uno periculo in aliud scienter me contuli ibique ad horrisoni undas oceani cum fugam mihi ulterius terrae postremitas non praeberet, saepe in orationibus meis illud revolvebam 'A finibus terrae ad te clamavi dum anxiaretur cor meum.'"—*Hist. Calam.* p. 34.

them with the means for their self-indulgence. This constant falling from one misery to a greater plunged him into a gloom which cannot be described. His whole life seemed a failure, and he felt that he had lived in vain.

During all this period of persecution and misfortune, the convent gates of Argenteuil have shut from our view the wife and nun, Heloise. The agony and dreary misery undergone by that fiery nature are not recorded for us. Stern, stoical fortitude, rather than Christian resignation, supported the wife of Abelard. The undaunted woman who, when beset by re monstrating friends on taking the veil, marched towards the altar, chanting the words of the Roman matron,—

> " O maxime conjux !
> O thalamis indigne meis !   Hoc juris habebat
> In tantum Fortuna caput ?   Cur impia nupsi
> Si miserum factura fui ?   Nunc accipe poenas
> Sed quas sponte luam," [1]—

was far removed from the pale, bloodless abnegation of personality which then was expected from "a sister in Christ." Whether she ever approached that ideal will be seen in the sequel. Meanwhile she was at this moment a houseless wanderer, having been, with the other nuns, driven out of her retreat at Argenteuil by the enterprising Suger, who had discovered that by virtue of old charters the convent belonged to the Abbey of St. Denis.[2] Heloise had risen to the dignity of prioress ; so that it is probable that her intellectual and adminis-

---

[1] LUCAN, *Phars.* b. viii. v. 94.

[2] When Suger was a young novice at St. Denis, he employed his leisure in examining the old charters by which the monastery held its lands. One which he discovered clearly established the right of St. Denis to the convent of Argenteuil. When he became abbot, and a man of importance, he determined to try and make good his claims. He sent his proofs to Rome, and begged for an investigation. The justice of his cause, he says, and the enormity of the nuns' lives, caused the Pope to decide the matter in his favour : " Tam pro nostra justitia, quam pro enormitate monacharum ibidem male viventium, eumdem nobis locum cum appendiciis suis, ut reformaretur ibi religionis ordo, restituit."—SUGERIUS, *De rebus in admin. sua gestis,* cap. 3.

trative powers had outweighed her deficiency of religious fervour. It must have taken some time before the remote Abelard in his lonely exile could hear of the misfortune. When he did, he appears to have acted with a decision not usual with him. It at once occurred to him that the deserted Paraclete could now be inhabited again. He hastened into Champagne. He invited his wife, and those of her nuns who still followed her, to occupy his old hermitage. He made a formal and legal concession to them of the oratory and all that thereto pertained. He prevailed on Atto, Bishop of Troyes, to confirm the donation. Misfortune had rendered him cautious and suspicious. To entirely preclude any subsequent cavil or machination of his enemies, he determined to get a papal letter to corroborate his deed. It will be remembered that Innocent II. made a lengthened sojourn in the north of France at the commencement of his pontificate. The most illustrious lords, both spiritual and temporal, gathered around him in his progress. At Morigni, a Benedictine monastery near Etampes, he stayed two days. There, surrounded by cardinals and bishops, he consecrated the high altar of the abbey church. In that company was Abelard. Shortly afterwards, the Pope published a bull which threatened excommunication against all who molested in any way "his dear daughters in Christ, Heloise the Prioress, and the other sisters in the Oratory of the Holy Trinity [*i.e.* the Paraclete], in the district of Troyes."[1]

At the period when Innocent was at Morigni Bernard never left his side : therefore he and Abelard must have met here, probably for the first time. Abelard had been convinced that part of his misfortunes was due to the enmity of the Abbot of Clairvaux. Thus, besides the natural repulsion of two such antipathetic minds, the notion of wrong would be present in one of them, to add to the discord. It is quite presumable,

---

[1] Innocent's letter to Heloise is dated from Auxerre, November 28th, 1131.—*Gall. Christ.* xii.; *Instrumenta*, p. 259.

also, that the little Bernard knew of Abelard was to his disadvantage. Such a loud-sounding career as his had been must have penetrated even a Cistercian seclusion ; and Bernard was now in the world. His old friend and adviser, William of Champeaux, ten years ago, in some of those mutual visits at Chalons or Clairvaux, would not be indisposed, perhaps, to remember some disparaging anecdotes of his former vanquisher. This meeting, therefore, was not, in all likelihood, a pleasant one.

We know of another instance in which their minds met, even if they did not meet in the flesh. It arose in the following manner. The Paraclete was not very distant from Clairvaux ; and on one occasion Bernard presented himself at Heloise's convent. He was received with all the homage the nuns could show to so distinguished a guest. He preached to them, and attended the office of vespers in their chapel. He was not a little astonished to observe, that in the Lord's Prayer a change was introduced, at variance with the custom of the Latin churches. They followed the version of St. Matthew throughout ; instead of taking from St. Luke the simple expression of "daily bread," they retained the text of the first Evangelist, and said "super-substantial bread." Bernard remarked to Heloise that the innovation appeared to him unnecessary. She gave as her authority the Abbot of St. Gildas. It does not appear that Bernard took any further steps in the matter ; he probably felt he had done enough, and that it was no business of his to supervise Heloise's devotions. Not so thought Abelard, when he heard of the remark made. He at once wrote a long argumentative letter to Bernard to maintain his point. He seems to exult in the opportunity of breaking a lance with him. This retiring, subtle enemy, as he supposes him, has at last laid himself open to a few dexterous thrusts. He begins with such excessive civility as to suggest the thought of irony far more than genuine good-will. He says that Heloise and her nuns had long wished to see Bernard, and that now he had visited them they felt comforted by his exhortations, not as if he were a man, but an angel. He then proceeds to show, with considerable force, why St. Matthew should be followed exclusively, in preference to an isolated deference to Luke. As he goes on he waxes warmer; he grows sarcastic. At last, like an old hunter hearing the hounds again, the disputant in him gets the mastery, and he breaks away into fierce invective. He forgets he is an abbot, writing to an abbot; he sees only an adversary, whom he is determined to knock down. After quoting St. Gregory, to show that he was right from authority as well as from reason, and claiming a certain licence of selection among the customs of the Christian churches, he says :—

"You Cistercians, indeed, are so vehement in your adherence to such a course, that you keep it and defend it against the practice of all the churches. You, forsooth, novel upstarts, and not a little proud of your novelty, have decided on celebrating the Holy Office in a way opposed to the ancient, universal, and long-continued custom whether of monks or clerks. And yet you do not expect to be blamed if this novelty or singularity of yours differs from antiquity, so long as you consider it consonant with reason and the tenor of the Rule; neither do you care for the wonder and objections of others, provided you follow what you think are your reasons.[1]

[1] "Vos quippe quasi noviter, exorti, ac de novitate plurimum gaudentes, praeter consuetudinem omnem tam clericorum tam monachorum longe ante habitam, et nunc quoque permanentem, novis quibusdam decretis aliter apud vos divinum officium instituistis agi; nec tamen inde vos accusandos censetis. Si haec vestra novitas aut singularitas ab antiquitate recedat aliorum, quam rationi plurimum et tenori regulae creditis concordare : nec cura tis quantacunque admiratione super hoc alii moveantur, ac murmurent dummodo vestrae, quam putatis, rationi pareatis."—AB. *Op.*, ed. Cousin, tom. i. p. 622. I have quoted this passage as M. Cousin, following all the editions, prints it. But I think there can be little doubt that a change of punctuation is required. I have translated as if it ran, "Nec tamen inde vos accusandos censetis, si haec vestra novitas," &c.

By your leave, I will mention one or two points: you have rejected the common hymns, and introduced others unheard of by us, unknown to the churches, and inferior also. Thus, throughout the year, at the vigils, whether of holidays or festivals, you are contented with one and the same hymn, whereas the Church, according to the diversity of festivals and holidays, uses different hymns and psalms, and whatever else pertains to these, as common sense dictates. Hence those who hear you, whether at Christmas, Easter, or Pentecost, singing always the same hymn,—i.e. '*Aeterne rerum conditor*,'—are filled with the utmost astonishment, and moved less to admiration than derision. Those prayers which follow the supplication and the Lord's Prayer in every church, and the *suffragia sanctorum*, you have entirely prohibited, as if the world were not in need of your prayers, nor you of the intercession of the saints."

Such a string of sarcasms at the end of an epistle could leave Bernard in little doubt as to the worth of the civilities at the commencement.

In the meantime matters were hastening to a crisis at St. Gildas. Abelard strove in vain to bring the refractory monks to a sense of duty, or even decency. They neither loved nor feared him. At last they came to a determination of getting rid of him by any means, however infamous. They tried to poison him in his food and drink; and when he showed caution and suspicion, they did not hesitate to pollute the cup of the Holy Eucharist by a similar attempt. They then corrupted his servant to assist them in their plans. They seized the opportunity of a visit he paid to his brother to make another attempt at poisoning. By mere accident Abelard refused the treacherous dish, but a monk who attended him ate of it and died, while the base hireling revealed his conscious guilt by immediate flight. To these dangers within was added constant peril from the marauders without. And as if

Fortune knew no limit to her enmity, he, about this time, had a severe fall from his horse, and broke his windpipe, he says, which caused him a long and debilitating illness. It cannot be wondered at, for he was past fifty years of age.[1]

He again resolved to try the effect of a change. Under the safeguard of a powerful chieftain of the country, he succeeded in making good his escape, the animosity of the monks leading him to fear a violent death at their hands. Whither he bent his steps on leaving St. Gildas we are not informed, for that extraordinary narrative, the " Historia Calamitatum," which has up to this point furnished us with facts, terminates here. Written in the form of a letter to a friend, it forms one of the most curious of autobiographies. Not the least interesting fact connected with it is, that it shortly afterwards fell into the hands of Heloise. It is extremely probable that even when he made arrangements for her occupation of the Paraclete Abelard did not come into personal relations with his wife. They each travelled their respective roads of trial and humiliation, and the smothered flame of their love had not been fed by meeting or letter. Since that harsh and terrible separation which had been caused by Fulbert's vengeance the two seared hearts had dwelt apart. The wife's external lot had indeed been less bitter than her husband's ; Heloise had in a measure prospered at the Paraclete. Abelard considered that she and her nuns had thriven more during one year "in worldly goods" than he should have done in a hundred. But "worldly goods" can little soothe a bleeding heart like that of Heloise ; they will rather give it warmth to bleed more freely. And now the sharpest pain a noble mind can know came upon her. While she had been comparatively peaceful and protected, he, she learns, has still been buffeted amid storms and

---

[1] " Dum autem in his laborarem periculis, forte me die quadam, de nostra lapsum equitatura, manus Domini vehementer collisit, colli videlicet mei canalem confringens." —*Hist. Cal.*

perils. The long, mournful recital of their common misfortunes, and of those which he had endured alone, was by some
chance thrown in her way. How the tomb of the past was
re-opened for her as she read, how the demure abbess became
again the impassioned mistress, how the last fifteen years of
sorrow and solitude dropped away like a vesture, and the days
when Abelard sang to her and wooed her rushed over her
again, may be conjectured by the letter which she wrote to
him immediately after :—

" To her lord, nay, her father ; to her husband, nay, her
brother ; from his handmaid, nay, daughter ; from his wife,
nay, sister ; to Abelard from Heloise."

She begins very quietly to say how his narrative, full of gall
and wormwood, had touched her. No one, she thinks, could
read it with dry eyes. She implores him in the name of Christ
to inform herself and her nuns, who are Christ's handmaids
and his, of his good or evil fortune, in order that " we who
alone remain to thee may be partakers of thy joy or grief."
He has discharged his duty to his friend by writing to him ;
he owes a greater debt to them who are not to be called
friends, but *friendliest*, not companions, but daughters, or any
other sweeter and holier name that can be thought of. " For,"
she continues, in words that seem saturated with love and
fondness, " of this very place, after God, thou art the sole
founder ; the sole constructor of this oratory ; this congregation is owing solely to thee. Thou hast built nothing on
another man's foundation ; all that is here is of thy creation.
This solitude, abandoned to wild beasts or robbers, had not a
trace of house or human habitation. In a den of thieves, in a
beast's lair, where God was not wont to be even named, thou
hast erected a holy tabernacle, and dedicated a temple to the
Holy Spirit. For this work thou hast had no help from kings
or princes, in order that all that was done might be ascribed
to thee. Thy clerks or scholars, coming hither in rival crowds

to thy teaching, supplied all necessities.   Thine, therefore, truly thine, is this young plantation."[1]

She then reproaches him for not writing to her or visiting her.   "Thou knowest, dearest one, all know, how much I lost in thee.   But the greater the grief, the more need of consolation, not from another, but from thyself; so that all my sorrow and all my joy may be alike owing to thee.   Thou alone canst make me sad; thou alone canst cheer; thou alone canst console.   Thou owest me this, who have so obeyed all thy words that I would not offend thee in anything, that at thy command I could lose my life.   At thy order I became a nun, to show thee thou wert the sole possessor of my body as of my mind.   Never—God knoweth—did I desire aught in thee but thyself; thee, not what was thine, I loved; I did not hope for the bonds of wedlock or marriage dower; not my wishes or pleasures, but thine, did I study to fulfil; and if the name of wife appears holier and more valid, the title of mistress has ever sounded sweeter to my ears.   I call God to witness that if Augustus, the ruler of the world, had offered to honour me with marriage, and to endow me with the universe for ever as a gift, it were far more precious and noble in my sight to be called thy harlot than his empress."[2]

She again recurs to his neglect as a proof that he had never truly loved her; that lust, not love, had bound him to her; "therefore, what he desired having ceased, his kindness had vanished with it."   "This is not so much my opinion, dearest one, as the common thought of all.   Would that I alone believed thus, and that thy love found others to vindicate it, by whom my grief could be allayed!   Would I could forge excuses to myself, which by relieving thee would cover my own vileness!   Listen to what I ask; it is little and easy to thee.

[1] Ab. Op. Epist. ii. p. 41.
[2] "Charius mihi et dignius videretur tua dici meretrix quam illius imperatrix."—AB. *Op.* Epist. ii. p. 45.

Seeing that I am robbed of thy presence, present to me by words—in which thou art rich—the sweetness of thy image. I believe I have deserved much of thee, I who have fulfilled all for thee, and now especially have persevered in obedience. Not religious devotion, but thy behest, subjected my tender youth to the asperity of monastic life. How vain is my toil if I earn nothing from thee. As if mindful of Lot's wife, thou arrayedst me in a nun's clothes and devotedst me to God before thou tookest vows thyself. For my mind was not mine but thine, and now most of all it is with thee or it is nowhere. Now, in the name of Him to whom thou hast offered thyself, restore to me in some measure thy presence, by writing to me some consolation, that I may be refreshed and be more ready for my religious duties. When in days gone by thou soughtest me for worldly pleasures, thy letters were frequent, and, through many a verse of thine, Heloise's name was in every mouth. The streets, the houses, echoed of me. Thou provokedst me to lust; wilt thou not urge me to God? Weigh, I beg, what thou owest me; give ear to what I ask. With an abrupt ending I close a long letter. Farewell, only one."

Abelard answers in the language of a man to whom all here below has become cold and colourless. He says he has not written, because he did not think she could need it. Divine grace had ministered all things necessary unto her; she who could teach and strengthen others, was hardly in want of exhortation and instruction from him. Yet quite free from that false humility which only waits to be importuned enough, he says if she will tell him in what she requires his advice, he will write back as the Lord shall direct him. "But thanks be to God, who, filling your hearts with solicitude for my perils, has made you sharers of my affliction, so that by the help of your prayers the Divine pity may protect me, and quickly crush

[1] Ab. Op. Epist. iii. p. 49.

Satan under our feet. For this reason, my sister, once dear to me in the world, now dearest in Christ, I have sent thee the Psalter which thou askedst of me. Mayest thou over it offer up a perpetual sacrifice of prayer to God for my great and numerous sins and frequent dangers." After establishing at some length the efficacy of the prayers of holy women, his sad heart returns to his approaching end. "If the Lord should deliver me into the hands of my enemies,—that is, if prevailing they should slay me,—or if by any other mischance when far from you I should enter the way of all flesh, I beseech you to convey my body, wherever it may lie buried or exposed, to your cemetery for interment, where our daughters and sisters in Christ, seeing my tomb, may be the oftener led to pour forth for me their prayers unto the Lord. Ye are anxious about my bodily dangers now; be not less anxious for my soul's welfare then. Show by your attention to the dead how great was your love to the living,—that is, by the special and peculiar intercession of your prayers. Farewell."[1]

To which Heloise replies :—"With no little wonder have we received thy letter, in which thou addest to the desolation of those whom thou oughtest to console, and tears which thou shouldest dry thou makest to flow again. For which of us could hear without weeping that which thou hast placed at the end of thy epistle ?—' If the Lord should give me over into the hands of my enemies,' &c. O, dearly beloved! how couldest thou harbour such a thought? how couldest thou endure to write it? May God never so far forget His handmaids as to allow them to survive thee, never burden us with a life which were more grievous than any death. Thou askest, only one! that whatever chance may terminate thy life, absent from us, we would carry thy body to be buried in our cemetery, in order that, ever mindful of thee, we may give thee a larger measure of our prayers. But how dost

[1] Ab. Op. Epist. iii. p. 49.

thou think that thy memory can pass away from us? Or how could that time be fit for prayer when perturbation of mind will leave nothing at rest? when the soul will lose all sense of reason, and the tongue all power of speech? when the unsound mind, rather angry than peaceful towards God, will rather irritate Him with complaints than propitiate Him with prayer? Tears, not prayers, will be alone left to us wretched ones, and we shall need rather to hasten after thee than to bury thee, and thus share thy tomb rather than place thee in it. The mention of thy death is a sort of death to us. Spare us, I beseech thee, spare thy only one, and use no longer words by which, as by swords of death, thou piercest through our souls!"

Then follows a marvellous and untranslateable passage, in which she reveals the "black and grained spots" of her soul.[1]   She goes on : "They call me chaste who have not discovered I am a hypocrite. They transfer purity of body to the mind. I may have merit in the sight of men, I have none before God. I am thought religious at a time when hypocrisy is no small part of religion, when he is extolled who does not offend the judgment of men. And, perchance, it is in a measure laudable and well-pleasing to God, to give an example of outward works, with whatever intention, to avoid scandal to the Church, that the name of God be not blasphemed among the heathen, and the profession of religion be not despised by carnal men. But it is vain to eschew evil, or to do good, if it be not done for the love of God. As for me, I have ever feared offending thee rather than God ; thee I strive to please rather than Him. My pretence deceived

[1] Mr. Lewes approvingly quotes Madame Guizot, "who excellently indicates the distinction between his [*i.e.* Abelard's] sensual descriptions and the chaster though more passionate language of Heloise. 'Elle rappelle mais ne détaille point.'"—*Hist. of Philosophy*, p. 297. Neither Abelard nor Heloise, indeed, had any scruple in their allusions on the score of decency. But that the husband should be blamed in comparison with his wife is what I cannot understand with Heloise's second and third letters before me.—See especially pp. 59—79 of Duchesne's edition.

thee, as it did many, for a long time; my hypocrisy thou tookest for religion.   Rather fear for me than trust in me, that I may have the help of thy solicitude.   I would not that thou shouldest exhort me to victory, to the battle, saying, 'Strength is made perfect in weakness,' and 'He is not crowned except he strive lawfully.'   I seek not the crown of victory; it is enough for me if I avoid destruction.   In whatever corner of heaven God may place me, it will suffice for me.   To use the words of St. Jerome, 'I acknowledge my weakness; I will not fight for the hope of victory, lest I at last lose victory itself.'"

So felt and wrote this extraordinary woman.   But she was speaking a language which Abelard had forgotten.   From his measured and methodical replies she saw her ardour could not be returned; she strove to follow and imitate him in this as in all else.   She asked for an account of the origin of nuns and convents; she begged he would write a rule for them, such as would suit and be specially adapted to women.   He complied with the gentle request.   The directions he gives are lengthy, and by no means indulgent.   After the whirlwind of passion which has hitherto enveloped them, the transition is strange to such quiet, matter-of-fact advice as the following:—" Let the ornaments of the church be such as are necessary, not super-fluous; neat rather than costly.   It should contain nothing made of gold or silver, except one silver chalice, or more if they be required.   Let no ornament be of silk, except the stoles or phanons.   Let there be no graven images; only a wooden cross may be placed over the altar, on which, if it be wished that an image of the Saviour be painted, it is not forbidden. But the altar may know no other images.   Let the convent be content with two bells.   A vase of holy water should be placed at the entrance of the church outside, that the sisters, entering of a morning or going out after compline, may be sanctified by it.   None of the nuns may be absent at the canonical hours, but as soon as the bell is rung, everything else being laid aside, let them hasten to the Holy Office, yet all in a modest gait withal.   On entering the church, let them say who can : ' I will go into Thy house, I will worship at Thy holy temple.' Let nothing be read or sung, except it be taken from authentic Scripture, especially from the Old and New Testaments.   In the middle of the night they must rise, according to the prophetic institution, to the nightly vigils ; wherefore they should go to bed so early that weak nature may be able to bear these vigils. . . . . On leaving the dormitory, they must wash ; and having taken their books, let them sit in the cloister reading or singing until the bell is rung for prime.   After prime, let them go to the chapter, and all then sitting down, the martyrology is to be read, the month being given out beforehand.   Afterwards, there should either be a sermon to edify, or else a portion of the Rule read or explained.   Then if aught needs correction or arrangement, it should be done."[1]

Their love dies, or rather is transfigured, at last in a prayer. A white, heavenly light falls on their faces, vanquishing the red flames of lust in which they once had moved.   At the conclusion of a long and eloquent letter, in which Abelard exhorts her to patience and resignation, he says : " I hasten to compose and send to thee a prayer, which ye (the nuns) may repeat, supplicating the Lord for me."

THE PRAYER OF HELOISE.

" O God, who from the first commencement of human beings, by the formation of woman out of the man's side, hast sanctioned in an especial way the sacrament of marriage ; who, through Thy birth from the espoused Mary, and Thy beginning of miracles, hast adorned it with immense honour, and who formerly didst grant it to me as a remedy for my incontinence ;

[1] Ab. Op. 159.

despise not, I beseech Thee, the prayers of Thy handmaid, prayers which for my own sins, and those of my beloved one, in the sight of Thy majesty I humbly pour forth. Forgive, O Most Clement! forgive, O Clemency itself! our sins, great as they are; and may the multitude of our offences experience the immensity of Thy ineffable mercy. Punish the guilty now. that Thou mayest spare them hereafter. Punish them for an hour, that Thou mayest spare them for eternity. Lift up over Thy servants the rod of correction, not the sword of wrath. Afflict the body, that Thou mayest save the soul. Cleanse, avenge not; be gentle, rather than just; a merciful Father, rather than an austere Lord. Prove us, O Lord, and try us, as the prophet asked for himself (Ps. xxvi. 2). As if he said, 'Examine the strength there is, and suit the burden of temptation to it.' Even as the blessed Paul promises to Thy faithful people, saying: 'God is faithful, who will not suffer you to be tempted above that ye are able, but will, with the temptation, also make a way to escape, that ye may be able to bear it.' Thou hast joined us, O Lord, and hast set us apart when it pleased Thee, and as it pleased Thee. Now, O Lord, that which Thou hast begun in mercy, do Thou in mercy perfect, and those whom Thou hast severed in the world join for ever unto Thyself in heaven. O Lord, our hope, our portion, our expectation, our consolation, who art blessed for ever. Amen.

Farewell in Christ, thou spouse of Christ; in Christ farewell, in Christ live! Amen."

CHAPTER III.

A.D. 1139.

THEOLOGY OF ABELARD—HIS VIEWS ON THE TRINITY.

A FULL account of Abelard's philosophy, and his position as a thinker in the history of the human mind, would require more space than can be spared in a "life of St. Bernard." All that is attempted in this chapter is, by a few extracts from his "illustrious work," as he calls it, his *Introductio ad Theologiam*,[1] to give some notion of the views and method which excited against him the powerful ones of his day, and caused the greater part of his life to be passed in sorrow and calamity.

It was this *Introductio* which led to his condemnation at the Council of Soissons. It was the same work that alarmed William of St. Thierry, who, by quotations from it, induced Bernard to declare himself the opponent of Abelard. This work shared in the anathemas pronounced against his writings at Sens. It was in reference to it that he himself said, that the outrage he had endured from Fulbert did not compare, for the pain it caused him, with the public burning of his book. It is thus evident that both Abelard and his contemporaries agreed in considering it one of the most important of his productions, and we shall probably not greatly err if we follow them in this respect, and regard it as a representative specimen of his religious philosophy, or rather, perhaps, his philosophy of

[1] Abelardi Opera, p. 1046.—Ed. Duchesne, Paris, 1616.

religion. He thus speaks in anticipatory defence of his method as applied to the doctrine of the Trinity :—

" But faith in the Holy Trinity we hold to be the foundation, so to speak, of every good, so that the origin of all excellence is derived from the very knowledge of God's nature. Whoever, therefore, shall succeed in sapping this foundation, leaveth nothing profitable to us in that superstructure which is to be erected upon it. For which reason we have taken care to raise against so great a danger a buckler, both of authority and argument, in firm reliance upon Him who comforteth His people, saying, 'When ye stand before kings and rulers, take no thought,' &c. (Matt. x. 12). In whose aid, verily, the stripling David trusting, slew with his own sword the boastful giant Goliath. Therefore we also turn the sword of human reasoning, with which both philosophers and heretics assail us, against themselves ; and with the help of God will demolish both their might and the force of their arguments, so that they may be the less arrogant in attacking the simplicity of believers, when they have once been confuted on such points as these (on which they consider their objections beyond refutation), as *e.g.* touching the diversity of persons in one wholly indivisible and purely Divine substance, and concerning the generation of the Word, or the procession of the Holy Spirit. Indeed we do not even ourselves undertake to teach the very truth of all this, it being a task to which we do not believe either ourselves or any other man to be adequate ; yet can we at any rate advance that which is probable, agreeable to human reason, and not opposed to religious belief, against those who vaunt themselves in opposing every creed by human rationalism, who pay no regard to any but such mundane arguments as they are acquainted with, and find many supporters from the fact that the majority of mankind are animal, but very few spiritual. For us, however, it is sufficient to overthrow the strength of our most powerful adversaries by any means what-

ever, especially as we are unable to do so in any other way
than by bringing against them arguments with which their own
arts have rendered them familiar.   For far from us be the
belief that God, who Himself sometimes useth evil for a good
end, hath not ordained all arts, which indeed are His gifts, for
His own glorification, notwithstanding their evil application by
the perverse."

In opposition to the narrow bigotry which denounced all
knowledge not connected with religion, he says :—

" Perhaps, however, you will say that the reading not only
of the poets, but even of such works as those which relate to
the liberal arts, should be forbidden to Christians, inasmuch as
the holy Jerome, in his epistle to Eustochius, declares that he
was severely chastened and scourged by the Lord for reading
the books of the philosophers.   But so, forsooth, it is not right
that a Christian should even study grammar, without whose
lessons neither the pages of Holy Writ, nor any other writing,
are intelligible ; or rhetoric, which marks the elegancies of
every kind of oratory with which Holy Scripture everywhere
abounds, insomuch that its beauties cannot be clearly discerned
without they are duly pointed out.   Why therefore, you will
ask, was the above-named teacher so grievously chastised for
perusing the works of Cicero, that he was compelled, under
declaration of an oath, to abstain entirely from the reading of any
secular books whatsoever ? Because, verily, he was aiming not
at any improvement, but was merely gratifying himself with
the writer's eloquence, to the neglect of his study of the Holy
Scripture ; being, as he himself said, revolted at its unculti-
vated style.   But I am of opinion that no scientific reading is
improper for any religious person, unless by this an obstacle
be presented to his improvement in graver matters ; as we
know is the case with regard to other literature, where, for
instance, trifling points are either discontinued, or even
altogether passed over, for those which are of more importance.

Provided, then, that the teaching be not erroneous, the language not impure, and there is some advantage in scientific knowledge, who deserves blame for speaking of or teaching such things, unless it be for the reason given above,—namely, for the neglect or contempt of some higher good? For no one can call any science evil, even though it be itself concerning evil, which an upright man requires; not indeed that he may work evil, but that he may be on his guard against evil prepared for himself; which, according to Boethius, he cannot escape unless he be forewarned. Thus the mere knowledge of the existence of falsehood and adultery is not a crime, but the committal of the acts themselves is; for the knowledge of such things is commendable, but their practice most base; and guilt consists not in the knowledge of a sin, but in its commission. But if any knowledge were sinful, then were it sinful to know certain things. So then God, who knoweth all things, could not be held guiltless of sin. For in Him alone is the fulness of all knowledge, whose gift all knowledge is. For knowledge is the comprehension of everything that exists; and in these He clearly discerns the truth, to whom those things which do not exist are revealed, even as though they were actually present. Hence, in the enumeration of the gifts of the Spirit, He is styled 'the Spirit of knowledge' [Isa. xi. 2]. But as the very knowledge of evil is a good in so far as it is necessary for the avoidance of evil, so it is plain that the power of being evil is a good, as a test of merit. For, if we were unable to commit sin, our merit in not sinning would be none; and to him who doth not enjoy free will no reward can be due for the performance of acts from which he cannot escape. But on the contrary, as saith the prophet, 'Who might offend, and hath not offended; or done evil, and hath not done it; his goods shall be established' [Eccl. xxxi. 10, 11]. Hence, therefore, it is clear that no knowledge or power is evil, however evilly it may be employed, since it is

God who bestows all knowledge and ordains all power. He it was who, speaking of the power of the unjust Pilate against Himself, said, 'Thou couldest have no power at all against Me, except it were given thee from above.'

"True science, therefore, we approve, but are opposed to those who abuse it by their fallacies; for they, as Tully bears witness, err in no slight degree who blame science on account of the wickedness of mankind. Thus, in his Rhetoric, when he is treating of the disparagement of arguments, he says, amongst other things, 'No part of an argument will be suited to that purpose for which it is intended, if fault be found on account of human wickedness, as if any one should object to learning in the abstract, on account of the vices of one learned man.' But I suppose that none who are well versed in Holy Scripture are ignorant that spiritual men have progressed in sacred learning more from the real study of science than from the merits of religion. Thus Paul, although his merits as an apostle do not appear superior to those of Peter, nor those of Augustine as a confessor to those of Martin, yet each of these exhibited greater graces in his teaching, after his conversion, in proportion as he possessed a more extensive knowledge of literature before it. Whence I conclude that the study of secular literature also is specially recommended by the Divine direction, not only on account of its inherent uses, but because it would seem unlike one of His gifts if He should employ it so as to serve no useful end. We, however, do not forget the saying of the Apostle, that 'knowledge puffeth up,' *i.e.* it begets arrogance. But this very circumstance proves that it is a good, inasmuch as it draws him who is guilty of arrogance to his own destruction; for as there are some good things which never issue forth but from evil, so again there are some evils which trace their origin to a good source. Thus repentance, or reparation and amendment, albeit they are good in themselves, yet are they so intimately associated with some evil committed, that they must of necessity be produced by it. Contrariwise, envy and arrogance, exceeding evil though they be, yet owe their existence to good. No one, for instance, suffers from his envy of another unless it be for his goods, and no one becomes puffed up with pride except for those goods which he is conscious of possessing. Whence, also, that Lucifer who is 'the son of the morning' was so much the more given to pride in proportion as he excelled the other angelic spirits in the brightness of his wisdom or knowledge. And yet it is not correct to designate that wisdom or knowledge concerning the nature of things which he received from God as evil; but he made an evil use of it through his pride. So, too, when any one is conceited on account of his philosophy or learning, we should not lay the fault upon the science itself, because of the vice which is united to it, but we should weigh each thing according to its own merit, lest, mayhap, by our want of discernment we should become liable to that curse pronounced by the prophet, ' Woe unto them that call evil good, and good evil; that put darkness for light, and light for darkness' [Isa. v. 20].

" Let thus much suffice to be said against those who, when we bring forward facts or probabilities founded upon philosophical teachings, so as the more clearly to demonstrate what we wish to prove, endeavour to find consolation for their own ignorance by raising an outcry against us; as if the very nature of things formed by God seemed opposed to holy faith and divine reasoning : whereas, in truth, the greatest knowledge of that nature, as it is derived from God, the philosophers themselves have obtained from Him. As when holy teachers trace mysteries and allegories to the very natures of animals, or something else, they enunciate them in almost the very words of the philosophers ; saying, indeed, that this is the *nature* of such and such a thing, using precisely the same terms as the writers upon physical science have done. But God is so far

pleased with this act, that He frequently prefers to be represented by the natural attributes of things which He has Himself created, to being expressed by our words, which we have
ourselves moulded or invented ; so that He takes a greater
pleasure in the actual analogy between things, than He does in
the fitness of our language ; and Scripture, for the adornment
of its style, chooses words taken from the very nature of things
according to some analogy, in preference to restricting itself to
the mere forms of ordinary speech.   Let no one, therefore,
presume to blame me, if, in order to demonstate my propo-
sitions, I shall employ either my own images or those of the
philosophers, with the intent of displaying more readily those
objects which I have in view."

The following arguments, prodigious in their originality in
Abelard's age, are not entirely wanting in appositeness even in
the present :—

" How far, therefore, are they worthy of attention who
assert that faith is not to be built up or defended by reasoning ?
especially when holy men themselves, in reasoning concerning
matters of faith, are accustomed to confute or check their
opponents by many arguments founded upon example or
analogy.   For if, in persuading a person to accept anything as
an article of belief, there is to be no discussion or reasoning as
to whether it ought to be believed upon such and such an
account or not, what remains but that we should give our
assent to those who teach falsehood equally with those who
teach truth, and put forward that defence of the heretic Faustus
by which he endeavours to protect himself from the attacks of
the faithful, and to confute them by the words of the prophet
and their own expressed opinion ?   Otherwise, as we have also
noticed above, the faith of any people, however false, cannot
be refuted, although it may have arrived at such a pitch of
blindness as to confess some idol or another to be the creator
both of heaven and earth.   But any one who accepts this as a

truth, immediately we begin to press him upon this point (as
the martyrs were wont to do in old times when they reproved
the heathen for their idolatry), will be able to answer, that
even according to our own admission we cannot reason upon
matters of faith, and that, therefore, we have no right to attack
others upon a matter with regard to which we think that we
ought to be ourselves unassailed."

Not less noticeable is the following :—

" Now very many persons, on the other hand, seek to console themselves for their ignorance, when they are endeavouring
to inculcate those points of faith which they are not even able
to discuss in intelligible terms, by recommending that exceeding zealous faith which believes before it comprehends what is
said, before it can perceive what the matter in hand really is,
and whether it should be acknowledged as worthy of acquiescence, or discussed before it is received.   But they assert
this chiefly in topics connected with the nature of the Deity,
and the divisibility of the Holy Trinity, which they declare can
never be thoroughly understood in this life ; but they say that
the very understanding of this is itself eternal life, according to
that word of truth which says, 'And this is life eternal, that
they might know Thee the only true God, and Jesus Christ,
whom Thou hast sent' (John xvii. 3).   And again, 'I will
manifest Myself to him' (John xiv. 21).   But, surely, to understand or believe is one thing ; to know or make manifest
another.   Faith, therefore, is defined as the evidence of things
not seen ; experience as the knowledge of existing things by
the presence of the very things themselves.   Between these
two St. Gregory distinguishes in his Sixth Homily on the
Gospels, book ii., when he says : 'It is manifest, because faith
is the evidence of such things as cannot be seen ;' for those
things which are seen are known, not believed.   Also the word
'intellect' is properly applied as concerning those things which
are invisible ; for there is a distinction between the natures of

things intellectual and things visible. Whoever, therefore, supposes that topics connected with the Trinity cannot be understood even in this life, is lapsing into that false doctrine of Montanus, the heretic, which Jerome condemns in the preface to his Commentaries upon Isaiah, where he says, 'Nor, in truth, as Montanus dreams, did the prophets speak in an ecstasy,' as men who did not understand what they were uttering, and as those who, when they learned from others, were ignorant of what they themselves were saying ; but according to the words of Solomon in the Proverbs : 'The wise man understandeth what he speaketh, and in his lips he will carry knowledge,' and 'they know what they say.' Again, 'How wisely have the prophets likened those to brute beasts who understand not that they utter !' Hence, also, this observation of Origen, who in his exposition of these words of St. Paul, 'according to the revelation of the mystery which was kept secret since the world began' (Rom. xvi. 25), remarks, 'But it will be asked whether I say this was so kept secret that absolutely no one knew it, not even the prophets who foretold it?' To me, in truth, it appears highly ridiculous to assert that the prophets so wrote about the Holy Sacraments that they did not understand their own words, whereas Scripture says, 'the wise man understandeth that which proceedeth out of his mouth, and carrieth knowledge in his lips.' But if they had not understood that which they uttered with their own mouths, then had they not been wise men. Whence if it be folly to assert that the prophets were not wise, it results that they must have understood what they advanced."

The following passage contains the analogy to the Trinity which he suggested, by which perhaps he incensed his opponents more than by anything else he ever wrote :—

"But the means by which the philosophers will be able to trace out and discover this distinction of persons in one Divine essence, by analogy of some earthly substance and its inherent qualities, will, I think, be easily exemplified by those things which, as they say, consist of matter and form, or something analogous to matter and form ; as, for the sake of illustration, brass is a substance in which, when a man works and fashions the likeness of a royal personage, he makes a royal seal, the impression of which is taken upon wax for sealing letters when-ever there is occasion to do so.   Now there is in such a seal the brass, which is the matter of which it is made, and the very figure of the royal personage, which is its form : and the seal itself is said from these two things to consist of matter and form, and by the conjunction of these two in itself it is com-pleted and made perfect.   So, then, a seal is nothing more than brass fashioned to such and such a form.   Therefore, the brass itself, which is the matter of the brazen seal, and the seal itself, of which that brass is the matter, are essentially one and the same thing ; yet the brass and the seal are so distinct in their properties, that the property of the brass is one, the property of the brazen seal another ; and though they are essentially the same thing, yet the brazen seal is made of the brass, not the brass of the brazen seal, and the brass is the matter of the brazen seal, not the seal of the brass.   Neither by any possibility can brass be its own matter, although it be the matter of the seal, from the very fact that it is brass ; for brass is not made up of brass, as the seal is made of brass ; and although that which is made up of the matter is made of the matter itself, yet by no means is the matter made into the material part of that seal, nor is the matter made into material part.   But when the seal is once made from the brass, it is of the nature of a seal (*sigillabile*),—that is, fit to be used for seal-ing, although it may not yet have been actually used for that purpose.   But when it happens that it is really employed for impressing the wax, then immediately in the one substance of the brass there are three distinct properties,—viz. the brass itself, its fitness for sealing, and its act of sealing.   Which

qualities stand thus in relation one to the other, that that
which is capable of sealing—in other words, the seal—is made
of the brass ; and that which performs the act of sealing is
conjointly made out of the brass and that which is capable
of sealing, together.   And so that which was at first made of
brass, at length arrives at this, that it is brass which is capable
of sealing ; then, afterwards, it is brass which is capable of sealing that it should be employed for the act of sealing.   Since,
then, its essence is the same, whether as mere brass, as brass
which is capable of, or as brass which is employed for, the act
of sealing, which are three distinct properties, these three
properties are conjoined one with another in such a manner
that the seal derives its power of sealing both from the brass,
and from the brass which is capable of producing an impression.   And if all these observations are applied in their
fitting proportions to the doctrine of the Divine Trinity, it
is easy for us, from the very arguments employed by the
philosophers, to confute those false philosophers who oppose
us.   For just as the brazen seal is made of the brass, and in a
certain way is born of it, so the Son has His being from the
very substance of the Father, and is thus said to be born of
Him.   For, as we proved in what we have said above, Divine
Power is set forth by the name of the Father, just as Divine
Wisdom is expressed by that of the Son.   But Divine Wisdom
is, if I may so say, a certain power of God Himself, of such a
kind, as that by it He can guard Himself against all deceit and
falsity, and through it can distinguish so correctly, and dis-
criminate so acutely, that it is impossible that He should be
mistaken or misled in anything."

The above extracts are sufficient for the purpose already
mentioned,—namely, of giving a sample of the views and
doctrines which Bernard felt it his duty to denounce and
oppose.

SUCH in brief outline had been the history and doctrines of
the man with whom Bernard was to be brought into conflict.
A shock between them was in the nature of things. They
looked at the shield from opposite sides. Reconciliation, or
attempts at it, however desirable, could only be superficial and
unsatisfactory. That efforts towards an understanding were
made by Bernard we are expressly told. After his Lenten
fasts and mortifications were over, he fulfilled his promise to
William of St. Thierry, and made himself better acquainted
with Abelard's "unwonted novelties in the faith." Whereupon
"he met him and admonished him secretly." Hopes were
entertained by Bernard's friends and followers that a pacific
settlement of the difficulties would take place.[1] Abelard, they
said, was so won by Bernard's modest and rational behaviour,
that he promised a general correction of his erroneous views at
Bernard's discretion. This, in all probability, was rather what
they wished, than what they had reason to suppose did take
place. Abelard, who regarded Bernard as a mere sciolist in
philosophy, doubtless kept silence while the latter was urging

---

[1] .... "Secreta illum admoni-
tione convenit. Cum quo etiam tam
modeste tamque rationabiliter egit,
ut ille quoque compunctus ad ipsius
arbitrium correcturum se promit-
teret universa."—ST. BERN. Op.
vol. ii. col. 1122.

what he considered irrefragable arguments, and this silence was interpreted to mean submission. In any case, the conference led to no good result; possibly, by causing disappointment, it exacerbated the opponents.

The time, indeed, was one of growth and ferment, and every sign in the heavens proclaimed change and strife. Bernard observed these portents before they struck the vulgar senses. He well knew what Abelard, with his " human and philosophic reasons," was about to lead to. His quick ear caught the distant thunder-roll of free inquiry, and a horror of great darkness fell upon him. He well knew what a bolt that remote but advancing cloud bore in its bosom for the Church and the Faith. The stag does not fear the hound, the dove does not dread the falcon, more intensely and instinctively, than the dogmatist fears and dreads the free philosophical inquirer. That at this period, in France, in Italy, and in Germany, a bold spirit of inquiry was abroad, Bernard could not allow himself to doubt. He had proofs in many parts of Europe of what Abelard's doctrines would lead to, if they could not be checked.

In the south of France, ever since the beginning of the twelfth century, a vigorous and encroaching heresy was propagated by Peter de Bruis, from whom his followers were called Petrobrusians.[1] Their doctrines went to the complete subversion of the Church's authority. (1) They were strongly opposed to infant baptism, saying that you could wash a young child's skin, but you could not cleanse his mind at that early age.[2] (2) They objected to the building and using of

---

[1] " Petri Venerabilis Epistola sive Tractatus adversus Petrobrusianos Haereticos." Praefatio, col. 722. —Ed. Migne. This highly interesting tract of Peter is the chief source of our knowledge concerning these curious heretics.

[2] " Otiosum igitur et vanum est, quando eo tempore homines aqua perfunditis, quo carnem quidem eorum a sordibus humano pro more abluere, sed animam a peccatis minime mundare potestis."—*Petri Ven. Tract.* col. 729.—Ed. Migne.

churches, declaring that God could hear us whether we prayed in a tavern or a church, in a market-place or in a temple, before an altar or before a stall. (3) They maintained that crosses, instead of being held in reverence, should be destroyed and cast away; that the instrument by which Christ had suffered such agonies ought not to be made an object of veneration, but of execration. (4) They denied the Real Presence in the Eucharist. (5) Prayers and masses for the dead they utterly ridiculed, and said that God was insulted by church singing. As He took pleasure only in holy affections, shrill voices and musical strains could neither win nor appease Him.[1]

These doctrines the Petrobrusians did not regard from a purely theoretical point of view, but were careful to reduce to practice when occasion offered. In one instance recorded they carried out their notions respecting crosses in a very horrible manner. Having collected, on a certain Good Friday, a vast number of them, they made a bonfire of the same; and not content with this insult to dominant opinions, they proceeded to roast meat at their sacrilegious fire, ate of it themselves, and gave it to the people whom they had invited to witness their doings.[2] With reference to the mass, they openly said, " Be careful, O ye people, and believe not the bishops and priests who lead you astray, for, as in many other things, so also in the office of the altar they deceive you— where they mendaciously pretend that they make Christ's

---

[1] " Additis, irrideri Deum canticis ecclesiasticis, quoniam qui solis sanctis affectibus delectatur, nec altis vocibus advocari, nec musicis modulis potest mulceri."—*Petri Venerabilis Tractatus*, col. 763.

[2] " Praevenistis scelestis operibus celeritatem verborum, et profundis in religionem odiis, quod vel cogitare scelus fuerat, insigne nostrae fidei tollere attentastis. Quod tunc factum est, quando ad inauditam Divinitatis contumeliam, magno de crucibus aggere instructo, ignem immisistis, pyram fecistis, carnes coxistis, ipso passionis Dominicae die Paschalem Dominicam praecedente, invitatis publice ad talem esum populis, comedistis."—*Ibid.* col. 771.

body, and give it to you for the salvation of your souls. They lie plainly, for the body of Christ was made once by Christ Himself, at the supper before the passion; and on that occasion only was it given to the disciples. From that time it has neither been made by, nor given to, any one."[1] It is not surprising that such teaching should have aroused the utmost resentment among the clergy and the orthodox faithful; and after twenty years of impunity, Peter paid for his temerity by being burnt at St. Gilles, in Provence.

Nevertheless his sect grew, and, under the leadership of one Henry, a Cluniac monk, spread into the northern provinces of France.[2] The reception this sectary met with at the town of Le Mans has been handed down, and is highly curious. Both "matrons and lads" flocked to hear him, and declared that they had never fallen in with such a man before, that he could bring even a heart of stone to repentance.[3] When he was about to enter the town on Ash Wednesday of the year 1116—profanely imitating the Saviour, it was said—he sent two of his disciples before him. These the people welcomed as though they had been angels. Bishop Hildebert, either through ignorance or approval of Henry's principles, received him in a friendly manner, and, as he was on the point of leaving for Rome himself, charged his archdeacons to grant him free licence to enter the town and preach to the people when he chose. Henry availed himself of the privilege with such success, that not only the people, but even numbers of the clergy, became his followers."[4]   A strong feeling of hatred

[1] Petri Venerabilis Tractatus, col. 787.

[2] For the history of Henry we are forced to rely on his bitter enemies—the writer of the Acta Episcoporum Cenomannensium (published in Mabillon's Vetera Analecta) for the beginning of his career, and St. Bernard for the latter part.

[3] . . . . "Cujus affatu cor etiam lapideum facile ad compunctionem posset provocari." — *Acta Episc. Cenomannensium, apud Mabillonii Vetera Analecta,* p. 315. Paris, 1723.

[4] . . . . "Plerique clericorum excaecati, plebeculae declamationibus alimenta ministrabant, tribunal praeparantes, unde concionator ille turbas alloqueretur obsequentium sibi populorum."—*Ibid.* p. 316.

was excited against the rest of the clergy who opposed him. The people, not content with refusing all social intercourse with them (they would not even buy of, nor sell anything to, the priests), at last began to threaten their lives and property, and would have stoned or gibbeted them, but for the protection of the feudal lords of the neighbourhood.[1]

The clergy, thus driven forth, drew up a solemn remonstrance, which they caused to be sent to Henry. It was read to him by a priest who bore the rude name of *Willus Qui-non-bibit-aquam*, "William Who-drinks-no-water." William, who appeared under an escort lent him by the Count, was enabled to speak plainly to Henry, and gladly embraced the opportunity. He said that the clergy had all been deceived by him; that he was a wolf in sheep's clothing; that he had given them the kiss of Judas; and ended by declaring if he should again presume to "emit poison from his execrable gaping jaws," they would at once excommunicate him. Henry took no notice of the threat, and daily extended his influence with the people, insomuch that they appeared to have no will but his, and were willing to lay down all they possessed at his feet.[2]

---

[1] " Qua haeresi plebs in clerum versa est in furorem, adeo quod famulis eorum minarentur cruciatus, nec iis aliquid vendere, vel ab eis emere voluissent. . . . Praeterea non tantum aedes eorum obruere, et bona dissipare, sed illos lapidare aut affigere patibulo decreverant, nisi princeps et optimates ejus, cognita illorum nequitia, ausibus suis vi potius quam ratione . . . resisterent."—*Acta Episc. Cenomannensium*, p. 316.

[2] He had most decided views concerning the relations of the sexes, female chastity, etc. . . . "Dogmatizabat novum dogma, quod feminae quae minus caste vixerant, coram omnibus vestes suas cum crinibus nudae comburerent; nec quilibet amplius aurum, argentum, possessiones, sponsalia, cum uxore sumeret; nec illi dotem conferret; sed nudus nudam, debilis aegrotam, pauper duceret egenam; nec curaret sive caste seu inceste connubium sortirentur." It cannot surprise us that these singular marriages did not turn out well. "Juvenes enim qui nequam ejus consilio uxores acceperant, parvo temporis dilapso curriculo, aut fame aut stupro compulsi mulierum ad alias partes transvolabant." Yet during all this period, "ex jussu tamen illius, plebis actio pendebat universa, et affectus. Tanta auri, tanta argenti affluentia, si vellet, redundaret, ut opes omnium solus videretur possidere."—*Ibid.*

X

In time, Bishop Hildebert returned from Rome; and, on entering his own cathedral town, offered to bless his people. To his infinite astonishment they received him with revilings, saying, "We don't want you or your blessing. Bless the clay; sanctify the mud. We have a father, we have a priest, an advocate, who excels you in authority, virtue, and knowledge. Your priests are opposed to him; they fear he will expose their vices with his prophetic spirit. But they shall quickly suffer retribution who have dared to forbid the saint of God to continue his celestial preaching." [1] The good bishop, however, persevered, and by degrees recovered his authority. He had a conference with Henry, in which, it is said, the latter betrayed the grossest ignorance of Scripture and ecclesiastical rites. Hildebert at last persuaded him to leave them; but, in spite of all that he or his priests could do, the memory of the itinerant preacher could never be quite obliterated from the minds and hearts of his flock. [2]

But these obscure provincial schismatics had been of late quite thrown into the shade by a young Italian, Arnold of Brescia, whose exploits in Lombardy had brought new troubles upon Innocent II., at the very hour of his triumphs over Anacletus. Arnold was a more formidable enemy than either Peter or Henry, for this reason, that while he denounced the hierarchy in the most vehement language, no erroneous doctrine could be laid to his charge. His own mode of life also, and personal austerity, extorted reluctant admission from his

---

[1] ". . . ejus signaculum et pontificalem respuentes benedictionem. Nolumus inquiunt scientiam viarum tuarum, nolumus benedictionem; coenum benedic, coenum sanctifica; nos habemus patrem, habemus pontificem, habemus advocatum, qui te excedit auctoritate, excedit honestate, excedit scientia. Huic clerici iniqui, clerici tui adversantur, etc. etc.; sed haec omnia sine dilatione in eorum capita redundabunt, qui sancto Dei vocem coelestis praedicationis, nescimus qua confisi audacia, interdicere praesumpserunt."—*Acta Episc. Cenomannensium,* p. 317.

[2] "Eos enim Henricus sic sibi illexerat, quod vix adhuc memoria illius et dilectio a cordibus eorum deleri valeat vel depelli."—*Ibid.*

most bitter opponents. He raised such a commotion in North Italy, that Pope Innocent procured his banishment from the peninsula at the second council of the Lateran. Passing into France for a time, he subsequently settled at Zurich, where he enjoyed the protection, and even friendship, of the Cardinal Guido, afterwards Pope Celestine II. Bernard became aware of the fact, and was filled with alarm by it. He wrote a remonstrating letter to Guido, and begged him not to harbour such a declared schismatic.[1]

While these popular preachers of rebellion against the Church were spreading their views among the multitude, in the cells and schools of the lettered few a more subtle spirit of disaffection was gaining ground. The learned Gilbert de la Porrée, Bishop of Poitiers, was already known to hold opinions on the Trinity which verged on Tritheism. Abelard had, shortly after this, the opportunity of giving him a significant warning of the results of his views. To conclude this short sketch of the heretical tendencies of the age, it is evident that Abelard's scholars developed or exaggerated their master's teaching in a manner that could not fail to cause alarm and animosity.

Thus in a letter written to Abelard by one Gautier de Mortagne, we read, " Certain of your disciples, while proudly extolling, far and near, your wisdom and subtlety, as they deserve, declare, among other things, that you have so thoroughly explored the profound mysteries of the Trinity, that you understand perfectly and completely how three persons can exist in one Divine essence, and how the unity of essence is compatible with the plurality of persons. They say, besides, that you are wont to discuss and impart to others how the Son was begotten of the Father, and how the Holy Spirit proceeds from both." [2] And this statement of a neutral

---

[1] St. Bern. Epist. 195, 196.
[2] Apud D'Acherii Spicilegium, vol. iii. p. 524.

is confirmed by Bernard himself, who testifies to the popularity and influence of Abelard's doctrines and disciples. "We have fallen upon evil times. Masters we have with itching ears. The scholars shun the truth, and turn them to fables. In France we have a monk without rule, a prelate without care, an abbot without discipline ; we have Peter Abelard disputing with boys, conversing with women. . . . . He does not approach alone, as did Moses, towards the darkness in which God was, but advances attended by a crowd of his disciples. In the streets and thoroughfares the Catholic faith is discussed. Men dispute over the childbearing of the Virgin, the sacrament of the altar, the incomprehensible mystery of the Trinity."[1]

The beginnings of a great change were there ; the human mind had again begun to move. Slowly, almost imperceptibly, like the gentle uprising of a vast continent from the ocean, the questioning intellect again rose up, approached problems, and tried to solve them.

Now, in Bernard's view, the intellect, if not carefully watched and guided, was not a friend, but a foe, to man's welfare ; not a pole-star to lead him, but an *ignis fatuus* to deceive him. To resist its questions and doubts was part of a good man's duty. They were carnal and devilish, even as lust and concupiscence were carnal and devilish. Truth had been given to man, once and for ever, in the teaching of the Church. No conclusions of his mind could add to its certainty ; none could diminish it. It was there, accessible and intelligible

[1] "Per vicos et plateas de fide catholica disputatur, de partu Virginis, de sacramento altaris, de incomprehensibili sanctae Trinitatis mysterio."—St. Bern. *Epist.* 332. This reminds one of what, according to Canon Stanley, occurred at the Council of Nicæa. "Every corner, every alley, of the city was full of these discussions. . . . . Ask a man, 'How many oboli?' he answers by dogmatizing on generated and ungenerated being. Inquire the price of bread, and you are told, 'The Son is subordinate to the Father.' Ask if the bath is ready, and you are told, 'The Son arose out of nothing.'"—*Eastern Church*, p. 86.

to all—absolute, complete, and final. To receive it, wholly,
unreservedly, and reverentially, ensured eternal life ; to reject
one jot or one tittle of it ensured eternal damnation.   It had
overarched man's life for hundreds of years now, capacious
and durable as the great vault of heaven.   The Omnipotence
which had revealed the one, had created the other.   And
now was a small human philosopher to advance with his
reasons and questions in opposition to it?   Were immortal
souls, for whom Christ died, to be stolen from the Church
and God by a profane heretic who had great powers of argument and speaking?   Was Satan to be assisted in his hostility
to man's salvation by their perverse minds, as well as by their
rebellious passions?   From his training, his character, his
position, Bernard could not avoid thinking thus of Abelard
and his philosophy.

   The Abbot of Clairvaux, therefore, arose in all his vehement
energy and resentment to stay the progress of this great plague.
He scattered broadcast over Europe his fiery appeals to Pope,
cardinals, princes, and bishops, to assist in repressing this
Arius, Pelagius, and Nestorius in one.   But Abelard was not
as friendless now as he had been twenty years before, or at
least his friends were in a better position to help him.   It is
with a cry almost of anguish that Bernard confesses that
Abelard has admirers and adherents even among the cardinals
of the papal court.[1]   The two chiefs were watching each other,
and the ranks of their followers, as they closed for battle.
War had begun, but was not yet openly declared.   Abelard
remembered the Council of Soissons, and resolved to anticipate rather than await the attack.   He sought Henri le
Sanglier (Henry the Wild Boar), that Archbishop of Sens

---

[1] "Ad haec gloriatur, se infe-
cisse curiam Romanam novitatis suae
veneno ; manibus et sinibus Romanorum libros et sententias suas in-
clusisse, et in tutelam sui erroris as-
sumit eos a quibus judicari debet et
damnari."—ST. BERN. *Epist.* 331.

whom Bernard had so recently scolded for his "hateful cruelty."[1] Henry was about to preside over a numerous synod, at which the holiest relics of his province were to be exposed to the veneration of the faithful. Abelard demanded to be heard publicly before the assembly. He insisted on being confronted with his accuser. He was prepared, he said, to answer all objections raised against his teaching. The archbishop, nothing loath perhaps to place his stern rebuker in a difficult position, acceded to the request, and summoned Bernard to attend the council.

Abelard, full of hope and exultation, gathered his friends and scholars around him. He published it far and wide that he was going to meet, in fierce logical combat, the great Abbot of Clairvaux.

Nothing in modern life can give an adequate idea of the interest and excitement such an announcement would produce. The two foremost men of the day in their respective walks, representing most divergent and even hostile principles of thought and action, were to encounter each other in the lists of controversy, with all the ardour of knights at a tourney. They and their partisans divided Europe between them. But would the contest take place? The challenger had thrown down his glove, but would it be taken up? It is not known as yet. Bernard, it is rumoured, hesitates. It is not only a rumour, but a fact. He not only hesitates, but refuses. "When all fly before his face, he selects me, the least, for single combat.[2] I refused," says the Abbot of Clairvaux, "because I was but a child, and he a man of war from his youth."[3] But Bernard's friends made him feel that this inaction could not be allowed. They represented to him how "all men had prepared

---

[1] See *ante*, p. 225.
[2] "Cum omnes fugiant a facie ejus, me omnium minimum expetit ad singulare certamen. . . . . Ille nihilo minus, immo eo amplius levavit vocem, vocavit multos, congregavit complices." — St. Bern. *Epist.* 189.
[3] "Abnui quia puer sum, et ille vir bellator ab adolescentia." — *Ibid.*

for the spectacle, as it were. They fear lest his absence should cause scandal to the people, and make grow the horns of the adversary." At last Bernard yielded, but with tears and heaviness. Not that he dreaded aught for himself; but how was that Church, that faith, for which he was ready to die, to be defended before such an adversary? Ill, as he always was, worn and weary, as he at this moment was, he girded up his loins to the trial, to his duty. Probably never crusader marched against overpowering infidels, never knight entered on a single combat, with more trust in God and less in man or himself than did Bernard when he left Clairvaux to be present at Sens. Without preparation or study; reflecting only on the promise, " Take no thought how or what ye shall speak, for it shall be given you in that same hour what ye shall speak," he set forth, and was at Sens on the appointed day. [1]

The original object of the meeting at Sens was a ceremony of unrivalled popular interest in the Middle Ages, viz. the exhibition of sacred relics to the eyes and adoration of the multitude. This occasion was intended to be exceptionally solemn. King Louis VII. was to be present; Count Theobald was to be present; and a crowd of bishops, abbots, and grandees from the northern parts of France were to assemble with them. Abelard came with a troop of disciples; Bernard came with two or three monks, as it behoved a Cistercian abbot to travel. At Sens, as at Soissons, Abelard and his pupils were in the midst of enemies. Bernard was not so much amid friends as worshippers. The one addressed

---

[1] " Disseminavit ubique, se mihi die statuto apud Senonas responsurum. Exiit sermo ad omnes, et non potuit me latere. . . . Cedens tamen (licet vix, ita ut flerem) consilio amicorum, qui videntes quomodo se quasi ad spectaculum omnes pararent, timebant ne de nostra absentia et scandalum populo, et cornua crescerent adversario. . . . Occurri ad locum et diem, imparatus quidem et immunitus, nisi quod illud mente volvebam, ' Nolite praemeditari,' &c."—St. Bern. Epist. 189.

the reason of the few ; the other inflamed the hearts and
passions of all classes.   Upon one had fallen the irre-
movable mortal blight of supposed heresy and unbelief.
Abelard, in the thoughts of many assembled at Sens, poisoned the air where he lived ; held familiar converse with
the demons ; deliberately had turned from heaven, and
marched towards hell.   Under Bernard's coarse woollen
cowl the seraph's wings were half-supposed to lie concealed.
Nature's forces felt and welcomed his approach. A child of
light, a man of God, he was now again to face the fiend and
worst him.

The first day of the council was taken up with the inspection and adoration of the sacred relics.[1]   The question of
Abelard's heresies was brought before it the second day.
The king, surrounded by his feudal lords, and the Archbishop of Sens (Henry the Wild Boar), in the midst of his
suffragans, met in solemn conclave in the Church of St.
Stephen.   Abelard entered, and walked up between the
ranks of monks, priests, bishops, and warriors on each side
of him.   His eye caught that of Gilbert de la Porrée, and,
as he passed him, he whispered the significant line—

> " Nam tua res agitur paries cum proximus ardet."

He moved on through the hostile crowd.   He stopped in
the centre of the building, and found himself opposite
Bernard.

In a pulpit, which was in existence up to the time of
the French Revolution, stood Bernard, holding before him
the incriminated work of Abelard.   He read, or caused to
be read, the passages he had marked for reproof, explanation, or condemnation.   But the lecture had hardly begun,
when, to the speechless astonishment of all, Abelard rose up,

---

[1] Abélard, par Charles de Rémusat, vol. i. p. 205.

said he refused to hear more, or answer any questions ; he appealed to Rome : and at once left the assembly.[1]

A cause for this extraordinary conduct has been variously and unsuccessfully assigned.   Bernard's friends declared that, when the heretic should have found his mind clearest and strongest, sudden darkness, confusion, and paralysis fell upon him, which deprived him of speech.   A more probable supposition is, that Abelard saw his hopes of a victorious disputation utterly frustrated by the temper of his audience and the conditions of his public defence.   He could not hope to win over that unsympathising crowd, on whom his subtlety would be lost, and his eloquence wasted.   The votes of his philosophic friends, however precious in *his* eyes, would be completely swamped in the multitude of his unscrupulous adversaries. Those ranks of hostile faces quenched enthusiasm.   Whereas an appeal to Rome, now intensely welcome to the growing despotism of the papacy, would cause delay and difficulty to his opponents, and allow time for his interest at Rome to have effect.   And it is quite certain that the manœuvre partly succeeded.   The assembly at Sens was in no small perplexity as to the course to be pursued.   Rome was the more jealous of her pretensions in such cases, that their legitimacy was as yet unsettled.[2]   Pope Innocent owed so much to Bernard, that he could hardly fail to dislike him ; and indeed, very shortly after these events, he did break off friendly relations with him.

To this extent, therefore, Abelard succeeded, that he checked

---

[1] " Dominus abbas (Bernardus) cum librum Theologiae magistri Petri proferret in medium et quae adnotaverat absurda, imo haeretica plane capitula de libro eodem proponeret, ut ea magister Petrus vel a se scripta negaret ; vel si sua fateretur, aut probaret, aut corigeret ; visus diffidere magister Petrus Abaelardus et subterfugere, respondere noluit."— St. Bern. *Epist.* 337.   This is from the minutes of the council, as drawn up by the French bishops and sent to Pope Innocent.

[2] " A new jurisprudence had established in the Latin Church the right and practice of appeals ; and from the north and west bishops and abbots were invited, or summoned, to solicit, to complain, to accuse, or to justify, before the threshhold of the Apostles."—Gibbon, ch. lxix.

his enemies in mid career, and caused them to pause. But the ruling spirit which presided there was not apt to renounce a deliberately chosen course of action. The person of the heretic was suffered to go free, in deference to the Holy See; his heresies and perverse opinions were condemned : they were read and re-read in "public audience, and were proven to be not only false, but plainly heretical, both by most evident reasons, and also by testimonies from Augustine and others of the Fathers, brought forward by the Abbot of Clairvaux. And because," the bishops continue, in their letter to the Pope, "because they draw many into most pernicious and damnable error, we unanimously beg, most beloved lord, with earnest prayers, that you will mark them with perpetual condemnation, and visit all who defend them with condign punishment.[1]

Such is the history of the proceedings at Sens, as related in Bernard's Epistles, and in the *Compte Rendu* of the bishops to Rome. A very different picture is presented by the sufferers from ecclesiastical censure, by Abelard's party, as made known to us by his friend and admirer, Berengarius of Poitiers. It is like passing over several centuries at once, to read his account after that of his antagonists. Soon after his master's condemnation, he wrote what he called an "Apology for Abelard," addressed it to Bernard, and made no effort to conceal his estimate of the actors and proceedings at Sens :—

"The renown of your fame, O Bernard, causes copies of your writings to be spread abroad everywhere. It is no marvel that they are placed upon the stage of popularity, seeing that, whatever they are, they are approved by the great ones of the present day. People wonder to see in you, a man ignorant of the liberal arts, such fertility of eloquence; so that your productions have covered the surface of the earth. To such persons the answer is, that 'Great are the works of the Lord.'

[1] St. Bern. Epist. 337.

But there is no reason why they should wonder; indeed the wonder would be greater if you lacked flowing words. For we hear that from your earliest youth you composed comic songs and polished verses. Do you not remember how you strove to surpass your brothers in rhythmical contests, and in subtlety of invention? And was it not especially painful to you to meet with any one who could answer you with impudence equal to your own?"[1]

This strain of sneering invective he carries to a considerable length :—

"Happy did we deem these modern times in being lit up by such a brilliant star, and we considered that a world doomed to perdition was supported only by your merits. We believed that on the words of your mouth depended the mercy of Heaven, the temperature of the air, the fertility of the earth, and the blessing of the fruits thereof. We thought the very devils roared at your commands, and we gloried in our fortune in having such a patron.

"Now, alas! what was hidden is revealed; you have awakened the sting of the sleeping snake. Neglecting everything else, you have placed Peter Abelard as a target for your arrows, on whom you might vomit forth the poison of your wrath. By your collection of bishops at Sens you pronounced him a heretic, you cut him off from his mother the Church. Whilst he was walking in the way of Christ, like a murderer rushing from an ambush, you have despoiled him of the seamless coat ; you harangued the people, bidding them pray to God for him, while in private you took means to get him proscribed by the Christian world. . . . .

"After dinner Peter's book was brought in, and somebody was told to read it in a loud voice. The fellow, full of hatred to Peter, watered by the vine—not of Him who said 'I am the true vine,' but of that which cast the patriarch naked on the

[1] Berengarii Scholastici Apologeticus.

ground—bellowed out louder than he was asked to do.   Presently you saw the pontiffs insult him (*i.e.* Peter), applaud with their feet, laugh, and play the fool, so that any one might see they were paying their vows not to Christ, but to Bacchus. Then the cups were saluted, the goblets filled, the wine praised, the episcopal throats moistened.   Horace's recommendation,—

> " Nunc est bibendum nunc pede libero,
>   Pulsanda tellus,'—

was executed from memory.   But their potations of the sleepy fluid had already drowned the hearts of the pontiffs.   When, during the reading, anything subtle or divine, but unusual to pontifical ears, was heard, they were all of them cut to the heart, and gnashed their teeth at Peter ; and these moles, judging a philosopher, exclaimed, 'Shall we suffer this wretch to live ?' Wagging their heads, as did the Jews, they said, 'Ah ! behold him who destroyeth the temple of God.'   So did the blind judge words of light ; so did drunkards condemn a sober man ; so did eloquent wine-cups attack the organ of the Trinity. . . . . These great philosophers had filled with wine their barrels of throats.   The fumes of it had so invaded their brains, that the eyes of all were drooping from sleep. Still the reader droned on ; the assembly snored.   One rested on his elbow, another procured a cushion, a third took his nap with his head upon his knees.   So when the reader came upon some thorn-bush in Peter's field, he exclaimed to the deaf ears of the bishops, ' Damnatis ?' (do you damn this ?) Hardly awake at the last syllable, in a drowsy voice, and with hanging heads, they muttered ' Damnamus.'   Others, however, roused by the noise of the damners, decapitated the word, and said . . . 'namus.'"

But although Bernard had not scrupled to employ authority to crush errors at which he was horrified, yet his mind was too powerful and noble to rest contented with a victory due to authority alone. **He prepared a succinct** but highly-wrought **treatise against the errors of Abelard.** In the form of a letter to Pope Innocent, he discussed "not all his errors, but such as could not be passed over;" **and whatever** may be thought **of** the tone of this tract, whatever may be **thought of the exalted** Bernard striking at the downfallen Abelard, **there can** be but **one** opinion as **to the** commanding powers which passed from action to speculation, from ruling men to **refuting opinions, with-** out pause or difficulty. Bernard's arguments are **triumphant, from his own point of view;** but the differences **between** him and Abelard **were of a kind which no argument can ever** really remove. **It is Abelard's method more than his results,** his tone more than his **opinions, which alarms Bernard.**

"**It is not wonderful if a man who cares not what** his words **may mean should rush in upon the hidden things of faith, and** thus profanely invade and despoil the concealed treasures of devotion, seeing that he has no feeling either of piety or allegiance to the faith. At the very commencement of his ' Theology,' or rather Fool-ology, he defines faith as being opinion. **As** if any one might think or say what pleased him concerning **it ; or as if the sacraments of our faith, instead of** reposing on certain truth, **depended without certitude on wandering and various** opinion, **and rested not upon most undoubted truth. If** the faith **is unstable, is not our** hope **in vain?** Therefore the **martyrs were foolish to** endure such **torments** for an uncertainty; for the sake of a doubtful reward, to pass through a painful death into everlasting exile. But God forbid that **we** should think as *he* does, that there is anything **in** our faith or hope which hangs on a doubtful opinion. Rather let us hold **that** the **whole** of it is grounded on certain, solid truth, preached divinely by oracles and miracles, established and consecrated **by** the childbirth of the Virgin, by the blood of the Redeemer, by the glory of the resurrection. These testimonies have **been** made too credible for us to doubt them ;

and if they fail in any way, 'the Spirit beareth witness with our spirit, that we are the children of God.' How then can any one dare to call faith opinion, except it be one who hath not yet received that Spirit, or ignores or disbelieves the Gospel? 'I know,' exclaims the Apostle, 'whom I have believed, and I am certain;' and you whisper to me, 'Faith is opinion.' You gabble on, and pretend that to be doubtful than which nothing can be more certain. Differently indeed writes St. Augustine: 'Faith,' he says, 'dwelleth in a man's heart, not by guessing and thinking, but by certain knowledge, conscience bearing witness.' God forbid, therefore, that Christian faith should have these limits! These ideas and opinions belong to the Academics, who doubt of all things and know nothing. Therefore I walk safely, following the Apostle of the Gentiles; and I know I shall not be confounded. His definition of faith, I confess, pleases me: 'Faith is the substance of things hoped for, the evidence of things not seen.' 'The substance of things hoped for,' he says, not the phantasies of empty conjectures. You hear, 'the substance.' You may not think or dispute on the faith as you please; you may not wander here and there, through the wastes of opinion, the by-ways of error. By the name 'substance' something certain and fixed is placed before you; you are enclosed within certain boundaries, you are restrained within unchanging limits. For faith is not an opinion, but a certitude."[1]

Bernard was right—a religion is a certitude. An explained or defended religion has half ceased to be one. In Bernard's devout, loving eyes, a man who could step forward as patron of Christianity, as upholder and protector of the Cross, was as impious as Uzzah, and deserved his fate. To render Christianity reasonable, to examine, anatomize, and then approve of the "mysteries of the faith," seemed to him only less horrible

[1] "Non est enim fides aestimatio sed certitudo."—*Tractatus de Erro-* *ribus Abaelardi.*—ST. BERN. *Op.* vol. i. col. 649.

than to deny them.   They were to be adored amid silent ecsta-
sies, to be brooded over by the unruffled soul, till the outer
world was lost in their brightness.   But the very thought of
sitting in judgment on them, of recommending their acceptance
in consequence, was revolting beyond words to Bernard.   For
with him faith was "not an opinion, but a certitude."

In the meantime, Peter's appeal to the Pope had been
unnoticed.   He proceeded towards Rome with the intention
of personally pressing his claim to more equitable judgment.
In his double character as a traveller and a monk, he rested
at religious houses along his route.   In time he came to
Burgundy, and put up at Cluny.

From Cluny's abbot, the wise, gentle, and loving namesake
of Abelard, he received the welcome of an unutterably guile-
less and sympathetic heart.   Nothing could exacerbate that
meekest of men ; nothing could sour that affectionate nature ;
nothing alienate that model of Christian charity.   Peter's
heresies were as horrible to him as to any one.   Nothing could
exceed his zeal for religion.   His leisure was devoted to the
literary defence of Christianity ; his life to the practical exem-
plification of it.   But all the commandments he thought subordinate to that " new one," "love one another."   So when
the downcast, sorrowful Abelard came his way, he saw only
the suffering brother ; the bold heretic was forgotten.   He
wrote thus to the Pope :—

" Master Peter, well known, I believe, to your wisdom, as he
lately came from France, passed through Cluny.   I asked him
whither he was going ; he answered that being oppressed by
the attacks of certain persons who had branded him with the
name of heretic, which he detested, he had appealed to Rome,
and was going thither for protection.   I praised his design,
and advised him to seek a refuge known and open to all.
Presently came the Abbot of Citeaux, who discussed, both with
me and Peter, means of reconciliation between him and the

Abbot of Clairvaux, who indeed was the cause of his making
his appeal. I also strove to bring about this reconciliation,
and exhorted him to seek Bernard, in company with the Abbot
of Citeaux. I added that, if he had written or said anything
offensive to Catholic ears, following Bernard's advice, and that
of other good and wise men, he should remove and expunge
it from his books. And so it was done. He went and
returned, and told us how, through the mediation of the Abbot
of Citeaux, he had met Bernard, and the old animosities had
been removed in peace. In the meanwhile, urged by me, or
rather, as I think, inspired by God, renouncing the tumult of
schools and lectures, he has chosen for himself a lasting
dwelling-place in your Cluny. I have assented to his wish,
thinking it suitable to his age, his weakness, and his piety,
while his knowledge, with which you are not quite unacquainted,
would be of the greatest use to numbers of our brethren ; and
if your permission were obtained, I with joy should give him
leave to remain with us, who are yours in all things. I, who
am devoted to you, the whole convent of Cluny, which is most
devoted to you, he himself, by and through us, beseech that
you will permit him to finish the remaining days of his life and
old age (which perchance are not many) in this your Cluny ;
and that he may not be expelled, at the importunity of any,
from that house which, like a sparrow—from that nest which,
like a dove, he rejoices to have found." [1]

And so the turbulent, audacious Abelard became a humble
monk at Cluny. His kind friend the Abbot was right ; his
days were not to be many more, but they were not the least
happy or profitable of his life. The Abbess Heloise one day
received a letter, of which this was the conclusion, written to
her by the lord of Cluny :—

"I write of that servant and true philosopher of Christ,
Master Peter, whom the Divine dispensation sent to Cluny in

---

[1] Petri Venerabilis Epist., lib. iv. Epist. 4.

the last days of his life. A long letter would not unfold the humility and devotion of his conversation while among us, and the witness Cluny would bear to it. If I mistake not, I never remember to have seen one so humble in manners and habit. When at my order he took a high place in our large company, he always appeared the least of all by the meanness of his attire. In the processions, when he, with the others, preceded me, I wondered, nay, I was well-nigh confounded, to see so famous a man able so to despise and abase himself. He was as sparing in his food, in his drink, in all that related to his body, as in his dress ; and he condemned, both in himself and others, both by word and deed, I do not say superfluities, but all save the merest necessaries. He read continually, he prayed frequently; he was silent always, unless the conversation of the monks, or a public discourse in the convent, addressed to them, urged him to speak. What more shall I say? His mind, his tongue, his work, always meditated, taught, or confessed philosophical, learned, or Divine things. A man simple and upright, fearing God, and eschewing evil, in this conversation for a time he consecrated his life to God. Having become more afflicted than usual by his bodily infirmities, I sent him to Chalons, because of the softness of its climate, in which it excels all other parts of our Burgundy. I had selected a place convenient for him, near the city indeed, but separated from it by the river Saone. There, as far as his malady would permit, returning to his old studies, he applied himself to his books, and, as is read of the great Gregory, he suffered not a moment to pass in which he did not either pray, read, write, or dictate. In the exercise of these holy works, the advent of the Divine Visitor found him not sleeping, as it does many, but on the watch. His disease grew worse, and in a short time he was in extremity. Then how holily, how devoutly, in what a Catholic spirit, he made confession first of his faith, then of his sins ; with what heart's desire he received the food for his journey, and pledge of eternal life—the body of the Lord Redeemer; how faithfully he commended his body and soul to Him, here and in eternity,—the religious brothers are witness, and the whole congregation of that monastery. Thus Master Peter finished his days, and he who, for his knowledge, was famed throughout the world, in the discipleship of Him who said 'Learn of Me, for I am meek and lowly in heart,' persevered in meekness and humility, and, as we may believe, passed to the Lord. And you, my venerable and very dear sister, be you ever mindful of your husband in the Lord, that husband to whom you were knit first by the bond of earthly love, afterwards by the stronger and better one of Divine charity, with whom and under whom you served the Lord. May God in your stead comfort him in His bosom; comfort him as another you, and guard him, till through grace he is restored to you at the coming of the Lord, with the shout of the archangel and the trump of God descending from the heavens." [1]

[1] Petri Ven., lib. iv. Epist. 21.

Note on St. Bernard's Sister Humbeline.

I have been guilty of an omission with regard to Bernard's sister Humbeline, which I would repair here, as she died about this time.

Humbeline had not shared the religious fervour of her brothers, when at Bernard's instance they devoted themselves to a monastic life. She was married, and unwilling to renounce the rank and affluence in which she was placed by her husband. One day she was moved to visit her cloistered kinsmen, and appeared with the pomp and retinue of a feudal lady at the gates of Clairvaux. She had especially come to see Bernard, but "he, detesting and execrating her as a net of the devil to catch souls," sternly refused to go out to meet her. Her brother Andrew, whom she encountered at the gate, treated her with equal harshness, and used very strong and unbecoming language concerning her fine apparel,—"cum a fratre sua Andrea quem ad portam invenerat monasterii ob vestium apparatum *stercus involutum* argueretur." Bursting into tears at such coldness from her brothers, she meekly said, "And what if I am a sinner? it is for such that Christ died. It is because I am one that I need the advice and conversation of good men. If my brother despises my body, let not a servant of the Lord despise my soul. Let him come and command; I am ready to obey." This speech brought out Bernard, who ordered her to imitate their mother's life; to renounce the luxuries and vanities of the world even while living in the world; to lay aside her fine clothes; and to become a nun inwardly, even if she could not be one in outward appearance. She returned home and literally obeyed his words. During two years she astonished her neighbours by her sudden and extraordinary change of life. Her fastings, prayers, and vigils were truly monastic. At the end of the above-named time her husband, wearied or enraptured with her religious practices, gave her full liberty to do as she pleased. She immediately retired to the convent of Juilly, where she passed the remainder of her life in a devotion austere enough to be considered worthy of a sister of St. Bernard.

It may be proper to state that Chifflet considers her death to have taken place in, or before, the year 1136. (S. Bernardi Illustre Genus Assertum, p. 156.) Manriquez and Mabillon adopt the date of 1141.

CHAPTER V.

(A.D. 1142. AETAT. 51.)

BERNARD AS A MONK AND RULER OF MONKS—SERMON ON THE PASSION.

To us, looking back on Bernard through a vista of seven centuries, he appears as one of the great active minds of his age—commanding kings, compelling nations, influencing and directing the men and things among which he lived;—in a word, one of the statesmen of history. And in truth he was all this. The twelfth century would have had another aspect if he had never lived. But it must not be forgotten that this external, mundane activity was an accident, an appendix, as it were, to his true career, to the career which he had chosen for himself. The central impulse of his being, the spring-head from which flowed the manifold streams of his public acts, had no necessary connexion with the outer world of men and events. He was, by intention and inclination, a prayerful monk, doubtful and anxious about the state of his soul, striving to work out his salvation with fear and trembling here on earth. The highest good he knew of, the ideal of Christian faith as he had been taught it—this was what in-flamed his heart, nerved his will, and braced his energies of mind and body to the extremest tension. To him and to his contemporaries this ideal was realized in the life of a pious monk. And a pious monk it was his desire above all things to be. That he failed to obtain the perfection at which he aimed, no one would have been more ready to acknowledge than himself: but that he also succeeded better than most, is proved by the almost concurrent testimony of his own and after ages. As a monk, therefore, he is to be judged in the first place; as an abbot, a ruler, and teacher of monks, in the second place.

It is difficult to judge of such a man, placed as we are with respect to him. He is quite below our ordinary intellectual horizon, and only by a considerable ascension can he be seen at all. What was considered wise in his day is accounted foolish in ours. What was thought true in his time is regarded as absurd now. Our planet has gone seven hundred times and more round the sun since he was on it; some billions of human beings have lived their lives through and died here in the interval; and it would be strange indeed if the human mind had remained unchanged amid ever-changing nature. Changes indeed have come and gone since then. Systems and philosophies have arisen and gathered broad populations under their dominion, and seemed so large, so complete, so true, that men have thought, as they had thought endless times before, that the goal was reached, the problem solved; that to them at last was the light given which would show and teach them all things; so different were they from their "unenlightened ancestors," who had no such golden rule. Alas! the hour of hope and triumph was short. The systems and philosophies were found as mortal as the men who made them. They, too, waxed old and shrunk, and from being (apparently) complete and true, became incomplete and false; till at last men would have them no more, and cast them aside as lumber, useless or obstructive. For behold, a new light is mounting in the eastern sky, rosy with the dawn of another hope. Again, it must be repeated that Bernard is far off. Not only his system and philosophy, but half a dozen other systems and philosophies, which have supplanted his and each other, have been cast aside as valueless since he lived.

To see through them is hard. It is not looking through the pure unrefracting ether, as we do at the stars ; but looking across the fogs and vapours of deep valleys and populous plains, which at times make observation difficult, or even impossible. It must be attempted, nevertheless.

To judge of Bernard, therefore, as a monk and abbot: we have not many means of attaining to such judgment preferable to his sermons. He spoke his heart in them, if he did anywhere. He spoke what he considered the purest truth attainable to him or to any human being. He spoke, in his conviction, the most momentous truth known to him, which neither he nor his hearers could ever lay too much to heart. It was for this truth that he and his monks, his church even, existed. Clairvaux and Cluny, clergy regular and secular, were but engines for its dissemination, and might, or rather certainly would, pass away ; but the Truth would remain. Another of his sermons will therefore be given here, spoken for different objects, to different hearers, from a different point of view, compared with certain modern discourses which go by the same name. Odd, almost grotesque, it and those already given will doubtless appear to the modern reader. It is not long ago that many a grand old Gothic cathedral was ridiculed, even despised, for its quaint gargoyles and portals. Without meaning to institute a rigorous comparison between Bernard's sermons and Gothic architecture, we may be allowed to say, that some of the antique solemnity and massiveness of twelfth-century aisles and choirs will also be found in the words which once awakened their religious echoes.

ON THE PASSION OF OUR LORD.[1]

" 1. Watch with your mind, brethren, that the mysteries of this season may not pass away without profit. The blessing

[1] I am happy to acknowledge my obligations to the Rev. W. B. Flower, B.A., who has translated a collection of St. Bernard's sermons, of which this is one. Mr. Flower has, on the whole, shown judg-

is plentiful ; offer yourselves clean receptacles ; show forth devout souls, watchful senses, sober affections, and chaste consciences for the gift of such graces. In good truth, not only does that special conversation which ye have professed admonish you of care in this matter, but it is the observance of the universal Church, whose sons ye are. For all Christians, in observance of these seven sacred days, cultivate holiness, show forth modesty, follow after humility, put on gravity, either according to or beyond what is usual, that they may in some sort seem to suffer with Christ's suffering. For who is so irreligious as not to be sorrowful ? who so proud, as not to be humbled? who so wrathful, as not to forgive? who so luxurious, as not to abstain? who so sensual, as not to restrain himself? who so wicked, as not to repent during these days? And rightly so. For the Passion of the Lord is here, this very day, shaking the earth, rending the rocks, and opening the tombs. Near also is his Resurrection, in which you will celebrate a festival to the Lord Most High, entering with alacrity and eagerness of will into the most glorious deeds which He has wrought. Nothing better could be done in the world than that which was done by the Lord on these days. Nothing more useful or better could be recommended to the world than that it should, by perpetual ordinance, celebrate year by year the memorial thereof with longing of soul, and show forth the memory of His abundant sweetness. But both were on our behalf; because in both is the fruit of our salvation, and in both the life of our soul. Marvellous is that passion of Thine, O Lord Jesus, which has removed all our suffering, made propitiation for our iniquities, and is found effectual for every one of our plagues. For what is there tending to death that is not destroyed by Thy death ?

---

ment and taste in the execution of his by no means inviting labour of translation. But I must, nevertheless, add that he has not shown a scrupulous regard for accuracy, and that I have felt compelled, in several cases, to correct his work.

" 2. In this Passion then, my brethren, we must especially
consider three things—the work, the manner, and the cause;
for in the work, indeed, patience is commended unto us, in the
manner humility, and in the cause charity. But unparalleled
was that patience, since, when, sinners made long furrows in
His back; when He was so stretched out on the cross that His
bones could be numbered; when that most powerful Defence,
which guardeth Israel, was everywhere wounded; when His
hands and feet were pierced;—He was led as a lamb to the
slaughter, and as a sheep before her shearer, so He opened
not His mouth; not complaining against His Father, by
whom He was sent; nor against mankind, for whom He
paid what He had not taken; nor yet, in a word, against His
own peculiar people, from whom He received so great evils in
return for so signal benefits. Some are punished for their sins,
and bear it with humility; yet this is set down to them as
a proof of patience; others are beaten, not so much to be
cleansed, as to be tried and crowned, and their greater patience
is approved and commended. How shall it not be considered
greatest in Christ, who, in the midst of His inheritance, was
punished like a thief by a most cruel death, by those to whom
He had especially come as a Saviour, though void of all sin,
whether actual or inherited, having indeed nothing in which
sin could grow? Doubtless He it was in whom dwelt all the
fulness of the Godhead—not in shadow, but bodily; in whom
God is reconciling the world unto Himself—not figuratively,
but substantially; who, in a word, is full of grace and truth—
not co-operatively, but personally; that so He may accomplish
His own work—'His strange work,' Isaiah says (xxviii. 21)—
because it was His work which His Father had given Him to
do, and a strange work that such a One should endure such
things. Thou hast then an example of patience in the work.

" 3. For if thou carefully considerest the manner, thou wilt
discover that He was not only gentle, but humble of heart:

for in humility His judgment was taken away, since He answered not a word to so great blasphemies and the many false charges which were made against Him. 'We saw Him,' it is written, and there 'was no beauty in Him' (Isa. liii. 2); not comely in appearance beyond the sons of men, but the reproach of men, and as it were leprous; the lowest of His race; clearly a Man of sorrows, stricken and humbled by God, so that there was no beauty nor comeliness in Him. O lowest and highest! O humble and exalted One! O reproach of men and glory of angels! None more exalted, none more humble than He! In fine, He was defiled by spittings, assailed to the full with revilings, condemned to a most ignominious death, and numbered with transgressors. And will that humility merit nothing which reaches such limits, or rather is beyond all limit? As His patience was singular, so His humility was admirable, and both without example.

"4. Yet the cause gloriously recommends both: and that is love. For, on account of the great love wherewith Christ loved us, neither the Father spared the Son, nor the Son Himself, to redeem His servants. Great indeed was it, for it exceeds all measures, passes all limits, clearly outstripping all. 'Greater love,' He saith, 'hath no man than this, that a man lay down his life for his friends' (John xv. 13). Thou, O Lord, hadst greater still, laying it down even for thine enemies. For whilst we were yet enemies, we were reconciled to Thee and Thy Father, by Thy death. What other love can be, has been, or will be like Thine? Scarcely for a righteous man will one die; Thou sufferedst for the unjust, dying for our sins, for Thou camest to justify sinners freely, to make slaves brethren, captives co-heirs, and exiles kings. And nothing surely so clearly sets forth alike this patience and humility, as that He gave up His soul to death, and bare the sins of many, entreating even for transgressors that they might not perish. A faithful saying, and worthy of all acceptation!

For He was offered because He willed. He not only willed and was offered, but it was because He willed. He alone had the power of laying down His own soul; none took it from Him; He voluntarily offered it. When He had received the vinegar He said, 'It is finished.' Nothing remains to be fulfilled : now there is nothing for which I have to wait. And bowing His head, being made obedient unto death, He gave up the ghost. Who could so easily fall asleep, on willing it? Death is indeed a great weakness; but thus to die is matchless power. For the weakness of God is stronger than men. The madness of man may lay wicked hands upon himself and kill himself; but this is not to lay down one's life : it is rather to destroy it by forcible means, than to lay it down at pleasure. Thou, wicked Judas, hadst a wretched power, not of laying down thy life, but of hanging thyself : and thy wicked spirit went out, not given by thee, but pulled by the rope ; not sent forth by thee, but lost. He alone gave up His soul unto death, who alone returned by His own power to life : He alone had power to lay it down, who also possessed the full power to take it up again, having the power of life and death.

" 5. Worthy, then, is love so inestimable, humility so wonderful, patience so insuperable ; worthy clearly is this so holy, unpolluted, and acceptable a victim. Worthy is the Lamb who was slain to receive power, to accomplish that which He came to effect, to take away the sins of the world. But I say that the sin which prevailed upon the earth was threefold. Do you understand me to mean the lust of the flesh, the lust of the eyes, and the pride of life?—a threefold cord, which is not easily broken : therefore many draw, yea are drawn by, this cord of vanity. But that former threefold cord has deservedly greater power among the elect. For how could not the remembrance of His patience repress all pleasure? How should not the recollection of His humility utterly extinguish the pride of life? for that love is beyond question worthy, the thoughts of which can so fill the mind, and claim the whole soul to itself, that it completely destroys the sin of curiosity. Powerful, therefore, against these is the Passion of the Saviour.

" 6. But I have been thinking of explaining how the power of the Cross blots out a threefold sin of another kind; and this perhaps you may hear with great advantage. The first I would call original, the second personal, and the third individual. Original sin, indeed, is that greatest one which we derive from the first Adam, in whom we have all sinned, for whom we all die. The greatest clearly, in that it seizes not only upon the whole human race, but upon every individual thereof, so that there is none, not even one, that can escape. It extends from the first man unto the last, and the poison is dispersed from the sole of the foot to the crown of the head. But in another way, also, it is diffused over the whole of life; from the day, I mean, on which his own mother conceived any one, to that on which the common mother receives him. Else whence that heavy yoke which is upon all, and the whole of the sons of Adam, and that from the day of his coming forth from his mother's womb, until the day of his burial into the mother of all? We are conceived in sin, cherished in darkness, and brought forth in pain. Before our birth we burden hapless mothers; during it we rend them in a fearful manner: and it is marvellous we also ourselves are not likewise mangled. The first cry we utter is one of lamentation, and rightly so; for we have entered the valley of pain, so that the saying of holy Job is thoroughly applicable to us : ' Man that is born of a woman hath but a short time to live, and is full of trouble' (Job xiv. 1). Not words, but stripes, have taught us the truth of this statement. ' Man,' he says, ' born of a woman;' nothing is more abject. And lest, perchance, he should be soothed by those delights of sense which he derives from outward objects, he is fearfully reminded at his very entrance into the world of his departure, by the words, ' hath but a short time to live.'

And that he may not regard the brief space of time which there is between his entrance and departure at his own disposal, it is added, 'he is full of trouble'—full of miseries many and manifold, both of the body and the heart; miseries when he is asleep, and when awake; misery wheresoever he turneth himself. Even He also, who was born of a virgin, nay, made of a woman—but blessed among women—who says to His mother, 'Woman, behold thy son,' lived only for a little while; and yet, in that brief space of time, was full of many miseries, aimed at by plots, questioned with insults, attacked by injuries, racked by punishments, and harassed by reproaches.

" 7. And canst thou doubt the sufficiency of His obedience, which absolved every one who was under the curse of the first offence. Truly not as the offence, so is also the gift. For sin came from one sin for condemnation, but grace for justification from many sins. And grievous beyond question was that original sin which infected, not only the person, but the nature itself. Yet every one's personal sin is the more grievous, when, the reins being let loose, we give up on every hand our members as servants to unrighteousness, being enchained, not only by another's, but our own sin also. But most grievous was that especial one which was committed against the Lord of Glory, when wicked men unjustly killed the Just Man, and wretched homicides, or rather (if any one may so speak) Deicides. laid their accursed hands upon the very Son of God. What connexion is there between the two preceding and the third? At this the whole of this world's frame paled and trembled, and all things were well-nigh resolved into primeval chaos. Let us suppose that one of the nobles of a kingdom had laid waste the king's lands in a hostile inroad; let us suppose another, who, being a guest and counsellor of the king, strangled, with traitorous hands, the latter's only son: would not the first be held innocent and free from blame in respect of the second? So stands all sin in relation to this sin, viz. Christ's crucifixion; and yet this sin He took upon Himself, that He who made Himself to be sin might condemn sin by means of sin. For through this all sin, personal as well as original, was destroyed, and even this very special one was removed by Himself.

"8. I take my argument from the greatest sin, as the two lesser are removed. It is this. He bore the sins of many, and prayed for the transgressors that they might not perish: 'Father, forgive them, for they know not what they do.' Thy irrevocable word, O Lord, goeth forth, and will not return without effect unto Thee, but will accomplish that for which Thou hast sent it. See now the works of the Lord, what wonders He hath done upon the earth! He was beaten with rods, crowned with thorns, bruised with staves, fastened to a cross, loaded with reproaches; and yet, unmindful of all these evils, he says, 'Forgive them.' Hence the many sufferings of His body, hence the mercy of His heart, hence the pangs, hence the compassion, hence the oil of gladness, hence the drops of blood running down to the ground. Many are the mercies of the Lord, and many His sufferings. Will the sufferings surpass the mercies, or the latter be greater than the former? Let Thy mercies of old time prevail, O Lord, and let wisdom over-come malice. For great is their sin; but is not Thy mercy greater, O Lord? It is greatly so in every way. Is not evil returned for good, saith He, because they have digged a pit for My soul? Plainly they dug a pit to catch impatience, furnishing many and the greatest possible causes for anger. But what is this pit of theirs compared with the depth of Thy kindness? Repaying evil for good, they digged a pit: but charity is not easily provoked, suffereth long; rushes not into a pit, and heaps up good for evil given instead. God forbid that flies about to die should do away with the sweetness of the ointment which flows from Thy body, because there is mercy in Thy breast, and plenteous redemption with Thee. The miseries, the blasphemies, and insults which a wicked and perverse generation heaps on Thee, are but as flies about to die.

"9. But what didst Thou do? In the very uplifting of Thy hands, when the morning sacrifice was now being changed into the evening offering—on the very strength, I say, of that incense which ascended into the heavens, covered the earth, and bestrewed even hell itself, worthy to be heard for Thy reverence, Thou criedst, 'Father, forgive them, for they know not what they do.' Oh, how ready art Thou to pardon! Oh, how great is the multitude of Thy mercy, O Lord! Oh, how different are Thy thoughts to our thoughts! Oh, how strong is Thy pity even over the wicked! A marvellous thing! He cries, 'Forgive them,' and the Jews, 'Crucify Him!' His words are soft as oil, and theirs be very spears. Oh, patient charity, and compassionate also! 'Charity suffereth long,'— this is enough; 'charity is kind' is more than sufficient. ' Be not overcome of evil' is abundant charity, but 'overcome evil with good' is superabundant; for it was not the patience alone, but the goodness of God that led the Jews unto repentance, because bountiful charity loves, and loves ardently, those with whom it bears. Patient charity puts off, waits, bears with the offender; but kind charity draws, allures, would have him converted from the error of his way, and, in short, covers a multitude of sins. O Jews! ye are stones, but ye strike a softer stone, from which resounds the ring of mercy, and the oil of charity bursts forth! How wilt Thou, O Lord, over-flood with the torrent of Thy bliss those who long for Thee, when Thou thus pourest out the oil of Thy mercy upon those who are crucifying Thee!

"10. It is evident, then, that this Passion is most effectual for the destruction of every kind of sin. But who knows if it has been given to me? It has been given to me because

it could not be given to another. Could it to an angel?
but he needed it not. Could it to the devil? but he riseth
not again. In a word, being made not in the likeness of
angels, much less of devils, but in the likeness of men, and
found in fashion as man, He emptied Himself, and took upon
Him the form of a servant. He was a Son, and was made
as a servant. He took upon Him not only the form of a
servant, that He might obey, but of a wicked servant, that He
might be beaten ; and the servant of sin, to pay the penalty,
though there was no sin in Him. In the likeness, He says, of
men, not of a man ; because the first man was created neither
in the flesh of sin, nor in the likeness thereof; for Christ
plunged Himself deeply into the universal misery of man,
that the subtle eye of the devil might not discover the great
mystery of godliness ; and, therefore, He was found in fashion,
yea in every fashion, as a man ; and, as far as nature was concerned, there was nothing particular about him. For He was
crucified, because He was so found. But He revealed Himself unto few, that there might be some who would believe ;
but He was hidden from the rest, because, had they known,
they never would have crucified the Lord of Glory. He
added ignorance also to their particular sin, that He might,
with some semblance of justice, be able to pardon the ignorant.

" 11. But that old Adam who fled from the face of God left
us two things as an inheritance, viz. labour and pain ; labour
in work, pain in suffering. He himself knew not this in
Paradise, which he had received to till and keep ; to till it
with pleasure, and to keep it carefully for himself and his
children. Christ the Lord endured labour and pain to deliver
them (i.e. men) into His hands, or, rather, Himself into
theirs, when fixed in the lowest depths, and the waters entered
even into His soul. ' Look upon My lowliness and labour,' He
says unto the Father, ' because I am poor, and in misery

from My youth up.' He toiled persistently, His hands were wearied in labours. 'Oh, all ye that pass by, behold and see if there be any sorrow like unto My sorrow, which is done unto Me' (Lam. i. 12). 'Surely He hath borne our griefs, and carried our sorrows' (Isa. liii. 4); a Man of sorrows, poor and afflicted, tempted in all points, yet without sin. He exhibited in His life passive action, and in His death endured active passion, while He wrought in the midst of the earth. Henceforth, as long as I live, I will bear in mind those labours which He endured in preaching; His weariness in journeying to and fro, His temptations in fasting, His vigils in prayer, and His tears of compassion. I will remember also His pains, the reproaches, spittings, blows, revilings, nails, and the like, which passed in great abundance through and over Him. Boldness, therefore, and resemblance are profitable to me, if there be also imitation, so that I follow His footsteps; for otherwise that righteous blood which was poured out upon the earth will be required of me, and I shall not be free from that singular wickedness of the Jews: since I should prove ungrateful to so great charity, do despite to the Spirit of grace, regard the blood of the testament as an unholy thing, and tread under foot the Son of God.

" 12. There are many who endure labour and pain, but it is of necessity, not of choice; and these are not conformed to the image of God. Others bear them of their own free will, yet neither have they part or lot in this discourse. The luxurious man keeps awake the whole night long, not only patiently, but willingly, to fulfil his pleasure; the bandit, clothed in mail, watches to seize upon his prey; the thief watches to break into another man's house: but all these, and the like of them, are far removed from the labour and pain of which the Lord takes account. But men of good will, who in a Christian spirit have exchanged riches for poverty, or even despised them when not had, as if they had them, leaving all

for Him, even as He also left all for them, follow Him whithersoever He goeth.   And imitation of such a character as this, is
in my opinion the most powerful argument that the Passion of
the Saviour, and His likeness to humanity, tend to my utmost
advantage.   For here is the relish, here the fruit of labour
and pain.

"13. See, then, how gloriously that Majesty has dealt with
thee.   As regards all things which are in heaven, and under
the heaven, He spake, and they were created.   What is easier
than a word?   But was it with a word only that He restored
thee whom He had created.   When He was seen for thirty
and three years upon the earth, and conversed with men,
He met with slanderers against His acts, and evil speakers
against His words, and had not where to lay His head.
Why this?   Because the Word had descended from its own
subtlety, and received a coarser clothing; for it was made
flesh, and therefore used a grosser and harsher form.   But as
thought clothes itself with a voice without any diminution of
itself either before or after the voice, so the Son assumed
flesh without any commixture or diminution either before
or after His incarnation.   He was invisible with the Father;
but here our hands have handled the Word of Life, and we
have seen with our eyes that which was from the beginning.
But this Word, because He had united to Himself spotless
flesh and a most holy soul, freely governed the actions of
His body, both because He was wisdom and righteousness,
and had no law in His members warring against the law of
His mind.   My words are neither wisdom nor righteousness,
but yet capable of both, which may be contained in them or
not; more easily perhaps the latter.   For it is far easier for
us to obey the faults of our flesh than to regulate its actions
and passions, since every age from youth upward is prone
to evil, and eagerly follows after its own pleasures, in the

midst of stripes and swords, and even with the risk of death itself.

" 14. Happy he whose thought (this is my saying) directs all his actions according to righteousness, so that his intention may be good and his acts right. Happy he who governs his passions for righteousness' sake, so that whatever he suffers he may suffer on account of the Son of God; so that murmuring be taken away from his heart, and thanksgiving and the voice of praise be in his mouth. He who has so uplifted himself, takes up his bed and walks into his own house. The bed is our body, in which we formerly lay languid, obeying our desires and lusts; but now we carry it when we are obliged to obey the Spirit : and we carry our dead, since the body is dead because of sin. We walk, however, but run not ; for the corruptible body presseth down the soul, and the earthy tabernacle weigheth down the mind that museth upon many things' (Wisd. ix. 15). We also walk to our own house. To what house? To the mother of all, because their dwelling-places shall endure for ever ; or, rather, to that our house which we have of God, not made with hands, eternal in the heavens. When we who walk under this load shall have laid it down, how shall we run, how shall we fly, think you? Clearly upon the wings of the wind. Our Lord Jesus Christ has embraced us through our labour and pain ; let us also embrace Him with corresponding returns on account of His righteousness, and according to His righteousness ; by directing our deeds according to His righteousness, and enduring suffering on account of His righteousness. Let us say also, with the Bride, 'I held Him, and would not let Him go' (Cant. iii. 4). Let us say also, with the patriarch, 'I will not let Thee go except Thou bless me' (Gen. xxxii. 26). For what now remaineth but blessing? what after embrace but a kiss? If I thus cleave unto God, how should I not now cry out, 'Let Him kiss me with the kisses of His mouth' (Cant. i. 2). Feed us meanwhile, Lord, with the bread of tears, and give us tears to drink in measure until Thou lead us to a good measure, full and heaped up, which Thou shalt pour into our bosoms, who art in the bosom of the Father, above all, God blessed for evermore. Amen."[1]

---

[1] St. Bern. Op. vol. i. col. 884. "In Feria quarta Hebdomadae Sanctae Sermo."

CHAPTER VI.

(A.D. 1142. AETAT. 51.)

THE IMMACULATE CONCEPTION—LOUIS VII. AND THE ARCHBISHOP OF
BOURGES—THE COUNT OF VERMANDOIS EXCOMMUNICATED—WAR
BETWEEN LOUIS VII. AND COUNT THEOBALD OF CHAMPAGNE—BURN-
ING OF VITRY—DEATH OF POPE INNOCENT II.

IT must have been nearly at the same time that he was
denouncing Abelard for his sceptical inquiries into matters of
belief, that Bernard wrote his celebrated letter to the canons
of the church of Lyons, to reprove them for just the opposite
vice, namely, a tendency to add without necessity to the
mysteries already generally held. The church of Lyons had
seen fit to celebrate a new festival—that of the Immaculate
Conception of the Virgin. Bernard addressed the canons in a
long letter on the subject, which is a temperate but vigorous
remonstrance against their proceedings.[1]

---

[1] In December, 1854, the Pope pronounced the dogmatic decree of the "Immaculate Conception of Mary," by which that was made a dogma of faith, which St. Bernard, St. Thomas, St. Bonaventura, and other great theologians of the twelfth and thirteenth centuries, had expressly condemned; as Gieseler says : " Die Lehre von der unbefleckten Empfängniss wurde von Keinem bedeutenden Theologen dieses Jahrhunderts angenommen." — GIESELER'S *Kirchengesch.* 2r. Bd. 2te Abth., p. 471, where a good collection of quotations will be found.

The difficulty caused by St. Bernard's and St. Thomas's condemnation of the doctrine is got over by the aid of a subtle distinction between (1) the active and (2) the passive conception : the transmission of the body being the first, and the infusion of the soul the second. Concerning St. Bernard Bishop Ullathorne says : "Yet it is evident, from the tenor of his language, that he had no idea in his mind beyond that of active concep-

In the intervals of quiet which Bernard now occasionally obtained, he vainly laid plans and indulged in hopes of

tion."—(*Exposition*, p. 141. London, 1855.) The great point is not to allow even a moment between her *animatio in utero* and her sanctification. "But, after a moment of sin, **she** is cleansed and sanctified, say **certain** objectors. But if we grant to **sin and the** devil but that one moment, we give up everything, and abandon her stainless honour."—(*Ibid.* pp. 89, 90.) It is this small but penetrating wedge which has made a breach in the doctrine of the great St. Thomas. "It is hard to say that St. Thomas did not require an instant at least after the animation of Mary before her sanctification."—(*Ibid.* p. 143.) The following extract from a letter of the celebrated Petrus Cellensis to an English monk of St. Alban's is curious on many grounds. The English monk, named Nicholas, had written in favour of the Immaculate Conception, and this was the reply he received from his correspondent, Peter:—

[vi. 23.] Petrus S. Remigii Nicholao Monacho S. Albani.— . . . . "Aggredior igitur phantasmata tua, lenocinantia quidem pulchritudinis specie, sed titubantia stabilis fundamenti egestate. . . . Nec indignetur *Anglica levitas*, si ea solidior sit *Gallica maturitas*. **Insula** enim est circumfusa aqua, unde hujus elementi propria qualitate ejus incolae non immerito afficiuntur, et nimia mobilitate in tenuissimas et subtiles phantasias frequenter transferuntur, somnia sua visionibus comparantes, ne dicam praeferentes. Et quae culpa naturae, si talis est natura terrae? Certe expertus **sum** somniatores plus esse Anglicos quam Gallos. Cerebrum namque humidius fumositate stomachi citius involvitur, et quas-

libet imagines in seipso depingit, quae ab animali **virtute** utcunque spirituali deferuntur, et ex occupatione omnium, tam naturalium quam animalium seu spiritualium virtutum, infra judicii veritatem confinguntur, ut phantasmata seu **somnia** appellentur. Non sic **cavernosa**, non sic aquatica Gallia, **ubi sunt montes** lapidei, *ubi ferrum nascitur*, **ubi terra** suo pondere gravatur. Quid ergo? **non** cito a suo sensu moventur, et veritatis auctoritatibus **tenacius** innituntur." —(Lib. ii. Epistola clxxi.) The tables have been strangely turned since. Nicholas, in answer, **wrote** thus [the anecdote concerning Bernard is not without interest, as showing **the** sentiment entertained towards him twenty years after his death]:—

[ix. 9.] Nicolaus Monachus **S.** Albani Petro Abbati S. Remegii.— "Ego autem . . . sic veneror beatum confessorem **Bernardum**, ut laudem et **amem** ejus **sanctitatem**, qui nec amem nec laudem ejus praesumptionem in Matris Domini conceptionem. Et ne putes me magis pertinaci quam bona conscientia dicere quae dico; audi quid ab ipsis Cisterciensibus vera **religione praeditis**, et Virginem in **veritate** diligentibus, acceperim de S. Bernardo, quorum nomina abscondo sub modio, ne odiosos faciam fatrum suorum collegio. In Clarevallensi collegio quidam con**versus** bene religiosus in visu **noctis** vidit abbatem Bernardum niveis indutum vestibus, **quasi ad** mamillam pectoris furvam **habere** maculam. Quem ex admiratione tristior alloquens: Quid est, inquit, Pater quod nigram in te maculam video? et ille Quia de Dominicae nostrae conceptione scripsi non scribenda, signum **purgationis** meae maculam

recovering that monastic peace and seclusion which had been his chief inducements to become a monk. The circle of his political and ecclesiastical relations was European. He had become a centre, around which the affairs and men of the Church had grown accustomed to revolve. While he lived, directly or indirectly he was destined to be brought into connexion with every matter of above average importance which occurred in Europe. Thus Master Peter's errors had hardly been condemned, the few remaining "years of his old age" had not yet run out, when Bernard's rest was again destroyed by a series of vexatious circumstances.

Alberic, Archbishop of Bourges, died in the year 1141. The chapter was divided about the election of a new Metropolitan, part of it voting for one Cadurcus, who also enjoyed the favour of the French king, Louis VII., part of it supporting Pierre de la Chatre, who was nephew of the Roman Chancellor Haimeric, and was supposed, with good reason, to have the countenance of the Pope.[1] Innocent's troubles had not humbled and chastened his mind; on the contrary, in the brief interval between the extinction of the schism and his death, during which he wielded the whole power of the papacy, he often appeared overbearing and unscrupulous. In this instance he threw the whole of his influence into the scale of his chancellor's creature. Without deigning to inquire about the wishes or feelings of the French

---

in pectore porto. Frater visa conventui innotuit, et aliquis fratrum in scriptum redegit. Relatum est in generali Cisterciensi Capitulo et de communi consilio scriptum periit incendio. Maluitque Abbatum universitas Virginis periclitari gloriam quam S. Bernardi opinionem. . . . . Et certe, ut credo, ea ratione sanctus in propria persona viro simplici et de talibus nil scienti apparuit, et culpam suam innotuit, ut totius Cis-

terciensis capituli discretio deprehenderet eum velle suum errorem damnari et virgineae conceptionis gloriam praedicari. Igitur si ego publico, quod ipse, ut credo publicari voluit, hoc non est ejus famam extenuare, vel gloriam evacuare, sed ejus voluntatem super delicti sui poenitentia exprimere."— Lib. ii. Epistola clxxii.

[1] Gesta Innocentii II. Papae ap. D. Bouquet, xv. p. 359.

king, he consecrated Pierre de la Chatre Archbishop of Bourges, and deposed his rival Cadurcus from every ecclesiastical office. Louis VII. was very wroth, and swore a solemn oath that Pierre should never enter any of his dominions. Innocent, with equal haughtiness, replied, "We must teach this boy-king a lesson, lest he should get confirmed in these bad habits," and proceeded to carry out his laudable design by excommunicating the son of his own faithful benefactor, Louis VI. He went further, and prohibited all celebration of holy rites in any town, village, or castle into which the king might enter, and during the whole period of his sojourn in it.[1]

Louis VII. was in no wise less hostile to Pierre de la Chatre for this measure on the part of the Pope. He resolutely prevented the Archbishop from entering his see. But churchmen had lately acquired in Theobald, Count of Champagne, a champion whose power to help them was only equalled by his willingness to exert it. He at once received and welcomed Pierre into his territories, who, from this safe retreat, administered the affairs of his province unmolested by the French king.[2]

Louis, who was never slow to anger, was deeply incensed. There had been a cause of coldness between him and Theobald before this, in consequence of the latter having refused to accompany him in an expedition against the Count of Toulouse. And now a third cause of animosity was to be added, far graver and more irritating than either of the preceding.

Queen Eleanor, the wife of Louis VII., had a sister named

---

[1] "Sic per triennium persona Regis interdicto subjacuit: in quamcunque civitatem, castellum vel vicum intrabat, celebratio divinorum suspendebatur."—*Radulfus de Diceto*, ap. D. BOUQUET, xiii. p. 183.

[2] "Rex vero . . . Archiepiscopum exclusit redeuntem, sed eum comes Campaniae Theobaldus recepit in terra sua. . . . Indignatus ob hoc Rex concitavit omnes fere proceres suos, ut una cum eo guerram inferent Comiti Theobaldo."—*Ex Appendice Roberti de Monte ad Sigebertum*, ap. D. BOUQUET, xiii. p. 735.

Petronilla.   Louis himself had a cousin named Ralph of Vermandois, and these two became deeply enamoured of each
other.   But an obstacle was opposed to their happiness by the
fact that Ralph was already married, and married to a niece of
Count Theobald, named Eleanor.   But Ralph, Petronilla, the
king, and the queen, all determined that this encumbrance
should be removed.   So they applied to the Bishops of Noyon,
Laon, and Senlis, and induced them to dissolve the marriage
of Ralph and Eleanor, on the ground of affinity ; whereupon
Petronilla hastened to the arms of the impatient Ralph, all
difficulties, it was supposed, having been removed.

It was now Theobald's turn to be indignant.   When he
heard of the treatment to which his niece had been subjected,
he made an application to the Pope, to have the matter
investigated.   The Pope sent his legate, the Cardinal Ives,
who held a council at Lagny, at which it was declared that
Ralph and Eleanor were still legally married, and that the
union with Petronilla was an adulterous connexion.   The
Cardinal then excommunicated Ralph and Petronilla, at the
same time laying the count's territory of Vermandois under
an interdict.   The three bishops who had assisted him in
his matrimonial schemes were suspended from ecclesiastical
functions.[1]

Louis zealously espoused his cousin's quarrel with Count
Theobald and the Pope, of whose conduct to himself he
thought he had such ample reason to complain.   His ambitious queen, the haughty Eleanor, was also quite ready to keep
alive his animosity, if it had been disposed to flag, as the posi-

[1] " Radulphus   Viromandorum comes   uxorem   suam   dimittit, et sororem Reginae Petronillam ducit : propter quod, instantia Comitis Theo-baldi, mittitur Romanae sedis Ivo Legatus, qui et Radulphum Comi-tem excommunicavit et Episcopos Laudunensem Bartholomaeum, No-viomensem Simonem, et Petrum Sil-vanectensem, qui divortium illud fecerant, suspendit."—*Ex alterius Roberti appendice ad Sigebertum,* ap. D. BOUQUET, xiii. p. 331.

tion of her sister, now branded as a concubine, was extremely painful to her. Both she and the king felt that Theobald was their most important enemy, not only because he was a great feudal lord, with power and territories of almost royal extent, but because of his intimate connexion with churchmen, and especially with Bernard, through whom he was known to possess no small influence at the court of Rome : " Leave me and my business alone," said Louis to him, "and occupy yourself with your estates, which are surely large enough to keep you employed." In the year 1142 Louis VII., at the head of a powerful army, boldly invaded the country of his hostile vassal, and laid siege to the town and castle of Vitry. The resistance was feeble. The king's people set fire to the houses, which were of wood, and a great conflagration ensued. Numbers of the besieged took refuge in a church, but the flames soon enveloped that also, and thirteen hundred persons were burnt alive.[1]

Although this event afflicted Louis even to the shedding of tears, yet he paused not in his career of conquest.[2] Theobald was not prepared for so much prompt vigour in the young king, and was unable to make an effectual stand against the invaders. The whole country was given up to destruction and pillage. Some people said it served Theobald right for thinking only of monks and nuns instead of knights and crossbowmen.[3] At an assembly of his friends, at which Bernard

[1] " Denique cum multo comitatu aggressus castrum ejus quod Vitreiacum dicitur, oppidanos et milites sibi resistentes aut cepit aut occidit.

" Oppido succenso, in tantum ignis excrevit, ut etiam castrum quod in eo erat valde munitum cum multo inhabitantium periculo concremarit. In hoc praelio vel incendio capti, caesi, aut concremati ad mille quingentos sunt aestimati."—(Ex auctore Gemblacensi, ap. D. Bouquet, xiii. p. 272.) " Cujus castrum Vitriacum cum Rex Ludovicus VI. cepisset, igne admoto ecclesia incensa est, et in ea mille trecentae animae diversi sexus et aetatis sunt igne consumptae."—(Ex Hist. Francorum, ap. D. Bouquet, xii. p. 116.) It will be noticed there is a slight discrepancy in the accounts. I have chosen the lesser number.

[2] " Super quo Rex Ludovicus misericordia motus plorasse dicitur."—Ibid.

[3] " Usque adeo de ejus evasione desperaretur, ut publice quoque jam

was present, the most melancholy views as to the future were expressed. A bishop said, "The Count Theobald is fallen into the hands of the king; we cannot save him now." "Stay," said another bishop, "there is one who can deliver him." "Who is that?" "God, to whom all things are possible." "Doubtless," said the other, "if He showed forth His might, if He seized His sceptre, and struck right and left; but up to this time He has done none of these things." Theobald's external dangers were aggravated by domestic treason; old friends and allies forsook him in his hour of need. After the long prosperity of his manhood, he was being deserted as useless and helpless in his old age.[1]

These misfortunes of Theobald were the cause of deep grief and anxiety to Bernard. People came and asked him what the issue of it all was to be; wanted to know what God had revealed to him on the subject. His kinsman, the Bishop of Langres, frequently made these inquiries. He replied, that nothing but tribulation on tribulation was manifested to him. Theobald he comforted by pointing out the uses of affliction, and by dwelling on the trials to which the saints of old were exposed. Theobald at once, to show that his faith faltered not, sent for two magnificent gold vases, a legacy of his uncle, Henry I., caused the precious stones to be knocked out, and the metal to be sold, the proceeds of which he devoted to the construction of monastic buildings.[2]

Nevertheless, Theobald's enemies had one design more at heart even than humbling him, to effect which was indeed their principal object in humbling him, and that was the removal of the excommunication which still weighed on Ralph

---

insultaretur religioni, pietati detraheretur, eleemosynis derogaretur. Monachi et conversi inutiles ejus milites et balistarii dicebantur."— St. Bern. *Op.* vol. ii. col. 1134.

[1] "In manu Regis est comes Theobaldus: non est qui possit eum eruere."—*Ibid.*

[2] "Aurum confringi praecepit ut venderetur et de pretio . . . . tabernacula fundarentur."—*Ibid.* vol. ii. col. 1116.

and Petronilla. For this purpose, they pressed him more hotly
than ever, and at last reduced him to such extremity, that he
was ready to sue for peace on almost any terms.   Their conditions were, that he should bind himself by oath to intercede
for them at the Roman court, and procure a raising of the
interdict which they lay under.   No questions were to be
asked or answered concerning the cause of the ecclesiastical
censure, viz. the illicit connexion of Ralph and Petronilla.
The latter may possibly have thought that to remove the
punishment was to remove the crime also.   Theobald, and his
clerical advisers, saw here an opening for a little artful diplo-
macy. They knew very well that Ralph and his concubine did
not intend to separate ; but they knew also that if the king's
troops were withdrawn, and time for preparations gained,
matters would wear a different aspect in another campaign.
Bernard wrote to the Pope, developing the scheme. He made
no pretence of concealing its craftiness and duplicity. "Count
Theobald," he says, "took the oath at the request and advice
of several faithful and wise persons.   They told him that the
raising of the interdict could easily be obtained from you,
without injury to the Church ; for it is in your power to renew
it, and immoveably establish it ; and thus cunning may be met
by cunning, and peace be obtained, while he who glories in
malice, and is powerful in iniquity, will derive no advantage."[1]

[1] "Ut non penitus desolaretur
terra . . . . compulsus est ille devo-
tissimus filius vester [i.e. Theobal-
dus] et ecclesiasticae libertatis amator et defensor, sub jurejurando pro-
mittere quatenus sententiam excom-
municationis, a legato vestro bonae
memoriae magistro Ivone datam in
terram et personam adulteri tyranni,
qui caput et auctor exstitit horum
omnium malorum et dolorum, atque
in ipsam adulteram, faceret amoveri ;
quod sane tamen praefatus princeps
fecit prece et consilio nonnullorum
fidelium sapientiumque virorum. Dicebant namque id a vobis facile et
absque laesione ecclesiae impetrari,
dum in manu vestra sit eamdem denuo sententiam, quae justa data fuit,
incontinenti statuere et irretracta-
biliter confirmare : quatenus et ars
arte deludatur, et pax proinde obti-
neatur : et qui gloriatur in malitia,
et potens est in iniquitate, nihil inde
lucretur."—(ST. BERN. Epist. 217.)
It is absurd to argue, as M. D'Arbois de Jubainville does, that this
is not a confession of intended du-

The Pope approved of the plan and withdrew the interdict. The king, conformably to the treaty, recalled his troops, and restored to Theobald the town of Vitry, which he had taken from him.   He had scarcely done so, when his eyes were opened to the clever deception which had been practised on him.   Ralph and Petronilla being still amorous and contumacious, were again threatened with excommunication, and a frenzy of indignation seized their royal relatives in consequence.[1]   Louis VII. wrote to Bernard to tell him that, if the sentence were pronounced, he should at once invade Count Theobald's territories.   In fact, he had found in the Count of Champagne a means of causing intense vexation to the Church. Theobald made energetic preparations for defence, and Bernard strained to the utmost his immense authority to prevent the king from breaking the recent truce.   Still the latter was determined to show the churchmen that he could annoy them, although they might excommunicate him.   He despatched his brother Robert to lay waste the church and diocese of Rheims. Robert installed himself in the archiepiscopal palace, with his knights, archers, and crossbowmen, and the country round was given up to their rapacity.   Louis kept both the sees of Paris and Chalons deprived of the presence of their bishops, and gave the ecclesiastics generally reason to regret their intention of slighting him.[2]

plicity on the part of Bernard and the clerical party.   The terms which the king and Ralph offered were, that they would withdraw their forces from Theobald's territory, if he would make their peace with the Pope.   Ralph was excommunicated, not as an assailant of Theobald in the field, but as a sinner, living in adultery with a concubine.   If the crime existed still—which it did—it was wrong to raise the interdict: if it had been condoned, as a condition of peace, it was wrong to renew it, which was soon after done, as the weaker party clearly foresaw.

[1] " Illusus est," ait, " comes Radulphus, et iterum relegatus est."— ST. BERN. *Epist.* 222.

[2] " Commisit Rex germano suo Roberto vices episcopi. . .   Remensem invadit atque in terra sanctorum iniqua gerit, non clericis, non monachis, non sanctimonialibus parcens . . . . terras fructiferas et villas populosas, ita in ore gladii devastavit, ut pene in solitudinem redegerit universas."—*Ibid.* 224.

In time the king grew tired of being excommunicated. He was willing to come to an agreement, and even to receive the Archbishop of Bourges; but the queen was still obdurate on the point of her sister's marriage. On one occasion she and Bernard met at the Abbey of St. Denis. He had come to settle terms of peace with her husband, but his efforts were baffled by the queen, who opposed all solution which did not recognise the marriage between Ralph and Petronilla. Bernard told her she ought to exert her influence over the king to better purpose than for the promotion of discord. Presently she complained to him on the subject of her barrenness, and begged he would pray for her. "If you," he replied, "will do as I shall advise, I will ask this of the Lord for you." She promised to acquiesce, and in the course of a year a child was born to the king and queen.[1] This difficulty of the queen's opposition being removed, Bernard was able to carry to a favourable issue his schemes of pacification. Ralph was still excommunicated, and remained so till the death of his wife, some years after. But the king and the royal dominions were to be freed from all ecclesiastical censure. Ambassadors were despatched to Rome to request officially the raising of the interdict. They met with a gracious reception from Coelestine II., for Innocent had died, and been succeeded by the Cardinal Guido di Castello, the friend of Arnold of Brescia. The Pope, in the midst of a large assembly of his councillors, rose up, and, turning in the direction of the

---

[1] "Erat autem vir sanctus apud Regem pro quadam pace laborans, et Regina in contrarium nitebatur. Cumque eam moneret desistere coeptis, et Regi suggerere meliora, inter loquendum illa coepit conqueri super sterilitate sua, humiliter rogans, ut sibi partum obtineret a Deo. At ille: 'Si feceris,' inquit, 'quod moneo, ego quoque pro verbo quod postulas, Dominum exorabo. Annuit illa, et pacis non tardavit effectus. Qua reformata, praedictus Rex, nam verbum ei Regina suggesserat, a Viro Dei promissum humiliter exigebat. Hoc autem tam celeriter est impletum, ut circa idem tempus anno altero eadem Regina pepererit."—ST. BERN. *Op.* vol. ii, col. 1137.

kingdom of France, gave his blessing; and the interdict had ceased.[1]

The friendly intercourse which had so long subsisted between Bernard and Innocent had given way, before the Pope's death, to coldness, or even anger, on the part of his Holiness. Cardinal Ives—he who had lately held the Council of Lagny, and excommunicated the Count of Vermandois and Petronilla —had on his death-bed appointed Bernard and two other abbots his executors, and charged them to make a distribution of a certain portion of his goods to the poor. The two abbots came to Clairvaux to settle the matter with Bernard; but he was absent on business of the Church, and they, deeming further delay objectionable, proceeded to carry out the wishes of their deceased friend. They did so in a manner which gave great offence to Innocent, who, however, at once laid all the blame on Bernard, whom he appears to have accused of unjustifiable presumption for his conduct in the matter. Bernard humbly and sorrowfully replied, that he could not be guilty, as the Pope supposed, inasmuch as he had done nothing; that he was absent on the Pope's business when the abbots came to Clairvaux; that they had done whatever had been done, and their warranty for it was the written testament of the departed cardinal. Innocent, it seems, had thought that he was entitled to the money which had been distributed to the poor, and at the same time believed that, whether Bernard appeared in the business or not, the "two abbots" would never have moved in it without his authority and sanction.

But it is evident that Innocent had no difficulty in finding grounds of quarrel with Bernard, so prejudiced had he grown

---

[1] "Ad hunc [i.e. Papam] Rex noster legatos pro pace incunda misit, quam ita dulcissima impetratione obtinuerunt, ut in conspectu illorum, multorumque nobilium, quorum frequentia Roma fremere solet, benigne assurgeret, manuque elevata, signum benedictionis contra regionem hanc faciens, ipsam a sententia interdictionis absolveret."—Ex Chronico Mauriniacensi, ap. D. Bouquet, xii. p. 87.

against his old friend and benefactor.   In the same letter in which Bernard repels the charge concerning the cardinal's property, he says he is sorry to hear that the Pope has had too many of his letters.   It is a fault, however, which can be easily rectified, and shall be, as far as he is concerned.   To give proof of his good intentions, he says that the dangers and difficulties which he foresees for the Church he has spoken of in letters to the bishops near the Pope's person, and not, as he had been wont to do, to the Pope himself.[1]

[1] St. Bern. Epist. 218.

Note on the Contested Election to the Archbishopric of York.

Dean Milman, in his history of Latin Christianity, vol. iii. p. 397, writes as follows :—"The Abbot of Clairvaux was involved in a disputed election to the Archbishopric of York.   The narrow corporate spirit of his order betrayed him into great and crying injustice to William, the elected prelate of that see.   The rival of the Englishman, another William, once a Cluniac, was a Cistercian ; and Bernard scruples not to heap on one of the most pious of men accusations of ambition—of worse than ambition—to condemn him to everlasting perdition.[1]   The obsequious Pope, no doubt under the same party influence, or quailing under the admonitions of Bernard, which rise into menace, issued his sentence of deposition against William.   England, true to that independence which she had still asserted under her Norman sovereigns, refused obedience.   King Stephen even prohibited his bishops from attending the Pope's summons to a council at Rheims ; the Archbishop of Canterbury was obliged to cross the sea clandestinely in a small boat.   William eventually triumphed over all opposition, obtained peaceable possession of the see, died in the odour of sanctity, and has his place in the sacred calendar."[2]

(1) "Epist. 241.   'Sævit frustrata ambitio : imo desperata furit.   Clamat contra eorum capita sanguis sanctorum de terrâ.'"   "St. William showed no enmity, sought no revenge against his most inveterate enemies, who had prepossessed Eugenius III. against him by the blackest calumnies."—Butler, *Lives of Saints.*
(2) "June 8th.   S. William.   Was Bernard imposed upon, or the author of these calumnies?   It is a dark page in his life."

This statement is open to several objections.   (1.) The "elected prelate" was not an Englishman, but a Norman, being nephew of King Stephen.   (2.) His rival was not "another William," but a Henry—Henry Murduch, to whom Bernard directed his 106th Epist. (see *ante*, p. 20).   He was, according to Mabillon, a professor in England before he became a monk at Clairvaux.   I find no grounds for supposing he had ever been a Cluniac before becoming a Cistercian. Bernard made him Abbot of Vauclair, and subsequently of Fountains, in Yorkshire. (3.) It was not an obsequious Pope, *i.e.* Eugenius, but a very haughty one, who first thought fit to condemn the election of William to the see of York. Innocent II. pronounced against it, and that at a time when he was nearly, or quite, estranged from Bernard, and more inclined to thwart than oblige him, namely, during the last years of his pontificate. (4.) There was ample ground in the manner of William's election for rigid churchmen to oppose it. It was confidently asserted that when the Chapter were on the point of choosing a new archbishop, King Stephen sent a message by the Earl of York ordering them to elect his nephew. "Comes Eboracensis in Capitulo Eboracensi praecepit ex ore regis, hunc Willielmum elegi." (*Acta Sanctorum die Octava Junii*, vol. ii. p. 138.) Simony was regarded by the austere Cistercians in the most odious light, and, rightly or wrongly, a number of the clergy of England considered William as lying open to the charge. Walter, Archdeacon of London, set out to meet King Stephen and expostulate with him on the subject ; but the Earl of York frustrated this intention by capturing him, and holding him prisoner in the Castle of Biham. Richard, Abbot of Fountains ; Cuthbert, Prior of Giseborne ; Wallevus, Prior of Kirkham ; and several others, declared that William had obtained the see of York by paying for it ; and Robert, Prior of Hexham, actually resigned his priory, and went abroad, rather than live under a simoniacal archbishop. The dispute was referred to Rome, and Innocent pronounced against William ; but, under the protection of his uncles, namely, the King of England and the Bishop of Winchester—the celebrated Henry de Blois, who was legate here— William was thrust upon the see of York, and appears to have enjoyed a tolerably peaceful possession for about two years. When, however, a Cistercian Pope ascended the papal throne in the person of Eugenius III., it cannot be wondered that Bernard became active in endeavouring to remove what he considered a scandalous outrage on the rights of the Church. He wrote according to his wont several fiery letters to his disciple the Pope, and succeeded in getting William put aside, and his friend Henry Murduch elected in his place. This enraged the partisans of William to such an extent that they attacked the Abbey of Fountains in great force, broke open the doors, plundered the premises, and then burned them to the ground. "Veniunt Fontes in manu armata, et effractis foribus ingrediuntur sanctuarium cum superbia, irruunt per officinas, diripiunt spolia, et non invento quem quaerebant abbate, sancta illa edificia, grandi labore constructa, subjectis ignibus redigunt in favillam." (*Monasticon Anglicanum*, p. 747. London, 1682.) I have little doubt that there was abundant party spirit on both sides, and that William was far from deserving all the reproaches cast upon him by his enemies ; but I think also that I have made it clear that Bernard's conduct was not so indefensible as Dean Milman is inclined to think, and that it can scarcely, with justice, be called "a dark page in his life."

BOOK IV.

BOOK IV

CHAPTER 1.

CONDITION OF SYRIA AND THE EAST UP TO THE MIDDLE OF THE TWELFTH CENTURY.

WHILE the nations of Western Europe were thus slowly rising out of barbarism, under the double discipline of Feudalism and Latin Christianity, great and stirring events had now for some time broken in upon the primeval apathy of the East. A new and aggressive religion had appeared.   In an ever-spreading wave of fanaticism and conquest, it had submerged great part of Asia, and, running along the shores of the Mediterranean, dashed itself into spray, which had fallen partly even on Southern Europe.   This rival and enemy of Christianity, although its junior by five centuries, had boldly attacked the followers of the Cross, and borne them down with its barbaric vigour, even in lands once hallowed by the presence of the Lord and His Apostles.   At last the fanaticism of the East had provoked the fanaticism of the West, and the First Crusade had been the answer of Europe and Christianity to the insolent defiance of Islam.   But at this period of our history, the fifty-fifth year of Bernard's life, nearly half a century had elapsed since the shout of *Dieu le veut!* from the warriors at Clermont had rolled and re-echoed throughout the

West. The heroes of the First Crusade had nearly all departed. Godfrey, and Tancred, and Baldwin were sleeping in Eastern graves. But the Latin kingdom of Jerusalem had, on the whole, progressed rather than declined during the first thirty years of the twelfth century. The two Baldwins had consolidated the conquests of their kinsman; and the other territories, viz. the principality of Antioch, the counties of Tripoli and Edessa, were in the possession of bold and able men, who were not likely to allow the Turks any permanent advantage over the Christian name.

One of the most important causes of the successes of the Franks in their daring enterprise of conquering the Holy Land had been the disunion and anarchy of their Moslem enemies.[1] The whole Mohammedan world was then, as it had been for centuries, the scene of an internecine civil strife. The great house of Seljuk, which, under the first rulers, had towered loftily over all past and actual rivals, was now crumbling to the same ruin which had befallen its predecessors.[2] The loose imitation of a feudal system, which the Turks established after their conquests, extended the boundaries of their empire at the expense of its vigour and durability. At the cheap sacrifice of a nominal allegiance to the Sultan every bold scion of his own house, every adventurous spirit in his wide dominions, might push his conquests and devastation in any direction he pleased. But these rapid

---

[1] "Il est certain, cependant, que si les Seljoucides avaient fait quelques efforts; s'ils avaient rassemblé toutes les troupes de la Perse; si le fameux Sulthan Sandgiar, le hero du Musulmanisme et Mohammed, eussent conduit eux-mêmes ces troupes dans la Palestine, jamais les Francs n'y auraient fait d'établissements."—DES GUIGNES, *Hist. des Huns,* vol. ii. p. 236.

[2] For the history of the house of Seljuk see Gibbon, chap. lvii., and the elaborate but ill-written "Histoire des Huns," vol. ii., by Des Guignes, Paris, 1750. But for a lively picture of Syria at the epoch of the Crusades consult the fourth volume of Michaud's "Bibliothèque des Croisades," where the narratives of the Eastern annalists are made to elucidate or correct the chronicles of the West.

and tempestuous onslaughts were as destructive and as transitory as the whirlwind they resembled. The conqueror's
companions had hardly aided him to make his conquest before
they thought it time to imitate his example. They soon
became his equals or rivals, and a murderous civil war
generally followed to ascertain if they should not be his
masters. Had not such discord enfeebled the Turks, the
Crusaders would have had but little prospect of subduing or
holding principalities in Syria. The Frankish empire, however, was slowly expanding both in length and breadth, and
the vanquished Moslems could only wonder at their deser-
tion by God and the Prophet.

But, in time, prosperity and adversity produced their usual
effects both on Christians and Mohammedans. The former
became careless and disunited, the latter grew vigilant and co-
operative. The great feudal lords, who had made themselves
Crusaders, were quite willing to do and suffer much for the
cause of the Cross;—they would expose their northern con-
stitutions to the Syrian sun, and wait and toil for opportunities
for slaughtering Paynims without a murmur; they would pray,
and fast too, like good Christian knights, and prostrate themselves on the ground till their hands and knees grew callous in
the process[1]—all this they would do, and feel they were only
"unprofitable servants." But there was one form of self-
indulgence, one direction in which the old Adam would break
out, which they found it impossible to withstand, and that was
the ineffable luxury of private wars. They were numerous,
they were neighbours, and how could they do otherwise than
fight? And, consequently, private wars were nearly as frequent
and a great deal more injurious in Palestine than they were in
France. The Count of Edessa and the Prince of Antioch

---

[1] Baldwin II., says William of
Tyre (lib. xii. cap. 4), was "religiosus
et timens Deum: in orationibus jugis,
ita ut callos in manibus haberet et
genibus, pro afflictionis et genuflex-
ionis frequentia."

were as hostile to each other as the Counts of Chartres and Vermandois. To the evil results which necessarily flowed from this source was now added a new one, viz. that as the older and abler Crusaders were removed by death, they were succeeded in their hereditary fiefs by heirs to their possessions, but by no means to their capacity and determination. We shall soon see how a notable misfortune befell the Christian cause by this means.

For the Turks were growing resolved to make a vigorous effort to restore their fallen fortunes. Suppressing their domestic rivalries and contests, they decided to elect a leader whose known courage and ability would give them some hope of vanquishing their enemies. "God," says an Arab writer, "had similar intentions. He was determined to raise up against the Christians a man able to punish them for their attempts, and visit them with condign vengeance. He was anxious to blast the demons of the Cross, as He had blasted the rebellious angels, and utterly crush and annihilate them."[1] The important point was, that the Emirate of Mossul should be in the hands of a man of energy and skill. On the death of the Emir Masoud, his brother, a young child of tender years, was his natural, but, under the circumstances, not a desirable, successor. Deputies, however, were sent to Bagdad to demand of the Sultan the usual investiture for the boy. Whereupon the politic Nasur-eddin induced them to change the nature of their petition entirely, and to speak to the Grand Vizier in these terms: "Thou knowest that Mesopotamia and Syria are a prey to the devastations of the Franks. Since the death of Borsaki the boldness of the Christian knows no limit. Our present ruler is but a child, whereas we want a man of discretion, and an able warrior. We inform thee of the state of matters, that no harm may happen to Islam; for it is we who should be culpable in the eyes of God,

[1] Michaud, "Bibliothèque des Croisades," vol. iv. p. 60.

and incur the reproaches of the Sultan." The Vizier having reported these words to the Sultan, the latter asked who was the Emir who, in the general opinion, was most able to defend the Mussulmans. The deputies replied Zenghis, the son of Ascansar. The Sultan approved of the choice, and appointed Zenghis Emir of Mossul.

Zenghis, the hope of Islam, and afterwards the terror of the Christians, had had a long apprenticeship in the school of adversity and hard-learnt experience. The son of a favourite of Malek Shah, he had been left a helpless orphan on his father's decapitation. He found friends, however, among Ascansar's servants and adherents, and, in the ceaseless civil contests which then raged, he soon mastered the art of war as then practised in Syria. The conviction that he was the only man capable of resisting the Christians grew among his countrymen without intermission, till they had the satisfaction of seeing their hero installed as ruler of Mesopotamia.[1]

He did not wait long before he made his power felt. Not far from Aleppo, which was still subject to the Mohammedans, was a castle, named Athareb, garrisoned by Franks. These latter were a source of great annoyance to their neighbours of Aleppo, and the enterprising Zenghis thought it would be advisable to dislodge them. He laid siege to Athareb. Young Bohemond II., Prince of Antioch, immediately took

[1] The Orientals set no bounds to their admiration of Zenghis's character and prowess. There can be little doubt that he was a man of most keen perception, and most rapid performance—a born leader of men. He lived on familiar terms with his officers, and promoted or disgraced them, having regard solely to their merits. He was particularly watchful over the honour of women, especially the wives of his soldiers. An insult to them he never forgave. He mutilated and crucified one of his emirs for gallantry. Discipline he maintained with an iron hand. One of his officers, on entering a town, took possession of a Jew's house, and turned the owner into the street. It was winter. Zenghis, in order to give his troops a lesson, made them evacuate the place, and pitch their tents amid the mud and water of the open country.—MICHAUD, *Bib. des Croisades*, vol. iv. p 78, *et seq.*

the field in force, with the view of defeating his design. Zenghis at once raised the siege, and giving battle to Bohemond, killed him, and utterly routed his troops. He then resumed his attack on Athareb, which he stormed and reduced to a heap of ruins. This so alarmed the men of Antioch, that they sent urgent requests for help to the King of Jerusalem. At this point an incident occurred which was highly significant of the demoralization which had seized the Franks in Palestine. Alice, the wife of the slain Bohemond, and daughter of King Baldwin II., on hearing of his defeat and death, at once revolved plans of independent sovereignty for herself, and determined to secure, if possible, the alliance of her husband's conqueror. With this object she sent to the triumphant Turk, " by the agency of a certain friend of hers," a present of a perfectly white palfrey, with shoes and bit-ornaments made of silver, and a snow-white housing of silk.[1] But the king, who had hastened to respond to the appeal he had received from Antioch, on his road thither, met this "certain friend" of his daughter convoying her remarkable palfrey. The unlucky wight, being made to confess his character and errand, was put to death by the king's orders. Baldwin then used more haste than before to reach Antioch, when, behold, his own daughter refused him admission, and prepared to offer a stout resistance if he attempted to force one. Faithful old servants, however, of the king, within Antioch, were not disposed to yield implicit obedience to an imperious woman, and Baldwin was soon admitted, in spite

---

[1] William of Tyre says that Alice was " nequam agitata spiritu," which is manifest enough. Her object was to exclude her little daughter from the principality of Antioch, to which the latter was heiress since Bohemond's death. As regards her present to Zenghis, these are the archbishop's words : " Miserat an-tem et praedicto nobili viro, per quemdam familiarem suum, palefredum albissimum, argento ferratum, freno et cacteris argenteis phaleris redimitum, *exameto* coopertum albissimo, ut in omnibus candor niveus consonaret."—(Lib. xiv. cap. 27.) Exametum = pannus holosericus. *Vide* Du Cange.

of his daughter's opposition. He punished her by restricting her authority to the cities of Gabala and Laodicea.

Zenghis's boldness and success encouraged other Turkish chiefs to make **an aggressive war against** the Franks. The Sultan **Masoud, of Iconium, attacked a** fortress belonging **to** the veteran Joscelyn de Courtnay, Count of Edessa.[1] Joscelyn **was** lying prostrate **on his** couch at the **time, in consequence** of injuries he had received shortly before. **As** he was be-**sieging a castle near Aleppo,** he incautiously approached too **near a tower which he had ordered to be undermined.** The tower fell, and buried **him beneath its ruins. Whether the** probability **that, in consequence of this accident, he would not encounter so renowned a champion of the Cross as Joscelyn, had any effect in determining the Sultan to make** the attempt **he was** now upon, cannot be ascertained, but the supposition is not unlikely. The old Crusader received the news of the inroad as he lay on his sick-bed at Edessa. Unable himself to grapple with the enemy, he commanded his son to hasten to the rescue with all the troops he could collect. But **young Joscelyn had** little of **his father's spirit—he demurred.**

---

[1] Joscelyn had had a wide experience of life, and the changefulness of fortune, during his long career as a Crusader. He and his cousin Baldwin du Bourg were taken prisoners by the Turks, and kept captive for five years.—(*Will. of Tyre,* lib. ix. cap. 8.) After they had recovered their liberty, Baldwin, who was then Count of Edessa, had reason to think that Joscelyn had shown an ungrateful disposition. So he sent for Joscelyn, and said to him, "What do you possess which I did not give to you?" "Nothing," answered Joscelyn. "Then why are you so unmindful of my benefits? You shall restore all I have ever given to you." Whereupon Bald- win—the excellent, gentle Baldwin —ordered his cousin to be seized and tortured till he had yielded up all he possessed.—(Lib. ix. cap. 22.) But this little incident produced no lasting coldness between them. Shortly after, Joscelyn was the first to vote for Baldwin's election to the throne.—(Lib. xii. cap. 3.) Baldwin and Joscelyn were soon again fellow-captives among the Turks; but when the latter was free again, he performed a great feat of arms, for he attacked and slew with his own hand Balac, the most valiant and able emir the Turks had, before the rise of Zenghis. —(Lib. xiii. cap. 11.) He succeeded his cousin Baldwin in the county of Edessa.

The Sultan, he said, was too powerful to be successfully attacked with the forces at their disposal. In a word, he objected to going at all. With bitter feelings of mortification and sorrow, the failing warrior listened to the degenerate youth. Ordering all his followers to be ready to march, he caused a litter to be made, and himself placed in it; and thus, the weakness of his body showing more distinctly the strength of his soul, he was carried at the head of his soldiers to meet the Turks. But such was the terror inspired by his name, that Masoud never waited to receive the attack of the dying Courtnay, but hastily raised the siege, and gat him into his own country. Joscelyn, when he heard that the enemy had fled, ordered his litter to be placed on the ground; then, lifting his eyes to heaven, he thanked God for the mercy He had showed him in his last moments; that, although he was almost passing through the portals of death, he was still formidable to the enemies of the Christian faith: and so, surrounded by his knights and men-at-arms, under the broad sky, he expired.

And now the important frontier stronghold of Edessa was in the hands of the young coward who had refused to attack an enemy who fled at the sound of his father's name. He soon did all that lay in his power to fulfil the evil promise he had already made. Edessa, he found, was a distasteful residence to him. Its proximity to the enemy on the borders disturbed his repose. The armed tumult of the fortress he could not endure. So he forsook the castle and town which his father and predecessors had bravely conquered, and fled, and betook himself to a luxurious retreat on the banks of the Euphrates, named Turbessel, where he gave free rein to his inclination for debauchery; and thus Edessa was left to the care of mercenaries and a mongrel population of traders and artisans.

This state of matters was not likely to escape the notice of such a chief as Zenghis. He doubtless would have assumed the offensive at an earlier period than he did, but for the civil commotions which again were raging among his countrymen. Twelve years of idleness and impunity were granted to Joscelyn, in which to repent of his wickedness. At last Zenghis, who had long had his eye on Joscelyn, felt he was strong enough to commence an attack. He laid siege to Edessa with a force of chosen warriors. He invested the town on every side, so as to cut off all relief from the besieged, if any were sent. He erected seven battering-rams to demolish the walls. He undermined the towers, and was met by the countermines of the garrison. The inhabitants, even the women and monks, showed the greatest courage, serving the soldiers with stones and other missiles, and also bringing them food and water. But Zenghis's archers sent such constant showers of arrows into the town, that the defenders had scarcely any rest by day or night.

At last two of the towers were so undermined that they tottered to their fall. They were supported by powerful beams, while the men worked under them ; and the application of a little fire would now complete their ruin. Zenghis offered terms to the inhabitants if they would capitulate. They rejected his proposals with scorn, being convinced that help would soon come, either from the count or the king. Joscelyn, as terrified after the event as he had been apathetic before it, could do nothing but run about imploring help. In the meanwhile, on the twenty-eighth day after the commencement of the siege, Edessa was being stormed. The fall of the towers opened a breach a hundred cubits wide, through which poured an excited throng of ferocious Turks, shouting their battle-cry, " God is great ! God is great !" For three days the carnage and devastation continued. But the prudent Zenghis saw the advantages which Edessa offered as a fortification ; he caused the walls to be repaired, and ordered his officers to treat the inhabitants with mercy and justice.

This was the last important achievement which Zenghis accomplished.[1]   Two years after the capture of Edessa, he was assassinated while he slept, by some of his own Mamelukes.[2] Count Joscelyn thought that the valiant Emir's death would be a good opportunity to recover Edessa.   He succeeded in gaining admission with his troops into the town, by the aid of the Armenian Christians, of whom it contained great numbers. The garrison, finding resistance hopeless, retreated to the citadel, for Joscelyn used his unexpected victory with savage ferocity, and gave no quarter to any enemies he met with. But within six days vengeance was at hand : Noureddin, the second and worthy son of Zenghis, appeared before the town with ten thousand men.   Joscelyn's head and heart failed him at the sight of their scimitars.   Plans of defence were hastily proposed, and as readily abandoned ; confusion and fear distracted the Christian councils, while the Turks were pursuing their one object with unflinching earnestness.   At last despair seized Joscelyn and his companions, and they resolved to evacuate the town as quickly as they could.   But now it occurred that many more were anxious to get out than had lately come in.   The Armenians, conscious of their complicity in the recapture of Edessa, had as much reason to fear the Turks as Joscelyn and his knights.   They therefore, with their wives and children, determined to attempt to join in the flight. At the darkest period of the night the gates were quietly opened, and the mixed throng of warriors, old men, women, and infants, noiselessly stole forth.   The imprisoned garrison now came out from their citadel, and giving the alarm to their allies outside, vigorously attacked the fugitives in their rear. The vanguard was also attacked with all the force of the

---

[1] For the siege and capture of Edessa see *Will. of Tyre*, lib. xvi. cap. 4, and " Bibliothèque des Croisades," vol. iv.

[2] The Latins expressed their delight in a venomous pun.   They called him Sanguineus :—

"Quam bonus eventus ! fit sanguine sanguinolentus,
    Vir homicida, reus, nomine Sanguineus."

Turkish army, and driven backwards through the gateway into the town. The carnage was appalling. The Christian knights, perceiving that their only hope lay in the courage of despair, clove their way through the opposing squadrons of Turks, and got into the open country. But the crowd of women, old men, and children, who still filled the narrow streets and avenues of the city, offered nothing but a yielding mass of helpless humanity to the sabres of the Turks and the hoofs of their horses. Very few escaped, or were able to follow the Christian army in its retreat towards the Euphrates. The triumphant Noureddin pressed closely on the retiring force, and his light cavalry cut them to pieces in their disorderly flight. Then Joscelyn ran for his life, and saved it in the fortress of Samosata. The rest of the people, casting aside all impediment and baggage, dispersed themselves in the directions which severally appeared to them the safest. And thus was Edessa lost a second time to the Christians. We must now turn our observation to the effect these events had on the public mind of Western Europe.

CHAPTER II.

(A.D. 1145. AETAT. 54.)

THE SECOND CRUSADE PREACHED BY BERNARD.

THE fall of Edessa was regarded as a calamity throughout Christian Europe. The conquest had seemed so complete, that men's minds were quite unprepared for the doleful tidings. In the Middle Ages, whenever the Crusaders were worsted by the Moslem, they attributed it to their own sins. They were undoubtedly cruel and wicked enough to make their contrition acceptable at any time. But the alternation of atrocious crimes with tearful repentance loses interest and pathos when too often repeated. Louis VII. was now about to enact the repentance, having committed the crime some three years before, at the burning of Vitry. He felt that the cruelty of burning above a thousand Christians could only be expiated by slaughtering several thousand infidels. He celebrated Christmas at Bourges with more than usual splendour. A large concourse of nobles, both lay and ecclesiastical, was present, and the king made known his wish to visit the Holy Land. Godfrey, Bishop of Langres, who had just returned from thence, made an affecting speech touching the melancholy capture of Edessa, and the sufferings and insults to which the Christians were exposed at the hands of the Turks. He urged the king and his court to hasten to the deliverance of their brethren in the East. Louis VII. was so wrought upon that he at once sent to invoke Bernard's counsel and assistance. Bernard replied that in a matter of such gravity he could not undertake to advise without the wishes of the Holy See being known. The king sent to Rome to learn the mind of the new Pope, Eugenius III.,—a Cistercian monk of the filiation of Clairvaux,—and also he appointed a general meeting at Vezelai for the following Easter. The Pope returned a long letter of exhortation to the good work, and delegated to his spiritual father, Bernard, the office of preaching the Second Crusade.[1]

Fifty-five years of age, and old for his years, was Bernard at this period. The last fifteen years had been full of heavy labour and gnawing care. Eight years of worry about the schism, three journeys to Italy, the controversy with Abelard, the recent vexations arising from the quarrel between Count Theobald and the king, and, finally, " that which cometh daily, the care of all the churches," had well-nigh broken down the feeble body, in spite of the strong spirit which supported it. In the year 1143 he had written to Peter of Cluny : " I do not intend to leave Clairvaux, except for the meeting of the chapter at Citeaux once a year. Here, supported and consoled by your prayers and good offices during the few days now left me to fight in, I am waiting till the change do come. May God not take away your prayers, nor withdraw His mercy from me. My strength is gone. I have the valid reason for staying at home, that I cannot now run about as I was once wont to do."[2] And to the Pope he says : " If any suggestion be made to you of adding to my present labours, I would

---

[1] The two principal authorities for the Second Crusade are—(1) Odo de Diogilo, or Odo of Deuil, a monk of St. Denis, who was chaplain to Louis VII., accompanied him on the expedition, and wrote a graphic account of it in seven short books, published by the Jesuit Chifflet, at Dijon, 1660, in his collection named " S. Bernardi illustre genus assertum ;" (2) and the anonymous narrative in vol. iv., p. 390, of Duchesne's " Historiae Francorum Scriptores."

[2] " Hic, fultus orationibus vestris, et benedictionibus consolatus, paucis diebus quibus nunc milito, expecto donec veniat immutatio mea."—ST. BERN. Epist. 228.

have you know that my strength is not equal to those which devolve on me already. My intention of not leaving the monastery, I believe, is not a secret to you."[1] Thus Bernard thought to prepare himself peace and rest before he lay down for the rest of the grave, when France and the Pope declare he shall preach to them, and "run about" for them, and go through more labour generally than he had ever done in all his previous life. Easter came, and multitudes flocked to Vezelai at the united bidding of the Pope and king. The town could not contain the ever-gathering throng. On the declivity of the hill which overlooks the plain of Vezelai the people were assembled. The king and the knights were there, the beautiful and haughty Eleanor was there, the crowd of poor hard-worked peasants was there, each grade by its dress and bearing showing to what class of society it belonged. But now nobles and courtiers, even the young king and his queen, have ceased to be the centre to which all eyes are turned, for Bernard of Clairvaux has come. Pale and attenuated to a degree which seemed almost supernatural, his contemporaries discovered something in the mere glance of his eyes which filled them with wonder and awe. That he was kept alive at all appeared to them a perpetual miracle ; but when the light from that thin, calm face fell upon them, when the voice flew from those firm lips, and words of love, aspiration, and sublime self-sacrifice reached their ears, they were no longer masters of themselves or their feelings.[2] This occurred whenever Bernard preached to great numbers, and the meeting at Vezelai was not an exception. At the top of the hill a

---

[1] "Propositum meum monasterium non egrediendi, credo non latere vos."—St. Bern. *Epist.* 245.

[2] The testimony of Wibald, Abbot of Stavélo, to Bernard's eloquence, and to the force which was in his bodily presence, is worth recording :—"Siquidem vir ille bonus longo eremi squalore et jejuniis ac pallore confectus, et in quamdam spiritualis formae tenuitatem redactus, prius persuadet visus quam auditus. . . . Quem si videas, doceris ; si audias, instrueris ; si sequare, perficeris." — *Wibaldi Stabulensis Ep.* 147. Martene, *Ampl. Collect.* ii. 153.

machine of wood had been erected, and on this platform
Bernard, attended by the king, appeared. Raised thus high
above the crowd, he could be seen, if not heard, from all
parts of the vast concourse. He spoke: the mere sound
of his voice was grateful to the loving admiration which
surrounded him. Presently rose a murmur from the sea
of faces, which rapidly swelled into a shout of "Crosses,
crosses;" and Bernard began to scatter broadcast among
the people the large sheaf of them which had been brought
for that purpose. They were soon exhausted. He was
obliged to tear up his monk's cowl to satisfy the demand.[1]
He did nothing else but make crosses as long as he remained
in the town.

The spiritual mind of Europe had spoken through Bernard.
The military mind was now to speak through Louis VII.
Addressing the people, he said:— "Great were our disgrace
if the Philistine should insult the son of David; if a devilish
nation should possess that which the chosen people of God
once had as their own; if dead dogs should scoff at living
courage, and revile those Franks whose valour has made
them free, even when in chains; which never, in whatsoever
straits it might be placed, could endure an insult; which has
ever borne prompt succour to friends, and ceased not to
pursue enemies, even after death. Let us not suffer this our
valour to melt away, but by a courageous assistance relieve
the friends of God and of ourselves, that is, the Christians
beyond the seas, while, by a severe punishment, we overthrow
our ignoble enemies, who are not even worthy to be called
men. Let us away, then, O valiant knights, let us check
these worshippers of idols. Let us visit those places which
we know were of old trodden by the feet of the God-man, in

---

[1] Odo de Diogilo, lib. i. cap. i.
. . . . "Coeperunt undique concla-
mando cruces, cruces expetere. . . .
coactus est vestes suas in cruces
scindere et seminare. In hoc labo-
ravit quamdiu fuit in villa."

which He suffered death, and which were thought worthy of
His corporeal presence.   God will rise up with us, His enemies
shall be scattered, and they who hate Him shall fly from before
our face.   They shall all be confounded, I say, they shall be
turned back who hate Sion, if we bear ourselves like men, and
our trust in God do not fail.   Know that a great devotion to
this war is come upon me ; wherefore I pray earnestly that
you will study to give strength to my resolution by your
company and assistance."   So spake the brave but rather dull
and confused young king of France on this great occasion.[1]

At Vezelai it was determined that preparations for the
Crusade should be made during a whole year.   Another
meeting was also convened at Chartres, which distinguished
itself by electing Bernard commander-in-chief of the Crusaders' army.   He almost cries aloud, in a letter to the Pope,
as in wonder where the popular excitement would stop.   He
superfluously demonstrates his ignorance of war, his unsuita-
bleness for the task.   The Pope had not much difficulty in
accepting a refusal which every man of sense among the Crusaders must have approved.   The more befitting office of
preaching the Crusade in Germany and north-eastern France
was deputed to Bernard.[2]

The weakness and exhaustion of which he had complained
were soon forgotten, when work, which he felt it was his duty
to do, came before him.   He left Clairvaux with the known
design of arousing the enthusiasm of the multitude for the
Crusade, and wherever he appeared the usual bonds of society
seemed loosed, and all moved round him as around a new
centre of life.   What remained of the summer of the year
1146 he spent in France.   Towards the autumn he began to
enter on the less known field of Germany.   The German
nation had, up to this period, taken a much less active part

---

[1] Ex Chronico Mauriniacensi, apud Dom. Bouquet, xii. p. 88.
[2] St. Bern. Epist. 236.

in the Crusades than the French, and it was believed that the emperor Conrad III. was strongly opposed to the present expedition. Bernard therefore prepared for a great effort. Friburg, Basle, Constance, Spires, Cologne, Frankfort, Mayence, and numerous other towns of north-western Germany, were visited and preached in by him. A daily repetition took place of the same phenomena — Bernard's appearance in a district ; the simultaneous rush and tumult of the whole population to see and hear him ; and then the assumption of the cross by the greater portion of the able-bodied male inhabitants. Bernard himself says that scarcely one man was left to seven women.[1] At Frankfort Bernard nearly lost his life. The crowd so beset him that he was in danger of being suffocated. Conrad for a time did his best to keep off the press, but it was more than he could do. At last, laying aside his cloak, he gripped Bernard in his brawny arms, and, hoisting him over his shoulders, carried him away in safety.[2]

But if we are to believe the testimony of eye-witnesses—ten eye-witnesses—there was that in Bernard's progress through the Rhine country which might well excite the intensest curi-

[1] "Vacuantur urbes et castella, et pene jam non inveniunt quem apprehendant septem mulieres virum unum, adeo ubique viduae vivis remanent viris." (ST. BERN. *Epist.* 247.) Gibbon, who is ever careful to pollute his notes with any filthiness he can find in his authorities, seems almost angry with St. Bernard for giving him but little opportunity to indulge his peculiar taste. He contrives, however, to extract an indecent pun out of the above passage. (*Decline and Fall,* cap. 59.)

[2] ... "tantus erat concursus, ut praedictus rex cum aliquando populum comprimentem coercere non posset, deposita chlamide, virum sanctum in proprias ulnas suscipiens, de basilica exportarit."—ST. BERN. *Op.* vol. ii. col. 1142. The Jew, Joseph Ben Weir, assigns Spires as the scene of Bernard's danger.— WILKEN, *Geschichte der Kreuzzüge,* Band iii. Beylagen, p. 7.

I am justified in attributing great strength to Conrad. When he was in the Holy Land he chopped a Turk in two. "Nam percussit eum inter collum et sinistrum humerum ictu mirabili ; ita quod ensis secuit totum pectus cum humeris, et descendit obliquando usque ad latus dextrum, taliter quod pars dextrior abscisso penitus cum capite, cecidit super terram."—*Gesta Ludovici Regis,* apud DUCHESNE, vol. iv. p. 393.

osity and admiration.   His journey, we are told, was marked
by a constant exhibition of miraculous power—a power not
obscurely or furtively displayed, but of daily recurrence before
large multitudes.   Herman, Bishop of Constance, and nine
others, kept a diary of what they saw with their own eyes :[1]
" Many miracles from this time shone forth, which, if we
should pass over, the very stones would proclaim."   Thirty-six
miraculous cures in one day would seem to have been the
largest stretch of supernatural power which Bernard permitted
to himself.   The halt, the blind, the deaf, and the dumb, were
brought from all parts to be touched by Bernard.   The patient
was presented to him, whereupon he made the sign of the
cross over the part affected, and the cure was perfect.   The
church bells sent forth a merry peal, and a chorus of voices
was heard singing, " Christ have mercy on us, ' Kyrie eleison ;'
all the saints help us."[2]   Indeed, this chanting was well understood to mean, by those too far off to see, that Bernard had
just performed a miracle.[3]   At Cambray, we read : " In the
church of St. John, after the mass, a boy, deaf and dumb from
his mother's womb, received his hearing, and spake, and the
people wondered.   He had sat down beside me deaf and
dumb ; and, having been presented to Bernard, in the selfsame
hour he both spoke and heard.   The joyful excitement was
scarcely over before a lame old man was raised up, and walked.
But now a miracle occurred which, beyond all others, filled us

[1] The diary to which reference
is made is one of the most curious
documents I have met with.   Miracles occur so much as a matter of
course in mediæval literature, that
one hardly notices them.   But this
account would seem to have been
drawn up with the express purpose
of avoiding cavil and of attracting notice.   The number and character of the witnesses are given,
and they solemnly assert that they
saw with their own eyes the miracles
recorded.   A very scanty *spicilegium*
has been given above.— See St. Bern.
Op. vol. ii. col. 1165, *et seq.*

[2] Wilken, Band iii. p. 67.

[3] " Multa ibidem facta arbitror
quae non vidimus.   Saepe enim can-
tantem audivimus populum, et nemo
ex nobis irrumpere potuit ut videret
quid agceretur."—ST. BERN. *Op.*
vol. ii. col. 1173.

with astonishment. A boy blind from his birth, whose eyes were covered with a white substance — if indeed those could be called eyes in which there was neither colour, nor use, nor even so much as the usual cavity of an eye—this boy received his sight from the imposition of Bernard's hand. We ascertained the fact by numerous proofs, hardly believing our senses, that in such eyes as his any sight could reside." In the same place a woman who had a withered hand was healed.[1] "In the town of Rosnay they brought to him in a waggon a man ill and feeble, for whom nothing seemed to remain but the grave. Before a number of the citizens and soldiers Bernard placed his hands upon him, and immediately he walked without difficulty ; to the astonishment of all, he followed, on foot, the vehicle in which he had just before been carried."

"On another day we came to Molesme, which is a monastery from which formerly our fathers went forth who founded the order of Citeaux. It was on Wednesday, and they received the man of God with great devotion. When Bernard was seated in the guest-house, a certain man, blind with one eye, came in, and, falling on his knees, begged his mercy. Bernard made the sign of the cross with his holy fingers, and touched the blind eye, and immediately it received sight, and the man returned thanks to God. About an hour afterwards, as it was getting dusk, the holy man went out to lay hands on the sick who were waiting before the doors. The first who was cured was a boy blind with the right eye, who on shutting the left eye, with which alone he had seen previously, discerned all things clearly, and told at once what anything was which we showed to him. And again, at the same place, a little girl who had a weakness in the feet, and had been lame from her birth, was healed by the imposition of hands ; and her mother bounded for joy, that now for the first time she saw her child standing and walking."[2]

[1] St. Bern. Op. vol. ii. col. 1184. [2] *ibid.* col. 1185-89.

Such is the record left by men who had probably as great a horror of mendacity as any who have lived before or after them. They thought they saw even as they have told us; they really saw what their fervid uncritical minds suggested to them. Deeply true is it that "the eye sees only what the eye brings means of seeing;" but scarcely less so is this, that the eye sees much which exists nowhere but in itself.

Far greater, in modern estimation at least, was the miracle of Christian love and fortitude which Bernard wrought at this time in favour of the persecuted Jews. That unfortunate race was now entering the darkest period in its long, dreary history of trial and sorrow. Before the Crusades, though often treated with cruelty, and always with contempt, the Jews of Western Europe had frequently known long intervals of comparative peace and happiness. The illustrious Charlemagne had openly shown himself their protector; and his son Louis imitated him in this respect. But, simultaneously with the growth of the new ideas of fighting and slaughtering the infidels abroad, hatred was developed against the Jews at home. They were miscreants as bad or worse than the Saracens, they were as rich, and far easier to kill—all excellent reasons for slaying them. At the commencement of the First Crusade they were so fiercely persecuted that they stabbed their own children, while their women jumped into the river. And now, on the preaching of this Second Crusade, the same tragedies seemed about to be repeated. A monk named Rodolph travelled through the towns on the banks of the Rhine, and by the most stimulating harangues inflamed the people to the highest pitch against the Jews. The massacres soon followed. Rodolph, emboldened and delighted by his success, waxed ever more violent. The Jews of those parts were like to be exterminated. Presently these events reached Bernard's knowledge.[1]

[1] How strong was the feeling against the Jews is best shown by the virulence displayed against them by the gentlest of men, viz.

His soul at once blazed into one flame of Divine wrath, as usually happened with him when he witnessed anything which he considered deeply unjust or wicked. He despatched messengers with letters to the various communities among whom Rodolph was preaching. He argued and demonstrated from Holy Writ that the Jews were not doomed to be slain for their crimes, but to be dispersed. To the Archbishop of Mayence he wrote a most impassioned letter in condemnation of Rodolph. In it occur some golden sentences, which, if they alone, of all he said and wrote, had descended to us, would proclaim Bernard a great man. "Does not the Church," he inquires, "triumph more fully over the Jews by convincing or converting them from day to day, than if she, once and for ever, were to slay them all with the edge of the sword? Is that prayer of the Church appointed in vain which is offered up for the perfidious Jews from the rising of the sun to the going down of the same, praying that the Lord God will take away the veil from their hearts, that they may be lifted up from their darkness to the light of truth? For if the Church did not hope

---

Peter of Cluny. It is with sorrow one sees that amiable nature excited into such language as this. After saying that the lives of the Jews should be spared, in order that they might be exposed to greater cruelty and insult, he proceeds thus :—"Sic de damnatis damnandisque Judaeis, ab ipso passionis mortisque Christi tempore, justissima Dei severitas facit, et usque ad ipsius mundi terminum factura est. . . . . Non inquam ut occidantur admoneo, sed ut congruente nequitiae suae modo puniantur exhortor. Et quis congruentior ad puniendos illos impios modus, quam ille quo et damnatur iniquitas et adjuvatur charitas? Quid justius quam ut his, quae fraudulenter lucrati sunt, destituantur."

He goes on to say that they never live by agriculture or any honest handicraft, but chiefly by receiving stolen goods; and of these the silver utensils and ornaments of the Church were the most lucrative. This insult, he considers, is felt very keenly by Christ Himself. "Sentit plane in his quae non sentiunt sibi sacratis vasis, Judaicas adhuc contumelias Christus; quia, ut saepe a veracibus viris audivi, eis usibus coelestia illa vasa ad ejusdem Christi nostrumque dedecus nefandi illi applicant, quod horrendum est cogitare et detestandum dicere." He concludes with a general advice to plunder them effectually. "Reservetur eis vita, auferatur pecunia."—PETRI VEN. *Epist.* lib. iv. Epist. 36.

that those which doubt will one day believe, it would be vain
and superfluous to pray for them; but, on the contrary, she
piously believes that the Lord is gracious towards him who
returns good for evil, and love for hatred. Is it not written,
'See that thou slay them not'? and again, 'When the fulness
of the Gentiles be come in, then shall Israel be saved'? Thy
doctrine, O Rodolph! is not of thee, but of thy father, who
sent thee. Nevertheless, it suffices thee if thou art like unto
thy master; for he was a murderer from the beginning; he is
a liar, and the father of it."[1]

But this was not an occasion on which Bernard felt inclined
to trust to letters, however vigorous and convincing: he determined to withstand the truculent monk face to face. He met
with him at Mayence, enjoying the tumultuous and vehement
admiration of the people. Bernard summoned him into his
presence and rebuked him for conduct so unbecoming in a
monk, and in time produced such an effect on him that he
persuaded him to depart home to his monastery. But the
people of Mayence were not so easily dealt with. They were
indignant at Bernard's treatment of their favourite. They
threatened to rise in rebellion for him. Thus here was Bernard, usually surrounded by an almost adoring crowd, facing
an infuriated mob of angry fanatics. How he bore himself
when the waves of popular passion rose high against him is
not described for us. One fact alone is transmitted to us,
that the people did not rebel, that the fury of the men of

[1] St. Bern. Epist. 365. The Jews were quite sensible of what they owed to Bernard. The most honourable tribute of respect he per-haps ever received is from a Jewish contemporary, who narrates the per-secutions his people underwent in Germany. "Had not the tender mercy of the Lord," he says, "sent that priest (Bernard), none would have survived." There is a transla-tion from the Hebrew in the third vol. of Wilken's "Kreuzzüge." Vol-taire and Gibbon display the "philo-sophy" of which they were so proud by tracing Bernard's opposition to Rodolph to a principle of *rivalry.*— See *Essai sur les Mœurs*, chap. 55; *Decline and Fall*, chap. 59.

Mayence was hushed into calm submission when met by the holiness of the Abbot of Clairvaux.[1]

Bernard had also a good deal of trouble with the Emperor Conrad III., who could not be induced to promise that he would join the Crusade. Indeed, so strong did the Emperor's resolution to stay at home appear, that at one time Bernard gave up all hopes of converting him. He was on the point of returning home from Frankfort, when Herman, Bishop of Constance, came and implored him to meet the Emperor at Spires during the approaching Christmas, and make one more effort to convince him of his error. Bernard went and argued a long time without effect ; he could only get the Emperor to say that he would give an answer on the following day. Bernard proceeded to celebrate mass, when "the Divine Spirit began to stimulate him, so that he declared—no one having asked him—that it were better not to pass the day without a sermon." He spoke, and towards the end of his discourse turning to the Emperor, he addressed him with all freedom, not as an emperor, but as a man. He pictured forth the future judgment of man before the tribunal, and Christ commanding and saying to him, "What is there, O man, which I ought to have done for thee, and have not done ?" And then, dwelling on the height and pomp of royalty, he enumerated the Emperor's riches, his councillors, his manly strength of mind and body. Presently the Emperor burst into tears, and exclaimed : "I acknowledge the gifts of the Divine favour ; neither for the future shall I be found ungrateful to God's mercy. I am prepared to serve Him, seeing that I am thus admonished of Him." A shout from the crowd greeted the Emperor's words. Bernard, from the high altar, invested him with the cross, and

---

[1] "Tandem ad hoc eum, ut sub promissa obedientia in coenobium suum transiret, induxit, populo graviter indignante, et nisi ipsius sanc- titatis consideratione revocaretur, etiam seditionem movere volente."— *Otto Frisingensis, De Gestis Frederici,* apud MURATORI, vol. vi.

gave him the standard which he was to bear when he marched at the head of the Crusaders.[1]

Thus the chivalry of Europe, commanded by a king and an emperor, was ready to advance towards the Holy Land. The Second Crusade had, in fact, begun.

---

[1] St. Bern. Op. vol. ii. col. 1172–73.

THE Abbot Suger had been from the commencement, and was still, opposed to the king's project of going to the Holy Land. He combated his sovereign's design with calm pertinacity. But he discovered before long that he was striving to stem a torrent.   Not only had he to withstand the impetuous zeal of Bernard ; he discovered that he was exasperating the king and the people equally against him to no purpose : he therefore desisted.   It was now necessary to take measures with regard to the government of the kingdom during Louis VII.'s absence. An assembly of notables had been convened at Etampes for this and other purposes.   On the third day of their sitting Bernard made a speech to them ; and, invoking the assistance of the Holy Spirit, they proceeded to the question of a regency. When they were agreed, Bernard came forth and said, " Behold, here are two swords : it is enough ;" at the same time pointing to Suger and the Count of Nevers.   This choice, which confided the ecclesiastical and civil government of the country to two able men, gave general satisfaction, which, however, was as soon destroyed by the count's declaration that he intended to become a Carthusian monk, an intention which he soon afterwards carried out.   Thus disappointed, the assembly saw no other course than to invest Suger with the sole regency of the kingdom.   His remonstrances were not listened to ; his refusal was overruled by the Pope's command to obey. As subordinate ministers, however, Samson, Archbishop of Rheims, and Ralph, Count of Vermandois, were appointed to assist him. The Pope also granted him full power to excommunicate all who should oppose his authority. Thus was Suger made great and powerful against his will.[1]

In the meanwhile Eugenius III. had come to Paris, and he and the king together celebrated Easter in the church of St. Denis, with the honour which became the occasion. Louis, we are also told, did a "laudable thing, which few could imitate; indeed, perhaps, none of his rank." In the first place, he visited all the religious of Paris, and sallying forth, he proceeded to the hospital for lepers. With them he stayed a long time, having only two witnesses with him; the multitude of his courtiers was excluded. While he was thus engaged, his mother and queen, and numberless others, hastened to St. Denis, and when he presently followed them, he found the Pope, the abbot, and the monks, all assembled. Prostrating himself on the ground, he adored his patron saint; and the Pope and the abbot, opening a little golden door, drew forth a silver case, that the king might see and kiss him whom his soul loved—namely, the relics of the martyr—"and thereby be rendered more sprightly. Then taking the standard from the altar,[2] and having received the pilgrim's scrip with a blessing from the Supreme Pontiff, he withdrew from the multitude

---

[1] " Eunt igitur ad consilium, et post aliquantulam moram, cum quod erat melius elegissent, sanctus abbas praecedens revertentes, sic ait : Ecce gladii duo hic: satis est."—*Odo de Diogilo, de Lud. VII. Itinere,* lib. i.

[2] Gaufridus de Ranconio is mentioned, "Qui gerebat Regis baneriam, quam praecedebat, prout moris est, vexillum beati Dionysii, quod Gallice dicitur Oriflambe."—*Gesta*

Lud. VII. Regis, apud DUCHESNE, vol. iv. p. 398. "As Counts of Vexin, the kings of France were vassals and advocates of the monastery of St. Denis. The saint's peculiar banner, which they received from the abbot, was of a square form, and a red or flaming colour. The oriflamme appeared at the head of the French armies from the twelfth to the sixteenth century."— GIBBON, chap. lix. note.

to the dormitory of the monks. The crush and numbers of the people did not admit of delay ; his wife and mother also were anxious to leave, for, what with weeping and the heat, they were ready to faint. On that day, with a few select friends, he dined in the refectory with the monks ; and having kissed them all, he afterwards retired, followed by their prayers and tears."[1]

Queen Eleanor had resolved to accompany her husband to the East. Her example did not remain without effect, and several ladies took the cross, arming themselves with the lance and sword. Men who were able to go, and remained at home, were regarded with contempt. Distaffs, from scornful acquaintances, were sent to them as presents.[2]

The Emperor Conrad and the King of France agreed to keep their armies at a considerable distance from each other. They feared, with more forethought than Crusaders usually exhibited, lest their undisciplined hosts should fall to quarrelling, or even to blows, if they marched in proximity. Conrad, therefore, started first, getting away from Ratisbon at Easter ;

---

[1] " Deinde sumpto vexillo desuper altari, et pera et benedictione a summo pontifice, in dormitorium monachorum multitudini se subducit. Non enim patiebantur moras oppressio populorum, et mater et uxor, quae inter lacrymas et calorem pene spiritum exhalabant."—*Odo de Diogilo*, lib. i.

During the Pope's visit to Paris on this occasion a great scandal took place in the following manner:—" Voluit Pontifex in ecclesia beatae Genovefae mysteria divina peragere, quia Apostolica dicebatur. Ubi eo ventum est, orta est contentio inter Summi Pontificis et hujus ecclesiae canonicorum ministros, adeo ut ad pugnos res processerit, et non solum Pontificis ministri sed etiam ipse rex Ludovicus, qui illos compescere voluit, a canonicorum illorum famulis verberatus sit." (*Ex vita*

St. Willelmi, abbatis Roschildensis in Dania, apud DUCHESNE, vol. iv. p. 421.) The King and the Pope punished the indignity by substituting those monks, "quos nigros vocant," in the place of the pugnacious canons; who, however, were allowed to retain their prebends as long as they lived, "erant enim inter eos non pauci nobiles et litterati."—*Ibid.*

[2] Michaud, vol. ii. Also Hist. de France, par Henri Martin. "La présence de la Reine Eléonore, des Comtesses de Toulouse et de Flandre, de la bru du Comte de Champagne, de beaucoup d'autres belles dames et de nombreux troubadours et trouvères, donnait à l'expédition une physionomie toute différente de l'aspect de la première croisade."—Vol. iii. p. 435.

Louis delayed till Pentecost.   After entering the imperial territory, he was received at Verdun and Metz with the most
cordial hospitality.   He then moved on to Worms, and after
that to Ratisbon, where he crossed the Danube, and also
shipped a number of his soldiers and a quantity of heavy
baggage.   Here, also, he was met by the ambassadors of the
Greek Emperor, Manuel.   These representatives of an old
civilization struck the rude Franks and Teutons very much.
After they had saluted the king, they awaited his reply in standing posture.   On being told to sit down, they did so, on
benches which they had brought with them for the purpose.
The servile obedience which they showed to their masters
attracted the notice of the Latins.   "They wear no cloaks.
Their garments are of silk, short, and closed up all round ; the
sleeves are tight: and they walk in the manner of boxers.[1] The
clothes of the poor are of the same cut, but differ in material
from those of the rich."   As regards the message brought by the
Greeks, it aroused a mixed feeling of surprise and contempt in
Louis and his followers.   The fulsome flattery which it contained would, in their opinion, have disgraced, not an emperor
only, but even a mountebank.   Louis listened to the extrava-
gant compliments till he blushed, but had no conception of
their motive or meaning.   Godfrey, Bishop of Langres, Bernard's kinsman, presently grew indignant, and, coming to the
rescue of his modest sovereign, he said to the envoys, " Be so
good, brothers, as not to rehearse quite so often the glory, the
majesty, the wisdom, and religion of the king.   He knows
himself, and we also know him well ; therefore please explain
your meaning with more clearness and promptitude."   At last
the ambassadors ventured to deliver their message.   It con-

---

[1] " Non habent amictus, sed vestibus sericis curtisque et clausis undique divites induuntur, strictis-que manicis expediti, more pugilem semper incedunt.   Pauperes etiam, excepto pretio, similiter se coap-tant."— *Odo de Diogilo*, lib. ii.

tained two requests : the first, that the king should refrain from
capturing any towns that belonged to the Greek empire ; the
second, that if the Crusaders should take any cities from the
Turks which had formerly belonged to the empire, such cities
should be restored to their original owner, namely, the Emperor
Manuel. The first demand was reasonable, and at once
acceded to ; concerning the latter an unanimous opinion does
not seem to have been come to by Louis and his councillors.
A convention on the part of the French to respect the rights and
property of the Greeks was then made ; the latter, in return,
undertaking to furnish adequate supplies to the army, and a
suitable rate of exchange. The remaining difficulties were
reserved to be settled at a meeting of the two sovereigns.

The Crusaders then pursued a peaceful and uneventful progress through Hungary, and entered Bulgaria, the territory of
the Greek Emperor. Up to this time they had experienced a
friendly reception from the countries they had passed through ;
but now they noticed a great change. The Greeks shut themselves up in their towns, and when the French wished to obtain
provisions, these were lowered down to them from the tops of
the walls by ropes.[1] The insufficiency and delay of this mode
of supply irritated the impatient Franks to the last degree, and,
in a short time, they betook them to plundering. The conduct
of the Greeks was partly excused and explained by the treatment they had received from the previous body of German
Crusaders who had passed through their country shortly before
They had taken to plundering from the first, without any preliminary attempt at traffic. The French discovered that they
had even burned the suburbs of Philippopolis. The Germans,
on reaching that place, had been met in a friendly manner, and
had dispersed themselves in the taverns to enjoy a carouse.
Presently a juggler came forth to amuse these strange guests.

---

[1] "Graeci autem suas civitates et
castella observabant, et per murum
funibus venalia submittebant."—
Odo de Diogilo, lib. iii.

To their overwhelming horror and astonishment, he drew from his bosom a charmed snake, which, after the performance of various tricks, he placed in a cup on the ground. The Teutonic mind, slow to apprehend, but in no wise slow to wrath, kindled into fury at the sight, seized the poor conjuror and cut him in pieces. Their impression was, that the Greeks meant to poison them all. The governor of the place, perceiving the tumult, hastily sallied forth unarmed to allay it. The Germans saw his cavalcade, but were too angry and too tipsy to see that he was defenceless. Thinking that their recent crime was going to be avenged, they rushed upon him and his escort and drove them back into the town. Whereupon the Greeks seized their bows, and, in their turn, became the assailants, and put the Germans to flight. But the latter presently returning in superior force, burned nearly all the suburbs without the walls.[1]

And this was not the only outrage of which the German Crusaders were guilty in their intercourse with the Greeks. On reaching Constantinople they committed an act of barbarism which might well make the inhabitants regard all western Christians with horror. Near the city walls was a spacious inclosure, in which nature and art had done their utmost to rival and assist each other. Aqueducts and artificial ponds, and caves and grottoes, among which every variety of game ran or flew, contributed to make this noble park the pride and delight of Constantinople. Into this fairy scene Conrad and his Germans ruthlessly rushed, and destroyed everything which was within their power. The Greeks and

[1] "Ubi cum tabernis insedissent Alemanni, malo auspicio adfuit joculator, qui licet eorum linguam ignoraret, tamen sedit, symbolum dedit, bibit, et post longam ingurgitationem, serpentem quem praecantatum in sinu habebat, extrahit, et scypho terrae imposito superponit. . . . . Alemanni quasi viso prodigio illico cum furore consurgunt, mimum rapiunt, et in frustra discerpunt."—Lib. iii. Odo of Deuil, who gives this story, seems himself to have had a sincere hatred of the Germans: "Nostris etiam erant importabiles Alemanni."

their emperor looked on from the walls, coming no doubt to
very decided conclusions respecting Crusaders and their ways.[1]
But Manuel was too much of an Oriental to manifest the
resentment which burned within him.   He asked for an interview with Conrad.   Conrad refused to go into the town, and
Manuel refused to go out of it.   And so matters rested till
Louis VII., who was coming behind as fast as he could, sent
messages to his imperial brother to wait for him on the western
side of the Arm of St. George, in order that they might arrange
joint plans of action.   But Conrad paid as little regard to the
wishes of an ally as he did to the honour and property of a
neutral.   He had obtained from Manuel—doubtless without
the least difficulty—a guide to direct, or rather to mislead, him
in Asia Minor : and he at once crossed the Straits.   Seventy
thousand horsemen clad in armour, besides numbers of foot-
soldiers and light cavalry, are said to have passed over.

By this time the French king and his host were nearing
Constantinople.   He also experienced the perfidy of the
Greeks, but appears on the whole to have acted with more
caution and discretion than his colleague the Emperor.   While
making the greatest show of cordiality and deference, the
Greeks plundered and attacked the French whenever they had
an opportunity.   They promised with the most solemn oaths
whatever was asked of them, never taking a thought about
performance.   It was their opinion that perjury committed for
the " Holy Empire " was in no wise criminal.[2]   Their various
forms of obeisance and respect filled the Franks with disgust,
especially the stooping or kneeling posture of body, and even

---

[1] "Erat ante urbem murorum
ambitus spatiosus et speciosus,
multimodam venationem includens,
conductus etiam aquarum et stanna
continens. . . .   In hunc, ut verum
fatear, deliciarum locum, Alemannus
Imperator irrupit, et undique pene

omnia destruens, Graecorum delicias
ipsis intuentibus suis usibus rapuit."
—*Odo de Diogilo*, lib. iii.
[2] " Generalis est eorum enim
sententia, non imputari perjurium,
quod sit propter sacrum imperium."
—*Ibid.*

C C

total prostration on the ground. Their abject fear when weak, and truculence when strong, were also noticed. To all these not illegitimate grounds of dislike was added the incurable one of difference of creed. If the Latin priests celebrated a mass in one of their chapels, the Greeks were careful afterwards to purify and wash the altar, as though it had been polluted. If a Latin wished to marry a Greek, they rebaptized him before marriage. Their other heresies, concerning the procession of the Holy Spirit and their mode of performing mass, did not escape the notice of the Catholic French. The impression was general among them that the Greeks could not be considered Christians, that slaying them was no crime, and plundering them was quite an innocent proceeding. But the chiefs of the army were too wise to indulge either the rapacity or bigotry of their followers.

As Louis VII. approached Constantinople the nobles, priests, and people came forth in a grand procession to greet him. They begged that the king would pay a visit to their emperor. Louis, pitying the terror in which he saw them, entered Manuel's palace with a few attendants. The Emperor received him with imperial magnificence under the porch, and, after the kiss of salutation, conducted him to an inner apartment. There they conversed by means of an interpreter. To judge by the manners of the Emperor, the pleasing smile on his countenance, and the polite and engaging expressions he addressed to Louis VII., nothing could exceed the cordiality of his heart: but, as an eye-witness says, such an inference could not be considered infallible. When this first meeting was over, the King was taken by an escort of nobles to the palace which had been provided for his reception.

The city of Constantinople filled the Crusaders with admiration and wonder. Its extent, wealth, and luxury surpassed their wildest dreams. But they evidently felt it was a very wicked place, and, as they might not plunder it, they had not

much wish to stay.[1] The King of France, accompanied by the
Emperor, visited the objects and places of interest or sanctity.
Then, overpowered by entreaties, he was induced to sit down
to a magnificent repast which had been prepared for him. The
French knights almost trembled when they saw their king sitting surrounded by the treacherous Greeks. However it was
not Manuel's design to irritate those ferocious warriors, while it
was still in their power to avenge themselves. Louis departed
without harm or hindrance. Indeed, in his simplicity, he seems
to have thought that Manuel had treated him very well. He
severely punished those of his followers who committed depre-
dations on Greek property, and cut off, in consequence, the
ears, hands, and feet of a great number of his followers. But,
even with such exemplary punishments before them, they could
hardly be restrained from burning houses and olive groves.[2]

But the Greeks were growing anxious that the French should
follow the Germans across the Bosphorus. They would have
been more anxious even than they were, if they had known of
the debates which were going on in the Frankish camp; for
one party, headed by Godfrey, Bishop of Langres, openly
advised the capture of Constantinople, as a prudent and
advisable preliminary step. This counsel was opposed, on the
ground that they had left their homes to fight infidels and not
to slay Christians. The discussion was still pending when
Greek astuteness got the better of barbarian valour. They
announced to the French that Conrad had had a battle with
the Turks, and slain fourteen thousand of them, with little or
no loss to himself;[3] that he had reached Iconium, from which

[1] "Quoniam autem in hac urbe vivitur sine jure, quae tot quasi dominos habet quot divites, et pene tot fures quot pauperes, ibi sceleratus quisque nec metum habet nec verecundiam, ubi scelus nec lege vindicatur, nec luce venit in palam."—*Odo de Diogilo*, lib. iv.

[2] "Faciebat eis rex aures, manus, et pedes saepius detruncare, nec sic poterat eorum vesaniam refrenare."—*Ibid.* Cutting off hands and feet was a favourite punishment in the Middle Ages.

[3] "Rumoribus Alemannorum nostros ad transitum concitabant.

the people had fled on his approach, and that he had written
to ask Manuel to come and take possession of his conquests,
as he was bent on hastening forward. The French fell into
the trap without a moment's hesitation. They complained to
their king of his delay. When they thought of the booty and
the glory which the Germans were acquiring, they were stung
with envy and impatience. Louis, pressed by the Greeks and
his own followers, consented to cross, though not without
misgivings, for all his forces had not arrived. With suspicious
alacrity Manuel provided the requisite transports, and the
French were soon ferried over.

They had not been long on the other side, when an incident
occurred which caused further delay and trouble to the French
monarch. A fleet of boats followed them, to supply the army
with the necessaries or superfluities which they were able or
willing to purchase. The shore was lined with gay and
attractive booths, presenting many an object of interest and
astonishment to the rude Franks. One day a "certain
Fleming," walking about among these treasures, was seized
with an impulse he could not restrain to lay violent hands
on them. Shouting out "*Haro, haro!*" he made a sudden
onslaught, and carried off a rich booty of stolen goods. His
example and its reward spread with swift contagion among his
fellows, and before long a general attack was made on the stalls
of the Greek merchants.[1] These hastened to their boats as

Primo retulerunt Turcos copiosum
exercitum congregasse, et Alemannos
de illis sine damno suorum quatuor-
decim millia peremisse." — *Odo de
Diogilo*, lib. iv.

[1] "Igitur, una die Flandrensis
quidam dignus flagris et flamma,
cernens immensas divitias et im-
moderata cupiditate caecatus, clamat,
haro, haro! rapiens quod cupivit; . . .
in prospectu civitatis illico suspensus
est."—*Ibid.*

Haro, a word of Norman origin.
"Rolloni primo Neustriae Duci ad-
scribitur. . . Quod si quispiam inveni-
retur vel homicida vel incendiarius
. . statim clamore sublato, indigenae
ac vicini in eum irruerent, captum-
que judici exhiberent. Erat autem
clamor iste : Ha Raoul ; qui ab iis primum edebatur ; . . . . tanquam Rol-
lonis Ducis auxilium implorantibus."
—DUCANGE, *sub voce* Haro.

well as they could, carrying off what remained of their property—and not only their own property, but also a number
of Louis's subjects, who were on board at the time buying
provisions,—to Constantinople. Louis was very wroth when
the facts were made known to him. He made a strict
inquiry for the criminal, and the latter being surrendered to
him by the Count of Flanders, he caused the too audacious
depredator to be hanged within sight of the city. He
threatened a like punishment to all who did not restore what
they had taken. The merchants were summoned to claim their
own, and whatever any swore he had lost was at once given
up to him. Many asked for more than they had any title to ;
but Louis rather chose to make good the deficiency out of his
own means than give the Greeks any reason to complain of
the conduct of his army.

Having thus done justice himself, he proceeded to demand
as much of others. His men were still detained in Constantinople, where they had been robbed and beaten. He therefore
despatched Arnulph, Bishop of Louvain, and his chancellor at
once to the palace ; but they could not get an audience of the
Emperor. They passed the day in his spacious halls, without
notice or any civility being shown to them. In place of food,
they had to satisfy themselves with looking at pictures, and during
the night, instead of beds, they were forced to be content with
the marble pavement.[1] In the morning, when the Emperor
had risen, they were admitted into his presence, but found his
manners mightily changed from the unctuous politeness he had
exhibited shortly before. After much difficulty, they procured
the release of their countrymen, without their property, which
was not to be extracted from the hands of the Greek thieves.

---

[1] "Illo die fuit alter alteri pro
solatio, intuitus picturarum pro cibo,
et instanti nocte marmoreum pavi-
mentum pro culcitra vel lecto."—
Odo de Diogilo, lib. iv. Odo calls
Manuel an idol : "Sed loqui cum
idolo nequiverunt." He never mentions the Emperor's name, declaring
from the first he would not, "as it
was not written in the book of life."

The bishop and his colleague then hastened back, anxious, if possible, to avoid the honour of a third day's fast in the Emperor's gorgeous but inhospitable palace.

Manuel then caused further delay to the French by means of protracted negotiations concerning two points. The first was a demand that a female cousin of Louis VII., who was in the suite of Queen Eleanor, should be given in mariage to one of Manuel's nephews. The second was a request for the homage of the French barons. By way of return, he promised Louis to furnish him with guides and supplies. Count Robert of Dreux, the brother of the king, soon showed what he thought of Manuel's conditions, by carrying off his cousin from the camp, and starting with a few followers for Nicomedia. The question of homage still remained to be decided. The Bishop of Langres again raised his warning voice, declaring that the perfidy of the Greeks was daily becoming more manifest. " Let us place honour above convenience," he said; " let us obtain by our own valour what he promises to our apparent cupidity and weakness." But the advocates of a more temperate course prevailed. They said there was no disgrace in the act of homage : it was a thing they were quite accustomed to do, when in their own country, to one another, and now, considering the price set upon it, altogether a most advisable step. " None of us know the roads or the country ; we cannot do without guides. Besides, our expedition is against the Pagans ; let us leave Christians in peace."

Louis was losing all patience with the Emperor and his delays. He gave orders to the army to march. This brought Manuel to a rapid decision. He named a castle for a conference, but, with a suspicious caution which well revealed his character, he provided for his own safety, in case of treachery, by the facilities it offered for escape by sea. Louis, mad with ambition to follow and emulate the German Emperor, would not delay the march of his army, but returned to meet

Manuel with a select company of knights and soldiers. It was not without a pang that he did homage to Manuel: "still he preferred subduing the stiff pride of his mind to throwing any difficulty or delay in the way of God's service." So they came to terms; Conrad's imaginary successes no doubt contributing to despatch. Louis promised to respect the Emperor's rights; the French barons acknowledged him as their suzerain. On the other side, it was promised that two Greek nobles should accompany the army, to act at once as guides and commissariat officers. The two sovereigns then parted, Manuel returning to Constantinople, while Louis hastened after his army. He almost immediately afterwards learnt that the Germans had been cut to pieces, and that Conrad had barely escaped with his life.

On leaving the shores of the Bosphorus, Conrad, trusting implicitly to the guides furnished him by the Emperor of Constantinople, had pushed on rapidly, as he supposed, in the direction of Iconium. His Greek deceivers, with specious candour, warned him of a desert he was about to cross, and advised that a supply of provisions calculated to last the army eight days should be laid in. The Germans plunged into Turkish territory, doubting nothing, marched forward for eight days, and came to the end of their supplies. Conrad called his guides before him, and pointed out to them the fact that the army had nothing to eat, and was still apparently far from Iconium. They had little difficulty in beguiling the simple German with plausible excuses, and promised faithfully that within three days he should reach the capital of the Sultan. On the following morning it was discovered that the Greeks had fled during the night. The Germans were without food in a desert country. The surrounding mountains swarmed with Turks.[1]

---

[1] The disaster which overtook Conrad's army is described both by Odo of Deuil and William of Tyre (lib. xvi. cap. 21, 22). The latter

The Crusading host, famished, exhausted, and overwhelmed
with disappointment, knew not which way to turn. Some
advised an advance, some a retreat. The onslaught of the
Turks stopped further discussion. Lightly armed with the bow
and scimitar, their nimble cavalry swooped down on the
ponderous knights, like eagles on a flock of sheep. They
poured volleys of arrows into the cumbrous mass, killing and
disabling their enemies without receiving a blow themselves.
When the Christians offered to attack them, they broke and
disappeared like a morning mist. When the Germans returned
to their disheartened camp, they found themselves again in a
circle of turbaned adversaries. The Emperor was struck by
two arrows ; his soldiers fell around him by thousands ; the rout
was pitiable and complete. After some fearful days of wandering flight, he succeeded in reaching Nicæa. About one-tenth
only of his fine army was ever seen again.[1]

Louis was plunged in grief when the sad news at last was
known. To Conrad's messages asking for help he lent a
willing ear. He despatched the Constable Ives de Niella to
his assistance. The constable found the Emperor and his
followers in the last stage of misery and despair. They confessed that but for this timely succour the hand of death had
been upon them. When the two princes met, they fell on each
other's necks and wept aloud.[2] Conrad ingenuously acknowledged his errors and his piercing remorse for them. Louis
comforted him as best he could, appointed a guard of noble
knights to attend upon him, and declared that he and Conrad
should for the future live under the same tent.

Conrad's failure to penetrate the interior of the country

---

author gives as a reason with the
Greeks for wishing the destruction
of the German army, that they resented Conrad's assumption of the
title of Emperor of the Romans.

[1] "Vix ut asserunt, qui prae-
sentes fuerunt, decima pars evasit."
—*William of Tyre*, lib. xvi. cap. 22.

[2] "Amplexantur igitur alter alterum, et infigunt oscula quae rora-
bant lacrymae pietatis."—*Odo de
Diogilo*, lib. v.

determined the French to follow the coast-line of Æolia and
Ionia.   Their progress, though slow, was not distinguished by
misadventures, except the constantly recurring one of short
rations.   They passed by Pergamus and Smyrna, and then
came to Ephesus.   Here the German Emperor, still suffering
from his wounds, left them, and retired to Constantinople, to
recover his health and spirits.   The French passed Christmas
Day in the rich valley of Decervion ; and while engaged in
the practices of devotion, for the first time were molested by
the Turks.   A prompt resistance dispersed their assailants,
" the firstfruits of whose heads they joyfully gathered."   But a
heavy fall of rain and snow, which swelled the rivers and
whitened the mountain tops, caused Louis to use additional
speed.   Forsaking the coast, he determined to make a bold
attempt to reach the port of Attalia.   With this object he provided himself with the requisite stores, and set out in the direction of Laodicea.   Presently he came to the river Mæander,
and found the opposite banks lined with Turks.   For two
days the hostile armies marched along the stream, in full view
of each other.   Then, when he was about to ford the river, he
was suddenly attacked in the rear, while the Turkish archers
disputed his passage in front.   But the French knights were
equal to the emergency.   Henry, son of Count Theobald of
Champagne, Thierry, Count of Flanders, who had succeeded
Charles the Good,[1] and William, Count of Macon, plunged
at once into the stream, amid the showers of arrows which
the Turks poured on them.   The flood was strong, the banks
steep, the enemy numerous and bold.   But the stalwart arms
of the Western warriors were too heavy for the light and active
Orientals.   They broke and fled.   In the meanwhile Louis had
hastened to protect his rear, where he had also routed his
enemies.   The victory was so complete, that the Christians
saw in it something of a miraculous character.   They had lost

[1] See *ante*, p. 113.

only one horseman, who was drowned in crossing the river. On the third day following they reached Laodicea.

After a short rest, they began their long journey to Attalia. The intricate defiles of the Phrygian mountains had to be passed, and both in front and rear they knew that they were surrounded by hostile Turks and Greeks, the latter having become more open in their enmity as the Latins grew weaker. On the second day of their march they came to a pass by which they hoped to emerge from the valley in which they were. Geoffrey de Rancogne and Amadeus of Savoy, uncle of King Louis, were sent forward to secure the summit of the mountain, while the main body of the army began slowly to ascend. Geoffrey and Amadeus unfortunately either misunderstood or disobeyed their orders ; for, instead of taking possession of the summit of the pass, they pushed onward till they had descended on the other side, where they pitched their tents. The steep and rocky side of the mountain was now gradually getting covered with the squadrons of the Crusaders. The peaks above them seemed lost in the clouds, while a boiling torrent roared beneath. The long array of knights and men-at-arms and pack-horses and pilgrims was spread over the vast slope, when the Turks rushed down upon them. A scene of awful confusion followed. The packhorses slid and fell over the slippery rocks, and, rolling with increasing velocity down the mountain sides, hurled men and animals into the abyss below. Large stones, also, loosened by the plunging of horses, caused by their swift descent much mischief. On the French, in the midst of these difficulties and dangers, was poured a well-directed shower of arrows : the Turks (and Greeks also it is said), from a convenient neighbouring eminence, threw their deadly volleys with undisturbed precision. The rolling masses of men, horses, and baggage, which shot over the precipice into the chasm underneath, threatened almost to fill it up.

The success of the infidels emboldened them to a nearer attack. Leaving their safe elevation, they rushed in upon the bewildered Christians, and slaughtered them like sheep. An effort was now made to retreat by descending the hill they had with such peril just gone up; but the steepness, their numbers, and the absence of all order, made this attempt only add to the confusion. Louis, who, though he was incompetent as a general, was at all times a most brave knight, performed prodigies of valour. The French chivalry imitated their king, although placed in a disadvantageous, nay, almost ludicrous, position. Seated on their cumbrous war-horses, and armed with their long lances, they were as helpless and nearly as motionless as ships on dry land. The horses dared scarcely move at all, much less go at the pace which would make a lance-thrust of any avail. Grim and mortified they sat, reduced to occasionally prodding those of their adversaries whom they could reach.[1] The King, separated from his escort, was attacked alone by the victorious Mussulmans. Unhorsed and surrounded, either his capture or his death seemed imminent. With great presence of mind and vigour he succeeded in climbing, by means of the roots of a tree, to the summit of a rock, where he turned upon his adversaries. While those nearest strove to take him, those who were at a distance made him a mark for their arrows. But his stout corselet kept out the missiles, while he buried his heavy sword, at every stroke, deep in some Turk's vitals, chopping their hands and heads off all round him.[2] Fortunately for him,

---

[1] " Ibi enim equus non poterat, non dicam currere, sed vix stare, et tardior impetus debilitabat ictum in vulnere. Vibrabant nostri hastas in lubrico suis viribus, non equorum, et illi sagittabant de tuto, innitentes scopulis arborum vel saxorum."— *Odo de Diogilo*, lib. vi.

[2] " In hoc rex parvulum sed glo-riosum perdidit comitatum, regalem vero retinens animum, agilis et viri-lis per radices cujusdam arboris, quam saluti ejus Deus providerat, ascendit scopulum. Post quem popu-lus hostium, ut eum caperet, ascen-debat : turba remotior eum ibidem

they did not know who he was; so, getting "convinced that his capture was difficult, and having given as much time to it as they deemed expedient, they forsook him, in order to collect their plunder before nightfall."

When the King got back to the main body of the army, he had no need to explain what had happened. Coming alone, exhausted, and splashed with blood, his knights saw at a glance that his escort had been cut to pieces, and that he had escaped by his own prowess. With silent grief they mourned over their lost comrades. They burned with desire to avenge them; but the enemy had retired to the fastnesses of his own mountains, quite out of reach. Few slept that night. Some in anxious watchfulness expected a friend whom they were never destined to see again; others experienced all the ecstasy of joy in the return of one for whom they had lost all hope.

But sorrow for the dead was soon replaced by anger against the living; for Geoffrey and Amadeus, whose culpable negligence had contributed not a little to the disaster, had overheard the clamour of the battle, and retraced their steps, reaching their comrades when the conflict was over. The opinion was general that they deserved to be hanged; and doubtless it would have gone hard with Geoffrey had he not had the king's uncle as fellow-culprit. But when the morning dawned, and revealed the opposite hill-sides crowded with Turks, the imperative necessity of taking active measures to save the remainder of the army dispelled all feelings either of anger or sorrow. The way in which the Crusaders set about this object was most remarkable; and the remedies proposed and carried out in the discipline and ordering of the army discover a state of things which not only easily accounts for

sagittabat. Sed Deo volente sub lorica tutatus est a sagittis, cruentoque gladio ne capi posset, defendit scopulum, multorum manibus et capitibus amputatis."—*Odo le Diogilo*, lib. vi.

their disasters, but makes it astonishing that they could ever have had successes.   First of all, it was agreed that they should keep together, and that, when attacked, they should not run away.   A solemn promise of mutual help was given and taken by all.   Secondly, it was agreed that they should appoint officers; and thirdly, that they should obey them. For this purpose a leader was elected, of whom we hear only on this occasion, named Gilbert, to whom the chief command was entrusted.   He chose for himself his lieutenants, to each of whom he assigned fifty subalterns.   With this staff to see to the execution of his orders, he proceeded to make them understand that they must keep their ranks; that a man belonging to the front must not be found in the rear; and that those in charge of the flanks were to avoid confusion by keeping to their own division as much as possible.   "Those whom nature or misfortune had made foot-soldiers were placed in the rear, armed with bows to reply to the archery of the Turks."   These and other wise measures were taken by Gilbert, and the immediate result was that they repelled their enemies with comparative ease—in one instance beat them soundly; and in time, though suffering grievously from short provisions, reached Attalia without further misadventure.

Attalia was garrisoned by Greeks, to the regret and misfortune of the Crusaders.   Provisions were doled out to the famishing host by the morsel, for which they were made to pay the most exorbitant sums.   Those who still had horses sold them readily for bread; but this resource was open to few, as the greater part of the horses had died of starvation and been eaten on the road.   And now was added to their actual sufferings the discomfort of incessant rain, from which they had no protection, their strong and large tents having been lost in their painful wanderings.   The King expressed a desire to move on; his barons said they were quite willing to do so, but also they declared that they must communicate a project

to him which had just occurred to them.   From Attalia to
Antioch they were told the distance was forty days' journey,
through a country crowded with enemies, and intersected by
rapid rivers.   From Attalia to Antioch by sea they learnt that
they could go in three days : they merely stated the fact, as it
was their intention to abide by whatever the King decided on.
Louis replied that no honourable man should want for anything while he had it to give him ; but at the same time, if
any refused to bear patiently with him those privations which
necessity imposed on them, of such he confessed he had a
bad opinion.   " Rather," he said, " let us collect all our
fighting men together, and travel over the road which our
fathers trod before us, winning for themselves at once earthly
fame and heavenly glory.   But the sick and helpless multitude
which has all along impeded us, and been a burden to us,
shall here take ship and depart."   The barons answered :
" We do not wish to depreciate the actions of our ancestors.
but they had an easier task than we have had.   As soon as
they had crossed the Bosphorus they attained their object.
They met the Turks, and were kept in good spirits by the
excitement of war, and became rich from the plunder of
captured camps and cities.   Instead of Turks, we had to deal
with fraudulent Greeks, whom, unfortunately for ourselves,
we spared as Christians, and among these, in idleness and
vexatious delays, we have spent nearly all our substance.
Some have been so foolish or so reduced as to sell even their
arms.   What your Majesty says is very noble, but, for the
reasons we allege, it is not safe."   And the barons gave him
to understand that he should go by sea, and that they would
not go by land.

The Greeks exacted four silver marks a head for every pas-
senger to Antioch.   The King made a vain effort to procure
ships for the helpless crowd of diseased cripples who still lay
in the stony plain round Attalia ; but under the circumstances

he could hardly himself have hoped to succeed. Even the barons, who had been so anxious to go by sea, began to despair of obtaining the transport promised them by the Greeks. For the poor pilgrims who could not pay enormous sums there was no alternative but the land journey. So Louis agreed to pay down five hundred marks, on condition that the Greeks conducted the pilgrims safely as far as Tarsus, the nearest town of the Christian principality of Antioch, and that the sick and helpless should be taken into Attalia, there cared for till they recovered, and then be sent on by sea after the others.

The Greeks readily took the money, and immediately the King was gone they informed the Turks of the helpless condition of the pilgrims. The Count of Flanders and the Sire de Bourbon had been induced to remain in charge of the poor wretches, who now, without money, clothes, or weapons, were expected to march for forty days through a hostile country. The escort promised by the Greeks existed only in the imagination of the credulous Louis. They would hardly suffer the Christians to come for shelter into their town, to which the Turks had free access when they chose. The Count of Flanders and the Sire de Bourbon were not heroes enough to endure this. They procured a ship and sailed for Antioch, leaving their countrymen to their awful and now very visible fate. The low wall under which they crowded offered no shelter from the Turkish archers, who, posted at convenient places, shot them down at their ease. In the meantime the Greeks crushed hale, and sick, and putrefying corpses into a narrow and filthy space, and quietly waited for the result. A body of three or four thousand preferred death by the scimitars of the Turks to a lingering suffocation by mephitic gases. They sallied forth, and attempting to cross a river, were repulsed and cut to pieces by the Turks. But, marvellous to relate, such was the scene of wretchedness presented by their camp, that even the fierce Moslem heart was touched with pity; they nursed the wounded, and fed the sick and starving.   This mercy of the Turks gives one a feeling of awe.   How unutterable must have been that woe which could pierce down to the humanity of a Turk, through his love for Islam, through his duty and delight in the slaughter of the unbelievers.   The Greeks made slaves of such of the pilgrims as were strong and serviceable.   The contrast between the Christians and Pagans of the East was so great that numbers of the pilgrims embraced the Mohammedan faith.[1]

The horrible scene at Attalia virtually closed the Second Crusade.   The French king, indeed, and a few courtiers had proceeded to Antioch, and from thence to Jerusalem; but much more in the character of humble pilgrims than bold Crusaders.   Louis gave himself up to devotion with a zeal more becoming to a monk than to the sovereign of a large kingdom which suffered grievously from his absence.   Suger wrote to him imploring him to return.   "The disturbers of the country have returned," he writes—meaning the barons— "and you, who ought to defend, remain as it were captive abroad."   The good abbot had reason to complain.   While the king was wasting both the blood and treasure of his kingdom in the East, Suger was administrating the affairs of the country out of the revenues of his own abbey.

---

[1] The conclusion of Odo's narrative is written with all the marks of intense anguish.   The generosity of the Turks reached to an almost incredible degree.   They actually bought up among themselves the specie of the Christians to distribute it among the poor of the French army.   "Quidam Turcorum a suis sociis nostras monetas emebant, et inter pauperes plena manu dividebant."

CHAPTER IV.

ACTS OF ST. BERNARD DURING THE PROGRESS OF THE CRUSADE—TRIAL
AND CONDEMNATION OF GILBERT DE LA PORRÉE—SECOND VISIT OF
ST. MALACHY TO CLAIRVAUX—HIS DEATH THERE.

THE various friends and disciples of Bernard who have left us
narratives of his life, or of parts of it, appear always especially
anxious to impress on their readers the singular humility and
gentleness of his character.   They seem to fear lest the great
Bernard of the world's stage, the dictator to popes and kings,
will keep out of sight the meek and affectionate father and
friend with whom they loved to be.   "He often used to tell
us," says his secretary Godfrey, "that when he was in the
midst of honours and flattering attentions, whether from
multitudes or the great, he seemed to himself to have borrowed
the personality of another man ; he could think of himself
as absent, and all that was going on before him as a sort of
dream.   But when he was conversing with the simpler among
his monks, then he rejoiced to find himself again, and feel, as
it were, in his own person."   For the innate modesty which
appeared in his youth adhered to him till the day of his death,
of which here is a singular proof :—In spite of his marvellous
gift of eloquence, and the triumphs which had attended it, he
often declared that "he never lifted up his voice in any
company, however humble, without a feeling of awe and fear

coming over him. He would by far have preferred being silent, had he not been urged to speak by the pricks of his conscience, the fear of God, and brotherly love."[1]

Utter fearlessness, coupled with deep humility—truly a very admirable combination, which will never want for influence while human nature remains what it is. "He seemed to fear no man, and yet to reverence all." He rarely reproved any if he could avoid it, preferring the way of advice and entreaty. Many were surprised to notice that a rough and insolent answer would as readily cause him to pause or interrupt his objurgation as a modest and humble one, so that some said he attacked those who fled, but yielded to aggressors. But the reply he made to this is not unworthy of notice. He said that conversations in which modesty appeared in both interlocutors were pleasant; where it appeared in only one, they were useful; where it appeared in neither, they were pernicious.[2]

Bernard's humility could bear rude tests, as the following anecdote shows:—A certain regular clerk one day came to Clairvaux, and asked with some importunity to be admitted as a monk. The abbot exhorted him to return to his church, and refused to receive him. "Why then," said the clerk, "have you in your books given such praises to a perfect life, if you refuse your help to one who wishes to lead it?" and, working himself up to a great passion, he continued: "If I had those books here, I would tear them in pieces." Bernard quietly answered: "I do not think you will find it anywhere asserted in my writings that you could not be perfect in your own cloister. If I remember rightly, I have everywhere in my books advised a change of manners, not a change of abode." Upon this the clerk rushed at him, and hit him a

---

[1] "Denique, sicut nobis saepius fatebatur, inter summos quosque honores et favores populorum et sublimium personarum, alterum sibi mutuatus hominem videbatur, seque potius reputabat absentem velut somnium quoddam suspicatus."— St. Bern. *Op.* vol. ii. col. 1126.

[2] *Ibid.* col. 1127.

violent blow on the cheek, causing a severe bruise.[1] Those
present were ready to seize the culprit with some degree of
roughness. But Bernard restrained them, and forbade any one
to touch him. He merely gave orders that he should be
safely and carefully led out, and that no hurt should be done
him. The poor wretch, overcome by Bernard's gentleness,
was taken away trembling with horror and amazement.

Such blows as these to his outward man Bernard could bear
without much effort. The pain they inflicted did not penetrate very deep. Much sharper was the pang which at this
date shot through his heart and mind, owing to renewed
reports of heresy. Heresy again, and evermore heresy. How
vexatious and horrible that men will not believe aright! No
sooner have we stamped out their infernal sparks in one place
than they appear in another. Peter of Bruis, Abelard, Arnold
of Brescia, heretics from Cologne, heretics from Italy, had all,
in one way or another, been answered, or vexed, or hunted out.
Still, such is the depravity of the human heart, more are ready
to follow in their evil ways. From Perigeux the most
shocking accounts are received. A monk named Pontius has
succeeded in seducing from Catholic verity nobles, clerks,
priests, monks, and even nuns. His views seem to have
coincided with those of Henry the Cluniac (of whom it is
probable he was a disciple), and consisted of the usual rejection
of the Church's doctrine on the Eucharist,[2] and the adoration of
crosses, coupled with vows of extreme poverty. Pontius and
his followers were believed to work miracles by the assistance

---

[1] "Tum vero impetum faciens, homo velut insanus in eum, percussit maxillam ejus idque tam graviter ut succederet statim rubor ictui, tumor rubori."—St. Bern. *Op.* vol. ii. col. 1127.

[2] "Missam pro nihilo ducunt neque communionem percipi debere dicunt sed fragmentum panis. Missam si quis cantaverit seductionis causa, nec canonem dicit nec communionem percipit, sed hostiam juxta, aut retro altare, aut in missalem projicit."—*Heriberti Epistola,* apud Mabillon, *Vetera Analecta,* p. 483.

of their patron the devil.   It was said that nothing could bind
them, for Satan always came to their rescue.   Even when
loaded with chains and stowed carefully in a wine-butt turned
bottom upwards, and well watched by a strong guard, however
secure overnight they might be, in the morning they were
found to have evaporated, as it were, and were not seen till
they chose to show themselves again.   They had the very
remarkable and enviable power of putting a drop of wine
into an empty bottle one day, and of finding it full of wine
on the day following.[1]   But their impiety was horrible ; and to
show their contempt for the Host, they were apt to throw it
about, sometimes behind the altar, or by the side of it, sometimes stuffing it in a missal.   Yet they rather courted than
shunned danger and death, and seemed to seek for those who
would torture them, and put an end to their lives.

To these sinister reports, coming from Perigeux, was added
the still graver intelligence that the heretic Henry, who had
been driven from Le Mans, had succeeded in alienating whole
districts of the south-west of France from the teaching of the
Church.   In his course southwards, he had passed through
and infected Poitiers and Bordeaux ; and now in Languedoc
his success with all classes was such that the churches were
deserted, the clergy despised, the sacraments neglected, or,
rather, carefully avoided.   Alberic, Bishop of Ostia, and
legate in those parts, saw, with helpless despondency, the
population forsaking him and his church.   The people would
take no notice of him.   When he celebrated mass at Alby, he
could hardly get thirty persons to attend it.   There was no
help but to send for Bernard.[2]

---

[1] "Faciunt quoque multa signa.
Nam sicubi ferreis catenis, vel com-
pedibus vincti, missi fuerint in ton-
nam vinariam, ita ut fundus sursum
vertatur, et custodes fortissimi ad-
hibeantur, in crastino non inve-
niuntur. . . . Vas vini vacuum, ex
suo vino parumper immisso, in crastino plenum invenitur."—*Heriberti
Epistola*, apud MABILLON, *Vetera
Analecta*, p. 483.

[2] "Cum signa pulsarent ad popu-

It cannot cause surprise that Bernard hesitated. He could hardly have recovered from the fatigues of preaching the Crusade, when this request to undertake a journey of several hundred miles was made. His health and strength were daily failing more and more. One of the wishes nearest his heart was to die surrounded by his brethren in Christ, his *carissimi Claraevallenses*. In so long and so exhausting a journey many chances might occur which would find him a grave in a distant land. He did hesitate; but not for long. Attended by his secretary Godfrey, he set out for Languedoc. All Clairvaux was in a state of alarm and anxiety about him, knowing his weakness and the distance he was going.

In time Godfrey wrote a letter to his friends at Clairvaux, giving an account of how it fared with him and Bernard in this expedition. As they approached Poitiers, he says, "The Lord Abbot" became weaker, and felt the fatigue very much. Still he would not give up his point after once undertaking it. From Poitiers he proceeded to Bordeaux, and performed several miracles. To one man who had had a fever for seven years he gave some water to drink which he had blessed. The man had no sooner drunk it than he experienced a sensation, he said, as if a vessel full of water had been dashed over his head. The fever had entirely vanished.[1]

At Toulouse and Perigeux his reception was enthusiastic. The heretics fled out of the towns as fast as he approached them. Bernard made the people swear that they would not harbour them any more. The promise was readily made. Henry had disappeared, but was searched for with such rigour that he was presently captured and delivered bound in chains

---

lum **convocandum** ad missarum solemnia **celebranda**, vix convenere triginta."—*Epistola Gaufridi*; ST. BERN. *Op.* vol. ii. col. 1194.

[1] "Ibidem burgensis quidam bibit aquam ab eo benedictam, et visum est ei ac si projiceretur super caput plenum vas aquae, et ex ea hora convaluit a febre, qua per septem annos laboraverat."—ST. BERN. *Op.* vol. ii. col. 1193.

to his bishop. Bernard's miracles astonished everybody, himself included. Godfrey gives the following instance of his abbot's supernatural power, of which he was himself eye-witness. "At Toulouse, in the church of St. Saturninus, in which we were lodged, was a certain regular canon named John. John had kept his bed for seven months, and was so reduced that his death was expected daily. His legs were so shrunken that they were scarcely larger than a child's arms. He was quite unable to rise to satisfy the wants of nature. At last his brother canons refused to tolerate his presence any longer among them, and thrust him out into the neighbouring village. When the poor creature heard of Bernard's proximity, he implored to be taken to him. Six men, therefore, carrying him as he lay in bed, brought him into a room close to that in which we were lodged. The abbot heard him confess his sins, and listened to his entreaties to be restored to health. Bernard mentally prayed to God : 'Behold, O Lord, they seek for a sign, and our words avail nothing, unless they be confirmed with signs following.' He then blessed him and left the chamber, and so did we all. In that very hour the sick man arose from his couch, and, running after Bernard, kissed his feet with a devotion which cannot be imagined by any one who did not see it. One of the canons, meeting him, nearly fainted with fright, thinking he saw his ghost. John and the brethren then retired to the church and sang a *Te Deum*." [1]

Indeed, immediately after this miracle, Bernard, we are told, became quite uneasy on the subject of his own extraordinary powers. He said : "I can't think what these miracles mean, or why God has thought fit to work them through such a one as I. I do not remember to have read, even in Scripture, of anything more wonderful. Signs and wonders have been

[1] Godfrey has given two accounts of this miracle ; one in the letter written home to Clairvaux, the other in his Life of St. Bernard.—St. Bern. Op. vol. ii. col. 1124.

wrought by holy men and by deceivers. I feel conscious
neither of holiness nor deceit. I know I have not those
saintly merits which are illustrated by miracles. I trust, however, that I do not belong to the number of those who do
wonderful things in the name of God, and yet are unknown of
the Lord." At last he thought he had hit upon an explanation.
It was this. That God in these cases has regard, not to the
sanctity of one, but to the salvation of many. Miracles are
not wrought for the good of him through whom they are
wrought, but for the good of those who see them or hear of
them. They are not meant to show the worker of them as
more holy than others, but to stimulate others to a more
active love of holiness. "These miracles, therefore, have
nothing to do with me ; for I know that they are owing rather
to the extent of my fame than to my excellency of life. They
are not meant to honour me, but to admonish others."
Godfrey, who informs us of these difficulties of his master,
considers that such a view of them is scarcely less miraculous
than the miracles themselves.[1]

Truly miracles had need to abound amid such a harvest of
heresies. Henry and his followers having been disposed of, it
is now Gilbert de la Porrée who stands in need of confutation.
Gilbert de la Porrée, Bishop of Poitiers, by common consent
was one of the most learned and subtle theologians of the age.
He was a Realist in Philosophy ; and, considering that Realism
had usually been regarded as orthodox, and that the opposite
of Realism, namely Nominalism, had been more than once
condemned by the Church as heretical, he may have presumed
to hope that the keen scent of theological suspicion would
discover nothing objectionable in his teaching. If he had
any such hope, it was disappointed. His archdeacons, Calo
and Arnold (*Qui non ridet* "who does not laugh") publicly
denounced his views on the Trinity as savouring of heresy.

[1] St. Bern. Op. vol. ii. col. 1125.

This was in the year 1147. Full of truth and vigour they hastened into Italy and proclaimed their bishop's errors before Pope Eugenius III. The Pope replied that he intended shortly to go into France himself, and commanded them to have all things ready for examination before a council he would preside over at Paris on the following Easter. The zealous archdeacons then went to Clairvaux, and succeeded in inducing Bernard to adopt their cause. The council at Paris did not proceed very far in the matter. In fact the aggressors did not appear quite prepared for the conflict. The Pope ordered Gilbert to appear before him at Rheims, in the Lent following; at the same time requesting him to send to him the incriminated work, as he meant to have it carefully examined. He also advised Gilbert to be prepared to give most explicit answers to all that might be objected to him.[1]

Eugenius having got Gilbert's book, had too much business or too little learning to master it, or controvert it himself; he therefore sent it to Godeschalc, then Abbot of Mont St. Elige, to make a searching examination of it. Godeschalc read and marked those passages which appeared inconsistent with Catholic doctrine, and appended a schedule of Patristic authorities which **overturned** Gilbert's heretical views. But, although Godeschalc could **thus** supply the learning and acuteness required to confute Gilbert, he was so deficient in the gift of ready eloquence, that he was quite unfit to attack an

---

[1] A luminous account of Gilbert de la Porrée's views as a philosopher will be found in M. Hauréau's work on "La Philosophie Scolastique," vol. i. chap. 11. As regards his condemnation before the Council of Rheims two authorities are extant: one is Otto, Bishop of Frisingen, in his history of Frederic I.; the other is by the monk Godfrey. Inasmuch as when these events took place Otto was with Conrad in the Holy Land, while Godfrey was on the spot, I have not hesitated, as a general rule, to prefer the latter. Otto's chronicle, which has not been often printed, is to be found in the sixth volume of Muratori's "Scriptores Rerum Italicarum;" Godfrey's account in St. Bern. Op. vol. ii. col. 1319.

adversary or defend a cause before a council. No one could doubt that for that purpose Bernard was the man. And so it was arranged. Bernard studied his brief, and the council gathered together at Rheims, both accuser and accused marshalling their adherents in great force.

Gilbert appeared, attended by a number of his clerks, carrying piles of ponderous volumes in support of his views; whereas the other side came with a single sheet, containing a few authorities in the form of extracts. The contrast attracted notice and comment; and Gilbert's friends said that Bernard brought only garbled evidence, while they adduced whole works, in which the context and its bearing on the points at issue could be clearly seen.[1] Thus fortified with his voluminous authorities, Gilbert wearied and bewildered the council by the interminable reading of long quotations from the Fathers, being careful to add, ever and anon, that his own views were identical with them. At last the Pope became very impatient, and said, "You speak a good deal, brother Gilbert, and cause a number of things to be read, which, perhaps, we do not understand. Now I would wish to know of you, quite in a simple manner, whether you believe that that highest Essence, in which you acknowledge the three persons to be one God—whether you believe that itself to be God?" Bernard addressed him in much the same manner. "This scandal has had its origin in this one fact, that many are of opinion that you believe and teach that the Divine essence, or nature, or divinity, or wisdom, or goodness, or magnitude, is not God, but the form by which God is. ' If you believe this, acknowledge it openly, or else deny it."

---

[1] "Ingredientibus vero nobis consistorium, prima die cum magnorum voluminum corpora per clericos suos Pictaviensis fecisset afferri, et nos paucas auctoritates Ecclesiae in sola schedula haberemus; occasione ac- cepta calumniabantur fautores illius hominis, quod decurtata testimonia proferremus, cum ille codices integros exhiberet."—*Epist. Gaufridi;* St Bern. *Op.* vol. ii. col. 1320.

Gilbert, fatigued and confused by the long discussion, answered rather hastily, " I do not. The form of God, the divinity by which God is, is not itself God." " Behold," said Bernard, " we have what we wanted. Let that confession be taken down in writing." Pen and ink were then handed to Gilbert, who, while in the act of writing, said to Bernard, " You also write down that divinity is God." " Write it," replied Bernard, " with a pen of iron, and with the point of a diamond, nay, grave it in the flinty rock, that the Divine essence, nature, form, deity, goodness, wisdom, virtue, power, magnitude, truly is God."[1] This terminated the first sitting; and immediately after the council rose Gilbert busied himself in an active canvass among the cardinals. Several were known to be friendly towards him, and he spent the remainder of the day, and even part of the night, in soliciting their good offices.[2]

Bernard's secretary Godfrey, on the other hand, proceeded to the library of the church of Rheims, and diligently examined the writings of the Fathers. St. Augustine, he discovered, used expressions almost identical with those which Bernard had just employed. On the day following Godfrey and Bernard appeared with such an array of tomes as quite struck a tremor into their adversaries, who were not prepared for so great a display of learning.[3] The investigation proceeded, and three more erroneous doctrines were entered against Gilbert. First,

[1] Dean Milman writes, "The Bishop of Poitiers, instead of shrinking from his own words in a discussion before the Pope, who was now at Paris, exclaimed, 'Write them down with a pen of adamant'" (Lat. Christ., vol. iii. p. 397). In attributing these words erroneously to Gilbert, the dean deprives Bernard of a highly characteristic speech. It is also wrong to suppose they were uttered at Paris; the incident occurred at Rheims.

[2] "Sic in haec verba conventus ea die dimittitur. Episcopus totum quod superfuit illius diei spatium, cum nocte sequenti, amicos suos ex cardinalibus, quos habuit non paucos, circuit."— *Otto Frisingensis*, lib. i. cap. 56. The Cardinals seem to have been very prone to heresy in these times. It will be remembered that among them Abelard reckoned his chief supporters.

[3] "Sequenti die codices tantos attulimus ad disputationem, ut obstupescerent fautores Episcopi."— St. Bern. *Op.* vol. ii. col. 1321.

for maintaining that neither one God, nor any one thing, was three persons, although three persons were one God ; secondly, that properties of persons and a multitude of eternal things had truly existed for ever without beginning, none of which, however, were God, or were from God ; thirdly, that it was not the Divine nature which assumed the human, but the person of the Son, who took our nature upon Him. When these points had been made clear, the council broke up, the cardinals saying at the same time, " We have heard the evidence, and we will, in the next place, consider what judgment we shall pass upon it." This announcement caused great anxiety. It was evident that Gilbert's friends meant to protect him if they could, and to dissolve the council without a decision at all. The French clergy, headed by Bernard, were not to be baulked in that way. Ten archbishops and a multitude of bishops and inferior clergy assembled in Bernard's lodging, and agreed to draw up a document of the most·unflinching orthodoxy. They first of all set forth Gilbert's heresies, and to these they opposed their own Catholic verity, using the greatest care and deliberation in all they put down. Suger of St. Denis and two bishops were commissioned to present the document to the Pope and cardinals, stating, at the same time, " Out of reverence to your Holiness, we have endured speeches by no means worthy of acceptation, until we heard that it was your intention to pass judgment upon them. We now offer to you ourselves and our confession, that you may be able to decide, on the showing, not of one, but of both parties. You hold that man's written confession ; it is proper that you should have ours also. He, however, gave in his, coupled with the condition that he would correct it, if you found it objectionable. We utterly exclude and repudiate any such condition, and would have you know that this is our belief, and in it we will remain, determined to alter nothing whatever." The Pope replied at once, that the Roman Church would never think of dissenting from the confession which they had made, and that, although some of the cardinals appeared to stand by Gilbert, it was the man, not the doctrine, they were willing to befriend. The council then reassembled in the " noble palace which is called Thau." The Bishop of Poitiers was questioned on the various points on which his orthodoxy had been denied, and recanted each successively, saying, " If you believe differently, so do I. If you say differently, so do I. If you write differently, so do I." The Pope then condemned his doctrines, and forbade any one to read or transcribe his book unless the Roman Church had previously expurgated it. Poor Gilbert added, " I will correct it according to your good will and pleasure." " Not to you," said the Pope, " will this office of correction be entrusted." [1]

A melancholy scene, sure enough. Over what dykes and ramparts has the current of human thought to force its way. Strange that men should prefer their stagnating ponds to the bracing stream of life and progress. Strange that they should account it a sin to slay the body, and hold it a virtue to slay the mind and the thoughts of the mind.

The cardinals, we are told, were highly incensed at the part played by Bernard and the French clergy. They made an indignant remonstrance with the Pope. " You ought to know," they said to him, " that considering you were elevated by us, on whom the fabric of the universal Church revolves, as it were, upon a hinge, from a private station to be the Father of all, you now belong, not so much to yourself, as to us. You ought not to allow private friendships to interfere with public ones, but to consult the common welfare of all; and both by position and duty you owe an especial care and regard to the Roman Curia. But what has that abbot of yours been doing, and, with him, the whole Gallican Church? With what a front has she dared to erect herself against the supremacy of the see of Rome? That see is the only one which shutteth and no

[1] St. Bern. Op. vol. ii. col. 1322.

man openeth, which openeth and no man shutteth. And yet, behold, these Gauls, despising us even to our faces, have presumed, without consulting us, to write down their faith on those points which have been recently discussed, as if thereby putting their hands to a final and abiding sentence. We request that you will speedily rise up against this bold innovation, and punish, at no distant date, this contumacy of theirs."[1] Eugenius gave a meek answer, and sent for Bernard to know what to do. Bernard declared that neither himself, nor their lordships the bishops, had defined anything on the mooted points; but that, because the Bishop of Poitiers had asked that his (Bernard's) belief should be taken down, he had been unwilling to appear alone in a confession of faith, but, supported by the authority and witness of the bishops, he had in a simple manner set forth his creed. This quieted the cardinals, who, however, declared that the confession of the French bishops should not be regarded as an authorized creed of the Church.

But although these conflicts with, and condemnation of, heretics had come so frequently on Bernard of late, as it seemed to him, in the plain path of his duty, yet to a mind such as his they could not fail to be the cause of pain and sadness. However unavoidable or imperatively necessary the public denunciation and confusion of false teachers might be for the welfare of the Church, it was still a sore and difficult duty, wrenching the mind from its peaceful haunts, interruptive of pensive meditation or fervent prayer, and dipping one's daily bread in the waters of strife. It must have been therefore a matter of no ordinary joy to Bernard that, in the autumn of this contentious year 1148, his old friend Malachy again made his way to Clairvaux.[2] He had been absent nine

---

[1] Otto Frisingensis, lib. i. cap. 57.

[2] Bernard's account of Malachy on his return home from his visit to Clairvaux is taken up entirely with the miracles and impossibilities which his friend performed. I do not think

years—years which had been well filled, in his case as well as
Bernard's, with hard work and fierce opposition, but with a fair
share of triumph over it all in the end.   He was again intend-
ing to go to Rome, on the same errand as had led him there
before, namely, to solicit of the Pope the use of the pallium.
Bernard's delight at seeing him again was unbounded. "Though
he came from the west, he was truly the dayspring from on
high which visited us.   What an addition was that radiating
sun to our Clairvaux!   What a bright holiday shone upon us
when he arrived!   How quickly did I, though trembling and
weak, spring forward to meet him!   how I hastened to embrace
him!   With what joy in my countenance and in my heart
did I lead thee, my father, into my mother's house, into the
chamber of her who bore me!   What days of festivity did I
pass in thy company ; but, alas! how few."   For Malachy had
indeed been only four or five days with his friend when he was
seized with fever.

A deep grief settled on Clairvaux when the fact was
known, and a universal emulation to help or relieve the
sufferer urged the monks to try every form of remedy.   But
in vain.   He grew steadily worse, and it was quite certain
that his hour had come.   When the monks whom he had
brought with him said he must not despair, that no signs of
death were apparent in him, he replied, "Malachy is this
year destined to leave the body.   Beloved, the day draweth
nigh which, as ye well know, I have ever hoped would be the
day of my departure.   I know in whom I have put my trust.
I shall not be robbed of the remainder of my desire, seeing

there is a page of non-mythical
matter in the latter portion of the
narrative, *i.e.* from cap. 16 to the
end, cap. 31. The first part, though
full of marvels, has here and there
the appearance at least of firm historical foundation. The difference may,
perhaps, be explained thus : that for

the first period Bernard had received
authentic material from Malachy
himself in conversation.   For the
second it is improbable that he had
anything of the kind, Malachy, as
it will be immediately seen, dying
soon after he reached Clairvaux on
his second visit.

that I already have obtained a part. He who in His mercy has led me to the place which I sought, will not deny me the last end I have wished for. As regards this poor body, here will it find a resting-place. As concerns my soul, the Lord will provide, who saves those who place their hope in Him." Malachy begged that he might receive the sacrament of Extreme Unction. He would not allow the brethren to ascend to the cell in which he lay, but came down to them, and, having received the viaticum, he returned to his bed. None could believe he was dying. "His countenance was not pale nor shriveled, nor his forehead wrinkled, nor his eyes sunken, nor his nose sharp, nor his mouth drawn, nor his teeth decayed, nor his neck slender, nor his shoulders bent, nor his flesh wasted on the rest of his body. Such grace was in his body, such glory in his face, as even the hand of death could not wipe away." [1]

On the Feast of All Saints he was visibly dying. Towards evening he called the monks to his bedside, and, looking up at them, he said, "Greatly have I desired to eat this passover with you. Thanks be to God, I have had my desire." Then placing his hands on each one, and giving his blessing to all, he bade them go to rest, as his hour had not yet come.

They went, and returned towards midnight. Several abbots who were staying at Clairvaux were present. "With psalms and hymns and spiritual songs we followed our friend on his homeward journey. In the fifty-fourth year of his age, in the place and at the time he had foretold and chosen, Bishop Malachy, taken by angels from out of our hands, happily fell asleep in the Lord. Truly he fell asleep. All eyes were fixed upon him, yet none could say when the spirit left him. When he was dead, he was thought to be alive ; while yet alive, he was supposed to be dead. The same brightness and serenity were ever visible. Death seemed to have no power over them,

[1] De Vita S. Malachiae, cap. 31.

nay, it seemed to increase them.   He was not changed, but we.[1]   Marvellously and suddenly the sobs and grief were hushed.   Sorrow was changed into joy, song banished lamentation.   Faith had triumphed."

"And, indeed, wherefore should we bewail Malachy above measure, as if his death were not precious, as if it were not rather sleep than death, as if the port of death were not the portal of life ? Malachy, our friend, sleepeth ; and shall I weep ? If the Lord has given sleep to His beloved one, and such a sleep, in which was the inheritance of God, the reward of the son, the fruit of the womb ; which of these tells me to weep ? Shall I bewail him who has escaped from tears ?   He rejoices, he triumphs, he enters into the joy of his Lord ; and shall I make lamentation over him ? "

"All things being prepared in the church of the Holy Mary, the Mother of God, in which he had been well pleased, Malachy was committed to the tomb, in the year of the incarnation 1148.   Thine, O Jesus, is the treasure which is entrusted to us.   We keep it to be restored to Thee when Thou shalt think meet to ask it.   We pray only that he may not go forth from hence without his companions, but that he who was our guest may be also our leader, to reign with Thee and him for ever and ever.   Amen."[2]

---

[1] "Et quidem omnium oculi fixi in eum ; nemo tamen, qui quando exivit, advertere potuisset. Mortuus vivere, et vivens mortuus putabatur."—*De Vita S. Malachiæ.*

"Our very hopes belied our fears,
  Our fears our hopes belied ;
We thought her dying when she slept,
  And sleeping when she died."
                          T. Hood.

[2] St. Bern. Op. vol. i. col. 689.

CHAPTER V.

THE LAST YEARS OF ST. BERNARD—THE BOOK OF CONSIDERATION—
TREACHERY OF HIS SECRETARY NICHOLAS—ILLNESS AND DEATH.

BERNARD had hardly turned from the grave in which he had laid his friend, St. Malachy, when the utter and hopeless failure of the Crusade became known in Western Europe. Rumours of misfortune had doubtless been moving about; but only when the crestfallen and vanquished Louis, attended by a few dispirited followers, entered his kingdom, as it were, by stealth, was the full extent of the calamity appreciated. Grief and lamentation possessed the land; and astonishment that God should put true believers to such confusion was not wanting. But presently the popular humiliation began to cast about for an individual victim on whom the responsibility of failure could be thrown, and thus a vent be afforded to the vague discontent and indignation which were oppressing every heart; and soon, from the broad population of Europe, a murmur of wrath and reproach was heard, which, rising in every swelling volume, at last broke into articulate utterance, and thundered out the name " Bernard " with every mark of anger and resentment.

It was so: Bernard was accused and reviled as the author of the calamities which had overtaken the Crusade. Why did he preach it? Why did he prophesy success? Why did he work miracles to make men join it, if this was to be the result? Bernard had never thought much of the praise or the blame of men, or else here would have been a sharp trial for him; after thirty years of eulogy and incense, to be thus held up as a subject of scorn and hatred. Fortunately for him, public opinion

E E

had not been the object of his solicitude. He had his own sorrows about the Crusade, and high and deep they were. The fact that men vilified and despised his name, which they formerly loved, was a small and unimportant matter, and did not require much notice in such a time of trial.

A year passed, and Bernard addressed a few words to Pope Eugenius, which he meant to be regarded in the light of an apology.

" We have fallen on evil days," he writes, " in which the Lord, provoked by our sins, has judged the world before its time, with justice, indeed, but forgetful of His wonted mercy. He hath not spared this people, nor hath He had regard unto His own name. Do not the Gentiles say, Where is now their God? And who can wonder? The sons of the Church, and men named Christians, have been overthrown in the desert, slain with the sword, or destroyed by famine. How confounded are the feet of those who bring good tidings, who publish peace! We said 'peace,' and there is no peace. We promised good things, and behold disorder. As though we had been guilty of rashness or levity in that undertaking! And yet with no uncertainty did I run that course, but at your command, or rather at the command of God, through you. The judgments of the Lord are righteous, as each of us knows; but this *one* is an abyss so deep, that I dare to pronounce him blessed whosoever is not scandalized in it."

He then seeks in the history of the Israelites for precedents bearing on the case in point. The misfortunes of the Hebrews, even under the leadership of such a prophet as Moses, are shown to be peculiarly apposite. " The sad and unhoped-for event cannot be imputed to Moses. He did all things as the Lord bade him, nay, with the Lord working with him, and confirming his work, with signs following. But that people, you will say, was stiff-necked, for ever contending against God, and against His servant Moses. Truly they were unbelieving and rebellious. But what are these men? Ask themselves."

Again, " Benjamin sinned ; and the other tribes gird them-selves to vengeance, not without the command of God ; the Lord Himself gave them a leader. Yet how terrible is He in His doings towards the children of men ! The avengers of sin fled before sinners, the many before the few. They return to the Lord. At His bidding they go forth again, and are again scattered. How, think you, would these Crusaders deal with me, if, at my exhortation, they again went up, and again were driven back ? And yet the Israelites, taking no account of their first and second discomfiture, went forth a third time, and were conquerors. But I may be answered, ' How do we know that this word cometh from the Lord ? What signs showest thou, that we should believe thee ? ' It is not for me to reply to this saying; my modesty must be spared. Do thou answer for me and for thyself, according to what thou hast seen and heard."[1]

It was during this dark and troubled time that Bernard con-ceived the plan of, and began to execute, the largest literary work he ever undertook, viz. the five books *De Consideratione*, addressed to his disciple, Eugenius III. His manner and sentiments with regard to his pupil, after his elevation to the papal chair, are curious to notice. At first he was vehemently afraid lest the cardinals had made a mistake in electing him. " May God forgive you, but what have you done ? " he wrote to them : " you have drawn into the world again a man who was buried ; you have plunged into crowds and cares a man who had fled from both."[2] And to Eugenius he wrote in a similar strain. In a long letter, in which respect, affection, and fatherly counsel are strangely mingled, he warns the new Pope to beware of the dangers to which such an elevation had ex-posed him. But, as time wore on, Bernard found that Eugenius was likely to make a very fair Pope, as popes went. He also took, as he said, a special interest in the son he had begotten. He was always ready to help his pupil with his advice and vast

<hr>

[1] De Consideratione, lib. ii.cap. 1.
—St. Bern. Op. vol. i. col. 416.

[2] Epist. 237. St. Bern. Op. vol. i. col. 232.

experience. Some people, indeed, said that it was not Bernard of Pisa but Bernard of Clairvaux who was pope.[1] Such a reproach was nearly sure to be made, in consequence of the relation in which Bernard and Eugenius had once stood to each other. But candid history will scarcely assert that the Abbot of Clairvaux's influence became greater when his disciple mounted the papal throne than it had been during the pontificates of Innocent, Celestine, and Lucius.

But although Eugenius appeared to be discharging his papal duties with zeal and discretion, Bernard thought there was no small error and confusion as to what those duties really were. The Pope, he observes, is occupied from morning to night in hearing lawsuits; "and would that the day were sufficient to the evil thereof! But the nights are not exempt. Sleep enough is hardly granted to exhausted nature, when you must be up again to hear quarrels and disputes." Eugenius, he says, can scarcely ever get an hour to himself; and when is he to pray, when to teach the people, when to edify the Church, if he is to be always disputing or hearing others dispute? Rome, whether the capital of the Pagan or the Christian world, continues as ever to be the centre to which "all things atrocious and shameful" find their way.[2] "The ambitious, the grasping, the simoniacal, the sacrilegious, the adulterous, the incestuous, and all such like monsters of humanity, flock to Rome, in order either to obtain or to keep ecclesiastical honours at the hands of the Pope." To consume all his time in settling the disputes of this crowd of petitioners, Bernard says, is unworthy of the exalted position of a Pope. A sudden and complete change he does not recommend. But he should certainly begin by degrees to introduce a better order of things. "Causes must be heard, doubtless, but let it be in a becoming manner. For the present fashion is plainly execrable, and one

---

[1] "Aiunt non vos esse Papam, sed me."—*Epist.* 239.

[2] " . . . . quo cuncta undique atrocia aut pudenda confluunt celebranturque."—TACIT. *Ann.* lib. xv. cap. 44.

which is unbecoming, I do not say to the Church, but even to
the market-place. I indeed wonder how your religious ears can
endure the pleadings of the advocates and the clash of words,
which lead rather to the perversion than to the discovery of the
truth. Correct this evil custom, cut off the tongues which talk
vanity, shut the deceitful mouths. These advocates are they
who have taught their tongues to speak lies, being eloquent
against justice, and learned in the service of falsehood. They
destroy the simplicity of truth, they obstruct the paths of
justice. Nothing with such facility makes truth manifest as
a short and unperverted narrative. I would wish you, therefore, to decide on those causes which must come before you
carefully, yet briefly withal, resolutely avoiding vexatious delays.
Let the cause of the widow, the cause of the poor, of him who
hath not wherewith to give, come before you. The rest you
can leave to the decision of others; indeed, many are not
worthy even to be heard. But such is the impudence of some,
that when their whole case bears on its very face the marks of
ambition and intrigue, they yet do not blush to demand an
audience. In a word, the whole Church is full of ambitious
men, and has no more ground to be horrified at their schemes
and plots than has a den of thieves at the spoils of wayfarers."[1]

This was not the first time that Bernard had lifted up his
voice against the evils which an excessive centralization was
bringing on the papacy. Several years before he had told
Pope Innocent what he thought on the subject, and pointed
out the injury which thence resulted to the Church. Priest
and churchman as he was in every fibre of him, he could not
endure corruption, incapacity, or injustice, even when they
borrowed the robes of the sanctuary for their protection. He
had no notion of making things smooth and pleasant. If a
bishop or a legate misbehaved himself, he denounced him,
and filled the world with tumult till he had brought him to

[1] De Consideratione, lib. i. cap. 10.

better ways.[1] He did not feel bound to defend, deny, or
extenuate notorious and manifest delinquencies, because they
happened to be committed by a clerical brother. He did
not think that evil and its consequences were removed by
simply denying that they existed. He did not think that
suppressing the symptoms on the surface was the proper
method to cure the disease below. On the contrary—and in
this respect he only resembles most of his illustrious contemporaries—he believed in outspoken honesty, as perhaps
the sharpest but also the most efficacious remedy in all cases
which affected the real health and excellence of the Church.
In other words, neither he nor his contemporaries were banded
together to defend a system *per fas et nefas* regardless of their
implements.   Doubtless he would not allow any tampering
with "Catholic verity," or permit any fundamental changes
in Church discipline. But the fact that a man pretended to
hold "Catholic verity," or was an ardent supporter of Church
discipline, was not enough to make Bernard think him perfect
in spite of grievous faults or even vices, in spite of narrow-
mindedness, licentiousness, and cruelty. Partisans were not
so scarce or so precious to him that he could not afford to be
particular in his choice of them. He called himself a Catholic,
and had some right to the title. In spite of sects in Normandy
and Languedoc, in spite of Abelard and Gilbert, he could feel
that the intellect and heart of the world was not against him,
but with him. His nature was not curdled by fear and hatred
of great masses of mankind. His soul was not withered by
the thought that the majority of his species regarded him as
an impostor and enemy, and a lie incarnate. Hence he felt
no necessity for concealment, artifice, or deceit, in reference
to clerical abuses. Hence he wrote those highly interesting

---

[1] "Pertransiit legatus vester de
gente in gentem, et de regno ad
populum alterum, foeda et horrida
vestigia apud nos ubique relinquens.
. . . . Turpia fertur ubique commi-
sisse ; spolia ecclesiarum asportasse ;
formosulos pueros in ecclesiasticis
honoribus, ubi potuit, promovisse ;
ubi non potuit, voluisse."—St. Bern.
Epist. 290.

passages in the *De Consideratione*, on the subject of appeals to Rome, which will be quoted here.[1]

That the papal supremacy in the Middle Ages conferred great benefits on Europe is a position which few will now be inclined to call in question. As a counterpoise to the brute force of feudalism, its services can with difficulty either be valued or overvalued. To grant, or rather maintain, so much does not preclude us from the further statement that the papacy had hardly reached its acme of beneficence before it began to be injurious to the world. Like the despotism of the Cæsars, the despotism of the Popes first relieved its subjects from intolerable evils, and then inflicted on them evils as great or greater. An unflinching centralization was gradually established, by which all independent life and energy were withdrawn from the members, and condensed at Rome. The episcopal office was lowered and weakened, both in reality and in public estimation, by the swarms of legates who were spread over Europe. These ecclesiastical proconsuls were chiefly employed to observe and to combat all attempts at local self-government in the provinces over which they were appointed. By their close connexion with the Holy See they towered high above the national bishops in influence and authority. If they were able and upright, they only added to the prestige and power of Rome; if they were rapacious and incompetent, they only humbled to a greater degree the local clergy, who bore their exactions as they best could; for an appeal against the Pope's legate was not a measure from which much could be hoped. As these pretensions increased, the pecuniary needs of Rome increased in a similar or greater ratio. The belief throughout the West was universal that any cause could be made to triumph at Rome, if well supported by money. As the popes wanted money very much indeed, and appeals to Rome con-

---

[1] On the subject of papal encroachments consult Gieseler's "Lehrbuch," 2 Bd. 2te. Abth. p. 236; where an admirable collection of contemporary complaints will be found.

tributed a great deal of money, it was their policy to stimulate
and foster the tendency to appeal to the utmost of their power.
The party which appealed had already secured the favour of the
Roman court. Wealthy culprits were naturally ready to hasten
before a tribunal where gold was more potent than innocence.
The revenues of the papacy were vastly increased; externally, the
monarchy of the popes rose in grander proportions of majesty
and power. But the seeds of the foulest corruption were planted
at the base of the mighty fabric, and grew with little interruption till the great catastrophe in the sixteenth century.

Bernard only saw the beginnings of these evils. But he saw
enough to make him give forth "no uncertain sound" with
regard to them. "It appears to me," he says, "that appeals
may become a great evil, if they are not managed with the
greatest care. Appeals come to you from all the world. This
is a testimony to your supremacy. But if you be wise, you
will not rejoice in the supremacy, but in its usefulness. Would
that appeals to you were as profitable as they are inevitable!
Would that, when the oppressed cry out, the oppressor were
made to feel it, and that the wicked could not wax proud over
the suffering of the poor! What can be more fitting than that the
invocation of your name should afford relief to the oppressed,
and, at the same time, offer no refuge to the crafty? What,
on the other hand, can be more perverse, more alien from the
right, than that the evil-doer should rejoice, while the sufferer
wearies himself in vain? Are you without compassion for the
injured man, the measure of whose injuries is filled up by the
labour of a journey to Rome, and the expenses attending it?
And will the author and cause of these calamities to his neighbour escape your indignation? Arouse you, man of God; when
such things happen, let your pity and your wrath be stirred.
The unchangeable law of equity, and, if I mistake not, of
appeals also, prescribes this rule to you, namely, that an illicit
appeal shall neither profit the appellant, nor injure his adversary. Why, indeed, should a man be vexed and wearied by

appeals for nothing? Nay, how just were it that he should
suffer himself who sought to injure his neighbour. An unjust
appeal is itself an injustice, and when it is attended with
impunity, it becomes the incentive to many other unjust
appeals. Every appeal is unjust which is not caused by a
denial of justice elsewhere. You may appeal, if you are
injured, not in order that you may injure. The right of appeal
is not intended to be a shelter for the guilty, but a refuge for the
innocent. How many have we known who, under the protection of an appeal, have enjoyed an impunity of crime as
long as they lived. What shall we call this but making that
a patronage of guilt which ought to be an object of especial
terror to guilty persons? For how long will you neglect or
refuse to notice the murmurs of the whole world? How long
will you slumber? When will you awake to this confusion and
abuse of the right of appeal? Appeals are made against law
and right, against custom and order. The good are appealed
against by the bad, in order that they may not do good;
and they refrain, fearing your voice of thunder. Bishops are
appealed against, that they may not presume to dissolve or
prohibit unlawful marriages, or punish or restrain in any way
either rapine, theft, or sacrilege. They are appealed against that
they may not depose or repel unworthy or infamous persons
from the sacred offices. What remedy will you find for this
disease? Now you will ask, perhaps, 'Why do not those who
are thus unjustly treated come before me, display their innocence, and expose the guilt of their adversaries?' I will repeat
what they are in the habit of replying: 'We will not be vexed
for nothing. At the Roman court are men who readily favour
appellants, and encourage appeals. As we must yield, it is
better to yield here than at Rome; cheaper to lose our cause
at home, than after a tedious journey across the Alps.'"[1]

Bernard mentions a curious instance as an example of the
extreme to which appeals were carried. A certain couple at

---

[1] St. Bern. Op. vol. i. col. 428. De Consideratione, lib. iii. cap. 2.

Paris had been publicly betrothed. The wedding-day came, all things were ready, numerous guests were invited, when, behold, a man who coveted his neighbour's wife suddenly comes forward with an unexpected appeal, declaring that the bride had been previously betrothed to him, that she was his wife by right. The bridegroom was struck dumb, the rest were confounded, the priest dare not proceed further, all their preparations were thrown away. Every one went home, and had his supper by himself; the lovers were kept from the nuptial chamber till a message could be sent to and received from Rome.[1]

He then draws the Pope's attention to another grievance, if indeed it be another and not the same. "I speak of the murmur and complaint of the churches. They declare that they are being mutilated and dismembered. None, or very few, are there who do not suffer from, or gravely fear, the wounds I speak of. You ask, 'And which are they?'. I will tell you. Abbots are withdrawn from the authority of the bishops, bishops from that of archbishops, and the latter from that of patriarchs or primates. By doing this, you prove that you have a plenitude of authority, but scarcely of justice. You act thus, because you are able to do so; but whether you ought to do so admits of question. You are appointed to preserve to others their grade and rank, not to envy them for possessing these. Is it not unbecoming in you to have no law but your own will, and, because there is no tribunal before which you can be called, therefore to exert your power and despise reason? Are you greater than your Lord, who said, 'I came not to do Mine own will'? What is more unworthy of you than that, while possessing the whole, you should not be content with the whole, unless you be busy in making your own certain small portions of a universe which is committed to your charge? I wish you would call to mind Nathan's parable of the man who, having exceeding many flocks and herds of his own, desired the little ewe lamb of the poor man. Remember

---

[1] St. Bern. Op. vol. i. col. 428. De Consideratione, lib. iii. cap. 2.

the deed, or rather crime, of Ahab, who was lord of all, and
yet lusted after another's vineyard. May God preserve you
from hearing the words which he heard: 'Thou hast killed, and
also taken possession.'" [1]

These passages have not only the merit of singular earnestness and force; they show also the lofty character of Bernard's
mind, and the far-reaching glance of his intellectual vision.
His mind almost seems to pierce through the gloom of four
centuries of the future, and to anticipate Luther's denunciations
against the sins of the papacy. Indeed, to any who can look
below the surface, to any who can see through the varying
costume which each successive age throws over the deeper
characteristics of human nature, there will appear much in the
Abbot of Clairvaux to remind them of the great Saxon reformer.
The same vehemence, not to say hastiness, of temper, the same
fearless disregard of consequences in denouncing falsehood
and sin, the same dauntless courage, the same real humility and
gentleness under all their divine wrath. This similarity becomes
almost startling if we compare the language in which they both
speak of Rome and its inhabitants. The Catholic abbot evidently remembered his visits to the metropolis of Christianity
with feelings differing but little from those which the founder of
Protestantism experienced there twelve generations afterwards. [2]

"Whom can you mention," asks Bernard, "in that vast city,
who received you as Pope without the intervention of reward
or the hope of it? Then especially your courtiers aimed at
authority when they made vows of servitude. They pretend
to be faithful, that they may the more conveniently injure
those who trust them. For the future you will have no plan
or determination from which they will consider you have a right

---

[1] St. Bern. Op. vol. i. col. 428.
De Consideratione, lib. iii. cap. 2.

[2] "I would not," said Luther,
"for a hundred thousand florins have
missed seeing Rome. I should have
always felt an uneasy doubt whether
I was not, after all, doing injustice
to the Pope. As it is, I am quite
satisfied on that point."—Michelet's *Life of Luther*, trans. by W.
Hazlitt, p. 17.

to exclude them, no secret into which they will not thrust
themselves; and if your porter were to cause only a little
delay to any one of them at your doorway, I would not like
to be in that porter's place.   And now judge from my description whether I do not know something of their manners.   In
the first place, they are cunning to do evil, but how to do
good they are ignorant.   They are hateful to heaven and
earth, on both of which they have laid violent hands; impious
they are towards God, bold with regard to holy things, seditious
and envious among themselves, cruel towards strangers, who,
loving no man, are loved of none; and as their pretension is
to be feared by all, they inevitably fear all.   They cannot
endure subjection, yet are they incapable of ruling; faithless
to their superiors, intolerable to their inferiors.   They are
shameless in asking favours, truculent in refusing them; importunate to receive, restless till they do receive, ungrateful when
they have done so.   They have taught their tongues to speak
great things, but they do very little.   They are great promisers,
but scanty performers, most subtle flatterers and most biting
detractors, natural dissemblers and most malicious traitors."

"Among such men you, their pastor, move about covered
with gold and gorgeous apparel: what do the sheep get of it?
If I might speak out, they are demons, rather than sheep,
which graze in these pastures.   The zeal of churchmen now
is never warmed, but for the preservation of their dignity.
Regard is now paid only to rank and honour; no notice, or
very little, is taken of sanctity.   Humility is so despised at
the Roman court, that you will more readily find men really
humble than willing to appear so.   The fear of the Lord is
regarded as simpleness, not to say as folly.   A thoughtful man,
and careful of his conscience, they declare to be a hypocrite
A lover of peace and retirement they pronounce to be a
useless person."[1]

---

[1] St. Bern. Op. vol. i. col. 436-37.   The book "Of Consideration," widely
De Consideratione, lib. iv. cap. 2.   discursive, not to say desultory, is

Such was the impression left on Bernard's mind by what he had seen at the threshold of the Apostles.

Another incident also occurred about this time, to add to the vexation which the failure of the Crusade had caused him. Among his secretaries was one named Nicholas. Nicholas had been a monk at Montiramey, but, by dint of perseverance and importunity, had succeeded in exchanging his monastery for Clairvaux. He was young, accomplished, and endowed with peculiarly winning manners. He was justly valued for his abilities by his new friends, the Cistercians, and a large portion of their vast correspondence devolved on him. Indeed, he rather ungraciously complained, in a letter to an old friend, that he was overworked in his new position. "While they," that is, his brethren at Clairvaux, "enjoy leisure for prayer and devotion, I am plying my pen. From morning to night I do nothing else." He had a *scriptorium* assigned to him, in which clerks, under his direction, worked and copied books and letters. He was on terms of intimacy with most of the distinguished men of his day in France, Peter of Cluny and Peter de la Celle being among his most valued acquaintances.[1]

Two years before his death Bernard discovered that his trusted and clever secretary had been guilty of the grossest treachery and duplicity towards him. As no doubt of his

not confined solely to the treatment of such public questions as those indicated by the above quotations. It would seem that the original plan of the book had been something far more esoteric and didactic. But while composing it, Bernard seems to have been led away by the vehemence of his feelings from his more peculiar topic "of consideration," to speak of the evils which he foresaw were coming on the Church. Consideration proper he divided under four heads : (1) Concerning oneself ; (2) concerning the things which are under one ; (3) concerning the things which are around one ; (4) concerning those things which are above one. The moral reflections scattered through the treatise, and the advice given to Eugenius, are marked by Bernard's usual sagacity and knowledge of human nature, but contain nothing sufficiently characteristic or excellent to detain us here.

[1] The reader will find in Mabillon's preface to the third tome of St. Bernard's works (vol. i. col. 712) a succinct and clear account of Nicholas and his doings.

fidelity was entertained, he had possession of Bernard's seal ; and of this advantage he had availed himself for the purpose of writing a number of letters to persons of every description, not only without his abbot's knowledge, but for objects which were most repugnant to Bernard's real wishes. He had even had the audacity to send some of his forgeries to Pope Eugenius III. When his misconduct became known, he fled from Clairvaux to England, and found a refuge, it was said, in the monastery of St. Alban's. The annoyance caused to Bernard by this incident was very great. He found that his name and authority had been repeatedly used to recommend men and causes often most unworthy of his patronage. He called this period of his life "the season of calamities ;" not without reason, in comparison with the earlier period of his career.

For, besides these external trials, the state of his health was daily growing more precarious and distressing. His weakness of stomach was such that he could take no solid food. Even liquids gave him pain. Sleep had left him ; his legs and feet were enormously swollen ; his debility was extreme ; yet not even for a moment did his unconquerable mind yield to his bodily suffering. He took the same interest in public matters —in the least equally with the greatest; as the following instances will show.

As Bernard lay on his bed of sickness at Clairvaux, the Archbishop of Treves came to him, in great tribulation about the state of affairs in his diocese. A ferocious and horrible contest had been and was still raging between the burghers of the town of Metz and the nobles of the country : the former had supposed that they were strong enough to withstand their knightly oppressors, and had ventured on a conflict, in which the citizens were cut to pieces. Exasperated by their defeat, they resolved, if possible, to wipe it out by a more successful effort, and made immense preparations for another struggle. The nobles, on their side, did the same ; and an exterminating contest seemed about to devastate the country, when the

Archbishop, utterly helpless by himself, thought he would do what nearly every one in Europe had been doing for a quarter of a century, namely, go to Bernard. As his friend and biographer, Godfrey, says: "Whenever a great necessity called him forth, his mind conquered all his bodily infirmities, he was endowed with strength, and, to the astonishment of all who saw him, he could surpass even robust men in his endurance of fatigue."[1] This despotic power of the spirit over the flesh he was destined to exert once more, and for the last time. He went with his friend the Archbishop to the banks of the Moselle, which were lined with the contending factions. The noble warriors would listen to no compromise or terms of arrangement. Elated with their recent triumph, they refused to hearken even to Bernard's exhortations. Indeed, they suddenly broke up their camp, and hastily retired, taking no further notice of Bernard; and this from no want of respect for him, but from a fear lest he should influence them and their followers even against their will; so they determined to avoid such dangerous proximity. Bernard told his friends to be of good cheer, that all would soon be well, in spite of these difficulties. And the reason of his confidence was this: "During the night," he said, "I had a vision, and thought I was celebrating a solemn mass. Just before the conclusion of the first prayer, I remembered that the *Gloria in excelsis* ought to have preceded it; commencing, therefore, the canticle which I had omitted, I sang it to the end with you." This was the ground of Bernard's hope. That same night, after midnight, a message came from the hostile nobles professing repentance, and offering terms of peace. A few days afterwards a complete reconciliation took place between them and their adversaries.[2]

In almost ludicrous contrast with this grand effort of charity

[1] "Quod quidem saepius erga eum providentia divina disposuit . . . ut quoties eum grandis aliqua necessitas evocaret, vincente omnia animo, vires corporis non decessent, miran- tibus qui videbant eum, et robustos homines in tolerantia superare."— ST. BERN. *Op.* vol. ii. col. 1152

[2] *Ibid.*

and zeal does it appear when he is seen writing to the Count of Champagne about some pigs which had been put under Bernard's care by the Abbot of Chatillon, and stolen by the people of Simon de Belfort, a vassal of the count. "I had much rather that they had stolen my pigs," says Bernard; "and I require them at your hands."[1]

Again, when his old friend and patron Theobald asked him to procure ecclesiastical preferment for his fourth son, who was still an infant, Bernard firmly but courteously refused. "I consider," he said, "that ecclesiastical honours are only due to those who can and will, by God's help, worthily fill them. For either you or me to procure such for your little son by means of our prayers, I consider, would be an act of injustice in you, and of imprudence in me. If this appears a hard saying to you, and you are still bent on carrying out your intention, you must be so good as to excuse me. I doubt not but that your other friends will be able to obtain what you wish. Truly I wish well in all respects to our little William; but God above all things: that is the reason why I am unwilling he should have aught against God's law, lest, by so doing, he may not have God Himself. Whenever anything occurs which he may lawfully have, I will show I am his friend; and if my assistance is required, I will not refuse it. But I need not be at great pains to defend before a just man an act of justice. Be so good as to excuse me to your countess, using the arguments which I have put in this letter to you. Farewell!"[2]

The interesting and pathetic letter which he wrote to his uncle Andrew here follows. It must have been among the last he ever wrote.

"Your last letter found me confined to my bed; yet I received it with longing hands, read it and re-read it with delight. But

_____
[1] ". . . . ecce ministeriales Simonis, homines de Belfort; abstulerunt porcos eorum. Maluissem dico vobis ut nostros proprios rapuissent."—ST. BERN. *Epist.* 279.
[2] *Ibid.*

with still greater delight should I have seen you yourself. I perceive your wish to see me. I also notice your fears of danger for the land which the Lord honoured with His presence, for the city which He dedicated with His blood. Woe, woe to our princes! They have done no good in the Holy Land. In their own country, to which they so hastily returned, they exercise an incredible amount of wickedness. Powerful are they to do evil, but how to do good they know not. We trust, however, that the Lord will not drive back His people, nor desert His inheritance. You do well in comparing yourself to an ant. For what else are we inhabitants of earth and sons of men but ants, exhausting ourselves upon vain and useless objects? What return hath a man for all the labour with which he laboureth under the sun? Let us therefore rise above the sun, and let our conversation be in the heavens, our minds preceding whither our bodies will hereafter follow. There, my Andrew, will be found the fruit of your labour, there your reward. You fight under the sun, but for One who sitteth above the sun. Our warfare is here, our wages are from above.

"You would like to see me, you say, and that with me it rests whether your wish shall be gratified or not. You also wait for my command on this point. And what shall I say to you? I wish you to come, and yet I fear your coming, alternately wishing and not wishing. I do not know which to choose. On the one hand, I should like to gratify your desire, and my own, of meeting. On the other hand, ought I not to defer to the general opinion that you are so necessary to the Holy Land that no little danger would attend your absence from it? Therefore what to say I do not know. Yet I hope to see you before I die. You yourself are better placed for judging whether you can leave Palestine without evil result. And it might happen that your coming would be attended with good effects. It is possible that, with God's assistance, some might be found who would accompany you back to the succour of the Church of God, since you are known and beloved of all men.   One thing I would add : if you mean to come, come quickly, lest you come presently and find me not.   For I am ready to be offered, and consider that my stay is short upon the earth.   Would that, before I depart, I might be refreshed by your sweet presence, if it be God's will !   I have written to the Queen, as you wished, and rejoice in the good report you give of her.   I salute all your brethren of the Temple, and those of the Hospital also through you.   I salute through you all the saints with whom you are able conveniently to speak, commending myself to their prayers.   Be my deputy with regard to them. Our Gerard, I hear, who for a season dwelt in our house, is made a bishop.   Him also I salute with the deepest affection."[1]

There was little left, of a truth, to attach Bernard very much to the earth in these last days.   To say nothing of the bright radiance of the hope which for him shone through the portals of the tomb, the world had darkened more and more as he had advanced in years.   And now his old friends and worthy compeers were dying, and preceding him to those realms beyond the sun he spoke of to his uncle Andrew.   First the good Suger died.   He had been rather strangely occupied of late. He had been actually preparing out of his own funds a Crusade to the East, which he meant to lead.   Opposed as he had been to the Second Crusade, its utter failure had filled him with sorrow and indignation.   He tried to get the French bishops to join him, but having "tasted their timidity and cowardice," he determined to carry out the expedition by himself.   He said nothing about his design, but the magnitude of his preparations betrayed him.   He made, through the Knights of the Temple, remittances to Jerusalem, to meet the necessary expense of such an undertaking.   He was seventy years of age, yet he was fully resolved to go.[2]

But it was not to be.   A slight fever set in and confined him

1 St. Bern. Epist. 288.
2 Vita Sugerii auctore Guillelmo, apud Dom. Felibien. " Hist. de

l'Abbaye de Saint Denis."   Paris, 1709.   Migne, Patrologia, tom. 186, col. 1193.

to his bed. His strength soon failed, and he perceived that his scheme was not destined to be carried out by himself. Supported by the hands of his monks, he addressed the assembled convent in words of solemn exhortation, and, falling down at their feet, he implored their forgiveness for any wrong he might have done to any of them. He confessed himself with assiduity to his friends the Bishops of Soissons, of Noyon, and of Senlis, and received the Eucharist for fifteen days without interruption. When Bernard heard of his condition, he wrote him a letter of tender sympathy "That peace awaits you which passes all understanding. Much indeed, dearest friend, do I desire to see you before you depart, that the blessing of a dying man may rest on me. I dare not promise that I will come, but I will do my best to visit you. I have loved you from the beginning, and will do so for ever. I say it boldly, I cannot be separated for eternity from one I have so loved. He does not perish for me ; he goes before. Only be mindful of me when you have arrived at that place whither you are gone before, that it may be granted to me to follow you swiftly, and to be with you again. Never think that your sweet memory can fade from my mind, although, alas! your presence is withdrawn from me. Yet is God able to grant you to our prayers, and preserve you to our necessities ; and of this we need not entirely despair."[1]

These last words indicate that the above letter was written before Suger's illness, which extended over a period of four months, had put on a hopeless character. Towards Christmas of the year 1150 he became rapidly worse. He prayed earnestly that his death might not happen till the festival was over, lest days of rejoicing should be turned into days of mourning through his decease. And it was piously thought that his petition was heard, for he survived till the 12th of January, when he died as he was repeating the Lord's Prayer.

Just a year after Suger's death occurred that of Count

[1] St. Bern. Epist. 266.

Theobald of Champagne, Bernard's lifelong friend and benefactor, in January, 1152.

Another year passed, and Pope Eugenius, Bernard's disciple, fell asleep, in July, 1153.

Bernard had no wish to remain behind these beloved friends. When, in accordance with his beautiful faith, he attributed a slight recovery to the prayers of his sorrowing monks, he said to them : " Why do you thus detain a miserable man ? You are the stronger, you prevail against me. Spare me, spare me, and let me depart." The unwearied activity of mind which had hitherto distinguished him gradually faded away ; the marvellous brain, which had grasped and influenced more or less every question and event in Europe for a whole generation, fell by degrees into peaceful repose. Public affairs ceased to interest him. When his cousin, the Bishop of Langres, came to him about some business, he found he could not attract Bernard's attention. " Marvel not," said the expiring saint ; " I am already no longer of this world." [1]

The weeping multitude of his friends, in the delirium of grief, implored him not to leave them—to have pity on them, and to stay with them. The last earthly struggle he ever knew had commenced in Bernard's soul. Things temporal and things eternal, his earthly and his heavenly home, the love of God and the love of man, contended with him. But for a moment. Raising up his " dove-like eyes," he said he wished that God's will might be done.[2] . . . . .

It was, for he was dead.

[1] " Ne mireris," inquit ; "ego enim jam non sum de hoc mundo." —St. Bern. *Op.* vol. ii, col. 1154.

[2] " Tunc vero flens ipse cum flentibus, et columbinos oculos in coelum porrigens . . . . testabatur coarctatum se e duobus, et quid eligeret ignorantem, et divinae totum tribuere arbitrio pietatis."—*Ibid* col. 1155.

INDEX.

INDEX.

THE END.

London: R. Clay, Sons and Taylor, Printers

MACMILLAN'S BIOGRAPHICAL SERIES.

Crown 8vo, uniformly bound.   Price 6s. each.

SPINOZA: A Study of. By Rev. Dr. James Martineau. With a Portrait Photographed from the Original Painting in the Wolfenbuttel Library. New Edition.

THE LIFE AND WORK OF MARY CARPENTER. By J. ESTLIN CARPENTER, M.A. With Steel Portrait.

CATHERINE AND CRAUFURD TAIT, Wife and Son of ARCHIBALD CAMPBELL, Archbishop of Canterbury: a Memoir. Edited, at the request of the Archbishop, by the Rev. W. BENHAM, B.D. With Two Portraits engraved by JEENS. New and Cheaper Edition.

BERNARD (ST.).—THE LIFE AND TIMES OF ST. BERNARD, Abbot of Clairvaux. By J. C. MORISON, M.A. New Edition.

CHARLOTTE BRONTË: A Monograph. By T. WEMYSS REID. Third Edition.

ST. ANSELM. By the Very Rev. R. W. CHURCH, M.A., Dean of St. Paul's. New Edition.

GREAT CHRISTIANS OF FRANCE: ST. LOUIS AND CALVIN. By M. GUIZOT, Member of the Institute of France.

ALFRED THE GREAT. By THOMAS HUGHES, Q.C.

BIOGRAPHICAL SKETCHES, 1852-75. By HARRIET MARTINEAU. With Four Additional Sketches, and Autobiographical Sketch. Fifth Edition.

FRANCIS OF ASSISI. By Mrs. OLIPHANT. New Edition.

VICTOR EMMANUEL II., FIRST KING OF ITALY. By G. S. GODKIN. New Edition.

MACMILLAN AND CO., LONDON.

MACMILLAN'S 4s. 6d. SERIES.

Now Publishing in Crown 8vo. Price 4s. 6d. each Volume.

Mr. Isaacs. A Tale of Modern India. By F. MARION CRAWFORD.

Doctor Claudius. A True Story. By F. MARION CRAWFORD.

Democracy. An American Novel. Popular Edition, Paper Covers, One Shilling.

Only a Word. By Dr. GEORG EBERS, Author of "The Egyptian Princess," &c. Translated by CLARA BELL.

The Burgomaster's Wife. A Tale of the Siege of Leyden. By Dr. GEORG EBERS. Translated by CLARA BELL.

Stray Pearls. Memoirs of Margaret de Ribaumont, Viscountess of Bellaise. By CHARLOTTE M. YONGE. 2 Vols.

Unknown to History. By CHARLOTTE M. YONGE, Author of "The Heir of Redclyffe." 2 Vols.

The Story of Melicent. By FAYR MADOC.

But Yet a Woman. A Novel. By ARTHUR SHERBURNE HARDY. Popular Edition, Paper Covers, One Shilling.

A Great Treason. A Story of the War of Independence. By MARY HOPPUS. 2 Vols.

The Miz Maze ; or, The Winkworth Puzzle. A Story in Letters by Nine Authors.

A Misguidit Lassie. By PERCY ROSS.

Camping among Cannibals. By ALFRED ST. JOHNSTON.

Memoir of Daniel Macmillan. By THOMAS HUGHES, Q.C. With a Portrait engraved on Steel by C. H. JEENS, from a painting by LOWES DICKINSON. Fifth Thousand. Popular Edition, Paper Covers, One Shilling.

Memoir of Annie Keary. By ELIZA KEARY. With a Portrait. Third Thousand.

Memoir of Sir Charles Reed. By his Son, CHARLES E. B. REED, M.A. With a Portrait.

Lectures on Art. Delivered in support of the Society for Protection of Ancient Buildings. By REGD. STUART POOLE, Professor W. B. RICHMOND, E. J. POYNTER, R.A., J. T. MICKLETHWAITE, and WILLIAM MORRIS.

The Burman. His Life and Notions. By SHWAY YOE. 2 Vols.

Folk Tales of Bengal. By the Rev. LAL BEHARI DAY, Author of "Bengal Peasant Life."

Essays. By F. W. H. MYERS, M.A. 2 Vols. I.—Classical. II.—Modern. Each 4s. 6d.

The Expansion of England. By Professor J. R. SEELEY.

Mrs. Lorimer: A Sketch in Black and White. By LUCAS MALET. New Edition.

French Poets and Novelists. By HENRY JAMES, Author of "The American," "The Europeans," &c. New Edition.

MACMILLAN AND CO., LONDON.

ENGLISH MEN OF LETTERS.

Edited by JOHN MORLEY.

"Enjoyable and excellent little books,"—*Academy.*
"This admirable series."—*British Quarterly Review.*
"These excellent biographies should be made class-books for schools."
—*Westminster Review.*

JOHNSON.
By LESLIE STEPHEN.

SCOTT.
By R. H. HUTTON.

GIBBON.
By J. C. MORISON.

SHELLEY.
By J. A. SYMONDS.

HUME.
By Professor HUXLEY, P.R.S.

GOLDSMITH.
By WILLIAM BLACK.

DEFOE.
By W. MINTO.

BURNS.
By Principal SHAIRP.

SPENSER.
By R. W. CHURCH, Dean of St. Paul's.

THACKERAY.
By ANTHONY TROLLOPE.

BURKE.
By JOHN MORLEY.

MILTON.
By MARK PATTISON.

HAWTHORNE.
By HENRY JAMES.

SOUTHEY.
By EDWARD DOWDEN.

CHAUCER.
By A. W. WARD.

COWPER.
By GOLDWIN SMITH.

BUNYAN.
By J. A. FROUDE.

BYRON.
By JOHN NICHOL.

LOCKE.
By THOMAS FOWLER.

POPE.
By LESLIE STEPHEN.

CHARLES LAMB.
By Rev. ALFRED AINGER.

DE QUINCEY.
By DAVID MASSON.

LANDOR.
By SIDNEY COLVIN.

DRYDEN.
By GEORGE SAINTSBURY.

WORDSWORTH.
By F. W. H. MYERS.

BENTLEY.
By Professor R. C. JEBB.

SWIFT.
By LESLIE STEPHEN.

DICKENS.
By A. W. WARD.

GRAY.
By E. W. GOSSE.

STERNE.
By H. D. TRAILL.

MACAULAY.
By J. C. MORISON.

FIELDING.
By AUSTIN DOBSON.

SHERIDAN.
By Mrs. OLIPHANT.

ADDISON.
By W. J. COURTHOPE.

BACON.
By R. W. CHURCH, Dean of St. Paul's.

Other Volumes to follow.

MACMILLAN & CO., LONDON.

MESSRS. MACMILLAN AND CO.'S PUBLICATIONS.

MACMILLAN AND CO., LONDON.